Bless Me Father

A Novel

Michael Deeze

outskirts
press

Bless Me Father
A Novel
All Rights Reserved.
Copyright © 2019 Michael Deeze
v2.0

This is a work of fiction. Names, characters, businesses, places, events, locales, and incidents are either the products of the author's imagination or used in a fictitious manner. Any resemblance to actual persons, living or dead, or actual events is purely coincidental.

The opinions expressed in this manuscript are solely the opinions of the author and do not represent the opinions or thoughts of the publisher. The author has represented and warranted full ownership and/or legal right to publish all the materials in this book.

This book may not be reproduced, transmitted, or stored in whole or in part by any means, including graphic, electronic, or mechanical without the express written consent of the publisher except in the case of brief quotations embodied in critical articles and reviews.

Outskirts Press, Inc.
http://www.outskirtspress.com

ISBN: 978-1-9772-0857-6

Cover Image © 2019 Lori Pecchia - Faith Tattoo Parlor. All rights reserved - used with permission.

Outskirts Press and the "OP" logo are trademarks belonging to Outskirts Press, Inc.

PRINTED IN THE UNITED STATES OF AMERICA

About the Cover

Lori Pecchia, cover artist
https://twitter.com/37zombies

Born in the suburbs of Chicago in 1978, Lori Pecchia grew up with a love for drawing and sculpting. She won numerous awards from junior high school through college for her abilities in pencil, charcoal, printmaking, and sculpture in multiple mediums. Lori began tattooing while in college, and a decades-long career followed. She has won multiple tattooing awards, but the real reflection of her art is the amazing clients she has amassed over the years. For Lori, tattooing creates a bond that lasts a lifetime.

In 2017, she followed her dream to move to the mountains with her husband, Peter, and daughter, Cora. She currently tattoos in a beautiful shop in historic downtown Golden, Colorado. Even though a thousand miles separate her from her Illinois clients, she returns regularly to work with them, while also expanding her new clientele in Colorado.

When she isn't tattooing, Lori enjoys both outdoor and indoor hobbies. She has completed the Chicago Marathon three times, and run every other type of race leading up to the marathon. Now she has taken on hiking and paddle boarding in her mountain surroundings.

Living on Bear Mountain gives her family a chance to see nature's beauty every day.

She has a passion for board and role playing games. Lori is involved in gaming convention culture. She loves the social aspects and shared experience of playing games. Most important to Lori, gaming is yet another place for making lifelong friends.

To my mother who taught me that 'you are only as happy as your most unhappy child' and to Kate, because after all, she's Kate.

Thank you to those few who saw how important this was for me and encouraged and supported me most especially Jo, Anna and Margaret, and the amazing and multi-talented Mary.

"Being Irish, he had an abiding sense of tragedy, which sustained him through temporary periods of joy."

— *W.B.Yeats*

Introduction

In my neighborhood, there were the *Ins*, and there were the *Outs* if you were lucky enough to have a nickname that meant you were one of the *Ins*. Otherwise, you were just the Jew on the corner or the Polack Janitor. A nickname meant that people knew you, and being called, Little Asshole or Hole made me feel unique so that I secretly liked it. Eventually, *Hole* stuck, and became a self-fulfilling prophecy.

Prologue

I shed my jeans and oily shirt on the small linoleum square inside the door and step back out into the hallway long enough to shake out all of the metal chips and grindings that have found their way into my pockets and waistbands. Once satisfied, I carry them into the bathroom to hang on the hooks on the back of the door, ready for another tomorrow. Turning, I spend a solid five minutes with dish detergent and a nail brush on my hands until only the cracks and fissures, and nail beds alone are highlighted by the black machine oil that they now bathe in daily. I don't bother to put anything else on, the curtains provide complete privacy. No one will be visiting. The phone will not ring.

It is much too early for dinner. The sun will not set for another hour or so, but I survey the refrigerator out of habit. I guess it is heated hot dogs or cold bologna tonight. It will depend on how stoned I am by then. From the butter compartment, I pull out a baggy of pre-rolled joints and light one up with my new fancy butane lighter with fake tortoise-shell finish. I lean against the stove, taking a much-needed hit. My brain sighs in relief.

I select a couple of joss sticks from the utility drawer. *Balsam and cedar tonight*, I think. Lighting one, I place it in the carved dragon incense holder on the counter. In the living room, I pull the chain on the red glass lamp that hangs from the ceiling next to the recliner and place the other joss stick in the ashtray on the single end table. A used sofa makes up the rest of the room's furnishings except for the massive component stereo system - my pride and joy.

The system is the only thing I brought home from overseas that I view with pride. It sits on two 2' X 6' planks supported by liberated bricks along the wall under the window. Two massive Bose 501 speakers sit on the floor at each end; their deafening output capable of vibrating the paint off of the ceiling in the third-floor apartments far upstairs. But sadly leashed in this environment, they are hardly ever allowed to show off their skills. Firing up the receiver, I turn on the reel to reel, put on my headphones, and sit down in the recliner. The cold pleather is stiff and hard against my bare back and legs. In the headphones, Deep Purple launches into the long, frenetic guitar solo of "Highway Star." I close my eyes while I finish smoking the dope. The roughly two hours of music on the tape will take me past sunset and into the night.

Later, I eat the last three hot dogs cold while standing at the open refrigerator door. I might need the last of the milk in the morning, so I drink water straight from the tap—all of the glasses are dirty. In the bedroom, I open the drawer of the dresser designated for socks and lift out the .38 Ruger long barrel revolver and make my way back to the recliner, which is still warm against my bare skin. In the red darkness of the lamp, I release the cylinder and drop it into my hand. Dumping the bullets into my open palm, I select one, replace it into the chamber, and line the other five up in formation on the table beside me. I reassemble the gun almost unconsciously, the movements automatic.

Settling into the chair, I lean it all the way back. With the headphones back in place, I listen as Pink Floyd begins the iconic "One of These Days"—a fitting song to match my mood. I rotate the cylinder by rolling it down my bare leg, each chamber distinctly clicking into position in line with the barrel and firing pin. I light another joint and fill my lungs, holding it tight in my chest. Closing my eyes, my demons are immediately present in the dimly lit room; my nighttime companions of terror and remorse. Lifting up the almost two-pound handgun, I place it under my chin, the end of the barrel cold against my skin. I exhale the smoke and close my eyes. The headphones mask the sound of the clicks as I thumb back the double-action hammer.

July 1970,
Central Highlands,
Republic of South Vietnam

There is a hum of countless noises and the wet vegetation that surrounds me drips with moisture. Night frogs and crickets and the constant trickle of the dirt that breaks away from the small berm that I am sheltered behind, the loose earth streaming down into the almost knee-deep water that I am standing in. Even the ground under the trees and grass sucking in all of the water makes a sound. Even in the thick fog that envelops me I can hear them all clearly. Although I am listening harder than I have ever tried to in my life, I cannot hear anything that I want to hear. I am hot. It is wet; the night sounds are pregnant with dread. The silence is deafening.

It is not the time to be anchored anywhere. I am standing in a ditch filled with water up to my calves. The clinging mud beneath the water forces me to shift constantly from one foot to the other. Standing still for too long captures the soles of my boots. Instead of helping to cool me, the water is warm—nearly the same temperature as the sweat running down my face—soaking my shirt and stinging my eyes. The air is stifling, hot and still; the overcast gray sky, like a thick blanket, makes the air seem more humid and the heat more claustrophobic.

The damp air along with the copious sweat I've been producing, have made my clothes wet. They now cling to me making movements uncomfortable, tight and awkward. My shirt feels too small, pulling between my shoulder blades and pinching under my arms. I shrug my shoulders to relieve the tightness created by the excessive moisture and fear. The clammy cotton in the crotch of my pants pinches the insides of my thighs, and my calves are beginning to cramp with the pressure of continually marching on the spot.

The fog, pea-soup thick, set in before darkness and is damp on my face. A small rock under the toe of my boot helps to stabilize me from the constant sink into the morass, but the pressure of standing on one toe causes my calf and arch to cramp with fatigue. I must shift back to the constant march of my feet in the water and mud to avoid having my boots trapped.

To the left of me, I hear Dugan doing the same shifting in the water and mud, slosh, suck and slosh—pause—slosh, suck, slosh. He's less than four feet away, yet I cannot see his face. I can't even see my own hand in front of my face.

I imagine Dugan as I last saw him, the whites of his eyes slightly bloodshot and mildly yellow in stark contrast to his expressive black face. His steel-pot helmet was pushed back on his head, sweat on his face, and the fear in his features as he stared into the gloom in front of him. Dugan, with a smart-ass comment for every situation, is now silent, except for the occasional whispered outburst, "This is BULLSHIT!" or "We are so royally FUCKED." I hear him breathing; pulling the high-altitude wet air into his lungs as if there isn't enough oxygen in it. Panting, just as I am: just as we all are. All of us afraid, all of us wet, and most of all—all of us trapped.

The quiet, like the air, seems oppressive. It is easy to imagine that we are alone. It is easy to believe that there is no one and nothing for miles in any direction. We all know different, that there is someone else here and not just generally but near, very near, less than fifty or sixty meters away from us, about half a football field, roughly as far as I can kick a football. We also know it is moving toward us. We know that when they find us, they are going to do their best to kill us. We know this because they already have.

We are trapped here in this puddle of water—this narrow furrow of safety. At our back, the land falls away, a sheer drop of several hundred feet. Far below, the forest reaches up toward us, but not close enough for us to chance a descent, even in daylight and certainly not blindly in the dark. There is no escape, and so, we march in place until our fate is decided by that something out in front of us. We wait, marching in place, soaked in our sweat, panting as if breathing through gauze, and we know with each second, death could be moments away. I can feel my fear pounding in my chest my heart racing.

We cannot call for help. The PRC-25, the radio pack, was on Spencer's back when the booby traps went off. Spence took the full blast. What is left of the radio and Spencer is twenty meters out in front of us. I saw him lying on his back, the front of his shirt and face smoking from the explosive charge that went off at his feet drifting slowly away from the gore of his ruined body in the still air. What was left of Spence was dead before he hit the ground. Whether the radio was damaged or not became immediately irrelevant, there was no time to retrieve it. Even if we had the radio, the night is too dark and overcast to call for air support. We are still four or five "klicks" (kilometers) from the forward operating base (FOB), and we are late getting back inside the wire. By now, they know why we are late, and will set a watch, but they will not come for us. There will be no help tonight. I offer a prayer that they come anyway although I know they will not. They must wait, just as we must wait—for the morning.

We started out this morning with twelve, now we are eight or nine. I am not sure of the exact head count of us that remain. A few of us didn't make it as far as this ditch. They're lying on the ground out ahead of us, some face-up and some face down. They make no sound lying there. We left them where they fell in our headlong rush to the meager shelter of this ditch. That seems hours ago. Since then we have maintained the steady march in the mud facing out; waiting, listening for them. We aren't talking anymore. We are frozen by the silence, which isn't silence, straining to hear anything. There are only the sounds we don't want to hear. The wet jungle sounds of the living earth, and none of the sounds of those that bring death.

The dirt bank in front of me is level with my chest and canted away from me, so there is nothing to lean on. There is nothing to assist us in the constant effort of standing while we march in place. Some grass and vine-like plants overhang the edge, but their roots are too shallow and provide no dependable handholds as they pull out without any resistance from the soil. The soil is loose as far as I can push my fingers into it all the way to my wrist without much effort. I withdraw my wrist, and I think about that for a while; no rocks so high up in the mountains. There should be more rocks. I could use a couple to stand on. My legs are tired from the constant dance to keep my feet free of the mud.

It is so quiet.

Sgt. Hobbs whispers somewhere from my right, "Everybody get ready — they're coming." His voice is calm, commanding.

I wonder how he knows they are coming. I don't doubt him for a second. I can see nothing, and I cannot hear anything except the constant dripping of the moisture and the dribble of the dirt cascading into the water around my legs. I drop my chest against the tilted face of the ditch and get my eyes level with the top. Impossibly, my heart increases its pace.

"Conserve your ammo, semiautomatic only. You FNGs got that?"

An FNG is what I am, a fucking new guy.

I start to nod until I realize he can't see me do it. "Got it," I reply, and my voice sounds tight, harsh in the dark. Even though I've tried to whisper, my reply is louder than I expected against the wet, still air. I realize that I sound as scared as I feel. How many of us are left? How many are already down? How soon before I'm one of the down ones? Hobbs took a roll call when we first got in here, but I couldn't hear all of the responses.

I've been in country thirty-three days. Dugan and I arrived together; a week to process, a week to assignment and then dropped into an FOB. Ours is Firebase Storm, 173rd Airborne Brigade, the Sky Soldiers. Sky Soldiers are the most decorated and the most shot-up group of fighting men in Vietnam, plenty of pride and a lot of fear. Storm is in the Central Highlands of the Republic of South Vietnam almost directly south and a little west of Pleiku, in the Dak Lak province, for what that is worth. More important, right up against the Ho Chi Minh Trail, the main supply route from North Vietnam into South Vietnam and a stone's throw from Laos.

Almost everything has been a jolt to my preconceptions—it is so beautiful here. The forests are vast, filled with mature growth trees and vegetation. The forest canopies overlap each other, rising over a hundred feet into the air and filled with countless forms of wildlife, some of them good, some not so good. The majority of the growth contains lush jungle vegetation. Where there are open areas, some of the grasses are astonishingly tall, well over a man's head. Elephant grass it's called, and it provides plenty of stealth cover for Charlie, the Viet Cong guerrillas. The vistas from the high ground into the valleys below are breathtaking. In the distance, forest-covered hilltops and neatly squared out and tended farm fields make up the rest of our view. It is a beautiful country, well worth fighting for, no matter which side you chose.

The old-timers and short-timers are just as afraid of FNGs as they are of Charlie. FNGs do stupid things with their lack of experience and overabundance of fear. Supplied with plenty of firepower FNGs cannot be trusted. The veterans avoid us when they can and do not step in front of us if they can help it. On patrol, FNGs are in the middle of the squad. They are the mules, strapped with bandoliers of fifty caliber machine gun rounds, ammo cans, and grenades. From that position, if the shit comes down, they can distribute ammunition to the fire teams and take someone's place if he falls. That way they stay out of trouble, and if they survive, they become more experienced.

It seems inevitable that the possibility of my own mortality seems ridiculously likely. This moment has the feel of a long march; not just with my feet but also with my adolescently short life to this final destination. It is my fault that I am here, and it has been seemingly inevitable from the beginning. I brought this on myself, and no one knows it better than I do. My memory of sunny Mifflin Street, golden autumn light, and the smell of dry leaves, hurrying to campus in the morning light, is shattered. Replaced by the nightmare that is now. How much I wish I had a chance to go back, to do it all over again. I rack the slide on the rifle—not much chance of that anymore.

Tonight is only my third patrol and my first skirmish. When you arrive in the country, you are considered a cherry until your first firefight. As of today, I am not a cherry anymore. I don't know how things are supposed to go in a firefight, I am pretty sure it is not this way. We are in trouble. The short-timers tell tales of their exploits and encounters, but I don't recall any of them telling one like this.

Dugan whispers, "Jesus, I'm scared. Ain't you scared Hole?" "Fuckin' A." I rasp back.

I am acutely aware that I am afraid, not just because of the circumstances but because I am afraid that I might be a coward. I have been afraid before and right now—*they* are coming.

February 1956,
Chicago Housing Projects,
Chicago, Illinois

It is very cold. I am sitting in my red Radio Flyer wagon outside of our Projects building with my back to the wind, waiting for my Da. It's overcast and blustery, so the winter darkness set in earlier. On Friday, my Da doesn't go to his second job. Instead, he comes home earlier because Friday night is special for us. On Friday night, my mother will have already packed our suitcases and they are lined up in the hallway inside our apartment door. As soon as he arrives, Da will carry them to our green, two-toned 1948 Pontiac Chieftain and load them into the trunk. My sister, brother and I—already in our pajamas—will climb into the backseat and we will be ready to go. From there, we drive from Chicago to Grandma's house in Madison, Wisconsin, and spend the weekend. Da will sit in the gridlock traffic with all the others escaping the city for the weekend far into the night. We don't spend weekends in the Projects.

Kate, Andy and I will be asleep when we arrive. Grandpa Quinn will grumble about how heavy we are as he carries each of us upstairs as we pretend to stay asleep. He will gently place us in between rough, cool, line-dried sheets that smell like fresh air. He will wake us in the morning chastising about wasting the *shank* of the day.

As I sit in my wagon, I am focused on the parking lot across the playground. The playground fills the space between the two massive Project buildings that comprise the part of the development where we live. It is an expanse of blacktop slightly dish-shaped. A large and frightening serrated storm drain cover sits directly in the center. There is a cement sidewalk that circles the entire area, making the walk to the other building seem far if you stay on it. I have walked the circle countless times, pulling my wagon.

Tonight, little tornadoes of whirling snow race each other away from me across the pavement. To my left and inside the circumferential sidewalk there are two swing sets placed next to each other with four swings each hanging by chains. The first set has flat wooden seats attached to chains that bang and clink against each other in the wind. I have recently learned how to hike myself up onto the seat by myself without tipping off onto the ground. The second set has four baby seats that are also wooden, shaped like baby high chairs with little steel bars that slide up the chains to allow parents to insert their children and then lower the bar to keep them safely in the seat. Tonight, the wind bangs these swings together in a clash of chain steel that disturbs the otherwise silent night. There is a steel slide with a ladder that I am still afraid to climb, a steel set of monkey bars and four perilous teeter-totters, which complete the playground setup. The sidewalk backs up to a six-foot cyclone fence and behind that, the *Milwaukee Road* railroad tracks are populated by the new diesel trains, running day and night, in and out of the city. Occasionally steam-powered locomotives still pass, but they are becoming increasingly fewer.

I watch as one by one, cars begin to nose into the parking spots. They will sit side by side, engines running, heaters on full. The drivers will wait for other men to arrive before they shut the cars off and exit into the lot. Friday night is payday, and the men are paid on Friday—in cash. Each man will stand in line at the paymaster window near the time clock as he leaves work for the day on Friday. The cashier will count out their pay in cash. The men have their pay in their pockets, and they know it is important to walk into the buildings together. There is safety in numbers. The men will wait until all of them arrive.

As the men start to get out of their cars, my Da has not reached the lot yet. They gather in a group at the rear of the nearest car and start across the playground, talking and laughing quietly. Halfway across the playground, the group divides, some of them peeling off to head into the other building. The rest continue toward me, seemingly unaware of my presence as they walk facing into the cold wind. When they arrive at the glass doors of our building, Mr. Tomaczak turns toward me and asks me if I want to come in with them. I just shake my head and continue to gaze toward the parking lot. Da will be here soon, I am watching for his car.

I am starting to shiver. I have been outside for a while, and it always seems a long wait. The wind is cold, biting through my clothes and down the back of my neck.

As they pull open the doors, a blast of warm air brushes the side of my face, and I think better of my decision. I awkwardly pull myself up, out of the wagon and turn it around, pulling it up the step in front of the building. Struggling against the heavy door, I wrestle it through the double glass doors. By the time I make it into the lobby, the men have all disappeared into the elevator, heading to their respective floors, homes and families.

The main reason that I pull the wagon everywhere I go is because at five years old, I am too short to reach the elevator button for the seventh floor. If I pull it up under the keypad, the wagon is the only way I can reach the button. Standing on tiptoe, I can just press the big black button next to the number. Pushing the button does not guarantee that the elevator will arrive. While I wait, I realize that the sudden movement into the warm air has made me realize that I have to pee, and I begin to dance from foot to foot. The elevator doesn't come, and the longer I wait the urgency in my bladder adds another factor of desperation. It is often stuck between floors or someone on the upper floor may have braced the door open, and when that happens, it may be long minutes before it becomes available, if at all.

There is an alternative to the elevator—a long concrete staircase behind the elevators, at the back of the building. It is a terrifying place. Eight steps to a landing to a 90-degree turn and eight steps to the first-floor landing. The next story a repeat of the first and so on until ultimately the seventh floor is reached. There are no windows, dim lighting is provided by a single incandescent bulb centered in the ceiling of each residence floor landing, casting the alternate mid-landings into shadow. I have often climbed up a few floors, only to discover the next floor shrouded in the blackness of a burnt-out bulb, dropping two whole sets of stairs into pitch-blackness. The thought of proceeding ahead into total darkness is terrifying, at those times, I have been forced to retrace my steps to the lobby and wait for a companion or another opportunity at the elevator. I don't like the stairwell.

I decide on the stairwell. Seven floors are a long way to drag a wagon, but I refuse to leave it in the lobby. There are too many opportunists in the building. I pull the wagon down the hall to the stairwell and push open the fire door. Standing at the foot of the stairs, I can see my breath as I contemplate whether to start the climb or go back and hope for the elevator. But my bladder has no patience. I need to pee. My need to pee overrides my reservations, so I start up the first flight, pulling the wagon along, yanking it up one step at a time. There is no sense in hurrying. I have let the wagon handle slip out of my hands before. When that has happened, it has rolled back down the stairs, rattling and banging until it crashed into the wall on the landing below, creating the most awful racket and completely paralyzing me with fear. I know the boom has awakened what-ever monster lives in the darkness on the floors above me, and now will be waiting for me.

When I reach the landing between the second and third floor my worst fear is realized, the light on the third-floor landing is out. Total darkness blocks my way, and I pause. I badly need to pee. The return trip down with the wagon is just as tricky as it is pulling it up, I am actually considering peeing in the stairway, but the darkness above me is terrifying. I am frozen in place when a dull red, pinpoint glow brightens above me briefly—a cigarette—followed by a disembodied voice.

"Come on kid. You're doin' fine. Don't be afraid, what floor you lookin' for?"

I swallow the lump in my throat, which I am not sure isn't my heart. "Seven."

"Come on by then, pal. We're just havin' a smoke."

There are two of them. I really must pee soon. I start to pull the wagon up the stairs one banging rattling step at a time, apparently too slowly for the voice above me.

"Come on kid. You need some help?" "No sir."

I try to hurry—bang, yank, bang, yank—and reach the third landing. I make the turn; there is only darkness. I sense one of the men standing against the door. I can smell the dank sweat of him, warm and close. I can't tell where the other one is, though I know they are there. They make no further sound. All I see is the glow of the two cigarettes, floating in midair, glowing momentarily brighter as they take a puff.

The stairway is cold, but I am suddenly very hot. I reach the next landing and turn into the meager light of the fourth floor above the men who make no further sound. Climbing steadily, sped by my fear of the stairs and the two men below, I increase my pace until I turn the corner between five and six and come face to face with pitch blackness above me again. The bulb is out on six too. I am trapped by what is ahead and what is behind me. I dance from one foot to another, clutching my crotch. Making a final decision, I abandon the wagon and start back down the stairs. Still afraid, I strive for stealth as I inch back down. I am close to the corner, descending back to the third floor when I hear far below the sound of the ground floor door slam shut and feet scuffing up the stairs quickly, running almost.

There are too many monsters in the staircase for me. I pee my pants.

Mortified I stand still as I can, urine running down my legs and puddling inside my rubber boots. The steps reach the turn to the third floor and pause when they confront the darkness ahead, then start up again at the same pace. On the third floor, there is an unfamiliar sound; a thud, then another and another. The sound of a gasp, then a groan, then a voice—the one I just heard.

"Just give us your money, shithead."

Then there is a long string of cursing from another voice.

Only one person can curse that creatively. It is my Da!

There are more noises, a fight—the sound of punches, blows connecting with bodies, more invective from Da.

More groans, gasps and then wheezing rise from below, feet shuffling. Then another steel door slams. Silence. I wait there endlessly unable and unwilling to move again. Eventually, I stumble down the last eight steps and stagger against the form, lying on the landing in the darkness that groans out, "Fuck your mother."

It is Da.

I sit down on the bottom step of the landing, helpless in the dark, ashamed in my pee-soaked pants. I should go for help, but I am too afraid.

We will not go to Grandpa's this weekend.

July 1970, Central Highlands, Republic of Vietnam

I have no idea how many rounds I have left. I have two sets of banana clips, four total. Each pair is inverted on each other, and duct taped together at their base so that when one is empty, it can be ejected and flipped over, and the second clip jammed into the magazine. Minimum effort, small chance for error. I am pretty sure that I have been using the rifle, but I haven't a clear memory of doing so. I don't know how many rounds I have left. In the unrelenting darkness, there is no way to count the rounds remaining. The two clips I have stuck in my belt feel heavier than the ones I have already loaded in the gun when I heft them. I'm guessing they are full, sixty rounds more or less. Definitely fewer in the rifle.

The M16A1 rifle is not mine; it belonged to Spic, our tunnel rat. His real name was Roberto Vega, but no one goes by their real name here. He won't need the rifle—or his name for that matter—except to put it on a headstone. He's lying behind me, on his back. Dugan and I dragged him to the ditch when we made a run for it. He stopped breathing hours ago. Claymore mines and machine gun fire at close range do that. You stop breathing.

I had never watched the process before. I watched him as he bubbled and coughed, watched him struggle for his last breath when there was no more room in his lungs for air, only blood. I recognized the panic in his eyes. I watched and learned about the swiftness of the Angel of Death.

January 1959,
Police Precinct House,
Chicago, Illinois, Late Afternoon

It is warm in the police station, hot actually. I've been sitting in a big, gray, steel-framed chair with some kind of fake, fat, green leather cushion seat and swinging my feet back and forth long enough to make me sweat. The chair is designed for a grown-up and not for an 8-year-old kid like me, dressed in two pairs of scratchy wool pants and a hand-me-down blue wool overcoat that used to belong to my sister.

The seat cushion has cracks along the seams that are sharp. When I try to hold on to the sides to keep from sliding off of it, I can feel them dig into my palms. Thanks to the two pairs of pants, the crack of my butt is now moist with sweat, and my legs and feet have started to itch maddeningly because the edge of the chair has cut off the circulation from mid-thigh down. Sweat is running off my scalp and down into my eyes, causing them to sting. I pull my wool knit hat off and hang it by the chin straps in my hand and use it to wipe the sweat from my forehead. My mittens dangle stupidly from the clips attached to the end of my sleeves, so I use one of them to wipe my nose. The slippery wool of the stupid coat keeps conspiring to dump me off the chair.

Every time my feet hit the floor, one of the three or four big cops sitting around the room at their gray steel desks swivels in his chair, offers me a stern look, silently pointing me back up into the chair.

Getting back up on the chair is not the easiest thing. It is high and everything I am wearing is wet, slippery wool. But I haul myself back up in the chair clumsily and settle. Then the cop goes back to whatever he was doing, which appeared to be nothing.

I've taken a lot of crap about the coat. It's nice and warm, but it is bright blue and has a little belt in the back to gather it at the waist with a big blue bow in the middle of it. Kate outgrew it last year, but it's a really warm coat so I have to wear it whether I hate it or not. Coats and money don't grow on trees. Because of the coat the guys on the block gave me a hard time, but they still keep me around. I get assigned to make the snowballs for the bigger boys, instead of getting to participate in our neighborhood snowball wars, and they let me chum with them when I'm not too much in the way.

It's a lot more than most of the boys my age get to do. They let me hang around with them because I am also useful for other things— things I'm good at but shouldn't be.

This is not the first time I've been here at the cop station. It's actually my third, I think, and I actually recognize a couple of the cops from previous encounters, but they are not chummy with me this time. I'm not being offered a candy bar or bottle of coke from the vending machines out by the water cooler this time. They don't stand around my chair and tease me, and I certainly didn't have to wait this long the last couple of times either.

On the first couple of occasions, I was given a little talk in the office at the back of the big room, back behind all of the steel desks. The office has a glass door and windows in the wall and window blinds in both that can be opened and closed.

The policeman who had given *the talk* is older and overweight, a big stomach overhanging his belt and he wears a tie and cream- colored shirt, not a blue uniform with a gun belt.

He made the talk good and scary about what happens to someone who adopts a life of crime and what going to a school for juvenile delinquents is like. Once he had the door of the office closed behind him, the older cop stood right in front of me - close enough to smell his sweat. Not as close as Monsignor Lavin, the Catholic priest at school does when I get *the talk* from him. The Monsignor smells like cotton and incense and tobacco smoke. This cop asked me questions about my neighborhood and threatened me with all kinds of stuff if I didn't tell him about how I landed in front of him.

Of course, he is not half as scary as what I knew would happen if I did tell him anything about how the neighborhood works. He doesn't have to live there, but I do. Neighborhoods have their own rules; rules that we all know, even when they aren't spoken aloud. Rules that have worse consequences than cuffs and juvie hall. In the past, by the time the squad car has driven me home I am in tears, and I have promised fervently to straighten up and never come back under any circumstances. Before, I got a ride back to my street in a squad car where they let me out on the corner, a block from my folk's two-bedroom walk-up apartment, now on the fourth floor, and that was pretty much the end of it.

This time though I can feel it is different. That is confirmed when my Da walks in and shake his hand. Instead of me, they take him to the glassed-in office at the back. Different tactics this time, a different outcome coming my way.

Da is in there a very long time before he comes out and walks straight to me. He takes a position in front of me, his feet apart, hands in his pockets. Da is not a very big man, but he fills my entire field of vision, literally and figuratively. He takes a deep breath and lets it all out with his lips only partly open.

He lets out a tight sigh, his breath aimed at the space between his shoes. It tells me he is disappointed in me, which is something I am used to. It also tells me he is exhausted. He is always exhausted—with trying to be patient, with working too hard and with worry, and maybe with life. He is gathering himself.

My Da and I get along pretty well. Our family isn't much for hugs and kisses we don't even make eye contact if we can help it. I can't remember him ever touching me in a nonviolent manner, except when I pretended to be asleep in the car. I do that, so he has to carry me into our apartment when we came home from Grandma's house late on Sunday nights. I liked it when that happened. Now, however, there are five other kids to carry up the four flights of stairs and seven people living in a small top floor apartment that need constant worry and groceries.

He stands in front of the chair for a few seconds before he says very softly, "You doin' okay?" Sometimes he will add my name to the end of this question. "You doin' okay, son?" that means he is concerned. If he asks the same question but uses my name, that means he is angry. If he asks me and uses my full name, that means deep trouble. Today—no name.

"Yes sir."

"You ready to go?"

"Yes sir."

He seems calm, and there won't be any conversation in the car on the way home, there usually isn't a conversation in the car, so that is not unexpected. We've ridden home together before under similar circumstances, usually after a little chat with Monsignor Lavin or the latest edition of whatever nun I've been exasperating at Our Lady of Grace. He doesn't ever talk much. I know there will be hell to pay when we get home though. My mother will wring her handkerchief in her hands and pull her grey cardigan tight, hugging herself as she paces from room to room. She will rant and rave; she will rearrange pictures on the mantle needlessly and pause in front of me to tell me that I am a rotten child or that I will never amount to anything but trouble. She will ask me why I do these things to her, she will cry and lock herself in the bathroom, where she will sit on the toilet and cry over the sink, the bathroom door doing nothing to mask her sobs. Afterward, the little balls of moist toilet paper will be left on the lid of the clothes hamper, probably just to make me feel guilty.

My brother and sister— they are the good kids—will avoid eye contact and make sure to stay out of the way. The smaller kids don't understand but they know it is me that makes Mother unhappy.

I'll get the belt again from Da. I prefer the belt, because once he used a wire coat hanger that he took from the closet and pulled out straight into a long continuous loop about two and a half feet long; it made a fearsome sound and had an equally fearsome result. I couldn't walk, stand or sit without a reminder of that event for the better part of a week. For my money, I'll take the belt. That belt and I are old friends.

Da is very businesslike about it. He and I go to the bedroom that I share with my brother. He does not yell or lecture, he merely pulls his belt off through the loops on his pants quickly and then starts to lay it on me, wherever he catches up to me in the room. I don't think he counts the number either. I certainly don't. He just whips the belt forehand, backhand, forehand until he has had enough. Sometimes, it takes longer than other times. On Saturday, he'll take me to confession and stand outside the confessional to make sure I tell Father O'Keefe what he expects me to confess to him, sometimes pulling the door open to remind me when my memory is too conveniently lax.

I get into trouble a lot. Sister Mary Loyola tells me I have ants in my pants or something, and I'm just trying to get attention. She hits me with a ruler across my knuckles, or a pointer, or whatever thing she has stashed under her nun's habit on any given day.

In truth, I seem to have a gift for being overly curious, which leads me to less than acceptable pursuits of knowledge.

Combined with a lot of unsupervised time, this produces a few too many audiences with authority figures. Or I am just overly social. I certainly don't look for trouble, but at the same time, I am interested in how trouble works and have a gift for being in the wrong place at the right time. As a result, I am thoroughly acquainted with every type of corporal punishment available from parents, relatives, neighbors and most especially, parochial school administrators.

Sister Mary Loyola is the most creative at this, but Monsignor Lavin is the most sadistic. In addition to spankings, slaps, and other hurtful inflictions, I have been made to stand in the hallway all day, holding armloads of books, locked in a cloakroom all day, a closet all day, the church confessional. I have been tied to my desk, taped to my desk, the teacher's desk, the flagpole in the classroom and made to kneel all day at the communion rail in the church. Most of the time, I am not even sure what I've done. I pray to Jesus and Mary to help make me easier to live with, I pray for forgiveness, but at eight years old, I already know that I am going to hell.

Our Lady of Grace parish is a considerable step up from our last church and school, Precious Blood. Precious Blood was only a few blocks from the housing project where we lived before, and where I had been born. PB was a poor church in a poor neighborhood in the inner city of Chicago. It was populated with the unstable mix of population, displaced when the Congress Expressway became an economic expediency after the war. The expressway, four lanes of concrete freeway designed in California and transplanted to the Midwest, provided access to commerce in the inner city. After World War II, it rapidly became a political and economic necessity for America's crossroads at the foot of Lake Michigan. The returning soldiers needed work and a way to get to that work, and the *Great City of Trains* needed to respond to the explosion of workers and commerce that commuted by roads instead of riding the rails. The new expressway bulldozed its way through all the insular ethnic neighborhoods from the west cutting its way through to the inner city of *The Loop*, what the locals call downtown Chicago, because of the circular track of the elevated train system.

The Chicago's city fathers answer to this displaced population of culturally diverse poor people was to construct the first of many housing projects and relocate those masses into them forcing them to co-exist, more or less against their will. The social and economic station of this populace and the conflicting social morays created immediate friction as the various factions established themselves and their respective territories. It was a violent place, and it was destined to be the breeding ground for what fifty years later, would become a second-generation hotbed of gang wars, drugs, gunrunners and insular poverty.

By comparison, Our Lady of Grace was a thriving money pit made up of working-stiff families composed of World War II veterans and their young broods, adjusting to civilian life and car payments. Just forty odd blocks from downtown Chicago, Our Lady of Grace featured two sacristies and two chapels, one upstairs and one downstairs capable of offering two separate masses at any time and on Sunday as many as ten before lunchtime. It had a flourishing Catholic school of grades one through eight and a full complement of rigid Dominican Nuns who resided on the campus to teach and maintain order. Each classroom had as many as sixty to sixty-five students and only one teacher. There was no room for a disciplinary problem of any kind and very little patience to deal with intractable, overly social eight year olds.

At eight years old, my life is a little more complicated than it should be. Little Mick, my Da, works in the city. A larger than life figure for us, he has a desk job that he goes to every day in a shirt and tie. What he lacks in stature, he makes up for in character. At night, he works down in the rail yards, loading Dunlop tires into freight cars so we can make ends meet.

He takes a change of clothes and two lunches with him when he leaves in the morning. When he gets home, he goes directly to the kitchen cabinet over the sink for his daily home-at-last ritual. He pours a shot of Early Times Whiskey and reaches in the refrigerator for a can of Schlitz. He stares out the back window and throws down the shot and opens the beer with the can opener that sticks to the side of the refrigerator with a little glued on magnet. No matter what goes down during the day, we all know not to address him until he is halfway through the can of beer and has poured the second shot.

My ma is sick all the time. She worries, and she stays in bed a lot. My sister Kathleen, Kate, is our rock. She is eleven; she can cook, clean and she packs a mean lunch. She knows how to bake a spice cake, and she bosses my brother Andy and I around as well as any Catholic nun. She also helps manage the three little kids. Trouble has a way of finding our family. Most especially— me.

Today was a perfect example. I like school, but not other kids as much. I like most kids, but I don't really have any friends. It is a funny kind of loop; the kids at school make fun of me because I am always in trouble and I get into trouble a lot because the kids all make fun of me. I like to watch them play on the playground, and I eye the girls and wonder if I will marry one of them someday. But I watch them from my spot along the church wall where I am guarded by the playground nun of the day. I am not usually allowed to play playground games.

I like the challenge of learning. When I was in first grade, I had trouble learning the alphabet. I would get some of the letters mixed up; L and J and p and b. Sister Mary Allen—who had a mustache like a man—was convinced that I was trying to be cute because I kept getting stuck on the same letters all the time. Sister Mary Allen had me stand in front of the class and tell everyone that I was pretending to be stupid just to cause trouble. That was when I first learned about standing in the hallway, waiting for Monsignor Lavin. I also took home my first note from the teacher. It asked for a teacher conference with my parents. I think that might have been the first time I got the belt for activities outside of the house. The meetings became a weekly, after Sunday mass, occurrence.

The belt and I became better acquainted on most Sunday afternoons.

January 1959,
Police Precinct House,
Chicago, Illinois,
Earlier the Same Day

It is a pretty long walk to and from school; about a mile and a half. Sometimes I walk with Kate, and sometimes I take a different way, so I won't have to. There is a fellow named Stosh that sets up his *shop* on the corner down the street from our fourth-floor walk-up apartment. Stosh is a self-proclaimed business man. He is large and loud, with slicked back hair and very shiny shoes. My Da says he is a Polack, but I don't know what that means. He has a big car—a Buick I think—with a grill like my buck-toothed cousin Seamus, and small, coiled springs that stick out from the wheel wells so that he can hear them scrape on the curb and know that he is close enough when he parks. The trunk and back seat are full of every kind of product he can attempt to sell to the neighborhood. The Buick pulled up tight to the curb is very shiny winter and summer. In the summer, there is a little strip of dirt between the curb and the sidewalk about five feet wide. It doesn't have grass that grows, although it is supposed to. It's where we play mumblety-peg and shoot marbles.

Right where Stosh sets up, a stray dog was hit by a car last summer. The cops stopped long enough to pull it out of thestreet and up into the strip of dirt, where they shot it in the head. It laid there for two weeks; its body slowly sagging into the dirt while its teeth got scarier by the day. Stosh had to move his operation down the block for a while when it was there, but I visited that dog every day.

22

Stosh ran a sort of a mobile Sears store on wheels. Mostly cleaning products—soap, a limited variety of cigarettes and pipe tobacco, small packaged goods that the housewives came out and picked through and occasionally, kitchen knives and utensils. Nobody ever admitted to buying anything from Stosh, but everyone did. You just couldn't beat his prices. His inventory varied depending upon available merchandise and the season of the year. Stosh knew his clientele, and he kept his stock accordingly. He would barter and trade, but mostly he liked cash.

Stosh also took custom orders. You could even buy shoes from him if you could remember which store you saw the ones you wanted. That's where I came in. Stosh had a good supply of candy, salted pumpkin seeds in a little red and blue box with an Indian on the front, and small bags of peanuts in the shell. For kids like me, he would run a tab, which he kept track of in a little spiral notebook and pencil that was jammed in his shirt pocket. He took empty soda pop bottles in trade, which were good for two cents at the supermarket, but they didn't like dealing with kids. Stosh was close by, handy and he paid one cent, no questions asked. Sometimes he had little jobs for us to do that he would even pay us for, or let us work off our tab. Sometimes he would pay twenty-five or thirty cents; a king's ransom for an eight-year-old kid.

Around the corner from Stosh, in the alley, was Leo Opramann's hangout. Leo was the building janitor. He was an elderly Kraut of impressive girth, with a strong accent and a permanent limp. He appeared and disappeared around the property with a gigantic pipe clamped in his teeth that smelled wonderful. During the winter, Leo would leave the furnace room door in the alley open. He had a couple of rescued, overstuffed chairs in there, facing the open door of the monstrous coal-fired furnace and boiler, which heated our water and building. Once he had shoveled the furnace full of black, dirty coal, he would sit in one of the overstuffed chairs and light his pipe, while staring into the blaze through the open door of the furnace, at peace in his one sanctuary. It was always cozy in the furnace room during the evenings, when the winter darkness came by four o'clock.

Leo was not particularly loquacious, but he welcomed company in the other chair. I logged a lot of hours sitting the copilot's seat, staring into the fire next to Leo but never exchanging a word. His wife, Lucille, was not particularly friendly to any of the residents and I suspected that that sentiment extended to Leo as well. Leo had particular tastes in pipe tobacco, which he consulted Stosh for on a more or less regular basis.

To ensure maximum profit, Stosh employed a few of us to acquire inventory that could be transported out of various stores by hand. I had demonstrated some originality and a knack for custom order acquisition, and I had picked up Leo's tobacco orders from time to time. In exchange, I had an open account with Stosh, and he was usually a little more welcoming of my appearance than some of the other block kids.

Walking home with my sister didn't allow me to loiter with Stosh. Kate was a good girl and had been warned about Stosh by the building housewives regarding his questionable character. She was also a tattletale. When people like my sister approached Stosh's corner, his trunk lid came down, and he would casually lean on the rear fender, facing the sidewalk, puffing on a cigarette until they passed by. Stosh knew his market, but he also knew the neighborhood.

This day Stosh was glad to see me, and as my sister kept walking, I held back. Stosh, just to be a pain, spun me around to check out the bow on the back of my hand-me-down coat. Once his teasing was over, he finally told me what he wanted.

He had orders stacking up, and his inventory was starting run short. Since I was small and wore the innocuous Catholic school uniform—dark blue wool pants and white shirt—I look right for the job. That day I had pulled on another pair of pants over the ones I wear at school to ward off the intense cold.

My mittens were attached to my sleeves by snap clips like the ones on suspenders, so I would have a harder time losing them. I still lost them, of course, it just took longer. I hated mittens—gloves were so much more grown up—but since I couldn't seem to hang onto mittens, my folks saw no reason to pony the extra dough for gloves.

My list for the day included a pouch of Amphora pipe tobacco (Leo Opramann's brand), one of the new squeeze-type can openers, two or three white handkerchiefs (just like my dad used), and a new smoking pipe, preferably one of the briar ones. All of the items are available at the Woolworth's 5 and 10, up on Fullerton, not far from the church, and Stosh suggested that I shop there specifically. Woolworth's is easier to get to than the Ben Franklin, which would require me to take the bus, but the Ben Franklins are much easier to fill a shopping list because they have a smaller staff and the store is bigger.

The best part about Woolworth's was that the candy aisle was nearly at the front of the store, directly in front of the cash register. The cashiers and managers watched kids like hawks in the candy aisle. As far as they were concerned, when it came to kids and the candy aisle, every kid had criminal intent so most of their attention was directed down that aisle. The items I needed were deeper in the store and once I passed the candy, employees relaxed their surveillance. Woolworth's was usually busy, but especially after school, so the candy aisle got a lot of attention. However, Woolworth's also had a wooden floor that creaked and groaned wherever you walked, so the staff was completely aware of anyone's location wherever they were in the store. The lighter the criminal, however, the less noise he made.

There is a hole in the bottom of both of my coat pockets. If I dropped something into them, it falls all the way to the bottom edge of the coat where the hem and the lining catch it. The coat functioned as a wool shopping bag, and items in the lining could be retrieved later on—if your arms were long enough.

I walked past the Zagnuts and Clark bars and moved to the back of the store. The handkerchiefs were easy to find individually folded in a little wire bin on the shelf under the Old Spice After-Shave and Wildroot Crème Oil. I put them in my lefthand pocket and looked around to be sure no one was watching me. Satisfied, I slipped three of them into my pocket, casually replacing one in the rack, just in case. The briar pipes are in another bin in the tobacco area, fifteen or twenty of them thrown randomly in a pile, and any one of them would do, they all looked the same to me. I got past the second item on my list and then felt a large hand drop onto my shoulder. I turned around and confronted, face to belt buckle one of *Chicago's Finest;* a beat cop. In no time at all, I was escorted to the Precinct House on West Belmont, deposited onto the steel chair with the fake leather cushion that was too slippery to sit on in wet wool pants.

The next Saturday morning, Momma stayed in bed again, Da came to the breakfast table, with a swollen and blackened left eye and an angry gash across the bridge of his nose. Kate cut up his eggs and buttered his toast because the knuckles on his hands were scraped and swollen. He leaned to the right at an angle in his chair and winced when Kate gave him a little hug. I never saw Big Stosh around the neighborhood again. Neighborhoods, you see, have their own rules.

July 1970, Central Highlands, Republic of South Vietnam

My weapon is a 40mm. M-79 grenade launcher. The guys call him Thumper. I'm out of rounds for it. They were the first to go. There had been one grenade in the weapon and eleven in my bandoleer. The Thumper is the weapon of choice for the FNGs; it's hard to fire accidentally, and it is usually pointed up in the air, not as much chance of someone accidentally stepping in front of the barrel of a nervous trigger finger. Thumper is handy when you want to convince someone to stay back and when he *thumps*, you'd better hope you are not underneath it when it comes down. It throws a grenade a long way and makes a big noise when it inevitably hits something. It creates impressive holes in things and plenty of trouble.

In the beginning, that is what we needed, distance and time; distance from them and time to run. Old Mr. Thumper is very good for that. We needed enough time to get to the ditch, time to turn around and some few seconds more to let our lives pass before our eyes. Thumper did his job, and I did mine.

At first, the hail of incoming rounds was withering, buzzing and zipping in on us, a steady pok, pok, pok, zwip, zwip, zwip into the dirt bank behind me, a swarm of high-velocity bees.

Concentrated, probing, only to be followed by an equally intense silence. The silence made worse by the sensory deprivation of the fog and anxiety.

I have no sense of what time it is. The quiet and fatigue of waiting in silence have made the minutes and hours pass, but not by any measure that I can track. I struggle to stay in the present and find my mind drifting back to high school and am shocked to realize that I was in high school less than a year ago. A mere twelve months and that I am still only eighteen years old. I feel so very far away from that kid, not aged as a measurement of time but older, like a tree weathered by a hard season. Yet, I can't tell how long we've been here. Where I am now is not a varsity sporting event and not gym class, not remotely related to the grab-ass games like Smear the Queer or Dog Pile. Games we used to play in the locker room, back in the day, so long ago.

Winter 1969, Western Chicago Suburbs, Illinois

I liked high school. High school classes were tailored to a guy like me; the classes only lasted fifty minutes, which was a stretch for my limited attention span, but not so long that I was motivated to entertain myself in what school administrators called an inappropriate manner. I liked mathematics and loved English. Math because it was a challenge, English because we got to read books, which took me away to somewhere else—anywhere else. The part of English that bored me was the endless discussions about the metaphors for life placed meaningfully in the stories we discussed, or the protagonist angst, providing an allegory to current, adolescent society. I liked the stories as they were, so I often zoned out the class, read the stories, aced the tests and went about my own business. Homework was another story entirely.

I had lots of themes and term papers in my head, but I lacked the commitment to put them on paper. I often had trouble sitting still long enough to finish dinner, writing a three- to-five page, typed, double-spaced term paper about whether Gene Forrester loved or hated his best friend Finny in the book "A Separate Peace" was beyond my scope of endurance. I personally thought Gene Forrester was a wimpy tag-along and didn't really give a shit what his motivations were, but I still meant to do the work. The problem was I couldn't.

I could sit in front of a typewriter for hours, procrastinating, doing anything to avoid doing the work. This fact was not lost on most of my teachers; A's on tests and oral reports, F's on papers, workbooks and science experiments made me a target. I was subjected to repeated good-intentioned but misguided attempts at mentoring and fostering, but was eventually rewarded with frustrated ambivalence.

On an unconscious level, I had developed behavioral tendencies that believed that any attention was better than no attention at all. I had learned this at a young age and reinforced it with every year that passed. Something inside of me believed that it was better to be noticed then just another face in the crowd. Being noticed for good behavior required a lot more effort than becoming notorious for activities outside of the structure of social acceptance. It became an unconscious habit.

I had inherited my ethnic proclivity for alcohol consumption and the ability to acquire it, which assured invitations to many of the high school weekend parties, but I was not popular. Kids with a future knew better than to befriend me, and girls who valued their reputations kept a healthy distance. I was not overpowered by overzealous attempts to alleviate puberty's hormonal imbalances, nor was I preoccupied with adolescent boy-girl social pursuits, so that I could fit in with everyone else. I avoided school functions like the plague, such as homecoming dances, basketball games, and the worst of them all, prom.

I took care of the pesky societal pressures personally and imaginatively; it was my attention span that tripped me up. With the few friends I did have, I feigned indifference for school subjects, for which I was regarded as both cool and misguided, depending on which particular clique I was hanging with. For my teachers, I attempted sincerity. Unfortunately, that permanent record that everyone tells you will follow you apparently does, and by the second semester of my senior year, I was failing most of my classes and written off by most authority figures with a shake of the head and the undeniable dread of having me repeat their class.

Illinois law required that you pass four years of English classes. Whether you learned anything from them or not was of no concern to the school system gurus. Learning was an issue altogether unrelated to high school educational standards. My senior English class was going to be my Waterloo. The end of the first semester found me without a passing grade in English— and without that, there would be no diploma, no graduation, and another year of school. Mrs. Riverton, my then senior English teacher, seemed sincere in her attempts to engage my participation in the class discussions at least. She was young(ish) and full of new teacher enthusiasm and she, like others before her, mistakenly thought she could salvage me.

I knew I wasn't stupid, in fact, I suspected that I was pretty smart. The endless discussions dissecting the real meaning behind passages in what I considered limp literature to begin with bored me stiff. I didn't care if the dragon in the epic poem Beowulf represented the devil or whatever embodiment of evil you chose. It was just a story that would have been much better written in our current vernacular. From my position at the back of the class, I usually expressed those particular sentiments in mumbled outbursts.

As a result, she called upon me—regularly. Mostly for my own entertainment, I dutifully replied to Mrs. Riverton that I believed Beowulf's *Grendel* represented the human psyche and the inability of the human self to defeat the evil demons within, during a class discussion. *Grendel* did not wish to destroy happiness; happiness destroyed itself by never being satisfied with what it had. The look she gave me and the class reflected her disappointment, and she moved on to other topics rather quickly, after advising me to see her after school. At least I was pretty sure she knew I had read the assignment.

I had been staying after class in one way or another for most of my educational career. The script seldom deviated, and I was well practiced in picking up my cues and in steering the dialog to its inevitable outcome. These *discussions* always began with a sincere plea for my academic soul, my personal welfare, and a general expression of bewilderment at what appeared to be a total lack of application. There would be some browbeating, which was dependent upon the gender of my assailant and then that would be followed up by the *What would your parents think?* monologue. They would then pry a confession out of me to buckle down, work harder, accept my full and obvious potential and eventually become president of the United States, all delivered with as much feigned sincerity as I could muster.

Mrs. Riverton was one of the more recent additions to the faculty, and as such, her office was relegated to the third floor at the far end of the academic wing. The prime office spaces were already taken by the teachers with tenure or testicles. Although the script for these after class, after school meetings seldom deviated, it was always a curiosity to see how the latest edition would be edited and augmented. Still, there was no reason to hurry the performance, so I dawdled my way to Mrs. Riverton's small office cubicle at the end of the day. The hallways were deserted within minutes after the last bell, the students rushing off to extracurricular club activities, sports team practice or just to catch their bus, and the teachers following quickly after to recharge for the next day.

The halls on the third floor didn't have student lockers as it was too far from the exits and bus stops. If there had been lockers, no one would have used them anyway. The stuffy, stillness was in direct contrast to the hustle and shouted conversations of minutes before. The expanse of empty hallway stretching out a half-block ahead of me, the monotony of club posters on the walls and forgotten litter on the floor only broken by the evenly spaced classroom doors. My shoes are the loudest thing in the otherwise silent double-wide hallway as I make my way to the far end. The classrooms to the right and left of me still lit but empty, filled wastebaskets standing sentinel outside their doors, awaiting the custodial night crew. The center of the vast hallway was taken up by evenly spaced enclosed office spaces for the teachers, an enclosed island of desks. These offices consisted of a walled-in space, just large enough for one desk at each end and a small space between them, barely wide enough to walk through, with a door marking the width of the path opposite of each other. The walls did not extend all the way to the acoustic-tiled ceilings but instead were topped by eighteen inches of glass windows, in a vain attempt to make the inside space less claustrophobic.

As I approached, I saw Mrs. Riverton sitting in her office with her back to me, her hands folded on her desk, silently regarding the wall in front of her. There was no way I could sneak up on her; my shoes made too much noise in the quiet hallway. I knocked on the metal door jamb anyway, the metallic booming overly loud in the deserted corridor. Her desk was surprisingly clean; In and Out boxes neatly stacked on one corner and a few books held in place by bookends of owl figurines gazing in opposite directions. She swiveled in her chair and gave me a long look.

"Please come in."

If I didn't sit, the room would be too crowded, and the two of us would be too close together for comfortable conversation, but she didn't give me leave to sit down. Instead, she got up and pushed the other desk chair out into the hallway and then closed both doors. Once she was seated again, she crossed her legs and cradled her elbow in her left hand and began stroking the base of her throat through the open neck of her blouse, apparently still in thought.

I was uncomfortable; standing in front of her while she looked me up and down. Somehow putting my hands in my pockets seemed too informal so I leaned back onto the other desk and crossed my hands over my lap. A full minute ticked by. The office was small and with the doors closed it felt too warm and the air stuffy.

After a moment's silent reflection while she took me in, she seemed to arrive at a decision. Leaning back, she crossed her arms instead. I couldn't hold her gaze, and there was nothing else to look at, so I looked at a spot on the floor between her gleaming high heeled shoes one of which bobbed up and down as she bounced her crossed legs. I really hated these talks, the sincerity on their part, the fact that their sincerity was destined to failure, and the feeling that I had, knowing that I was going to disappoint another person that I actually respected and admired. The whole situation was filled with a negative déjà vu.

After a long pause, she fired the first volley.

"I was interested in your comment in class today, Robert. Is that how you truly think? That people are inherently evil and in a turmoil with themselves that they will eventually succumb to?"

This was not the way most of the *talks* usually opened, so I was momentarily at a loss for words, not sure how to respond.

"I think people use their demons conveniently," I supplied tentatively.

"You mean in order to justify their disappointing behavior? You are either a profound thinker or a truly an odd duck. Wherever did you arrive at such a thought?'

I couldn't argue with the question or the following first statement, and I had a lifetime of Roman Catholic guilt to back up the second.

"I think when people do whatever they want to—whether it is correct behavior or not—they give in to their inner devil. I think people soothe their conscience by telling themselves those actions are not really who they are. That the devil made them do it. Then they go to confession, or they say their prayers and go to sleep at night absolved of their responsibility. They are still ashamed of their actions but they will still get to heaven, and they got to eat the cake too."

"I think I am impressed," she paused and then with a wry smile added, "or appalled. That's some pretty deep thinking on your part. I hope you are not really that jaded because that is a pretty negative perspective for someone your age." She paused again, looking me up and down. "But do you think that is true, always?"

"I haven't known anyone in my life that doesn't function that way."

"I see that you seem to go out of your way to make things difficult for yourself in school? You seem to have more than a bit of a reputation, and I have witnessed the way you interact with your peer group. I am somewhat amazed at your ability to always be around trouble but never quite in it. Either you are very clever or just very bored. Yet you don't seem to be overly friendly with the other kids, so your actions don't seem motivated by a need for attention or approval. You seem to be a loner by all accounts."

She leaned slightly forward and lowered her voice.

"Tell me. Are you really the one who lowered half of the band into the orchestra pit during their winter concert?" She half smiled and then added, "I don't want to turn you in, I'm just curious."

This last question changes the dynamic in this tiny room a little, and accidentally I smile at her, just a small, half-cocked smile.

"I see," she continued, "how did you escape apprehension I wonder? I am sure that the dean's office also asked you about the stolen school bus? Or maybe the eight-foot-tall penis snow sculpture next to the flagpole this winter?"

"The school bus was not stolen. Turned out it was just. Relocated. Someone must have left the key in it." Then I added, "From what I've heard anyway."

I am well aware of your reputation among the students, so why in heaven's name do they all call you Hole? The boys admire you, but they also keep their distance. The girls get unbelievably stupid around you, yet you ignore them. How do you manage it?" I shrug my shoulders and say nothing, holding her gaze.

"Is it because you are bored with it all? Does it move too slowly for you?"

"They call me that because that's who I am. It's short for asshole, and according to them, that's the way they think I act. Like an ass-hole—but in an amusing sort of way, I hope. The nuns in Catholic school called me Robert, but if you don't mind, I prefer Emmett." *That should help shorten up this interview.* Just in case it didn't, I added, "No, I actually like your class. What I don't like is the parsing and dissecting that teachers insist upon, because to me it destroys the ef-fect and meaning of the sentence, paragraph or story. When I read something, I enjoy the reading for the impact it has on me. Taking it apart and discussing it to death takes the joy of discovery out of it for me. Teachers try so hard to help the students understand the point of the reading that they break it down to such an elementary level that anyone with any brains at all can't help but to go away to their happy place. I think as a student you either get it or you don't, and if you don't, you can always take metal shop."

"Hmmm, not everyone should or can take metal shop, Robert. I think you are an interesting individual and certainly one of the most challenging students I have been graced with so far. I also sus-pect that you are probably more than a little misunderstood. But—and this is a big but—you are now between the proverbial rock and a hard place. You are required to pass fourth year English, in order to graduate. It doesn't matter that you already have enough class-room credits to meet the necessary requirements." She paused, looking over her shoulder at a piece of paper on her desk, "You have already failed the first semester, and you are well on your way to failing the second in my class. Your other grades are more than adequate, but English is going to be your downfall. If you don't find a way to put aside your smart-aleck, just don't care attitude and buckle down, you will be here again next year. I hope you realize how much I want to try and help you though. I don't want to waste my time, but if you don't let me help you, this conversation I'm afraid, is also an ultimatum."

This part of the talk I get. Now comes my sincerity part, and then my promise. I will be out of here inside of five minutes.

"No," I replied, "I think you are doing a great job. All of the kids like you and your class. I like you, and I really like your class. I have read and re-read the assigned reading. In fact, I finished it over a month ago." I paused, briefly looking at the floor, "I will try harder to apply myself, I promise."

"Oh boy, you are going to apply yourself harder?" The sarcasm in her voice makes me tense. "Mr. Casey, you really are well-practiced at throwing the bull around. You and I both know that five minutes after you walk out of this office, you will slide straight back into the persona that you have perfected. Tomorrow you will arrive in my classroom with the same chip on your shoulder, and we will have this conversation again and again."

She paused and looked around the tiny cubicle for a moment and then unexpectedly she rose to her feet and stepped toward me.

"You seem to at least try to cast yourself as a loner. You admit that you don't have many friends, but I sense that you aren't really happy with that. I think you are very misunderstood, I think you have been in the role of an outsider for so long that everyone has accepted it. The administration is not concerned with your emotional health or if that is the reason that you don't apply yourself. You've managed to paint yourself with the bad-boy image enough so that the students are willing to stay at a distance. What I see is an old man in a young man's body. I think you probably are looking for acceptance and affection, but you don't know where to look for it, and that is why this conversation and the situation that required it exists."

I was not expecting or prepared for any kind of psychological evaluation. I had come here to fulfill my obligation of a mandatory academic dressing down and then go back to my regular routine as soon as possible. My family did not discuss emotional issues, and I didn't waste a lot of personal time trying to understand my deep-seated emotional motivations. I was seventeen years old and already had enough problems without thinking about them too.

"I see a very handsome young man who could have half of the girls in his class but doesn't. You seem distant, but something in you attracts people to you at the same time. I feel that attraction too, so I know it's a real thing."

She placed her hand on my chest and ran it down over my stomach making my muscles flutter and involuntarily I shuddered.

"Don't be afraid, Emmett. I think that the reason you don't respond to the accepted teaching standards is that you have needs that aren't being met at another level. I have an idea about how I can help with those, and also help you graduate. I am going to make you an offer, and I suggest that you take it. If you don't, the consequences are quite clear for you. Whether you have experienced consequences of your own making before or not, this one will not just go away if you ignore it. Honestly, the school district would very much not like to see you back here next year for a number of reasons, and not the least of which is they don't want you personally."

Her hand continued to roam across my chest. It was impossible to ignore the faint touch of her perfume.

"I would like to arrange to tutor you privately for a while. I think two nights a week, but three would be ideal if we are to make enough progress by the end of the year. I have a special project in mind, an experiment if you will. I think you might be well-suited for it. But I need to be sure that you will apply yourself. Otherwise, your graduation or lack of graduation in June will be out of my hands."

My mouth was so dry I couldn't swallow the tight lump in my throat. I was already backed against the desk behind me. I could feel it digging into the back of my legs as I leaned back.

"I'm not sure what you mean Mrs. Riverton. If you think that I can find a way to get my grades up I think that would be pretty good though. I don't think I could tell my parents that I can't graduate. If history is any kind of indication, they would not handle it very well."

"I was hoping you would be interested, but I need to have your promise that this will be just between you and me. You aren't the only student who has trouble with English; however, I'm beginning to understand that the problem with you is not English but motivation. I have motivation in mind, and I think I might be able to provide it, in what may be a more innovative way for you. Since you don't socialize much with the other students already, I wouldn't want this type of attention to become common knowledge. Too many other students might want to participate."

"Whatever you say Mrs. Riverton, I won't mention it to anyone."

"You have to promise that you will follow my instruction. There will be instruction, and benchmark tests, you will have to pass each one before you can move on to the next, some of it may not be very easy for you. If you don't try your hardest, the consequences are already laid out for you Emmett. Can I have your promise?"

"I promise. Cross my heart, hope to die."

"Let's hope it doesn't come to that. Alright then, moving on. Please take a seat."

I sat down in the chair she had occupied, and she leaned back against other the desk, crossing her arms.

"You don't seem to date, Emmett. Any girlfriends?

"No."

"You are good looking and very smart. Why don't you have a girlfriend?"

"The girls that I think are interesting are too popular, and the ones that like me think that going steady and getting a date for prom are the keystones of society. Either way, they all think that being popular is the most important thing in their lives. I'm not interested in that kind of stuff."

"Again, a not surprising answer on your part Emmett. So— you're not having sex with anyone?"

I felt the sweat in my palms and armpits spring out of my pores.

"What? I mean. Excuse me? I'm not sure if I know what you are asking me for Mrs. Riverton."

"Emmett, you are not the only person that has demons, if that is what you choose to blame your behavior on. Everyone has them, and I have some of my own. Being a grownup isn't any easier than being a teenager the consequences are just heavier. You may not think so, but like most adults, I have personal issues that I must deal with every day. For instance, on more than one occasion I have noticed you looking down the front of my shirt when you stand at my desk. I have also noticed that you stare at my legs when I am in the front of the class. These are things that I am aware of every day and must deal with maturely."

Mrs. Riverton was the youngest teacher that I had had in a number of years. She was also pretty. She wore stylish clothes and seemed tall and slender in the high heels and skirts that she wore every day. She was a total babe, and she knew it. The mystery of what women kept inside of their shirts and under their skirts was a preoccupying fixation for me, just like most other boys my age, and I certainly was thinking about those things right now. Still unable to swallow the monstrous knot in my throat I opted for silence.

"I want to tell you that it is perfectly natural for a boy your age to do those things. I would be more surprised if you didn't. In my case, it is particularly troubling. It bothers me more than it should, and I have struggled with it recently more than I like. That is why I wanted you to come here this afternoon and that is the special project I will be working with you on. I would like you to help me with it."

"I don't understand Mrs. Riverton. Am I in trouble?" My voice croaked. "I really apologize. I don't know what to say. I am a little uncomfortable talking to you about this kind of stuff."

She gave a small smile that only lifted on side of her mouth and leaned farther back against her desk and uncrossed her arms placing them on the desk behind her, the twin cones of her breasts pushing the material of her blouse out and gapping the space between the buttons so that a tiny portion of her bra appeared in the space. "Do you think it is okay to stare at my breasts or my legs?"

"I don't mean to offend you, ma'am. I really can't help it. You are really pretty," *Oh my god what am I saying?* "I'll try not to do it anymore. I promise."

She bit her bottom lip with her top teeth. I hadn't noticed her teeth before. They are very white and even; pretty teeth, surrounded by red lipstick which I was suddenly transfixed by.

Outside, there was the unmistakable ding of the elevator arriving at the third floor. She cocked her head to the side and listened for a moment. The sound of a wheeled cart rattled off the elevator and began to roll toward us from the end of the hallway. She leaned forward and flicked off the lights. The cart was accompanied by the shuffle of one pair of shoes as it passed by and proceeded down the hallway, and eventually into the distance. Then she smiled and continued in a less nervous voice that was soft and a little throaty.

"Emmett, you are looking at your world as a constant need to decide between good or bad, right or wrong because that is what society wants you to do. Society wants you to choose to be good or right, and it has built-in life penalties for when you don't make the proper choices. But life choices aren't always right or wrong, good or bad, often it just is what it is. If you struggle with this to and fro battle constantly your mind will eventually try to shave off the sharp corners of those decisions, you will begin to rationalize how you can split hairs and have it both ways. You will be pulled one way and then the other, and eventually, you will lose your free will. You will become controlled by your own guilt and doubt. Instead, it is essential, I think, for people to understand that there is no right and there is no wrong, no good or bad, there are actions that the voice inside of us directs us to perform. When we listen to our inner voice, choices no longer need to be made, and we enter into the flow of life. Our inner voice innately knows our own path, and that way is then of our own choosing.

"Everyone has demons, Emmett. Some people like you fight against them. They fight against them their whole lives. Other people learn to embrace them. They learn to make them a part of their lives; separate but allowed to exercise themselves occasionally. I have demons Emmett, and I have learned that if I accept my devil and allow it to express itself, then I do not have to worry about it popping up at an unexpected and perhaps inappropriate times which might create an embarrassing situation."

"Oh, you're not offending me, Emmett. I kind of like it. In fact, I was wondering if you would like to touch me in those places. You know the places that you look at, that you think about." As if a sudden thought occurs to her, she cocked her head to one side and broke eye contact. "Do you think about me when you masturbate? I wonder?"

I tried to swallow, but my mouth was dry and my tongue wouldn't cooperate.

"You see Emmett even though I am your teacher and a grown-up I know my demon very well, and I have learned how to give her/it expression. My demon has taught me that there are certain things that I must have. I give in to it, and I stay happy. I like to be happy and I work very hard at my job which creates an awful lot of stress for me. If I don't release that stress, I am afraid that it might find some form of expression that would not be creative or helpful to my career and my life. With your help on this project, I think it will help me be a better teacher and a more creative person. It has been very hard to find just the right person to help me with this. It must be someone I can trust and who is willing to do the work to become proficient at this task, and I am sure that I can make you more than proficient. I think you might be that person."

With that she reached down and clutched the hem of her skirt and gently gathered it in her hands as she raised it slowly up her thighs, rolling it up in her hands as they steadily rose. I expected pantyhose, but instead, she wore stockings that ended three-quarters of the way up her thigh. The stockings were attached with little elastic straps that continued up under her skirt. Garters I learned later.

"Why don't you put your hand here?" She said indicating the space above her stocking where her smooth pale skin showed soft light that filtered in from the hallway. "I think we will start with the basics for your first lesson."

The bright hallway lights were muted by the skylights at the top of the walls and took on the grey muted tones of the inside of the small room. Turning to the desk, she bent down and opened the bottom drawers on either side. Turning slowly back to face me she slowly hiked her skirt up above her waist. Black panties highlighted the flair of her hips, and above that, a garter belt holding up her stockings circled her waist. Never taking her eyes off of my face she hooked her thumbs into the waistband of the panties and lowered them slowly, first one side and then the other, an inch at a time. When the panties reached her ankles, she gracefully stepped out of them one high heel at a time, in a stunningly feminine movement. Taking the small black bundle, she reached for her purse and dropped them in.

Turning back to face me she took a seat on the edge of her desk and hooked her heels into the open drawers on either side and leaned back onto her hands. Throughout the mesmerizing performance, I was transfixed. Her eyes had never left mine. Now she broke the contact and pointedly looked down at displayed femininity then back at me. There for the first time in my life in the half-light of the room a warm, fragrant and fully three-dimensional pussy was staring me in the face. The real thing far more fascinating than any pictures that I had seen up until now. I looked at her face again, and she pointedly directed my gaze back down with her eyes.

"Remember Emmett, this is the way for you to manage your graduation. It is the answer to the problem, and because it is in my hands, it will be the only way. Roll your chair closer, Emmett. It will be important for you to remember that whatever we do, and no matter what we do, I always come first—always. That will be your first lesson. There is a treat at the end if you learn your lesson well. Come closer now, and I can show you how to begin."

⸺⸺◦⟨◉⟩◦⸺⸺

For the rest of the winter, the spring and well into the summer of that year, I attended Mrs. Riverton's extracurricular classes. Some classes were impromptu; others were well- planned and anticipated. These classes could take place after hours in the school library, the front seat of her car or the park down near the lagoon. During school hours, we were usually restricted to the projection room in the auditorium, or the fallout shelter in the catacombs beneath the gymnasium. We met among the tiers of stored drinking water, where the accumulated dust would stick to my clothes and make me sneeze for the rest of the day. When her husband was out of town, the weekend would be spent working on my lessons in her apartment. Some of her methods were innovative and even enjoyable, but she was a taskmaster and demanded perfection. I learned quickly not to disappoint her.

I rerouted my commute to classes in order to pass by her classroom. I lived for the subtle eye contact that we shared as I passed; the small smile, the almost imperceptible nod. I told myself that it was not just sex; it was that she cared. I reveled in the touch of skin on skin, but more important, that I was special. I felt it inside, and I could not work hard enough to make her happy, because she cared about me, just me. My Catholic upbringing would not let me enjoy it completely though. Contentment and serenity were at war with shame and sinfulness. I knew all about guilt, and I knew that it had a way of catching up to you. That primary tenet of Catholicism had been drilled into me since my baptism. Retribution was out on the horizon—but I would worry about it when the time came.

I learned an awful lot in my second semester of English, to say the least. I doubt that it noticeably improved my vocabulary and I am reasonably confident that none of it had anything to do with English. I graduated from high school with a C in English for both semesters. My name was not listed on the graduation program between Catherine Canfield and John Custis, yet I walked across the stage. My name did not appear in the graduation program, but I accepted the empty folder from the presiding administrator. The folder should have had a diploma in it, but there had been no time to print one for me once the administration realized I was qualified to graduate.

I wasn't eight years old anymore, but I knew that my reservation in hell had experienced a significant upgrade.

July 1970, Central Highlands, Republic of South Vietnam

There is a sudden break in the stillness. Tracer rounds come zinging out of the night. There is thwip, thwip, thwip as they and their invisible brothers flash past. The rounds leave a long bright blind spot in my night vision after they pass. Tracers help you direct your fire in darker situations. You can see where the tracer rounds end up. When you can't see the sight on the end of your rifle, you can use the tracers to help you hit what you are shooting at. These tracers are from the tree line above us. Back at home, when I used to hunt, I learned that when you are shooting from high ground to a lower target, it's difficult to aim low enough. You always assume that the drop is not as steep as it really is. So, these shots are too high to do us any damage physically, but the message is clear. They are still there—waiting. Don't go to sleep on us now.

The tree line is eighty or ninety meters above us. It's not a great distance if it is daylight and you can see your target, but it is impossible at night to hit anything smaller than an elephant. Between the tree line and where we are huddled, the ground slopes in a steady, steep incline, a twenty or thirty percent grade, I would guess. It is a wasted area, burned by a previous napalm barrage, littered with trees blackened and broken and at varying heights. The ground is so steep that the spring rains have washed large patches of grassy sod loose. It has sloughed off and slid down into wrinkled rolls of soggy grass and mud to pile up around the feet of the murdered trees like a prom dress dropped in haste leaving behind exposed earth as large as a helipad.

The footing on the hill was slippery and untrustworthy. The ditch we are in is almost twenty meters long and at the very bottom of the slope, constructed mostly of a berm of piled sod that had slid down into uneven heaps, creating the meager shelter we huddle in. It doesn't appear to go anywhere or drain anything. Behind us—the cliff and the forest canopy far below.

No one from our side returns the fire. After the volley, it's quiet again.

October 1895,
Oklahoma Territories

My Grandfather Padraig O'Casey—the son of Oklahoma Sooners—dropped the O from his last name, thinking it might make him sound less Irish, and at the very the least, less Catholic. As a young man, he was hired onto the railroad, only to discover that most of the Irish immigrant railroad workers were known as Paddy anyway. By the time he regretted his decision, he was, and we were forever—Casey's. Railroad life—with the exception of providing his family with an abundant source of heating and cooking coal, which he liberated from the various engine tenders in the winter—was not the occupation for Grandpa Paddy. Neither was store clerk, grader operator, church custodian, carpenter, steeplejack and several other jobs, he tried for varying periods of time and with varying degrees of enthusiasm. He did acquire a working knowledge of how most things work in the world and a multitude of manual skills. Already clever minded and charming, there was little he could not turn his hands and mind to. Eventually, at twenty-eight years old he had wandered far enough north to find himself in the lumber camps of Wisconsin and Upper Michigan where he plied his now considerable expertise as a teamster and moon-shiner, with adroit enthusiasm. He got hired on with the Tigerton Lumber Company, where he started as a swamper and moved up quickly to roustabout which best suited his problem-solving skills and mechanical talents.

Turn of the century northern Wisconsin was a rolling land of glacially deposited stone and seemingly limitless pine to be harvested. There was minimal elevation and it was dotted with swamps and peat bogs. Still largely unsettled and unoccupied, the view from what little high ground there was did not change in any direction. Miles of dense forest with varying shades of deep green in summer, and in winter hues of black, gray and evergreen. Given the harvesting and transporting methods of the time, there was no way to estimate the vastness of the forested hills of Wisconsin, Michigan and Minnesota.

But Wisconsin was considered to be the richest of the three. It was thought that the timber barons would never be able to cut it all and what they did cut would replace itself in short order. The resource would be available forever. This belief was proved wrong in less than twenty years when vast tracts of clear-cut were left covered only in pine slashings. The top soil, already thin and poor, was left to erode and wash down the great water-shed of the north and into the mighty—and now muddy—Mississippi River, to eventually become part of the Louisiana delta, far to the south.

The Tigerton Lumber Company, like many of the other lumbering concerns, set up camp in these wooded tracts of timber every winter. The frozen ground allowed for the easier transport of cut logs on the ice and snow by the horse or oxen teams and out to the logging roads. The ground supported the wide-decked sleighs once on the logging roads so that they could be sledded to the river, where massive quantities of logs were dumped onto the ice to await the spring thaw and ice-out. The spring thaw made the logging roads a morass of rutted mud and the active logging operation ceased for another year. The youngest and most athletic men, armed with peaveys and cant hooks, rode the logs downstream, to the sawmills that awaited them. River hogging—or riding the logs downriver—was a dangerous job and many men were lost between the logs when chancy spring currents produced an unexpected opening in the floating raft directly under their dancing feet. Once under the logs the chances of finding another opening or being able to drag oneself to safety before it closed and crushed you were almost impossible.

Once downriver, the logs were placed in the lee of a river bend, or into a log pond. They were sequestered from the river by a surround of logs, chained end to end on the current side of the log float known as a log fence and the rest of the spring, summer and early fall were spent debarking the logs, and sawing them into railroad ties and board lumber. The sawed wood was dried and loaded, board by board, onto boats or railroad cars and shipped to all points of the compass. America was growing faster than the building and railroads could keep up with, and the market for wood was unquenchable. The lumber barons of the north became fabulously wealthy, but the lumberjacks were not part of that loop. They worked, got paid, and eventually their bodies could not support the substantial cost of their tasks.

For six months of the year the lumber camps were home for the men. The lumber camps were self-supporting, a town unto themselves and most men who went to the camps in November did not return home until late March. Sometimes small communities sprang up near the more permanent camps and supplied alcohol and women of easy virtue. For the most part, the camps were solitary, self-contained entities; remote and lonely. It was not uncommon for wolf packs to wander between the buildings in deepest winter night searching for any scrap of food carelessly discarded. Harness gear, shoes, gloves and even the leather straps nailed to the doors for handles were quick to disappear when the wolves driven by hunger entered the camp. More than one night's sleep was ruined when a rifle was fired out the window of a bunkhouse or mess hall in the dead of night. In the morning, a wolf skin was soon stretched and nailed to the barn for drying safely high enough to remain out of reach of its former brothers. A barn and stable for the draft animals, sometimes several bunkhouses; a mess hall, which was also used for any group activities; and church services when a priest was available; a blacksmith; and saw filer shop made up the entire life of a *jack*.

The cook in Grandpa Paddy's camp was a laconic, half-breed woman of questionable temperament and skill. As a woman in the northern lumber camps, she was a rarity, occupying a position and job usually reserved for men. Mary Agnes O'Donnell was half Irish, by her father Seamus, a displaced Irishman who mistakenly ended up on the Canadian frontier at the end of a dying fur trade. She was French Canadian and Ojibwa on her mother's side and had inherited her mother's strong work ethic, her sense of humor and a universal distrust of all things male. A spare framed, olive skinned woman with large hands, a strong back and constitution, she stood a mere five feet tall. The only woman in a lumber camp, she discouraged amorous advances and casual conversation with negative enthusiasm and exceedingly poor hygiene. For slow learners, she was also handy with a ten-inch deer antler knife that she carried in her left boot. She brooked no nonsense and rarely displayed any semblance of humor. She skinned what she was brought by the hunters, applied salt and grease liberally then served it up with plenty of beans and salt pork. What she lacked in the culinary skills, she compensated for in portion control. It wasn't delicious, but there was plenty of it. Mary Agnes was never inclined to marry but nonetheless had produced a daughter, Margaret Elizabeth, the holy terror and darling of the camp.

Maggie was a wild thing. She was welcomed everywhere she went and had free rein to roam and explore the deep forests at her leisure and charm every man within one-hundred miles. Comfortable in the company of men her entire life, Maggie learned to chew tobacco by the age of twelve and could roll her own cigarettes with one hand. She could shoot the eye out of a squirrel at twenty yards with the 25-caliber Sharp's camp rifle, which she always carried with her. Maggie could handle a two-horse slip-tongue log skidder, run the log boom, man her end of a buck saw and was an easy hand with a team of oxen. She cursed as creatively as anyone in the camp, but she could turn on the charm when she needed something done that she couldn't or wouldn't do herself. She kept her flaming red hair covered with a man's battered, soft-brimmed felt hat and could freeze a man with eyes bluer than the winter sky. She displayed a cruelly liberal dose of freckles, roughly calloused hands, flannel shirts untucked at the waist, baggy men's trousers tucked into cast aside strapped jackboots, a hunting knife, a sharp wit and a sharper tongue.

By sixteen years old, she was a formidable fixture and more than a match for any man woman or woodland creature. As a result, the entire camp adored and feared her. As the only available woman for miles around, Maggie could have had her pick of any man in the territory.

Until Paddy Casey arrived in the camp, the thought of romance had occurred to her only as a passing thought. She had always been able to get what she wanted from any man, with a smile or a pout, which to her was a natural talent and had never entered into a rational analysis of action and outcome. To a woman, Paddy Casey was hard to overlook. He was darkly handsome, clever with his hands, capable and popular. He had quickly become the man to seek out when a difficult job presented itself. She watched as Paddy plied his double occupations with skill and wit, always available for any transaction that came his way. In truth, Paddy moonshined only because it ensured him an endless supply of drink for personal consumption.

Suddenly Maggie found herself finding her path crossing Paddy's more frequently. She found herself thinking about him when he wasn't around. He was a man's man and everything about him stood out from the other men. When they spoke he was polite, clever, and engaging, but he knew his place, and never overstepped polite conversation and an easy smile for her. Paddy looked very much like her ticket out of lumber camps—the shoulder-high snow in winter and black flies in summer. A full three inches taller than Paddy and twelve years his junior, Maggie set her cap for Paddy, and the deal was as good as done. She approached him in the same way she did most things—straight on. She challenged him to a night of drinking and simply sat down and in her charming, disarming way, drank with him until he was good and drunk, while she only pretended to match him drink for drink. In showing off for Maggie, Paddy only succeeded in drinking himself unconscious. Once he had, she merely removed his pants, rearranged hers and hollered at the top of her lungs.

The rest of the camp men, hearing the alarm came on the double and listened with a mixture of concern and no small amount of admiration to how poor Paddy Casey had stolen her virtue.

A tear-streaked face and disheveled appearance sold the camp and wedding plans were soon put into motion. After all, Margaret Elizabeth was a good Catholic girl, and these things had consequences. That Saturday, in the mess hall/chapel of the camp, Father Pierre presided over the wedding of Margaret Elizabeth O'Donnell and Daniel Padraig Casey. It was the first time she had ever worn a dress, and many caught their breath at the sight of her with her hair combed out and her small feet pushed into stylish slippers that her mother had surprisingly saved for that very day. Paddy, for the most part, was bewildered by the whirlwind process, and not exactly sure of what role he had played in his unexpected arrival at the altar. Seeing his newly appointed mother-in-law-to-be in the front left seat of the chapel, idly thumbing the handle of her boot knife left little doubt of how the event would play out.

In truth, although they recognized Paddy's indiscretion, the men's already high estimate of Paddy rose further as most, if not all of them, had fantasized the same scenario that apparently Paddy had just enjoyed accidentally. Paddy, of course, could not remember a thing, and when pressed for details, simply smiled knowingly as he was thumped on the back and pressed for details. He freely distributed his liquor after the wedding, and that quickly quieted any call for further detail, as he tried to enjoy this unexpected turn of events. A glance at the surprisingly beautiful bride was certainly encouraging, and he looked forward to a repeat performance of his most sinful act—this time without the angry mob scene and knife-wielding camp cook.

May 1908,
Near Gagen, Wisconsin

The following spring after the ice went out of the river and the logs were floated out, Maggie drove Paddy to a small farm in Oconto County and told him to go to the bank and arrange the purchase. They bought a cow, a brood sow and ordered chickens by mail. In the fall, Maggie delivered little Catherine in the morning, early enough that she could still milk the cow afterward and Paddy butchered one of the spring piglets. The farm was sixty-five acres of poor, sandy soil. It grew potatoes only with enormous effort and struggled to give them a passable kitchen garden. The nearby woods had plenty of blackberries, wild plums and currants, which they gathered. Maggie canned, jellied, and managed the smokehouse meat. Paddy—when he wasn't working in town as a handyman and farrier—put up the hay crop and what little corn they were able to raise.

Paddy stepped into the harness of marriage surprisingly well. He was already a hard worker and used to making whatever tools he needed. Maggie was spirited and although their arguments were legendary and not always private, resolving their conflicts often proved to be worth the trouble. Ultimately, they got along well. Paddy always affable; Maggie, a head- turner when in town and a demon worker when at home, had little patience for laziness or indolence. When she was not busy with farm chores or housework, she went to the woods to hunt. The forests provided plentiful game, and for Maggie, a respite from the kitchen work. Thanks to her mother, she could cook it if she could skin it, so the dinner table had plenty of variety from venison, waterfowl and porcupine.

Paddy was proud to display his handsome bride and growing brood at church and local functions. Maggie, for the most part, raised in the company of raucous men, understood and overlooked Paddy's more fraternal moments, which became fewer with each passing year. Evenings were more frequently spent shelling peas or pitting cherries on the front porch, rocking in chairs of his own making and smoking cigarettes that Maggie could still roll with one hand. The years passed and their family grew.

In short order, there had followed Mary, Seamus, Fiona, Brigid, Arthur, Andrew, Danny and finally Michael in 1925. Seamus was the delight of his mother's eye and could do no wrong. Fiona and Brigid were ginger-haired, white skinned beauties who took to housework and farm work like little ducks to water. Art and Andy loved the woods and everything about it. From an early age, it was clear that Danny was and would ever be a sure and steady hand at farming the land.

——»«(◊)»«——

In the summer of 1917, there was a train wreck at Glyem Spurr near Goodman and Paddy was asked to assist in getting the train and the track repaired and back in service. While he was away, Maggie had to stop hoeing the beans and go into the house long enough to deliver Catherine's little sister, Mary Evelyn. There was a war in Europe, and a letter from Oklahoma told them that Paddy's brother Emmett was killed. Maggie bought another cow and a small buggy with the train wreck money and began to sell her butter and eggs around the neighborhood. The hay crop was good enough to sell some to the livery stable in town, little Catherine died of the influenza. She was buried on the hill above the church; Paddy drank in the barn for three days.

From early on they were taught chores and to help each other. Little Mick played in the sunshine and followed his sisters wherever they went. Small like his father, he mostly took after his maternal grandmother with her darker complexion, deep-set brown eyes and black as coal hair, he was as different from his siblings as night and day. He liked the farm and the woods, but his eyes always looked beyond it. In Little Mick, Paddy found the salvation he had lost when Catherine died, so he and Little Mick could be seen everywhere together.

When Little Mick was five years old, The Depression hit and soon after, Paddy and Maggie lost their little farm to taxes. They heard there were more sympathetic Irish living in southwestern Wisconsin and not as many hard-nosed Scandinavians. The ground there was hilly, rocky but cheap. In Mineral Point, there were the lead mines run predominantly by Welshmen. The Caseys loaded what they had left in their Model A Ford and moved lock, stock and barrel to southern Wisconsin and a hopeful new start.

In Lafayette County, they found many of their kind in similar straits, and they settled down near little St. Michael's church, built by good Irishmen to resemble the churches of western Ireland, near the town of Fayette. Times were hard, money was nonexistent, Paddy bartered and traded. It was prohibition, so the still was busy, which made Paddy popular. He got on with the township, plowing and grading the roads, and it served as an excellent way to have a delivery route without the expense of maintaining his own vehicle. Seamus hired out as a farm hand and worked at the cheese factory, bringing home two dollars a week. Fiona and Brigid milked cows at the big Wiegel dairy farm, each milking fifteen to twenty cows twice a day and each bringing home a dollar a week. The Caseys were poor, and they knew it.

The hard times lingered, and their Irish luck continued. When Andy broke his leg in a fall, and it didn't mend correctly, he limped for the rest of his life, with one short leg. Fiona married at age sixteen and Brigid at fifteen; both lost their first children. Paddy built two tiny coffins, and they were buried, side by side at St. Michael's. Maggie's hands began to swell, and her knuckles reddened. Soon, Paddy had to roll her cigarettes for her. Little Mick learned to swim when his brothers threw him out of the boat while fishing one summer.

Paddy heard there was work in Madison and left to find it. He was killed while working at the Oscar Meyer meat plant, when the ladder he was standing on was knocked over by a stampede of frightened hogs. He fell to his death among them. He was forty-eight years old. Seamus and Arthur brought his body back in the old Ford pickup, and he was buried next to his two tiny granddaughters on the hill behind St. Michael's. Maggie rocked on the front porch for two days and stared out across the pasture. Always with an upward view and hungry for more knowledge Seamus decided to go to college.

Himself and Herself

By 1940, Seamus had become the first person on either side of the family to finish high school or attend college. After college, he went further still, starting at medical school at the University in Madison. Arthur and Andy had followed him, working nights and attending school in Madison and soon, both graduated too.

Maggie fared less well—her rheumatism had reached a point where she could no longer move without difficulty. Varicose veins—the result of too many children too close together—had created a network of ugly purple lumps that wound their way from her ankles to her groin. Her hands and feet were swollen and red and caused her to be unable to stand or manipulate many things without severe pain. Her large gnarled knuckles wouldn't allow her to perform the tedious morning task of pulling on the support wrappings to prevent the formation of dangerous blood clots in her legs. Mary Evelyn who slept in the bed with her would stop her morning duties to do it for her.

Far from once being able to roll her own cigarettes, she stooped to buying Lucky Strikes. When she could no longer hold the cigarettes between her fingers, she finally quit them altogether.

Her days soon became an abbreviation of the numerous activities she had used to perform. Now she could only shuffle to the kitchen to shake the clinkers into life in the stove before daylight then heating the water for tea—this for Danny and his young wife Martha as they headed to the barn for milking and chores. Then a brief shuffle to the front room and her rocker relocated from the front porch so it could be closer to the photograph of a young Paddy which was placed on the side table, under the schoolhouse clock

Danny had quit school in the eighth grade and now worked the farm with Martha. They now owned eight mixed breed cows, which provided two full cans of milk for the cheese factory every day and four good brood sows, which provided table meat and market hogs.

Little Mick helped with the chores and attended the Dobb's school through eighth grade. He was an average but unenthusiastic student and an average worker. Little Mick finished grade school but was ambivalent about high school. He was not lazy; he was *overly deliberate*. Danny soon learned if he wanted something done right he asked Mick, if he needed it done rapidly, he did it himself. Mick could turn a one-hour job into an all-day project; it wasn't that he dawdled, but every choice he made was considered, deliberate, and precise. His work was suited to things that needed to be perfect. Feeding the pigs often could extend his stay down at the hog house through breakfast-time. And unlike the rest of the family, Mick was quiet and reflective. If he were older, he would have been called diplomatic in his dealings with family members and the few neighbors he did talk with. Mick finished the eighth grade without a single fistfight. He didn't make friends readily, preferring instead to spend his free time walking in the woods or fishing, unconcerned about whether he caught anything. It was clear that farming was not an enthusiastic aspiration, but not because it was difficult.

Setting the table and cooking were now tasks too delicate for Maggie's red-knuckled hands. Mary Evelyn—now well into her twenties and considered to be an old-maid in the neighborhood—would handle that before they returned from the barn.

Mary Evelyn did the canning, gathering and gardening. She brought in the water for washing and cleaning, drawing it from the pump-stand that stood next to the milk house. She tended Maggie's needs; helping her to wash and dress, pulling on her stockings and shoes, making beds and maintaining the still bustling household. She helped butcher and smoke the meat and gather the eggs. She did all this before her two-mile walk to the one-room schoolhouse on Dobbs's Road where she would again start the stove, sweep the room, arrange the desks, ring the bell and teach her charges.

Andy got a teaching position at the high school in Madison. Arthur followed him and got a job at the Ray-O-Vac battery plant. The war in Europe meant that there was plenty of call for supplies from overseas. Everyone agreed that America should stay out of the fight but probably would not. The war was a distant concern for the family though, and they concentrated on their lives, making the best of everything.

With his teaching position securing his life a bit more, Andy put money down on a duplex house on Northern Court, on the east side of town and married a pretty Italian girl with a temper. That summer it was decided to move Maggie to the city along with Little Mick. On the farm, the ground was too uneven for her unsteady gait, and the house in Madison had a boiler in the basement and radiators in each room for heat, so no wood stove was required. Danny and Martha could handle the farm, and it would be one less worry for them. Mick could attend a high school that was within walking distance, and he and Maggie could occupy the first floor of Andy's new house. After much discussion, Mary Evelyn came too, and the Caseys became city folks.

Directly across the street with their front door facing the Caseys' front door was the Quinn house. The Quinn's had recently arrived in Madison themselves and welcomed the Caseys as kindred spirits. Thomas Quinn—a carpenter by trade—was constructing the new steeple at St. Patrick's Catholic Church, several blocks closer to the capital, after the previous steeple burned after a lightning strike. He and his wife, Theresa, had six children, three boys and three girls, five of them were married and far-flung. The last—a tail-ender called Dorothy Elizabeth or Lizzy for short—had come to them late in life almost twelve years junior to the next youngest sibling.

By the age of fourteen, Lizzy had become a full-figured beauty and had proved to be a bit precocious. A fact that boys were quick to discover and her parents a little too slow to notice. Subsequently, she had been sent to live with a married brother for a season and had only recently returned to live again with her parents. Now at fifteen, Lizzy was an eyeful for anyone no matter what she wore, but she was also shy and emotionally delicate as her parents called it. Prone to nervousness she craved approval and so was an excellent student, bright but not inventive. She was not athletic or prone to joining clubs or organizations lest she face teenage society's judgments and drama. She preferred her adventures to be limited to books, and she took walks along the Yahara River that passed by the end of their street. That is where she found Little Mick fishing and reflecting, and that is where he learned to converse with girls—quickly.

Lizzy and Mick became friends; a natural thing for Mick as he was provided with companionship and entertainment without the requirement of much reciprocity. For Lizzy it was someone to be with, who provided no judgment, was readily available and at a price she knew she could afford. It was not a torrid affair, just easy for both. Mick was his own man even at age fourteen; he consciously didn't seek out company and preferred his own.

Lizzy sought him out for companionship when she was lonesome or anxious for approval—which was often—and when it suited him, he was available. It was a relationship of convenience, and it supported them both through the difficult, socially fraught process of high school and maturing into adulthood. It provided both an outlet for the emotional and physical pressures that accompanied puberty and a buffer from the necessity of socializing with others.

In 1941, Seamus finished medical school and immediately enlisted in the Army, where he was given a commission as a Captain and assigned to Fort McCoy near Tomah, Wisconsin. The war had come to the United States, and to the Caseys—they heeded the call of the draft.

Arthur signed up as well and was commissioned into the signal corps as a lieutenant. Andy had a bad leg and was disqualified, although he tried to enlist anyway. Brigid and Fiona's men—Robert and Charlie—discussed it along with Danny but decided to wait and see whether they would be needed more in the war than at home farming the land and raising their broods. Within weeks though, the draft board called Danny and Charlie, but Robert was spared.

Seamus was soon deployed to Europe, working in field hospitals in England and eventually France. Arthur was assigned to the Aleutian Islands and spent the war at a listening post to guard the homeland against the incursion of the Yellow Hoard. Danny served in the Pacific working with the Army Corps of Engineers, building airstrips, roads and cleaning up what the marines finished destroying. All of them witnessed the horror of war from a moderate distance but were spared ongoing battle, much to Maggie's relief. All would return home heroes. Charlie came the closest to peril, fighting his way from Anzio to the Rhine River. A small flag banner in the front room window proudly showed four blue service stars for all in the neighborhood to see.

Life went on for those remaining behind though. Mick attended high school and mowed yards up and down the street as well as taking a job delivering for the Sunshine Market grocery store up around the corner. Every night, he—along with Andy, Rosalie, and Maggie—gathered around the Philco Radio to hear Edward R. Morrow give the news of the war. On the wall of his bedroom were maps of the world; faraway places he hoped to visit someday and small pins placed where he believed his brothers now stood. The world and its vastness had become close, which was both frightening and exciting.

Ten days before he turned eighteen he reported to the enlistment office to sign up with Maggie by his side. At the induction center, he was rejected. He was too small. Weighing only 117 pounds, he was three pounds under the minimum weight requirement. But he was determined to enlist and would not be deterred. He went down the hall and drank as much water as he could hold and returned to the nurse and demanded to be weighed again. At 121 pounds he passed and was assigned to the new Army Air Corps, where his small size and build made him ideally suited for the suicide position of tail-gunner on the new B-17 Flying Fortress bombers that were soon to be deployed overseas.

He would not come home the same boy that left Wisconsin.

Little Mick went to war.

July 1970,
Central Highlands,
Republic of South Vietnam

I am jolted out of my reverie as a sudden, deafening explosion rips through my daydream and backlights the fog to my right. I might have fallen asleep on my feet. I'm shocked and dazed. Stupefied by the sound, I gaze into the glow, momentarily paralyzed by the concussion and its brightness, transfixed by the shadows dancing within it. I briefly think the lingering light must be a flare, but then I feel the searing heat of a hundred bee stings on my arms, chest and hands. It is Willy Peter, a white phosphorus grenade; the liquid metal fragments burn into me with such searing intensity that it instantly jars me back to reality with a jolt. Immediately to my right, Hitchcock's rifle opens up with a volley, on full auto, and his yell makes me realize that they are upon us. Among us, in our ditch—with us. Between us.

A colossal shadow rears up in front of me, eight feet tall, running directly toward me. A demon, backlit by the flaring grenade making it larger than life. It is carrying a monstrous rifle at the shoulder, attacking my position. I raise my rifle and pull the trigger, nothing; jammed by too much mud or too much water. There is no time to pull the slide and clear the weapon. He is already on me. Reflexively I raise the gun up to ward off the onslaught, pointing the useless gun at the oncoming behemoth out of habit and training. He plunges himself onto my bayonet; the sound surprisingly like a pitchfork entering a bale of straw. A crunch, with a soft penetration. The rifle is wrenched from my hands

64

as he plunges into the ditch directly on top of me, his blood-curdling scream cut short by the bayonet. Together, we fall backward into the water, his contorting body bearing me down under him. I am helpless to defend myself, and immediately my open mouth fills with water, choking me, filling my nose.

The body on top of me continues to writhe, struggling against the rifle bayonet still buried in its guts making it impossible for me to throw him off me. I panic sinking down into the clinging, suctioning mud; drowning. I wrap my arms around him, trying to gain purchase to push him away and feel the bayonet stab through the palm of my left hand where it has emerged from his back pinning me to him. In my blind panic, I wrench my hand from the blade and grab the fabric of his shirt, tearing and scrambling to get away in frenzied desperation.

While still under the surface, I feel as much as hear the explosion of another grenade. In my disoriented state I don't know which direction it detonated from, but immediately, I feel something thrust into my right leg above my knee with tremendous force. I am shielded from the rest of the shrapnel halo by the body above me, and almost immediately he violently convulses once and then stops struggling. I struggle against the dead weight of him above me, and with a spasm of effort, I finally throw him aside, gasping and coughing for air, as I rise from beneath the water. At the last moment, my attacker has saved my life.

I come up out of the muddy morass, scrambling with my hands and feet up the ditch side behind me and out of the water. I emerge into a hell on earth of noise and carnage; tracer fire splitting the dark and the sounds of struggle to either side of me. Satan has come for me. I have no money to pay the ferryman.

In a rush of panic, I suck a lungful of air, almost unable to decipher the violence in front of me. Inadvertently, I scramble up on top of the body that used to be Spic, the Tunnel Rat, Vega, but is no more. Clawing at the muck in my eyes I brace my hands against the dirt preparing to push myself up to my feet, maybe to run. My hand comes down onto Spic's sidearm, and in the darkness, it's instinctively familiar in my hand, though I don't know that I've taken it at first. Stupefied, I regard the automatic in my hand, barely able to see it in the haze of flares and smoke and darkness, but I know what it is.

The beast that sleeps inside me with one eye open awakens—something clicks—suddenly I know what I need to do. Muscle memory and practice take over, as I thumb the safety off and rack the slide to bring a round into the chamber. The feel of it somehow reassuring, and reality is restored. A feeling of exultation washes over me. I feel my muscles respond and swell in the jubilation of power and strength. A red mist washes through my vision, hot and empowering; there is no more fear.

I scream at the top of my lungs.

I scream, not in fear or despair. I scream with the absolute knowledge that I am going to die and it is too late to care. I scream my rage and fury and feel the joy and lust of it. It blisters through me like fire.

And finally, I realize someone else will have to pay the ferryman if he wants me tonight because at last, I know why I am here. I have come to die.

I transfer the automatic to my left hand, the blood from the bayonet wound making the grip slippery, but my finger finds the trigger. I release my bush knife from my utility belt with my right hand. Motion and sound envelop everything around me, and everything slows to a crawl, my fear and fatigue have vanished in the mist. I feel the pure clarity and joy of discovery.

My demons and I are one after all and finally, we are in a place where we may have that final dance with the devil. I wade across the water in the ditch and scale the dirt bank in front of me. I will not wait for Death to find me; I will go to meet him. It is time that we finally shake hands.

Late October 1969, Mifflin Street, Madison, Wisconsin

The pounding, nauseating pain in my head finally crescendos to a point where I have to acknowledge it. I open my eyes to a strange room. The air in the room is stagnant; ripe with the odor of sweat, dirty laundry and ashtrays full of stale cigarettes and pot. It assaults my senses. The single window in the room is covered by a poster of Che' Guevara, which dims what little light is available from the outside. A rumpled bed sheet hangs from above the window frame, thumbtacked directly to the plaster. The lower edge is stuffed in a wad across the lower window sash and above the poster of Che'. The mottled and chipped plaster walls of the rest of the room are tacked with random Day-Glo posters, and a rumpled American Flag hangs directly above the bed instead of a headboard.

I am hot and sticky, wrapped up in the rumpled bed sheet. A naked leg draped across my lower body is making me feel claustrophobic and reminding me that my bladder is way too full. As carefully as possible, I extricate myself from the tangle of muggy cotton and sweaty flesh, pushing myself into a sitting position on the edge of the bed. Once in the upright position, the pounding in my head shifts forward and centers behind my eyes. I might need to throw up.

The floor of the room is a disaster of clothing and pizza boxes, while other debris hangs over and about on the minimal furniture, forgotten wherever it landed. My foot bumps up against an empty fifth of 101-proof Wild Turkey Kentucky Straight Bourbon, and there are several empty cans of Pabst Blue Ribbon in view. Some I see have been used as ashtrays and immediately, I need a cigarette and aspirin—a lot of aspirin.

I carefully rise to my feet, aware that I am still drunk enough to be unsteady and my vision still slightly doubled. I search through the detritus for my own clothes and a cigarette. There are plenty of empty cigarette wrappers, crumpled and tossed in corners or left among the rest of the rubble but there are no cigarettes. A purse lies open on the counter near the sink and yields a bottle of Midol. I take three tablets, washing it down with a half can of stale, room temperature beer and I smoke the longest cigarette butt that I can find—a slightly soggy Virginia Slim.

Dancing around the kitchen area on one leg I yank on my jeans and Rolling Stones Sticky Fingers T-shirt over my head and turn back to the room. Two bodies lie side by side in the bed, their hair in disarray. One girl, the blonde; supine, arms flung out in surrender, head tilted back, mouth open, breathing deeply. The other and owner of the naked leg—a brunette, lies on her side, her back curled into the other girl, spooned. One arm pillows her head, while her thumb of the other hand is corked firmly in her mouth. Sisters, I recall them telling me. Still pretty in the new day's light. One light, one dark; a smorgasbord of breasts, pale flesh and contrasting pubic patches, both oblivious to the hangovers that await them. One is named Karen, I think, and the other I cannot immediately remember if I heard it at all. They appear younger than I recall, almost childlike in repose.

Brief flashes of the night before come back to mind, and fuzzy on the edges, and in washed-out pastels. A party, a bonfire, loud music, joints being passed to me. Hysterical, unending laughter and eyes meeting from across the fire. These come back to me now, disjointed and out of sequence. With sudden clarity, I realize this is their apartment.

I step into the bathroom and after noisily emptying my bladder, I sit down on the stool to pull on my army surplus boots. Standing, I face myself in the bathroom mirror. My hair auburn and wavy spreads out over the collar of my T-shirt, shaggy bangs overhang my brows. It is long enough that the curled waves have to be contained with a rubber band from time to time and the bangs have to be pushed up out of my eyes. A shaggy Fu Manchu mustache that is a little too blond stands out among a week's worth of stubble and eyes so bloodshot that the ordinarily blue irises appear purple under the fluorescent light. There are two toothbrushes in a 'Juicy Lucy' coffee cup on the back of the toilet along with a half box of tampons, a box of Q-tips and a tub of Vaseline Petroleum Jelly. There is no toothpaste, but I use the pink toothbrush and some hand soap to scrub the funk out of my mouth as best I can.

After running my fingers through the hopeless tangle of my hair, I sigh, turn and grab my field jacket from the floor and let myself out of the efficiency apartment, closing the door as quietly as I can. I try to move softly, but my balance is still iffy, and soon, I am banging down the stairs to the street below. The racket my shoes make on the wooden staircase and the creak of the ancient banister booms and echoes hollowly in the empty stairwell and compounds my headache.

On the street, I am greeted by a glorious fall day; intense, unappreciated, bright sunshine and balmy weather. I note the position of the sun and reckon that it is still early morning before 10 a.m. for sure, more likely around 9. There is a light breeze coming in, off the lake to the north, which cools the air only slightly. The air itself is filled with the smell of dry leaves and Saturday's mown grass. Gazing up and down the tree-lined street, l realize that I am on Mifflin Street, a good eight to ten blocks from campus. I have no memory of this place; it must have been quite a night.

Throwing my jacket over my shoulder, I begin the walk back to campus. There is no reason to head back to my place; I have no food, aspirin or beer there. The campus offers the best chance for relief, and it is Saturday. A football game Saturday. The Student Union, specifically Der Rathskellar is the best destination on any Saturday, but better still during football weekends. There, I know I can grab a bite to eat, get a healing beer and settle in with my back to the wall and listen to the political speeches against the war that are a weekly staple. They also broadcast the radio play of the Badger football game on the in-house speaker system and today, they are supposed to play Indiana. The Fieldhouse is a short distance from the Union, and if a fellow is enterprising and appears confident, he can walk right in grab an almost clean towel and catch a shower.

So, I do.

A short time, later after a shower is secured and I've satisfied my hunger purloined out of the vending machines I settle down on the Union lounge furniture to wait until game time and when Der Rathskellar will start serving beer.

I am woken some time later, startled and jangled momentarily, not sure of my surroundings again. My hangover still makes my head feel like it is two feet wide and has been slapped by a plank. The side of my face is wet with spittle that has drooled out of my mouth and puddled on the table where I had rested it. The steady drone of the football play-by-play over the in-house speaker system gives me a sense of what time it is but is being drowned out by the usual high-pitched harangue of the peaceniks in Der Rathskellar. From the sound of it, the speaker has a full head of steam and is whipping the crowd into a frenzy of self-righteous indignation with shouted hyperbole. It grates upon my sensibilities, and I am unable to make sense of the rhetoric.

I rise stiffly and with some difficulty, shuffle to the doorway to see the commotion. A small man, wearing black framed glasses and a Roman collar is standing at the bar, waving a copy of *The Daily Cardinal* —the liberal campus daily rag—exhorting his audience in protest. It is none other than Father Groppi himself, and members of the Students for a Democratic Society, the SDS. Their rant today centers on the presence of the Dow Chemical Company's recruiting efforts on campus, the Demon Dow; makers and distributors of napalm. It is their conviction that nothing short of a march to the capital will be sufficient to communicate *our* outrage.

As I am leaning against the post inside the door, an angel dressed in jeans, a tie-dyed caftan and a smile, drifts to me with a full pitcher of beer and a tray, full of empty mugs. I am immediately much more interested in the proceedings and gratefully accept the beer. Instead of continuing to circulate through the crowd, she lingers at my side and between pauses for breath by the speakers, suggests that the walk to the capital is our patriotic duty, that we must draw the line with the war-mongers. She seems fervent and implores me and the other interested males surrounding her to make a statement to the university bigwigs to stop burning babies to death in Vietnam. Although I cannot speak for the others, I am ready to walk to Milwaukee with her if she asked me to.

The furor in the tavern reaches a fever pitch in no time. It is a beautiful fall day, balmy and we are young, full of youthful exuberance and most are moderately drunk. With the speakers in the lead, there is a rush to the doors, and with nothing else to do, I find myself joining the melee. After a brief organizational grouping on the sidewalks, the vanguard of students starts down Park Street and makes a left onto State Street chanting.

"Hell no, we won't go! Hell no, we won't go!"

As the grouping proceeds, many students join the mob, stepping in off the curb and the steps of the various campus buildings. By the time we pass Calvary Church, several dozen students are part of the throng. I have been swept up in the enthusiasm of the moment; I chant along with the others my hangover forgotten momentarily anesthetized by the infusion of new beer and the enthusiasm of the group.

The few short blocks to the Capitol building are not enough distance to cool the enthusiasm of the crowd. In fact, the short march in the beautiful afternoon took on a slightly festive feel as the people along the street gathered at the curb to watch and cheer or jeer. The appearance of Madison Capitol Police cordoning off the Capitol steps and live television crew's cameras at the ready, increased the energy of the moment and the opportunity for newsworthy demonstration swelled in our breasts. We are oblivious to the Paddy Wagons quietly parked along the side streets as we pass, the city cops leaning against their vehicles watching quietly with arms folded as we file past exercising our right of free speech.

A skinny male with frizzy, wild, afro-style hair and an American flag T-shirt brandishes a bullhorn in front of the cops and begins to shout, "Down with Dow, Down with Dow!" which was picked up by the crowd until it died down. Then he begins again "Hell no we won't go!," "One two three four, we don't want the fucking war!" This chant is picked up in earnest by the crowd, and they continue with enthusiasm for far longer while they began to march in a massive circle around the west side of the Capital green. At last he shouts, "Eighteen today, dead tomorrow! Eighteen today, dead tomorrow!" This chant is repeated as a dirge by the group, and instead of marching we slow our pace and drag our feet in our slow circuit that deliberately coalesces into a tighter circle and finally runs out of energy, facing the bullhorn-carrying speaker.

He calls for silence and begins when it finally mostly falls. "Let us bow our heads for our brothers that they have already taken from us. Let us show our reverence for the lives that are lost to the profit-seekers and the war pigs. What brother will step forward? We are here for you brothers, step forward, make your case. Hell no, you won't go!"

Heads turn from left to right in the crowd, looking for someone moved by the march and after a quiet murmur from the assembly one fellow—probably a student—young and obviously nervous steps forward. He holds up a small piece of paper the size of a business card and as we watch, digs out a steel Zippo lighter from his jeans pocket and lights the paper on fire. He lets the paper burn in his hand until finally, he drops the hot cinder and stamps it out. The cops regard the display passively while a cheer erupts from the crowd.

There is a shift as others push forward and I find myself moving too. I am buoyed by the energy and tension of the moment. I pull out my wallet and find the same small piece of paper. It has a date near the top of two months ago, a long number which is my Social Security number, and down near the bottom, my typed name—Robert Emmett Casey. It is a bifold card on the opposite face is a stamp and signature that says that I am duly registered with the local draft board. In the very center are the characters that cause so much concern, 2-S, my student deferment classification. But I already know it will soon say 1-A.

I step forward to the front and then out among my other brothers that have queued up at the bottom of the stairs and finally face the crowd. I reach into my pocket for my Zippo, snap it open and flick it, setting the flame to the bottom corner of the card. It doesn't burn very well; slightly damp from the depths of my wallet and made of heavier paper instead it slowly curls as it blackens in my fingers with little or no smoke. A cheer goes up from the crowd, and I smile at the recognition, a television crewman with a huge shoulder mounted camera moves in and directs the focus on my face. I hold the remains of the card up to the crowd and for the camera. I don't even feel the first nightstick hit the back of my head.

October 25, 1969, Police Paddy Wagon, Madison, Wisconsin

Motivation is a funny thing. I am not an anti-war peacenik hippie. I don't hate the war, I don't understand it. Because I don't understand it, I am afraid of it. At the core of my being, I have fantasized about being a hero but worried about the finality of death. Above all, I suspected a deep-seated cowardice that might betray me when my bravery was called into question. In high school, I admired the brainiac kids who would sit in the cafeteria and argue with three-dimensional clarity about the political aspects of the Vietnamese conflict. I listened to their arguments, not just to educate myself on these multifaceted issues, but because I admired the rhetoric and well-turned phrases that these teenage geniuses could manufacture. I gathered from these discussions that the war was fomented by economic greed and misplaced patriotism. However, it did not stir my guts or create heated animosity for the political administration that was supposedly reaping the benefits of the slaughter. If anything, it further increased my ambivalence. It wasn't until much later that I discovered that those so-called geniuses' primary motivation was also fear.

As it had become increasingly evident that I would probably graduate from high school, I had been suddenly confronted with a need to contemplate the future. In the past, I had moved forward in my childhood, buoyed by a tide of natural progression of institutional education, moving from one grade to the next without conscious planning or thought of the end of the line. The foundation of the elementary educational system seemed most successful in instilling a herd consciousness in its students. Sitting still in classes, learning to behave and regurgitate lessons on command and in turn be rewarded with progression to the next grade, only to repeat the exercise at the next higher level redundantly. It seemed that more than anything else, school taught students not to expect too much and to be patient because adulthood is a number measured by years and grades, not wisdom or experience.

A male student scheduled to graduate from high school in 1969 had only two real options for his future. He could enroll and attend college. Or he could join the military. The military draft was not a roll of the dice; it was a sure thing, a waiting game. Most young adult males expected that anyone with half a brain would follow the herd and join the procession through the next four years of regurgitating education at the college level and most agreed, surely by that time the war would be over. It was survival by education.

I had no vocational aspirations beyond my feeble attempts to garner peer acceptance. I had not given any real thought to life after high school. My summers at the farm taught me to love the land but I lacked the financial backing and sufficient knowledge of agronomy beyond adolescent fantasy and, reluctantly, I realized that this was not an option. However, when all was said and done, I opted for the path of least resistance; I enrolled in college.

That summer, I attended the requisite parties and exchanged future campus addresses with others, everyone hopeful of their bright, grown-up futures. Once at college, I discovered that enrolling in college and attending college were not the same things. Attending college required going to class, studying, and doing your own research prior to rote regurgitation and apparently, not drinking to excess. These two different approach requirements and my total lack of self-control had soon netted me a certificate of nonattendance, a

written request to vacate my dormitory room and a soon to be realized 1-A draft board classification.

———◈———

There are five of us in the Paddy Wagon and all of us handcuffed.
The back of my head hurts when I lean back against the wall. So,
do other parts of my body. My ribs and arms throb from the multiple
nightstick blows inflicted before the police dragged me to the waiting
wagon. I feel what must be blood running down the back of my neck
spreading out across my T-shirt and when I look down, I see that I also
have blood on the front of my shirt. The open mouth and tongue of my
Rolling Stones Sticky Fingers logo appears to be lapping it up. I cannot
raise my hands to the back of my head to assess the damage because
of the cuffs. The rest of the passengers appear to be like me. None of
them look very happy, and I am sure I look the same. Directing my
gaze to my left, toward the front of the vehicle, I see two cops through
the glassed, steel-latticed window, talking quietly. They are resolutely
gazing forward. I have been arrested—again. The wrong place at the
right time—again.

The police vehicle slows and begins a left turn, bumping up over a
curb, before it reverses direction and executes a three- point turn and
then jolts to a stop. In a moment, there is a metallic clatter of the lock
on the rear door, and it is unlocked. With a screech, the double rear
doors are pulled open and one of the cops, palm up, twitches his fingers beckoning those of us inside to climb out. Heaving myself up off
from the bench without the benefit of my hands, I discover that I have
other aching spots. The ceiling in the van is too low to stand upright,
and the stooped position as I walk to the rear of the wagon makes my
head pound even more—the combination of hangover and a probable

concussion. I join the small procession out onto the loading dock of the police station and then through the steel rear door, as one of the two cops holds it open.

We are taken directly to a holding cell area where another unsmiling and very businesslike officer confiscates my belt, shoelaces and field jacket so I won't hang myself in the cell. After what seems an overly thorough search of my pockets and groin area, he unlocks the handcuffs and directs me into a cell. I drop gratefully onto the bench in the corner and lean my face against the cool, concrete wall. My head was already hurting before someone hit it with a stick, and now the room keeps tilting under my feet. Closing my eyes to the pounding in my head, I am overwhelmed by a sudden wave of fatigue that steals the last of the strength from my legs.

Around me, I listen to the other voices as their angst is vocalized. Terrified at the unfamiliar circumstance they are in, fearful of parental reprisal, institutional censorship and university expulsion, they bemoan their situation in a circular, shared diatribe. I have no such fear. I have an extended history of parental disappointment, a laundry list of institutional censorship and have been released from any university connection with the posting of my grades and attendance records.

Once again, I have managed to find myself in exactly the right place at the wrong time. In my exhausted and hung-over state, I reflect on another lousy decision made from a subconscious desire to please someone and garner, if not affection, then at least acceptance. Once again, I recognize with finality that none of those I had hoped to impress will share the penalties of my behavior. I make myself as comfortable as possible in the cell corner and lose myself to self-recrimination and regret.

Sitting in the holding cell with my headache rapidly expanding to fill the available space I was aware that my life options were narrowing. As far as I was concerned, I had left Chicago for the last time. I had no intention of returning those dirty streets. My adolescent fantasies of a brighter future through education had mostly been centered on my desire to put home as far behind me as I possibly could and take it from there. To me, Wisconsin had represented the *Promised Land* of opportunity with its clean air, lack of traffic and above all people that were actually more interested in what you had to say then in picking your pocket. I had fallen victim to one of the most common of the immature misconceptions of youth. In my mind, I had believed that changing geography equaled changing your life. My Uncle Danny had a saying that he had repeated so often that I had stopped hearing it a long time ago.

"Wherever you go in life you always take your own worst enemy with you." He would say things like that while sitting on a milking stool his face inches away from the cows right hip his hands slowly stroking the last of her milk into a five-gallon pail. The comment would usually be in response to some other unspoken conversation that he was having in his own head while he worked, but occasionally would be directed at something I had brought up several hours before. It took Uncle Danny a long time to answer a question because he needed to consider it for a while. Aunt Martha had once told me that if you wanted to know the weather was this morning, you had better have asked Danny last Tuesday.

This comment was always directed at my latest 'pie in the sky' dream. When he originally began to say the phrase, I hadn't understood who he was talking about. Later, when I was convinced that success in life eluded me because of the people and circumstances that surrounded me, I just believed that he didn't know anything about life. He was a simple old man who had lived his entire life on a sixty-seven-acre truck farm in the middle of nowhere. I, like most people my age, believed that a change of clothes equaled a complete change in personality. I knew with certainty in my gut that a drastic change in geography would guarantee a new life with a different future. In the span of just a few short months, even with a radical change in geography, somehow bad luck and past experience had pursued me right into this holding cell.

A police officer in a starched white shirt with a narrow blue tie entered through the steel door at the other end of the corridor. His shoe heels loud on the cement floor as he walked in a measured stride toward the holding cell. He had a clipboard in his right hand, and with his left, he idly ran his fingers across the bars of the cells. When he reached our cage, he signaled the overly diligent cop to unlock the cell and stood in the cell doorway. After consulting his clipboard, he called a name and one of the boys—already in tears—was taken down the hall and through the steel door at the end of it. It is apparently a slow process wherever they take him because the span of time before they come for the next victim seemed protracted. I am glad that I didn't go first, but I don't want to be last either. I dread the consequences of what is beyond the door at the end of the hall. The sound of that door closing portends inevitable doom.

Whenever the officer returned for another subject, the previous one does not return to the cell with him. That inserted an air of finality to the proceedings. Even though I am reasonably sure that you won't be executed for burning your draft card, I don't know for sure that you can't be. In the cell block, as far as I can see in either direction, there is no clock and no sound once the steel door at the end of the hall closes. After so long in the cell, the few that remained were completely talked out, no one wanted to look at the door at the end of the hall, but we couldn't help doing so, glancing and waiting, another glance to the door another wait, five minutes—taking forever.

When it is down to myself and another fellow, the snappily dressed officer came through the steel door and sauntered down the corridor again, requisite clipboard in hand. From his expression I couldn't tell if he is enjoying the proceedings or not; he appears utterly expressionless although I suspect he is not neutral in his opinions. After consulting his clipboard again, he regarded the two of us. After a moment's consideration, his gaze fell on me, and he said, "How about you hippie? What's your name? And please don't tell me it's Ray O'Sunshine or I will personally kick your ass, all the way down the hallway."

"Robert Emmett Casey. Sir." Again, he looks at the clipboard.

"Casey, hmm, it seems that you already have a little history here Mr. Casey. You're one of those troublemakers, are you? The University doesn't even have you on their rolls so—Are you even a student at the University?"

The inflection in his voice makes it sound like a question, but it was evident that he already knew that I was no longer a student. It occurred to me that you don't have to be a student at the university to demonstrate against the war, but my intellectual reflexes were just fast enough to stop me from saying so. It would have just made the situation worse and worse I didn't need right now.

I remain as silent and as still as possible, so after a long pause, he finished with, "I guess we need to have a little talk?"

He looked at the other boy in the cell and addressed him briefly. "That's the lot, Cunningham. See the disbursement officer at the front desk. Thanks for your help today, we appreciate your cooperation."

I was stupefied by the realization that this Cunningham kid was one of the cops, not one the kids in the cell. I stare at him and realize that he bears only a slight resemblance to the other boys in the cell. His hair is shorter and neater, his army surplus jacket is much cleaner than mine, and his tie-dyed T-shirt and bell bottom pants are color coordinated, even the embroidered hem at the end of the pant legs matched his shirt. Cunningham is one of them. One of the cops.

Officer Clipboard obviously enjoyed my reaction, and his gaze never left my face as he watched me go from stunned to realization to anger. This may have been the most fun he had had all day. I could tell he had been saving the surprise for me.

If I had to admit it, I probably would have acknowledged a measure of grudging admiration for ingenuity. I doubt I would have thought of that strategy. For whatever time span we had been sitting in this shit-hole, Cunningham had been sitting in the same shithole, watching the rest of us and probably ready to report. I was glad that I spent my time in self-reflection and not talking to anyone. There would be no telling what I might have said that now might be held against me.

As for having a little talk, I was entirely sure he knew I didn't want to have a little talk. I have had plenty of these little talks. Police stations have changed over the years. The equipment is more modern, and most cops will tell you that their methods are more efficient, but not much has changed as far as I can tell. The desks in the bullpen are all still big bulky grey steel. There are always a few cops sitting at the desks, staring off into space or twiddling a pencil while they hold a phone to their ear. The office at the back of the room with the glass windows and the closeable blinds is still there. This is where the little talk used to take place. Nowadays, it takes place in a tiny little win-dowless room with a steel topped table and two or three steel chairs. There are small, steel rings in the floor under the chairs, where they can attach their *guests* by their ankle chains, and there is a tape record-er on the table. I would suppose that the tape recorder and room suf-fice as more efficient methods and I would hazard that they get more serious once you are legally an adult.

Officer Clipboard stepped back far enough into the walkway along the cell fronts to allow me to proceed ahead and then pointed the way toward the steel door. An officer who is watching from the other side of the six by six-inch window pushes the door open for us, and I enter the police station proper. Ahead of me, down a short hallway, there is the bullpen, with the standard grey desks and the normal chat-ter of ringing telephones, men laughing around the water cooler, and typewriters clacking. In the bullpen, it was just another day; nothing special.

In the hallway were four closed doors—two doors to the right and two to the left. The uniformed policeman squeezed past me and with his hand on my right shoulder leaned forward and opened the right-hand door, closest to the bullpen. Ushering me in, he steers me by the shoulder into the room and into a chair opposite the doorway and behind a small table. Both of the men then left the room. There is no knob on the inside of the door. The walls of the interrogation room are bare except for a hand-printed sign stapled to the drywall next to the door informing me that there is no smoking or spitting tolerated in this room. To my left, a mirror is set into the wall that is about two feet square. Since I cannot smoke or spit in the room, I guessed the next logical activity must be to comb my hair.

July 21, 1970,
NSA Station Hospital,
Danang, South Vietnam

The following is a verbatim transcript of the audio tape debriefing of Private E-2, Anthony Dugan, Company C, 173rd Airborne Division, 2nd Battalion, 503rd Airborne Infantry regarding ambush and skirmish encounter of July 18- 19, 1970. Taped interview: 0915 hours, July 21, 1970, in the presence of Major George M. Lundt, 2nd Battalion Executive Officer, and Corporal Wallace Charles, Battalion Clerk.

———◦‹(◦)›◦———

Private Dugan:
We was out all day on recon. It wasn't too hot for a change, but everything was just real wet. We were all soaked to the skin ten minutes after we were outside the wire. Most of the day we were walking downhill so it wasn't too bad, and we didn't see nothin'. Man, nothin', just wet, you know, wet grass, wet bushes, wet trees, all of 'em drippin', you know, not like what come later. When we stopped for chow, Sarge (Staff Sergeant Hobbs) told us all to change socks. Man, your feet are wet here all day, every day, like I don't want to get that foot rot stuff, you know. *"Just a nice walk in the woods"* what the Sarge said.

We were going pretty slow though all day cuz our Point, (Specialist Vega) was checking for traps, (booby-traps), and rat holes in the thick stuff. Coming back was uphill, ya' know, and it got hotter. I was getting shagged out, cuz I was carrying a lot of shit.

As far as I can tell we came back in a sort of circle, we were supposed to be checking the trail, (Ho Chi Minh Trail) for any activity, but we didn't see much that I could tell. All of a sudden, all hell busts loose. I was about halfway between the front and back, you know, of the squad 'cuz that's where they put us FNG's (new replacements), so's we can't get into trouble and (deleted) stuff up. Me and Hole (PFC Casey) were carrying all of the heavy shit. Hole had the 79 and, you know, the grenades, and we both had a couple of bands of chopper rounds. That shit gets pretty heavy slogging all day with wet feet I tell ya'.

Anyway, they must'a daisy-chained four or five claymores in front of us cuz man when they popped it (deleted) knocked me down from the blast. I couldn't hear nothing, Jesus (deleted) there was (deleted) smoke everywhere and all of us was laying around on the ground. Spence (Specialist 4 Spencer) was lying right there next to me on his back, and his shirt and his face were all smoking, and I knew he was a goner but you know it didn't seem real or nothing just kinda slow and quiet-like. I was looking around, and Hole looks at me, man we were like twenty feet apart, and just a minute ago we were right next to each other.

Then Hobbs was there, and he's pulling on my arm and pointing to this big ditch about thirty or forty feet down the hill, and I swear to God his mouth is hollering but I didn't hear a sound, there was nothing coming out of it. Sarge, he's got blood all over his face, but he's got his piece out, and he keeps pointing so I'm thinking we better get in that ditch but you know I can't get my feet to do it. Then, it's like all of a sudden I can hear again and (deleted) I wished I couldn't cuz all I can hear is sounds like a whole swarm of bees or wasps or something flying around and the grass, and the brush is getting all chopped to bits and these little pieces of grass and leaves are flying around and it's like a big lawnmower that you can't see or something, you know? Like it's cutting the shit all around us, and I can smell grass like it's just been mowed all fresh-like.

Then we wuz running, and I got Spence by the ankle, and he's so (deleted) heavy, and me and Hitch (Specialist 4 Hitchcock) are pulling and scrambling, and Gonzalez is yelling for us to leave him he's dead. I can see Conny (Specialist 4 Connelly) make the ditch and then Spic (PFC Vega) goes down right in front of us and he's like trying to get up, and Hole grabs him and helps him up, and we're running. Man, I mean, we are running, and the bees never stop, and we jump into this (deleted) ditch, and the (deleted) thing is full of water right up to my ass.

Jesus, it was so noisy. Hobbs is hollering, you know, telling us to turn and fire. Hitch and Conny start settin' up The Pig, (M60 machine gun), and all of a sudden Hole opens up with that Thumper, (M79 grenade launcher), Jesus there was so much noise. The incoming is so thick we can't get our heads over the edge of the ditch you know, just to see what's what. We're all leanin' with our backs against the dirt, and we can't get up to shoot back, so Hole keeps lobbing grenades. Then we watched Vega die. He's looking right at us on the other side of the ditch, and then he's dead, and I can't stop looking at him you know, he just laid there all night, and he watched us, and I hope he's proud of us cuz we did our best and he just could only watch, you know. I always liked Vega, he was cool man. He didn't deserve that. I shoulda closed his eyes cuz pretty soon it got really bad in that ditch you know. He shouldn't've seen it. I coulda done that but I didn't think of it. I coulda' closed his eyes.

Hobbs didn't look too good, you know, he's like pointing us into position but he's just sitting about halfway down the bank and he is coughing a lot, but he's cool you know, like it's normal or something.

Once we're like down in the ditch and Conny fires up The Pig it starts to quiet down a little and we start to take peeks over the top, and Hole is throwing those grenades way out there and for a while, we are giving them a little bit of hell back, ya know. But then Hobbs tells us to stop shooting cuz we don't have enough ammo, and just return fire once in a while like so's they'd know we're still sharp-like.

Then it got dark. Like all of a sudden, you know, all day it's like foggy/cloudy and then it's just dark, like we didn't notice it coming on or something and now we don't just hear them wasps flying by, now we can see em' cuz of the tracer rounds and they're zipping all around but we don't have enough ammo to direct fire and Hobbs, he keeps telling us that they'll be here soon enough and we (deleted) better be ready, and I'm pretty scared for first time that day.

Pretty soon you can't see your hands or rifle or nothing and it gets pretty quiet and Hobbs keeps telling us to get ready. We're standing there in the water, and it's quiet, and we can't hear nothing except Hobbs coughing and frogs and crickets and shit. Then they're in the ditch and Hitchcock is hollering like he's on fire and shooting and they're all down at that end, and we go and help him out. Then a Willy Peter goes off, and we can see a little bit, and you can see the tracers only go a few feet before they disappear into something. Then a couple flares get lit up, and the shadows turned into people, you know, and Hitchcock is up on top, and he's swinging his rifle like a baseball bat and yelling like he's a crazy man, and all of sudden Hole comes out of that ditch and he's all business man he's got that big (deleted) bush knife and a pistol and he shoots a guy right in the face and then damn near cuts him in half, and he and Hitchcock are standing next to each other and they're fighting.

(pause)

Jesus, I never seen nothing like that before they were all around him and he started screaming like Hitchcock and swinging that big (deleted) knife and snot were flying out of his nose, and he was killing them with both hands and I just found myself next to him, and we stood there. We stood our ground man. They were on top of us, they were like right *here* man. I could see their eyes, I could smell them, Jesus man, I could tell what they ate for breakfast, they were *right there* man.

(pause)

Hole and Hitchcock, you never saw nothing like that, I hope to god I never do again. We did the best we could, sometimes we were in the ditch, and sometimes we were up on top, and we did the best we could. And then it just stopped. It just stopped.

(pause)

Then there wasn't any shootin', Hitchcock stopped screaming and one by one we kinda did a roll call. Gonzalez didn't answer, and Hobbs had a coughing fit, Hale said he was shot. Then there wasn't any sound, and you could feel the fog on your face, and my legs were so tired, and you know what? I'm thinking about how I hate my feet being so wet, and if I knew where my pack was I could change my socks, can you believe it? I was thinking about dry socks.

Hobbs told Hole and me to look for weapons and ammo, so we crawled out, and there were like VC lying right at the top of the ditch, and maybe some of us too, but we got a couple rifles, one was Spence's for sure, and I picked up a couple grenades too. The rifles had banana clips that still had rounds in them. Then there was quiet, long quiet, there was still incoming, but man I don't know, they didn't come right back, they waited us out. That was pretty good cuz I don't know if we could've stood another one.

Pretty soon we could see, and then we could've shot too cuz we had more ammo. When the light came, they went back into the trees, and we got back in the ditch, and I was thinking that this was the way it was going to be.

(pause)

You know? Just be in that ditch, and I didn't know why we were trying so hard to keep them from being in the ditch too cuz we wuz all gonna die anyway.

(pause)

I looked at Spic, and his eyes were all cloudy like, and I could see Hobbs, and he was lying face down up on top, and I figured he'd got it. Then there was more incoming, and I peeked up over the top, and it was the grunts from the FB, and they were firing into the trees, and they lit it up, and it was so nice cuz I knew that now I could go to sleep. That's what I remember except that it took so long to happen.

October 1969,
Police Headquarters,
Madison, Wisconsin

This is an interrogation room. I have seen them before, and I know the mirror is a two-way window. It appeared that they were taking my arrest as seriously as I was, so I decided to rehearse my sincerity speech—which had worked practically never—just in case it came to that and realized I didn't yet know what I would be apologizing for. I decided to work on my sincere face instead but knew better than to practice it in the mirror. However, meeting my reflection derailed that briefly as I surveyed the damage they'd done. A scraped and bloody lump was coloring nicely on the right side of my forehead, and dried blood had drawn a ragged line, down the left side of my temple to my chin. My eyes were still bloodshot, and there were dark circles underneath them. I told myself I wouldn't look half as bad if I would spend more time sleeping at night.

While examining the damage, the door burst open and two new officials entered the room brusquely, followed by Officer Clipboard. The first man unclipped his badge from his belt and laid it on the table in front of me—a silver shield with an eagle sitting on the top and a blue circle with an insignia in the center. Around the outside of the blue circle the words Marshal on the left Service on the right bracket a large U.S. in silver and again Marshal at the bottom. Shit, this guy was a fed. He did not introduce himself but sat down behind his badge at the end of the small table, facing the mirrored wall he leaned back in his chair and crossed his arms.

The second gentleman was dressed in a brown suit, white shirt and a narrow tie. By that time of day, he should have loosened the tie and maybe even dispensed with the jacket, but his tie was knotted tight at his neck, and his suit and shirt looked as if he'd just arrived.

He introduced himself as Mr. Hamesworth, and I immediately assumed that his butthole was probably puckered as tight as the rest of his outfit. Before I could school my expression to ensure it wasn't giving that thought away, he sighed and dropped a laminated identification card onto the table facing me so that I could read it. The small card has a cut-out hole in the top with a lanyard snaked through it. His picture was a mirror of his current expression; sour. I skimmed to the bottom where it stated that he is a duly sworn member of the local Selective Service board. He took the seat directly across the table from me, putting him between the door and me and pointed me into the chair.

The officer with the clipboard and sense of humor casually leaned in the corner of the room between the door and the mirror on the wall and folded his arms while still gripping the clipboard in his right hand.

"This young man is Mr. Robert Emmett Casey, he is charged with disturbing the peace, inciting a riot, destruction of U. S. government property, and willful violation of the Military Selective Service Act. All in all, a nice package that—with a conviction—carries a maximum sentence of two to three years hard labor at Fort Leavenworth, Kansas."

"Wait a minute," my voice an octave higher than normal, "I didn't start a riot and what government property did I destroy?"

The marshal on my right snorted through his nose and leaned forward in his seat and uncrossing his arms he put one hand on the edge of the table. "Easy now boy, you don't want any more trouble. Do you?" He left no doubt that he was the enforcer here.

"Go ahead, Mr. Hamesworth."

Mr. Hamesworth cleared his throat and actually gave me a little half-smile. "Well then, although I cannot speak to the charges regarding the subsequent riot and arrests, I can help you understand how much trouble you have created for yourself Mr. er, uh, Casey.

The draft card that you burned actually qualifies as government property. It is your government classification and an official document of the United States Government. It is just as illegal for you to wantonly destroy that document as it would be for you to burn the United States Flag. In addition to destroying your draft card—which by the way you were kind enough to do on camera and in front of dozens of witnesses—you have refused to be registered for the Selective Services and to serve our country. I will state for your information and the record, that knowing and willful refusal to present yourself for the draft and to serve if called upon is a federal offense."

"You don't understand; I was just caught up in the moment. I wasn't really thinking about all that stuff."

"Be that as it may Mr. er, uh, Casey, when we begin to prosecute you, your case is going to be open and shut. You have actually done me an enormous favor. Normally, when we make an arrest, it is difficult to prove that a person is willfully refusing the draft, but in your case, we have witnesses and news footage," he paused for a second and met my eyes, and the smile became more wolfish, "and we thank you for that. A federal judge in the U. S. District Court for Western Wisconsin—which, by the way, is a few short blocks from here—will have no trouble indicting you on those charges. Your case will be *nolo contendere* which means you will have no defense to present. Once you finally get to court, you will be on your way to Fort Leavenworth Prison, in Kansas very shortly."

He uttered his speech in almost a single breath. After he finished, he dropped back into his chair and took a deep breath, straightened his tie which wasn't askew and pulled down the lapels of his suit jacket. I am looking at him, stunned and as I don't speak, he holds out his hands in front of him, palms up, and as if to say it is as simple as that. When I still don't speak, he leans back, crosses his arms with a smug smile, and relaxes in his seat.

At first, I expect someone to add something, maybe throw me a bone, a lifeline, but the silence that stretches out increases my discomfort. My more than slightly addled thought processes were now in a complete shutdown. A few short hours ago I was partying, getting laid, and enjoying myself—a lot. Suddenly, three very serious grown-ups were looking at me like a three- course dinner and talking about three years of hard labor, and in prison no less. I struggled to connect the dots; my head hurt, and I felt like my tongue was two sizes too large.

"Can I get a drink of water?"

The cop leaning against the wall, holding his clipboard, spoke up.

"In a few minutes, you are going to be processed over to the marshall here. That will save us the trouble of formally booking you and processing you for a bail hearing. The U.S. Marshals can hold you until your court date without a hearing for bail if they so choose. Saves us a lot of trouble for dirtbags like you, and we get you out of our system without a lot of headaches. Marshall Goodman, he's all yours."

With that, he made a small note on his clipboard and passed it to the burly U.S. Marshal. Goodman unhooked his pen from his shirt pocket, clicks it half a dozen times and then signs the paper that is presented. Signature secured, Officer Clipboard smiled at me and gave me a little wink, then knocked on the door, which opened and out he went. I never got his name. Marshall Goodman pushed away from the table and stood. Plucking his badge off the table in one movement he hooked it to the left side of his belt in exact line with his shirt pocket. To Hamesworth he said, "I'll go get his paperwork and be right back. Shouldn't take more than ten or fifteen minutes."

He returned in less than a minute with a large Dixie Cup in each hand. One hand had coffee, the other water and he set them both in front of me. I made eye contact with him, probably for the first time.

"You've got ten minutes son. Think about using them for something smart."

The water went down in less than a second. The coffee was hot, burnt from sitting in a pot on a hot plate far too long. I took a long sip and felt circulation begin to return to my face and scalp. Hamesworth reached down to a paper bag near his feet that I hadn't noticed before and pulled out my pack of Marlboro's and my beat-up Zippo lighter and slid them across to me. I was surprised but grateful by the unexpected humanity from the stiff.

"No ashes on the floor." He reminded me. "Use the cup."

Two long inhales of life-giving tobacco and half a cup of burnt coffee, and I began to return to some semblance of intelligence. Hamesworth pushed back from the table to avoid the cloud of cigarette smoke that seemed magnetically attracted to him, a look of slight discomfort on his face. I regarded him with the benefit of better critical thinking, and he returned the gaze. I thought about Goodman's remark, "…use it for something smart." What did he think that would be, I couldn't walk out could I? Or can I?

"Am I missing something here? I never got my phone call, you know."

"It is my understanding that you don't usually get a phone call until after you have been booked and processed. Neither of these will be done until you are under Marshal Goodman's jurisdiction. Which will be in just a few minutes."

"So, in a few minutes I will be arrested by a federal marshal and formally charged, but until right now?"

"As of right now you are still in limbo; suspended animation as far as the system is concerned, Mr. Casey."

"There are no options other than, um, Marshal Goodwin?"

"You can always consent to serve your country."

He said this in a quiet half whisper, with his eyes directed at his nametag lying midway between us on the table.

"What? What do you mean?"

"Mr. Casey, you are going to be charged with refusing to register with the Selective Service System, and subsequently refusing to serve in the military. Both are technically federal crimes; however, both are predicated upon you refusing to serve your country. Should you change your mind . . ."

"So, you're saying if I just enlist in the Army, this goes away?"

"Yes, that's true. Not the Army necessarily, all you need do is to volunteer for the draft. Technically, you would be an enlisted man, but only be obligated to serve the two years required of a draftee."

I visualized the marshal processing my paperwork with a small smile, looking forward to making me uncomfortable, locking me in a cell in a federal jail; bread and water, humiliation. I thought about my parents, ashamed. Again.

"I could do that. Could I volunteer, if it's not too late?"

"It is certainly not too late. It would avoid a lot of unnecessary trouble, and you can walk out of here a free man."

"Okay."

I paused. My palms were sweating, and my head was swimming. The inside of my mouth tasted of bile and bad coffee. I tried to find some spit to moisten my tongue, and I managed to croak out.

"Gimme two!"

Another day had just kicked me in the balls.

April 1958,
Kimball Square,
Chicago, Illinois

I'm curled into a tight fetal position on the cold cement. My arms are wrapped around my knees, and I struggle to hold on to them as tightly as I can. I cannot protect my head though, and the kicks are landing in a flurry of fevered brutality. The punching is over now that I have fallen to the ground. The three boys, about my age, stand over me. Their hands are on the wall of the building I am sheltering against, kicks landing as quickly as they can, without losing their balance. Two older boys, fifth or sixth graders, supervise from a few feet, their arms folded as they lean against the wall on the other side of the passageway. My assailants are *in training*.

Apartment buildings line most of the streets from block to block, identical in every respect except for the shade of brick used in their construction. They are nondescript, anonymous, and unremarkable in every respect. To get from the street side of the building to the rear courtyards of each, there is a small walkway that enters from one side or the other of their street- facing edifice and passes through a short tunnel under one of the second-floor apartments. Twenty feet of darkness that opens into a narrow courtyard.

The courtyards are where the wooden staircases wind through the consecutive floors to the back entrances of the apartments they serve. It is where the housewives lean over the banister railings to yell at their kids and hang their wash to dry on long clotheslines that traverse the open spaces. The clotheslines tether the various staircases together across the expanse of the courtyard. Each floor shares one or two sets of clotheslines, and each is festooned with their limit of white cotton squared diapers, perfectly uniform and hanging limply in the doldrums of unmoving air between the back-to-back buildings.

"That's good enough," one of the older boys says. "Get him up."

With one final kick to the side of my head, there is a moment of relief before I am pulled to my feet. I cannot get my breath, and I am dizzy. I feel puke rise in my throat. The feet and legs of one of the older boys swim into my line of sight. I push myself back against the rough bricks of the passageway and straighten up as much as my labored breathing allows, sobbing mostly silent tears causing me to gasp as much as the inability to breathe properly. Snot is flowing freely from my nose mingling with plenty of blood. I am afraid that I will puke on his shoes and provoke more beatings. He shoves me hard in the center of my chest, his hand holding me up and leans in, inches from my face.

"You're on the wrong side of Fullerton, punk. You know better than that. If you didn't, you do now." He paused, and the pushes hard on my chest increases, as he continues, "Tell those sons-a-bitches Conway and D'Angelo to make sure you stay on your side. This is what happens to shit stains like you when you walk on our street."

He brings his knee up into my crotch with so much force it lifts me off my feet, and I drop like a sack of cement onto the sidewalk. The damage to my nuts is not what it could have been ten years from now, but I don't know that yet. Instead, pain explodes into my brain. I puke.

I am strangled by the combination of sobbing and crying; can't pull in a full breath, continuing the cycle. As my right eye is swelling shut, I look through the slit and watch the five sets of shoes run down the tunnel and into the courtyard beyond.

I lie there until my breathing slows, knowing I should try to get up but the cement is cold, and my body refuses to respond. After a time, maybe a long time, my vital functions slowly return. My heart rate slows while the cool sidewalk feels refreshing on my face, which feels like it is on fire.

It is early afternoon. I should be home from school by now, but I chose a different route, without considering the consequences. At the end of the school day, all eight grades of Our Lady of Grace march out of the school in an orderly fashion. When they are all assembled in the front of the church, the children that go north line up to cross Altgeld. The children that go south line up to cross Fullerton, this is my group. Once the mass of children crosses the street, we are on our own to make our way home. I am supposed to find my sister Kate so that she can keep an eye on me, but I have to stay after school so often that she doesn't wait for me anymore.

Miss Graham is my third-grade teacher and the first teacher that I have had that is not a Dominican nun. She is the most beautiful woman I have ever seen. I plan how I will marry her as I watch her teaching the class. I find ways to aggravate her, so she will give me individual attention. I worship her from afar whenever I can. Miss Graham is the line monitor for the group that goes north across Altgeld. If I get into that line of students, I can pass within a few feet of her. I look forward to that moment with fevered anticipation every afternoon. After dismissal, I take my place in the single-file line and gaze openly as I approach her. She keeps her gaze focused straight ahead, somewhere between the line on the right side of the sidewalk and the line on the left side of the sidewalk, alert to any shenanigans that might disrupt the ordered discipline. I don't even try to avert my glance or keep her in my peripheral vision; I have no sense of subtlety. I stare in open admiration, her facial profile stunning in its incredible beauty. I imagine that she watches me out of the corner of her eye, knowing that our fates are intertwined, awaiting that time when we can be together. Forever.

After those fleeting moments of romantic bliss, I cross Altgeld and am on my own. I must double back to find my way home. I cannot return the way I came and make my way down to Fullerton because I assume that my devious scheme will be discovered by the suspicious nuns. I must circle down three blocks east to come up to the traffic light at Fullerton and Central Park. Fullerton is a big avenue, four lanes wide, with trolley-bus traffic as well as a lot of car and truck traffic. I can't get across the street without the lights.

I have made this trip many times, and I have the route down. Today was different. Typically, I would have about a thirty-minute head start on the kids that go the public school in the neighborhood, Kimball School. Today those kids didn't have school. Pulaski Day, no public school for the kids that live in Chicago—unless of course, you attend a Catholic school. I hadn't even gotten to the end of the first block before they had caught me.

I pull myself up into a kneeling position and then, using the tips of my fingers to grip the rough bricks, I work my feet underneath me and eventually, stand up. My right arm does not work correctly, and I can feel the pulse in my right eye, and it will not open beyond a fevered slit. I stand there, too hurt to assess myself, and too dazed to perform such a complicated inventory. I have just enough sense to realize that I must go toward the light at the end that the boys did not go out of, so I turn that direction.

The first step is agonizing and the second is no better. With each step, the pain in my crotch causes me to I suck my breath through my teeth trying to adjust to it. By the time I reach the sidewalk, I settle into a shuffling bow-legged gait. Each step requires concentration. My lips are bruised and torn and, as I run my tongue over them, they sting and make my eye hurt even more. One of my back teeth on the right side moves back and forth when I prod it, making little squishing sounds. I don't pause when I reach the pavement, concentrating instead on making my next step. I am still crying. I keep shuffling focusing on the sidewalk directly in front of my feet, making myself move from square to square, seeing the texture of the aggregate, moving on to the next square, sucking air through my teeth.

Finally, I can't make myself take another step, I stop walking. It is not a conscious decision; I just cannot walk any further. I look up and around. Strangely, I have walked back to the church and school. The grey marble church steps just to my right are inviting, and I slump down on the second one, leaning my head against the cool steel post that supports the brass handrail leading down from the huge, oaken double doors. The cold steel is refreshing on the throbbing right side of my face. I just need to rest for a minute I close my eyes the world spins and tilts. I know if I open my eyes I will puke again, so I don't try. I rest my face and drift.

"This is no place to be sitting at this time of night, son."

I must have dozed off—or worse—because when I open my good eye, darkness has fallen, and the temperature has dropped significantly. My gaze falls on a pair of dark shoes and the hem of a cassock, and as I tip my head up, I take in an impressively long frame until I am squinting into the street light at a very tall figure. The man is not only towering above me but is also as wide as a car door across the shoulders. His face is in shadow as the street light backlights him and shines in my eyes over his right shoulder.

"Lord have mercy!"

He drops into a squat, and I make out the features of the broad, Slavic face, framed by blond hair buzzed into a crewcut. His nose is almost flat and wide at the bridge, and his eyes wide like saucers. It is Father Kowalski, and without another word, he reaches underneath me and heaves me into his arms. I gasp at the explosion of pain in my head, my ribs, and my shoulder. Waves of pain pounds into my chest with every step he takes. He is walking, and he is making very good time. I lean my head against him thinking that he will take me home.

I feel every step telegraphing a shockwave up through his massive frame and shaking me in his arms. I watch as the landscape jounces past through small slits, my teeth clamped tightly together in anticipation of the next blast of pain. At speed, we pass the school and turn up the first set of steps across the alley. Father Kowalski takes the steps two at a time and hits the doorbell on the run. There is a brief wait, and the door opens slowly, too slowly for him, and he shoves the door with his foot so that it bangs against the wall and rebounds.

"Father Kowalski! Oh, dear God, what has happened!?!"

He rushes into the front room where he very gently lays me in a deep red leather chair and then turns to the nun wringing her hands behind him.

"This was not a fight sister. Someone has seriously kicked this boy's ass. Call the police, then call over to the rectory and have Monsignor come immediately. Then call Dr. Giannini; he will be in the church directory I am sure."

He turns to look at me at last, "If I am not mistaken this is Mick Casey's boy is it not?"

"I am not sure Father, but Sister Mary Ellen is here, she will know. I will get some warm water and towels. Dear me, is he going to be alright?"

"I do not know Sister. Have Sister Mary Ellen come straight through, and then we should get Owen Carter from the Holy Name Society on the phone as well."

I have trouble taking a breath through my nose, but somehow, I get the impression of warm wool and sweet vanilla. The chair is soft and warm, and I feel like I will never stop sinking into it. It is like sitting in a warm bathtub, and I feel myself drift into a blissful state of relaxation. I could sit here forever if they let me. I drift away as the pace of activity around me in the room continues to accelerate.

In what seems hours later, I am still in the wonderful chair. A cop came with his notebook and squeaky leather gun belt. He sat on the footstool and asked me questions. I was glad my mouth hurt so much so that I didn't have to answer them. I know better than to talk to the cops. Then Mr. Carter from the Holy Name Society sat on the footstool and asked me questions. He was smarter than the cop and probably tougher too; he asked me to nod or shake my head when I answered. After that, he and Father Kowalski left together and seemed in a hurry. I drifted again.

I didn't notice that Doctor Giannini had arrived, but the hiss of the air being pressed out of the footstool roused me as he sat down in front of me. He sat there with his black bag smelling of oiled leather resting on his knees and squinted at me through his half-glasses before finally placing his bag on the floor. He rummaged in the bag, taking out gauze and tape and bottles that smelled like rubbing alcohol. He worked a long time, mostly wrapping or taping something silently. The Dominican Nuns hovered, hanging back in the hallway, their hands rattling beads under their habits. Doctor Giannini raised, patted my hand, and left. I could hear his low voice outside in the hall with the nuns before I drifted again.

The next time I opened my eye my Da was sitting on the footstool; somehow, he made no sound when he had sat down. His hands were clenching and unclenching, and his mouth was in such a tight line that I could not see any of his lips. He looked me up and down and then went into the hallway to speak to Monsignor Lavin, who stood with his hand on his shoulder, as I slowly began to focus on everything around me again. When he came back, he noticed that I was awake, and he leaned toward me to make eye contact. His eyes flickered with something that I had never seen on his face before, and he leaned back quickly, maybe afraid that I saw it.

"Well, I guess that school shirt is ruined for sure." His statement is flat and without any of the emotion that I had just seen.

At last, the dam breaks and I burst into tears.

October 1969, Early Morning, Da's House

Even before I open my eyes, I can tell that there is a thick, low-lying fog outside the window. The late fall air wafting in through the open sash is warm and damp, it makes the bed and the blankets uncomfortable, cloying. It is still hours before sunrise and the morning is waiting to rain. The room is still deeply dark as the outside fog blocks whatever ambient light might have filtered in from the outside. I kick off the covers and lie on my back, gazing up blankly at the ceiling. The room is tucked in under the eaves on the second floor, and the pitch of the roof means the ceiling is less than a foot above me, but I can barely see it in the dark. The prospects of the coming day are as dim as the light in the room.

Turning on my side, I look at the luminous hands of the alarm clock on the nightstand between the two twin beds. It is just minutes before four a.m., and the alarm is set for four. I know I will not be dozing off again, so I push the alarm button to the off position and push myself up to sit on the side of the bed.

I do not need light to negotiate in this small space. This is the bedroom of my childhood. I could close my eyes and walk anywhere in this house without colliding with a single stick of furniture or stepping on one squeaky floorboard. Nothing in this house has changed in all the years that we have lived here. The years of practice during my alcoholic fueled high school career have helped me become a walking ghost. Nothing ever changes in this house.

The twin bed across from me is unoccupied. It was my brother's bed. He is long gone from beneath the shadow of family. He also seized the first opportunity to escape, putting as much emotional distance and geography as he could behind him. The others would follow; each avenue of escape suiting the individual it was meant for; college for some, jobs for others, and in my case wanderlust and a misspent youth.

For one last night, I have returned to this room tucked under the eaves of this house that is too large now and was too small when we all occupied it. I have returned for this one night, and after this night I will not return again, perhaps for a long time. I know unconsciously that if and when I return, I will not return the same man I am this morning.

Today will change many things. Today I feel much more like a boy than a man as I face another life change and experience again the fear of the unknown.

There is a slight shuffle in the hallway, and a pale shadow appears in the doorway, not a ghostly apparition but my father, standing uncertainly in his pajamas just outside the door. I see him more in my mind than with my eyes.

"I'm already up Da," I say, trying to sound bright and chipper.

"I'll get dressed in a minute or two. I would like to go with you if that is okay?" He whispers into my dark trying not to disturb the ghosts of the other long-gone residents. It is not like him to speak meekly or respectfully to one of us.

"Umm, are you sure Da? It's not that big a deal you know."

"Yes, I am sure, and yes, it IS a big deal. I'll be ready in twenty minutes. The coffee is already on."

Now, that's more like the father I know.

It is only after he says this that I recognize the wafting coffee aroma of the percolator boiling on the stove downstairs, barely detectable at this great distance from the family kitchen.

Today will be bad enough, but now Da will be going with me.

I've had years of my father going with me, or worse my father coming to get me. There have been those nights of being picked up by the police for those mandatory juvenile offenses, of highway breakdowns that occurred miles and hours from where I was supposed to be, days upon days of parent/teacher, parent/priest, and parent/neighbor conferences. My father is a man of few words and I already know that today there will be less.

I have been told that most fathers have words of wisdom, or a pat on the shoulder and an easy camaraderie with their grown sons. There are many times I have longed for that father. My father had no use for those ploys for acceptance. Instead, he was a walking, not talking guilt machine who could hold his peace even in the middle of the worst shit-storm. You could wait for days and sometimes weeks for the other shoe to drop with Da only to get a three or four-word summation that would verbally eviscerate you on the spot and stay with you forever.

"Can't fix stupid," one of his favorites, because as he would tell my mother "Stupid doesn't run in my family so he must be retarded." And of course, my personal favorite, "You're not the first loser I've ever met."

I've come home to say goodbye to them, Himself and Herself; my parents. Today, I am to report to the Armed Forces induction station so that I can begin my "sentence" as an American Soldier. Today it feels like an even worse idea than it did last weekend when I "volunteered" for the draft. I have no choice though, the papers are signed, and I am to become G.I. Joe before the end of this day. I have fear, regret and worry, and now I have a spectator. He will ride the train with me, not speak to me and I will wish he would, for just this once, say what I so need and want him to say. Only, I don't know what that thing is that I so want to hear.

After a quick dress and face washing, teeth brushed and a cup of scalding hot, burnt coffee, we step out of the house. The damp air immediately settles on the back of my neck. The yard light, so engulfed in fog, looks more like a haloed candle. The glow of its edges well defined by the deeper dark of the night, making the fog seem thicker than it would if there was no light. I have my small gym bag in my hand, with its two pairs of clean underwear and socks, my razor and shaving cream, and deodorant. I'm not even sure if I get to have deodorant, but I packed it nonetheless. This is all I am taking with me, yet feel I am leaving nothing behind.

We walk the five blocks through sleeping suburban town to the commuter train station. We shuffle along the sidewalks choked with the fallen autumn leaves and the damp air heavy, even at this hour, with the smell of them. I've listened to the trains coming and going most of my young life. It seems we have always lived near the train tracks. Maybe it is a genetic salute to our Irish ancestors who laid the rails over so many Midwestern miles. I have never put any particular importance on where the trains took people or where the freight trains went. In my early teens, my brother and I would hoard food stolen from the dinner table and plan our escape from home. We hoped to jump on a westbound freight train and ride the rails to our freedom. From what we needed to escape, we never verbalized. We only shared the unspoken agreement that we truly needed to do it. We even tried it once and made it all the way to Indiana before Da had to come and rescue us from the railroad police.

At the commuter train station, Da sits on the wooden bench that is up against the track side of the station, his hands laid flat on his thighs his gaze directed at the ground somewhere out in front of his feet, his thoughts much further away. There are dozens of people already on the platform all exhibiting varying degrees of boredom or routine acceptance. They hold their lunchboxes or briefcases, some with newspapers, some women with headscarves and shopping bags. It is the beginning of an ordinary day just another work day for them, and they have none of the angst-fueled urgency that I feel. We are heading into Chicago, into town.

I pace the platform, watching the tracks to the west, waiting for the inevitable headlight I will see long before the train with its clanging bell will roll up in front of us, with its thudding, stupendous bulk and the whine and hiss of its air-brakes. I want the train to come right away, though, at the same time, I wish it would never arrive. Somewhere in the recesses of my consciousness, I realize that if it never arrived, I would not have any other place to go, no prospects, no future plans. There is only the promise of the dim bedroom, tucked under the eaves, and the crushing long-suffering silence of my parents' house if I do not get on this train. If I do get on this train there is only the unknown ahead of me and fear. Fear of war, fear of death, and most of all, fear of failure.

When it finally rumbles and clangs its way into the station, Da stands and I follow him, climbing the steps into the car and taking the first double seat available. I don't know what I would have done if we had had to sit separately. Da sits nearest the window, and I sit facing him, facing away from the inevitable, riding backward toward my fate much as I have most of my life. Da's hands go palms down on his thighs and he looks straight ahead, showing no interest in the other passengers as they make light conversation with other frequent riders. His gaze is far away but seems fixed on the center of my chest. It is still dark outside and the bright lights of the railcar make a mirror of the window on my right. I avoid the opportunity to look at my own face and regard him in the reflection as he sits expressionless in front of me.

I don't often get the chance to look at him in any kind of depth, and I am self-conscious about my curiosity. He is a good man—a hard worker and steady provider, cursed with the Irish luck that forever drags at our feet and our futures. He probably was handsome once, with his wiry, muscular frame, his hair has thinned and started to gray without my notice, and I can see his scalp shining through where his hair is parted in the window's reflection. His face, although lean, has started to sag a little with lines and creases around and under his eyes; fatigue that is deeper than the early morning rising can cause.

I know him as a loner, never comfortable in groups or family affairs. He seldom displays interest in small talk or gossip. He is friendly enough and my uncles all look to him when they need help or someone handy with a tool or a task, but he has never sought their company. His only comfort and relaxation seem to be in his own company. His one weakness seems to be his little granddaughters whom he dotes on, carrying them everywhere and taking them on his frequent trips to the hardware store. I have never seen him hug, kiss, or touch my mother and yet here we all are, my siblings and I. I am sure that I can count on two hands the number of times he has physically touched me with emotion. Yet I have no doubt that he loves us deeply, although I don't know how I come by that knowledge.

This morning we have not spoken, and I wonder if he is with me because he feels an obligation to see me off or that maybe it will be a relief to him to have me in a structured environment that will control my random acts of stupidity.

Today, I will go into the army, and today there is a war. Many years ago, he did the same. There was a war to end all wars, and he went to do his duty. He was only an eighteen- year-old boy but failed the physical at first because he was too skinny. He doesn't weigh much more now, but back then he apparently didn't have any muscle on his frame at all. He has told us about his own induction and how he struggled to volunteer. He came up about three pounds short of the minimum weight, so he went to the water fountain and drank water until he could hold no more and demanded that they weigh him again. The second time he passed—barely. He took the fight to the Nazis and returned with multiple decorations and photographs that lined my grandmother's dining room breakfront. He has never spoken about it, his time in the service.

His enlistment is the only story I have from him of his time in the service. I know because of his small stature he became a tail-gunner on the B-17, Flying Fortress. The only crew member guaranteed to die if the plane went down because tail-gunners left their parachutes in the bomb bay to squeeze into their tiny turrets. I also know he flew missions out of Africa and Italy and that he lived in a two-man tent throughout his time overseas. I know these things, but nothing else. I know them mostly because my Granddad—his father-in-law—told me about them on the rare occasions when he and I talked.

Other men, other fathers, other boys' uncles could and would regale us with frightening and heroic tales of their wartime exploits. Tales where bullets fly, bombs drop, and medals are won. These stories stir and excite young boys. During those stories my Da only becomes a polite listener and to my knowledge has never added a footnote or highlight of his own. The same held true for my uncles—Da's brothers—a united front of stolid silence. Uncle Danny had once told me that "if they have to talk about what they did over there, it probably never happened."

One of the pictures on my Grandmother's breakfront is of Da. In it is a handsome young man, in his leather bomber jacket and leather flying helmet and with a bright smile that appears to come easily and maybe often. Looking at that picture, it is easy to imagine my Da as a flying ace and a hero of the war, but I have no reliable information and only my imagination to go on. I learned as a small boy that if I asked him about the war, he would get a faraway look and then change the subject, and after, no matter what the setting or event was, his mood would darken, and soon he would disappear to be alone for a time.

Today must be the same thing, no conversation, no eye contact; change of subject.

Once we arrive at monstrous Union Station in Chicago, we join the press of commuters, like a stream of cattle jostling for position moving as quickly as the mass will allow unconscious to the individuals that surround them. The stream sweeps through the station, with its aroma of coffee, wet wool, caramel corn, and cigarette smoke. As I flow along with the fast-paced stream of traffic, I remember the last time that I visited a train station with my Da. It was a long time ago and only once. It was a different station but still in Chicago - the tremendous subterranean Randolph Street Station, several blocks east of Union Station and the home of the mighty Illinois Central and South Shore Line.

On that day we were there for a similar circumstance too.

May 1958,
Randolph Street Station,
Chicago, Illinois

Standing in the low light of the train platform, the air is cool, and a light breeze blows in from the daylight-illuminated opening at the end of the tunnel to my right. I am dressed in a new pair of blue jeans and a red checked shirt with buttons. I have never had a pair of blue jeans before, and the pant legs are stiff and hang heavy from my waist. The shirt, my first ever casual shirt that buttons, is one of a pair. The other, a blue checked one is carefully packed in the cardboard suitcase that rests on the platform under my right hand. The suitcase is a dandy. Brown with darker brown stripes and a real leather handle that just fits my hand. It is part of the set that my parents have, the smaller of the two, but is mine, at least for the time being.

To my left stands my Da, straight as a string. Together we both face the monstrous train car which rests on the track in front of us. It rises in front of us, almost to the rusted steel girders of the roof above. It is hard to decide what color the car is in the low light, possibly brown with an orange undertone with gold lettering and highlights spelling out Illinois Central underneath the curtained windows along the side. This car is one of several extending toward to the engine far to my right. The snub nose of the engine aimed toward the opening and the late afternoon sunlight beyond.

People bustle down the platform from the station in twos and threes. Some couples holding hands, others with children in tow. They make their way past us and after a pause; they each climb aboard the car of their choosing. Disappearing from sight only to reappear in the windows as they make their way down the aisles toward their seats. The suitcases and other luggage that they carry or push on trolleys, are left on the platform and porters dressed in deep blue uniforms and caps with red piping promptly carry them into the car behind the passengers.

As if suddenly thinking of something, Da rouses from his reverie and reaches into his pocket. Holding his hand out to me he places a dime in my palm.

"Put this is in your pocket and make sure it goes all the way to the bottom, so you can't lose it."

I look at the dime—still warm from his pocket—and do as I am told.

"When you get to Warren you will need to call Uncle Danny, so he can come and pick you up. You know how to use a pay phone right?"

"Yes Da, I've used the one at the school before."

After another longer pause, Da takes out his wallet and fumbles through it. He draws out two dollar bills and also hands them to me.

"Put these in a different pocket, all the way to the bottom. You are going to be gone for a while, and you might need to get yourself some things. This is only for necessities, not candy or other crap. Ok? You're a Casey, and Casey's pay their own way. Understand?"

"Yes sir."

My right arm is still hanging in a sling, so it is difficult to stuff the bills in the opposite front pocket of the stiff jeans I slide the two bills into the back pocket on the same side as the dime. I look up to see my Da watching me. He raises one eyebrow, which is a skill that I have yet to perfect, even though I've practiced it in the hallway mirror enough, and then shrugs and looks somewhere else.

I can't remember the last time I had two whole dollars or if I have ever had that much money entrusted to me. Once in a while, Da will give me a dollar and send me to the tavern down on Fullerton and Central Park to buy him a pack of cigarettes, or a couple of bottles of beer. At those times though he always writes a note and wraps the dollar in it. The note tells the bartender what the dollar is for and that it is alright to give whatever it is to me so that I can bring it home. Those times though I don't really get to hold the money in my hand like it is mine.

A tall man in a blue uniform with a military cap steps down out of the train car and approaches us. Above the patent leather bill of his cap, Conductor is printed in gold lettering. He approaches Da and I,

"How far are you folks going with us tonight?"

"Only one rider, going to Warren."

"Is this our passenger?" He tips his head in my direction. After a curt nod from Da, he continues.

"One child fare to Warren, Illinois comes to three dollars and twenty-seven cents." He doesn't consult anything but apparently from a broad knowledge of all of the possible fares that could be charged on the train. Da could have purchased the ticket at the ticket window inside the station but, if there is one thing I know he hates is standing in line. In fact, when we go to church and communion time finally rolls around he is the first out in the aisle so he can get to the head of the line. If we were late getting to church and we have to sit in the back, he waits until the priest is at the last couple of people before he starts up the aisle.

There is an exchange of money, and he produces a booklet of tickets from a small pouch on his left hip and a hand punch from a holster on his belt. Tearing out a ticket, he punches it ferociously letting the chads fall to the platform and stoops and picks up my suitcase.

"Well then, come along son, we'll find you a seat." Turning to Da. he adds, "I'll keep an eye on him myself and see he doesn't miss his stop."

With that, he turns and climbs the nearest set of steps and drops my new/old suitcase on the landing at the top. In no apparent hurry, he turns and waits at the top of the steps.

Da places his hand on my shoulder and gives it a shake.

"No foolishness now. Not on the train and not when you get to Uncle Danny's. They work for a living, and if you are going there, you have to work for a living too. I expect nothing less."

"I will Da."

Without anything else to say, he turns left and walks back down the platform toward the station. He does not look back - other responsibilities beckon. I don't know if I expected anything else or not, but there is nothing left for me to do but mount the steps and let the conductor find me a seat. This action seeming less like an adventure and more like a sentence, the outcome of a long stride toward banishment.

After the beating I had taken at the hands of the north side kids, a life with not enough money, too many kids, and no family members close enough to help had exacted a final toll on my mother. The crescendo of stress brought her to the breaking point, and one morning while we hustled to get ready for school she collapsed in the doorway of the kitchen, moaning and twitching. Da had pushed us out the door telling us to hurry, or we would be late for school. Once outside we heard the siren of the ambulance as it approached and lingered on the street corner until it pulled up and the ambulance drivers hurried inside with their stretcher. At school, I asked the nuns if we could include Herself in our morning prayers but didn't understand the look I got in return.

When we got home from school that afternoon Aunt Evelyn, having driven all the way from Madison, met us at the door and ushered us to the front room. Once seated and our books were stowed she served us fresh baked chocolate chip cookies and milk, a real treat. She folded her hands in her lap and then launched into a lengthy litany regarding our need to pull together and time to grow up and finally that our mother would not be coming home for a while and that when she said a while, she meant a long while. She reminded us that we were family, and as a family we would come through alright because Casey's always came through. Then she told us that I would be going away too, to live at the farm. The little ones would be sent to other aunts and uncles and that Kate and Andy would stay here along with her.

The men from the Holy Name Society had come to the house and spoken to Da in the living room. They brought boxes of assorted canned and boxed goods that were donated. Ironically, most of it had the big Manichewicz label indicating that it had been processed and boxed kosher. Doctor Giannini came with them and took out the stitches above my left eye and retaped my broken collarbone. After they left, Da spent a long time on the phone in the little foyer outside of the bathroom. Today I didn't go to school, and Da didn't go to work. Instead, we went to Sears, where he bought me my new blue jeans and some underwear, socks and my two button-up shirts.

The blur of changes culminated in this train ride. I'm being sent to Uncle Danny's. Uncle Danny is my Da's older brother, and he still lives on the farm where Da was born. I love the farm, it is the one place that I feel I was born to be. Uncle Danny bears almost no resemblance to my Da. He and Aunt Martha are larger in size and gesture, hardworking rawboned relatives with quirky, refreshing humor and a smile for everyone and everything and especially each other. I should be excited and happy, but instead, tonight it feels like abandonment.

Eventually, the train moves forward out of the station and into the late afternoon sun. It rolls northwest through the neighborhoods of the inner city, and I watch from my seat as the identical homes with their backs to the tracks move past faster and faster. In short order, the train clears the city. Once through the more rural suburbs where the houses are still identical, but with more space between them, we speed out into the countryside, and I discover why they call this train the "Land of Corn". Cornfields seemingly without end stretch out away from the train as far as the eye can see, broken only by the occasional farmstead with its outbuildings and requisite silo.

The conductor smiles at me each time he passes by but leaves me alone on the leather seat. The few other occupants of this car soon tire of the monotony of the landscape and disappear behind newspapers and into books. The newness of the train and the moving view out of the window soon bores me, and I begin to doze. I rouse only a little as the train makes its stops in Broadview, Rockford, Freeport and Lena. Finally, a gentle hand on my shoulder rouses me, and the conductor retrieves my suitcase, and we exit into the noisy opening where the stairs go down. Then, hanging out into the evening air while holding on with one hand, he signals with an arm wave and the train brakes and slows to a stop. Swinging down out of the car, he sets a small stool below the last step and waves me down onto the ground. After handing me my suitcase, he holds out his hand to me, and I tentatively shake it, just like a grownup would. He hops back up on the first step the stool in his hand waving toward the front of the train, and it immediately begins to move forward, out of my life. The entire time of the 'whistle stop' took less than a minute.

Darkness is falling, and across the track, in front of me the main streetlights and storefronts of Warren, Illinois fall away from me down a hill for only a couple of blocks, and beyond that, there is darkness.

There is activity on the street, but not much, there is no bustle like the city. These people work for a living during the day and go home to dinner. After dinner time, which it is now, they sit on their front porches and rock or listen to the radio. In Warren, Illinois—like most of the Midwest—television has not replaced family life yet. The broadcasting stations are too far away for the signal to reach these little outposts of humanity, so people were left up to their own devices.

The darkened station stands alone on my side of the tracks, and behind it, the flat corn-laden fields disappear into the night. A small incandescent light with a tin shade over it lights the pay phone, mounted on the side of the building and I make my way to it. I pick up the receiver, and the dial-tone blares in my ear. I fish the dime out of my pocket and stick it in the ten-cent slot listening to the clink of the coin and the ding-ding as the phone registers the deposit. Reaching into my shirt pocket, I dial the number for the farm from a piece of paper that Da wrote and put there. I wait impatiently as the dial slowly rotates its way back through the numbers.

"Operator, may I help you."

"Um, yes please. I'm trying to call my Uncle, Danny Casey."

After a long pause.

"I'm sorry, but I do not show a listing for a Daniel Casey. Is there another name?"

"Um, I don't think so. He lives in Fayette."

"I'm sorry; this is the operator in Warren, Illinois. Fayette is in Wisconsin, and that is a long-distance call. Please deposit twenty-five cents for the first three minutes."

"Oh. I only had a dime, and I put that in the phone already ma'am."

"I cannot place the call until you deposit the necessary twenty-five cents."

"I don't have twenty-five cents."

"Would you like to reverse the charges?"

"I don't know what that means."

"It means sir, that you will place this call collect."

"I don't know what that means either."

"It means sir that I will place the call for you, and when and if someone answers I will ask them if they will accept the charges for the call. That means that if they agree, they will then pay for the call. Would you like to do that?"

"Yes please, can we do that?"

"One moment please."

After several clicks and tones, a phone rings at the other end. Suddenly, I realize I have to pee, and I begin to dance while I hold the receiver to my ear. Once, twice, three times, and finally on the fourth ring, an answer, a woman's voice.

"Hello?"

"I have a collect call from, excuse me, please state your name, sir."

"Robert Emmett Casey."

"I have a collect call from Robert Emmett Casey. Would you like to accept the call?"

"Collect? How much is that going to be?"

"I do not have the exact fee ma'am, but it should be less than a dollar."

"A dollar? Oh alright. Yes, I'll accept the charge. Emmett dear, where are you?"

"I'm at the train station in Warren, Aunt Martha."

"Oh dear, we didn't expect you until tomorrow. Well shit!" (*shit? She actually said shit!* I can't help it, I smile a little into the phone.) "Well, Danny is still up in the barn, choring. He'll finish soon enough, and I'll pack him something until he can get back and have a proper dinner. I'll send him right along then. It will be while though Emmett, Warren is close to thirty miles and it's dark now, so you just sit tight there. He'll be there soon as is sensible, don't wander away from the station. Alright?"

"Yes, Aunt Martha."

There was a click and a buzz as the phone disconnected the call. I reached up and hung up the receiver. I checked the coin slot and to my utter amazement found that Da's dime had been returned. I looked up and down the track and then across the tracks, toward the soft homely glow of the streetlights. The little town, like an elaborately prepared Christmas time window at Marshall Field's, fascinating and cozy, but always on the other side of the glass.

I stepped behind the station into the darkness more than a little afraid of what might be back there and relieved my full bladder against the side of the empty building. Finishing, I struggle with the brand-new zipper trying to get it all the way up. With a sigh, I turned my little suitcase on end and sat down on it, near but not under the small incandescent bulb of the payphone with my back to the wall. There was no sense letting something sneak up on me from behind.

October 1969, Union Station, Chicago, Illinois

The press of commuters winds its inexorable way through the bowels of the cavernous Union Station. We are engulfed in the press of traffic; in it but not a part of it. Eventually disgorged onto the wet, filthy pavement of Canal Street the city smells of garbage dumpsters, diesel exhaust and most of all, damp. Daylight is now coming up and promises fog, overcast, and a dreadful outcome. The dampness from the air has collected on the sidewalk combining with the grime of the city and making multitudes of shoeprints amid the discarded cigarette butts and empty gum wrappers. Without hesitation, Da turns right, and we walk the five blocks, to the AFEES station on Van Buren. There is already a press of young men like myself, climbing the few steps to the doorway. I count the six steps as my gaze slowly rises to the entrance, where the door is held open by a uniformed soldier who greets each one without a smile.

We pause on the sidewalk. For my part, I see the doorway at the top of the stairs as a gateway to the unknown filled with doubt, excitement and fear. Da looks at the doorway then turns and scans the traffic on the crowded street, checks the tops of his shoes and then turns to face me. He has been carrying my little overnight bag, and I reach for it, but he pulls it back from me. Surprised by the gesture, I look up to meet his gaze. Placing his free hand on my shoulder, he actually leans toward me. He has to raise his gaze to look me in the eye. He holds the eye contact for a long moment. Again, he raises only one eyebrow, which I am proud to say I have now mastered as well. This time I see something I have not seen before; there is fear in his eyes.

I'm taken aback by the unaccustomed intimacy of the gesture, but in the next moment, I am stunned speechless. With his next statement a lifetime of worldly experience and pain pass between us, and suddenly I understand him. Still maintaining eye contact, he says to me from over the years, "If you want to go to Canada, I will drive you, son."

June 1970,
Central Highlands,
Republic of South Vietnam

The morning sun fondled by the fingers of distant clouds clears the distant mountain ridgeline to the east with fierce intensity. Reclining with my back against the dirt bank, I sit in filthy water up to my waist and slit my eyes against the glare. The cloud fingers caress the new arrival, as its entire form continues to climb. Soon it will be time to milk the cows and feed the pigs. I wonder why I don't hear the cows mooing up near the barn, calling me to chores. I can hear the sound of the compressor coming from the barn as Uncle Danny readies to run the milking machines, and I think about getting up to help—but I don't. I am so tired, so very tired. Instead, I continue peeking through my squinted eyes at the bright ball that now hangs in front of me, and I listen to the sound of the milk compressor getting steadily louder.

From the mists of the valley below, a dark green Cobra gunship rises. It climbs directly up the cliff face, right in front of me. In slow motion, it rises to block the new rising sun. It is so close that I can see the expression on the faces of the pilot and gunner. Behind their mirrored sunglasses, they appear grim, maybe even angry. I think I am happy to see them as they hang right in front of me the roar of the engine and the rotors pounding. It is not a compressor for the milking machines that I've been hearing. Their expressions don't change as they regard me through their dark sunglasses. I would wave, but somehow the action would require thought and effort. So I sit there my back to the dirt bank, fascinated by how it just hangs there motionless, making so much noise. In my confused thinking, I can't understand how this gunship got to Uncle Danny's farm.

The nose of the chopper rises slightly, and from the side mounts rockets explode, and a blast of exhaust erupts behind them, and in less than a second, they rush directly at me. The rockets, trailing com trails, pass over my head close enough that I actually feel the concussion of the air as they pass above. The Cobra drops its nose and with amazing agility, giddy-ups, rushing past with impossible wash from its rotors chasing down the trail left by the rockets. I hear the miniguns open up, a familiar sound, like someone pushing a refrigerator across linoleum. Another Cobra rises and sweeps past with another prop wash. Explosions reverberate behind me over my shoulder, and I feel the ground shake under my back. I imagine that they are giving somebody some serious hell. I hope it isn't anyone I know, but I don't feel compelled to stand up and look.

Moments later, two Hueys drop down out of the sun, and one turns left and the other right. They make a pass over the cliff face. This time I wave at the door gunner. He seems too busy to return the wave, but it doesn't even piss me off. I guess some people just don't have social skills I reflect. There is so much noise; the roaring in my ears makes my head hurt, and my eyes ache from staring into the rising sun. I close them and think about other sunrises; standing in the barn door, listening to the cows chewing their cud, the milking machines chugging, the dew so wet on the pasture that it looks like snow. Steam rising from the roof of the old truck parked in the morning sun as the moisture evaporates. I drift away.

Suddenly there is someone standing right in front of me, splashing in the water, roughly grabbing the front of my shirt. I lunge for him, grabbing for my bush knife. He is too quick for me and pushes me back into the dirt bank, leaning into me.

"Easy soldier, easy I'm a friendly. *Comprendo* motherfucker?

I squint out of my good eye. He has a helmet with a red cross on the side of it, and for a moment I wonder where my helmet went. His head is turned to the right and then swivels back to me.

"Jesus-fucking-Christ," he mutters, "what the fuck? What's your name soldier?"

"Hole." I manage with my dry throat.

"That your last name or your first?"

"Neither." I croak. "We're out of ammo, I hope you brought some. I can still go, sir. As soon as I finish my chores, but I think the Sarge is fried."

"Easy soldier, I'm no sir. I work for a living." Bending over, he gets eye to eye with me. "We're all done here, you've done good you hear, we're all done soldier. Stand down. Stay with me for a little while. You hear? Stay with me now, where are you hit?"

That makes me smile, and I squint up at him. "Fuck you asshole, just pick a spot."

"That's better, that's more like it. Hang in there Hole, papa's coming. I'm going to give you something for any pain you have okay? Then, I want you just to wait for evac. 10-4? Jesus fucking Christ what the fuck happened to your hands!"

All on its own, my left hand rises up in front of me. The skin on the knuckles is torn open, and two of the fingers are bent at odd angles. It looks like there is a hole clean through the middle of it.

"Ran out of grenades I guess, I don't know where the Thumper went. We don't have a radio anymore either I guess."

"It's okay buddy, I got one. Just be cool, I got some other business here. You're gonna be okay, Sky Soldiers are here, we got your six buddy. Just hang on."

I can't argue with him. I should know who the Sky Soldiers are, but I can't remember. I wonder if they are coming for breakfast. He wipes my arm with something and shoves a needle into the space below my elbow. I have to smile, I don't even feel it. Then, he takes something out of his shirt pocket, a marker, and writes something on my forehead. Then he leaves me. Well shit, I didn't think to tell him to look at the beautiful sunrise. I close my eyes and memory washes over me.

October 1969,
West Van Buren Avenue,
Chicago, Illinois

Once inside the AFEES station, all of the new arrivals are queued into a line. One by one, we are shuffled to individual desks. Each is manned by a soldier in khaki dress uniforms with their rank—which means nothing to me— displayed on their sleeves. When it is my turn, I take my seat, and recite my name and Social Security number and surrender the small package of paperwork that the draft board guy— Hamesworth—had given me back in Madison. I answer a few perfunctory questions and sign a few papers and then am sent through a seemingly endless number of other desks and stations, where little by little, I surrender various parts of my self-respect and individuality.

Eventually, we all end up standing only in our underwear, with our toes on a line taped to the floor on one side of a large room, facing a group of other soldiers armed with stethoscopes and rubber gloves. As a group, we turn, face the wall, bend over and spread our butt cheeks. This exam is a first for me, and I sincerely hope there is not a repeat. Apparently, we all pass this inspection because we are then prodded and probed in various less invasive ways. At one point, one of the examiners notes that my left arm is about five inches longer than my right and that the left elbow is cocked at an obtuse angle. He calls someone else over and together they bend and flex my arm.

Speaking to the first man, he says, "This is known as a gun- stock deformity, caused by a crushing injury to the elbow joint itself, but he seems to have a full range of motion." They both nod at one another, continuing to manipulate my arm.

Addressing me, he asks, "How did you do this?"

"Got it caught in a PTO shaft while I was grinding corn." Not exactly sure what he was, I added, "Sir."

"A PTO shaft? What is that?"

"It's the power take-off on a tractor it spins and transfers power to the piece of equipment that you are using."

I didn't want to get my hopes up too high, but inside of me, it stirred all on its own. *Maybe, just maybe, I might flunk my physical.*

"Let's see you do a pushup."

I drop down right there on the floor and do a push-up.

"Good job. You pass."

Shit!

The rest of the day goes by in a flurry of shuffling. Already we are beginning to accept the anonymity of the herd consciousness. The boy in front of me seems no different than the one behind me. We all accept what will come next and there is almost no conversation and certainly, no humor—from anyone of us. At length, we are dressed and again lined up in the largest room yet. Another soldier, this one with a different bearing and attitude addresses us. We don't have to be told this is an officer because he acts like one.

"Gentlemen you have completed the necessary physical to enter into the service of your country. In a few minutes, I will perform the swearing in that will officially begin your term of service for whatever period you have elected to serve. Before we perform that obligation, it is my duty to inform you that all of you have been selected to serve in the United States Army. Up until the time that you raise your right hand and swear allegiance to our United States Army, you may opt to begin your service in any other branch of the service of your choice. Representatives of our Marine Corps, Navy and Coast Guard, are present to discuss these options with you if you so choose. If you had wished for the Air Force, that choice should have been made before today."

He spoke the whole paragraph, seemingly in one breath. His voice never changed inflection, and his gaze never shifted from a place on the wall directly over our heads. If I weren't already pretty sure that it wasn't up there, I would have sworn he was reading it directly from the wall.

Everyone shifted and shuffled but no one departed from the line. We duly raised our right hands and were administered the oath, which confirmed the inevitable doom we had been anticipating all day long. In very short order, we were right faced and marched out the doorway, directly onto tour buses. We were each given a small cellophane-wrapped lunch which we ate en route to the airport. The trip to the airport consumed a little less than an hour. Once we arrived at the terminals, a very large soldier with a black MP armband and an absolutely no-nonsense countenance and voice boarded the bus. He addressed us, again in a memorized monotone.

"Good evening, I am Corporal Willem. I am part of a detail of military police that will escort you through the airport and onto the waiting aircraft. Once aboard the aircraft, you will be flown to SeaTac Airport in Seattle, Washington. We will shortly deboard this bus and enter O'Hare International Airport. From the moment that you depart the bus until you are actually on the aircraft, you will maintain a single file and will follow your escorts. There will be no talking during the trip through the airport. You are not here to sightsee, and no you may not use a restroom or buy a coffee. Anyone who does not do exactly as the escorts directs you to do will be dealt with accordingly. You are in the army now, and as such, you are subject to the Uniform Code of Military Justice. That means until those airplane doors close your asses are mine. There are no quibbles gentlemen, so follow me out of the bus."

We filed off the bus and fell into line. It was hard to say whether I was more worried about what was at the other end of the trip or afraid of stepping out of line and facing Corporal Willem, one-on-one. In single file, we negotiated the blindingly lit terminal with no hindrance. If anyone even noticed as we passed, I couldn't say because I was so fixated on the back of the head directly in front of me I wouldn't have seen. We moved down a long concrete staircase and stepped through a steel security door directly onto the tarmac where a United Airlines jet sat with stairs pulled up to the aft door.

Corporal Willem took a position at the top of the steps with a clipboard in his hand. As each of us passed, he asked our last name and the final four numbers of our Social Security number. Once we supplied this, he checked our names on a list, and we were allowed to enter the plane. Stowing my little AWOL bag in the overhead compartment, I took a seat and buckled my seatbelt immediately. The plane was warmed up, and with no preamble, the doors closed, and we taxied for takeoff. Like the others, I fixed my gaze on the seatback behind me, trying not to show my anxiety, much less feel it. As the plane taxied and then powered-up into the sky, everyone strained to see out the window—a last look; a memory to be imprinted as we sailed toward an unknown fate.

A beautiful stewardess handed out packaged meals right away along with cans of Coke. The kid next to me told her that they had fed us on the bus, so I ate his too. I had flown once before to New York City and back, so the excitement of the push back into the seat and the rumble of the landing gear lifting off the ground were soon over. I settled into the chair, folded my arms and was asleep, almost immediately. It had been a long day.

October 1969, Sea-Tac Airport

The only excitement during the flight was some turbulence as we passed over the Rocky Mountains and as midnight approached in Illinois, we arrived in Seattle. Unlike Chicago—where the weather had been cool and damp—the rain fell in torrents and sheets that swept across the open expanse of the disembarking zone. After taxiing to the buildings, I watched out the window as a wheeled staircase was pushed up to the side of the aircraft. As it was put in place, I watched as a lone figure emerged out of the doors of the terminal, sprinted across the rain-darkened space toward the plane, and vaulted the steps two or three at the time, arriving at the hatch almost before it was pulled back out of the way.

Once on the plane, he hurried up the aisle from the rear galley his rain gear rattling against each seat back as he passed and leaving behind a swirl of cold rainwater, which flew in every direction with his haste. Once he arrived at the front of the cabin between the first-class section and the coach seats he turned to face the rear of the plane and pulled his rain poncho up over his head and unceremoniously dropped the dripping garment into the laps of the two boys sitting just behind the bulkhead.

He is dressed in green army fatigues and has a black armband on his left arm that says SP. Unlike the MP at O'Hare Airport, he is not an imposing figure. Instead he is a little guy, barely five feet five and rail thin, with a thin face and eyes that never seemed to stop darting about the cabin. He took a deep breath and blew it out. Brandishing another clipboard, he addresses us. Unlike the first two speeches we'd gotten already today, his speech is not a monotonous litany, but instead, it is excited and high pitched, almost manic in its delivery with dramatic hand gestures and constant pacing up and down the aisle.

"Good evening pukes; welcome to Seattle. I'm Corporal Stoopes. I am detailed to see that you arrive at Fort Lewis Army Base. My crew and I are not in the mood for any bullshit. If there is bullshit, my crew and I will become your worst night-mare. When I tell you to move, you move; when I tell you to stop, you stop. If I tell you to shit nickels, you shit nickels. I don't want to get to know you, I don't want to make conversation, and I don't care if you miss your mommas. There will be no talking, there will be no grab-assing, and I want to be in my bunk, warm and dry, while this man's army finishes fucking with you tonight. So, I will take a roll call here on the plane, and I will take a roll call when we get on the buses. If you have any questions, save them. I'm not your momma and I'm not your friend. When I call out your name you holler out—**HERE!**" He looked around, skimming over each set of eyes glued to him. "Now, when I give the word—and not before—when I call your name you will get your asses up out of the seat, grab your bag and move to the exit. Once you are in the order that I call, you will not change position in line. You will remain in single file and alphabetical order. Alright, pukes?!"

Instantly, he begins calling out names in alphabetical order. Armstrong, Jeremy, Axelrod, James, and on and on until Casey, Robert, and throughout the alphabet each name met with a resounding **'here'** from various locations in the cabin. There is no hesitation, we had gotten the message.

In silence and in perfect order the procession begins; we retrieve our small bag of possessions and file off of the plane in perfect order. The rain is not just rain, it is an intense cloud-burst. Within seconds of stepping out of the shelter of the plane, we are soaked all the way down to our socks and freezing. There is no talking; we are all too tired and cowed by the speech of the little corporal. In the terminal, we meet the rest of the detail as they line us up against the inside wall where we stand shifting in the puddles we make around our feet while shivering from the cold and wet.

Corporal Stoopes blows in the door with the rain and whips his poncho one more time.

"Alright, fuckheads, now we are going to march up these stairs to the terminal floor. When we enter the terminal, we will turn to the right and march directly to the end of the causeway. At the end of the causeway, we will turn left and exit the terminal. Outside the terminal, there are buses lined up at the sidewalk. You are to enter the buses in the order I have put you in. You will not select a seat. You will move directly back into the bus as far as you can go. You will then take a seat and shut the fuck up. There is a cart next to the bus, and you are to put your AWOL bag on the cart as you enter the bus. Do not take the bag with you, do not fuck around; do not talk. Now, march!"

We do exactly as we are instructed. We filed up the stairs, afraid to use the handrail because he did not say we could. At the top of the staircase, another SP holds open the fire door, and we enter the terminal proper and begin to make our way down the causeway silent like convicts walking a chain gang. The silent SPs are keeping pace with us. In short order, we reach the end of the causeway and make the left turn. The double doors hiss open before of us. In front of us, lined up on the edge of the sidewalk are three shortened school buses, their doors open, their engines running, their lights on. These are not yellow school buses though, these are probably green but appear black in the darkness glistening in the torrential rain.

The Little Corporal stations himself at the door of the first bus, clipboard in hand. We reach the buses, and the first few guys climb aboard after placing their little gym bags on the cart sitting outside the door. The kid in front of me—who looks like he is about fifteen years old—looks up at the bus as he arrives and quips, "Well, I guess there won't be any more tour buses."

Like a bolt of lightning, Corporal Stoopes falls on him. Grabbing him by the back of the neck, he slams the kid's face into the open door of the bus, cracking the glass and probably breaking his nose.

"I said no fucking talking, puke. That means no fucking talking. Get the fuck on the goddam bus. And you, dipshit," he says pointing at me, "Name?"

"Casey, Robert Emmett" He checks me off his list.

"Wait until the bags are all on the cart, then push it to the back bus and load them into the back."

I have seen violence before, I have even participated in violence, but I had never seen unprovoked violence and cruelty that served no purpose. Even back in my youth, those boys from the north side of Fullerton had a reason for their behavior. Back then it was a neighborhood thing, this display shakes me to my core.

I remember my Uncle Danny telling me he had seen it rain so hard once the chickens had drowned standing up. This is that kind of rain. It is so intense that I have trouble keeping my eyes open against it and unless I lean my head forward, I cannot draw a breath that is more air than water. I step out of line and watch as the first bus is loaded and the second and then finally, as the line peters out the third bus. When the last bag is on the cart, I push the cart around to the back of the bus, where the emergency door is open. I toss the bags in three and four at a time. I have no interest in being in this rain any longer than I have to be. When the last bag is in, I think about following it in and shutting the door behind me, but it is a long way up into the bus from here, and my clothes are heavy with rain. I also remind myself that I am supposed to be on the first bus. Slamming the door shut I pound it with my fist so that they know that I am done loading.

I hurry around the corner at the back of the bus and head back toward the front of the line. Only to see that the first two busses have already pulled out, I hadn't heard them go with the roar of the falling rain on the metal roof of the bus. Making for the door of the third and last bus I watch in horror as the bus roars to life and accelerates away from the curb the doors slamming shut as it pulls away. I stand there in the rain, abandoned, overlooked and soon to be in trouble—again.

Gasping a little, with the rain in my eyes, I turn and look back at the pneumatic doors of the airport terminal. There is nothing back there for me to return to. I suck water out of my mustache while I recognize the only future I have is whatever is still in front of me. Time is short, and a life decision should take years instead of minutes. Consequences should be weighed, and outcomes assessed, but that has never been my style. I pause long enough to unzip the collar of my old army fatigue jacket pull the hood out and pull it as tightly around my face as I can. It is my understanding that California is very nice. It can't be that far. I am already on the west coast, and I have never seen the ocean. Straightening up, I give the terminal one last look, and I shove my hands deep into my coat pockets and start walking south.

July 1970, Central Highlands, Republic of South Vietnam

The Huey lifts off the ground with an unworldly roar and lumbers into the air. I am sitting, strapped into one of the jump seats at the back of the chopper. It occurs to me I am on the port side, not that it matters. I look across at a stretcher where they have Sgt. Hobbs propped while they work on him. He looks like hell. His big, flat, normally white face is black with mud, and his bare chest is stuck with bandage plasters that are starting to change color. The left side of his face from his hairline to his chin and from his nose to his ear is covered with a big Maxi-pad bandage that is taped on with several laps of gauze around his head. The medic is busy still working on him. Hanging a bottle from a hook above Hobbs' head, he attaches a hose to it, the other end of which disappears into the big man's arm. The bottle is shaking wildly in the baritone vibration of the big bird trying to get airborne and out of range.

Hobbs catches me looking at him and gives me a thumbs up. He grins out from under the Maxi pad, and mouths "We're going home, -------" I can lip read enough to know that the last part is a bad word, or two.

Going home? Can that be? I lean my head back, going home? I just got here. Going home sounds pretty good.

The medic crab-walks over to me. He starts messing with my leg, and cuts my pants leg open. Then he shoves another Maxi-pad bandage into the opening he has just made. He tapes the whole thing in place and climbs up the seat so that our faces are inches apart. He shines a light in my eyes, and looks in my mouth, then looks down and makes a face. He leans right next to my ear, yelling above the ungodly din of the rotors.

"Take it easy now, okay? I'm gonna have to cut your shirt off to get at some of this stuff." He gives me a little wink and smiles. "Looks like you've ruined your good school shirt for sure."

I look down at the shirt and see it is definitely ruined. It is caked with mud and blood and what are probably pieces of my friends. *If my Da could see this shirt, oh brother,* and then I start to laugh, then I laugh harder, and for a while, I cannot stop.

1969, Late October, Sea-Tac Airport, Seattle, Washington

A short distance from the airport terminal, the sidewalk comes to an end. Signaling the end of the terminal's grasp on the surrounding area, I stand on the edge of it, looking stupidly at the expanse of grass and weed that extends ahead of me toward what must be a road. I assume this road must eventually lead to some kind of civilization. There is a small, dark ribbon of a dirt path where the grass has been worn away by foot traffic, but looks slick with mud and standing water. Instead, I step off the curb and continue toward the airport exit walking in the street.

The rain continues its unrelenting onslaught, and I start to regret my decision. No matter which way I turn my face, the rain is pouring directly into my eyes, nose, and mouth. Drawing a breath either through my nose or mouth is a wet, sputtering experience and I am soaked through every nook and cranny of my clothes and private parts. As a result of the downpour, I end up walking with my face down, watching my boots slosh through the accumulated water on the street. I reach the intersection and look in both directions, trying to decide which course will be the lesser of two evils. Traffic is steady in both directions and because of the rain, the time of day, and the disorientation of the airport, I cannot determine north from south, east from west.

I have no idea of the actual time of the day. It was late afternoon when we left the AFEES Station in Chicago, and now, it is many hours later. The distance between Central Time in Chicago and Pacific Time in Seattle granted me two more hours, so it isn't as late as it feels to me. But I don't really have a good feel for it. My stomach tells me that it is past my dinner time, and I feel the effect of rising early this morning because I feel my brain slowing down. There is nothing to go back to, going forward even without a plan seems like the only option, and I have the rain to keep me company. I turn right and start walking. There have been other rain storms.

October 1963, Darlington, Wisconsin, Uncle Danny's Farm

The clouds that have promised rain all day are still holding back any precipitation, but it won't be long. There is not a whisper of wind. In spite of the heavy cloud cover and lack of breeze, the air is cold and feels wet. The barnyard is muddy as a result of the earlier autumn rains and a mire of torn up mud and turf roiled by the passage of farm equipment and tractor traffic. The greasy ground challenges casual foot placement and the various pieces of running equipment crowd the available walking space.

Two tractors parked side by side roar at high rpms doing what they were made to do; produce massive amounts of power. The noise the tractors create is amplified by the side of the barn they stand parked shoulder to shoulder against. It echoes back into my ears and deafens me to any other sound. The roar and its reverberation resonate into a cyclic, harmonic rhythm that my hips and shoulders and the machinery pick up. I dip and rock along with the cacophony. Almost mechanical myself, I go about the business of this chore that I love so much.

Both tractors are running machinery that is coupled to their power-take-off shaft. The four-inch solid steel shaft extends from the rear of the tractor, under the driver's seat. The power take off—or PTO—is a rigid shaft that runs directly out of the transmission case that can also drive the wheels of the tractor when properly engaged. Instead of moving the tractor, when the transmission is shifted into the proper position, the engine turns the shaft to power whatever piece of machinery is in use for the current task. With the PTO of a tractor, the monstrous farm equipment can operate at maximum rpms and efficiency anywhere, at any time.

The larger of the two tractors, a muscular John Deere 4020, is coupled to the big red Gehl mill. The Gehl is also portable in that it can be towed anywhere necessary. The Gehl consists of a massive set of relentless gears that grind and toss the contents about thoroughly, mixing them in a large cone-shaped bin, roughly six feet wide at the top. It holds the product until it is delivered to its destination, whether a feed trough or silo for storage. The job of the mill is to take whatever is fed into it through a ten-inch screw-like intake auger and grind it into particulate. Depending upon the chosen setting, the mill can either grind feed, mix it or both at the same time. The amount of time it is allowed to stay in the mill and the setting determines the size of the particulate. In this way, any grain—oats, beans or in this case ear corn—can be fed into the mill whole and emerge out the other side in the chosen format. The fearsome growl of the grinding and the cyclic sound of the ground corn striking the sides of the mill mix with the roar of the tractors.

The smaller of the two roaring tractors—the one closest to the barn—is coupled with the PTO to the feed blower. The blower is nothing more than a massive fan with a huge flywheel, three feet in diameter, with blades that are turned at an acute angle, geared to revolve at extremely high speed. The ground feed is fed into the intake where the fan blades grab it and literally blast it up an outtake tube and into the top of the silo or grain bin where it is piled up and stored. Silos can be sixty feet tall, the blower with its massive torque flywheel and powerful fan blades are capable of delivering huge amounts of cubic feet of heavy, wet silage at a high velocity without any problem at all. The blower is hard to stop once it is going at full speed due to the heavy flywheel and because of this, it is one of the most dangerous pieces of farm equipment there is.

It is fall, and time to bring in the corn. All year we have watched the corn grow from the time it pushed out of the ground in mid-May, through the spring while we cut and baled hay. Then, all summer long while we harvested oats and baled the straw, while we vaccinated the feeder pigs and shoveled out the pens and into September while we accomplished one more hay harvest before the night frosts began. We watched for when it was knee high. We waited until it tasseled, we listened at night when it was so hot we could hear it growing, and we counted the ears when they finally pushed out and began to sag and point toward the ground signaling that it was ready to be taken in.

Uncle Danny strips the corn from it's now brown and raspy leafy covering and twists the kernels out into his knobby gnarled hand. He puts one or two in his mouth and chews them with a look of concentration on his face. He finally he tosses a small handful of the kernels onto the surface of the water in the stock tank out in the cow yard. Together with Aunt Martha, we watch the kernels waiting for them to tell us their message. If the kernels submerge in the water, the moisture content of the corn is still too high to harvest. If the moisture content is too high, the corn feed will mold and become toxic and cannot be used for feed. If the kernels float and keep floating, then it is time. Uncle Danny could take the corn into town and have the moisture content tested, but that was cheating as far as he was concerned.

Once the kernels reveal their readiness, Uncle Danny pulls the old John Deere B into the equipment shed and with a lot of jockeying, manages the tractor into the ancient, two-row corn picker. The anticipation of harvest is tempered by the moderate angst of concern about whether the old picker will operate properly for one more season. There are multitudes of moving parts and fittings that require ample application of grease from the handheld grease gun, bolts to check for wear, and belts and gathering chains to tighten. All of these tasks are performed by Uncle Danny, with meticulous care and concern, as if to an old friend that he has known for years. He would not trust anyone else to this most important job.

The ancient green and rusty picker once harnessed to the tractor bears a resemblance to something medieval, with long, pointed snouts and metallic armor. It is a mechanical beast with a complex array of moving gears, pulleys and long chains that run up between the chutes, called headers, and each side of the tractor, rising high above and behind the tall rear wheels and returning underneath the twin chutes to cycle over and over again. Its simple task is to pass down the corn row and cradle the corn stalks as they are gathered into the twin headers. The stalks are combed by the gathering chains at the bottom, and the ears are plucked off, leaving the stalks to fall broken and trashed to the ground. Then as the ears pass up the channel, the chain mechanism strips the husks and finally, at the apex of the machine, the ear of corn is clean with no other plant matter attached. All of that is tossed backward in a shower of husk and stalk material that drifts away on the breeze. The relatively clean cobs land with a bang and a clang into a big steel wagon towed behind the little tractor as it chugs along at a fast walk.

It is a procedure not of speed but of efficiency. The machinery is a huge step above the previous way of harvesting the corn by hand. The old tractor chugs along at a speed only slightly quicker than a person could walk through the field. It makes an incredible racket of chains, gears, and crushing, and the steady banging of the tractor's engine cylinders, the stripped ears of corn banging and bouncing into the steel gravity box wagon in tow. The steel wagons are solidly built and heavy, constructed roughly in the shape of an inverted pyramid. At the apex of the upside-down pyramid is a steel door with a geared crank that allows you to open the door slowly in increments. The shape of the wagon coupled with the smoothness of the sheet metal lining allows whatever is inside to flow or slide out the opening fed only by the pull of gravity. Hence the name, gravity box.

The ear corn is stored either in cribs that are open on the sides to ensure proper ventilation and prevent the corn from molding, or it is ground down into feed and stored in a bin or a silo. Uncle Danny has two wagons in the field with him, and he fills each one individually. Once he fills them, Danny brings them back to the yard and unhitches them from the picker, drops them off, picks up two other now empty wagons and heads back out to the field. It is my job to empty the wagons. What should be a simple job of emptying the wagons and having them ready for the next rotation becomes quite a production given the amount and size of the machinery involved.

Since we only have the three tractors, I pull the wagons up to the mill with the old GMC farm truck, lining up the gravity box door with the mill's intake auger chute, which rests directly on the ground. Once in position, it is a simple matter to turn the geared wheel on the box and let the ear corn begin to spill out and into the auger. There is a small sheet metal shoot which folds down and positions directly below the door to make sure that the grain is directed below the opening. If it were loose grain, like oats, only opening the door a small amount would be sufficient to empty the wagon. But because it is ear corn, the task is more complicated.

The corn, thrown into the wagon haphazardly, is an impossible tangle of ears that jam up against the edges of the door and prevent easy flow. I stand precariously in the relatively small space between the intake auger of the mill in front of me, the spinning PTO shaft behind me and the now open door of the Wagon. I hold a three-tine silage fork, pulling and pushing the corn out the doorway and into the shoot. If the corn exited the wagon too quickly, the mill overloads and bogs down and the tractor has trouble turning the grinding wheels contained in the belly of the huge red beast and causes the tractor to start to stall out. If I unload more carefully, the wagons will not be empty by the time Uncle Danny arrives back with the next couple of filled wagons. Uncle Danny does not suffer delay very well. Striking a balance between the two extremes is both tricky and somewhat tedious, but the tremendous racket created by the roar of the engines and the whine and crushing of the equipment allows my mind to be free to wander while my hands remain busy, and my body and feet dance to the rhythmic pulse of the machinery. It is times like this that I truly find my bliss.

Without preamble, the rain begins; large drops the kind that only fall during the last warm days of autumn. The drops are large enough that I can almost hear them above the roar of the machinery as they hammer off the hoods of the tractors and the top of the mill. Within minutes the already saturated ground refuses to absorb any more, and the water begins to stand wherever it can find refuge—in the tire tracks and boot prints in the barnyard. I must hurry now, or the corn in the wagons will become wet before it goes into the mill and be damp when it is blown into the silo where it will mold.

I turn the crank on the gravity box door, opening it all the way, allowing the corn to rush out into the hopper of the mill. Too late I realize the auger that pulls the ear corn into the mill is too full and with a change of note the mill starts to bog down. I step over the spinning PTO shaft and reaching up past the tractor seat I shove the throttle lever higher to get more power and RPMs to the mill. As I step back over the shaft, my foot slips out from under me in the mud of the downpour, and I almost lose my balance.

A shockwave hits me, and for a moment I stand stunned, not sure what it was. Out of the corner of my eye, something flutters in my vision. I look down at it, confused. Something is spinning on the PTO shaft but too fast to recognize what it is. I bend slightly to look more closely and watch as dull dark drops fall onto the ground, mixing with the rain already puddled there. I try to raise my arm to clear my suddenly blurred vision and am surprised that I cannot lift it. Staring stupidly at my arm I see it is bent at an odd angle and hanging limply at my side. I look down at my shirt and see blood has now covered most of the front of it. In a confusion of shocking clarity, I know now that it is my old raggedy sweatshirt spinning on the shaft. I can't understand how it got there. I look back down at my chest. I thought I was wearing that sweatshirt, but I see I am not, except for the sleeves. Somehow, I am still wearing the sleeves of my sweatshirt, but it seems that the rest of it is spinning on the PTO shaft. It was old and threadbare just something warm to wear in the barn while milking on cold mornings, the front pouch already torn halfway off and covered with aged, frayed holes. But I still liked to wear it.

It is a mystery how that shirt got there, and my mind is suddenly stupid. I decide to lie down and think about how it got there. As I lie flat on my back, Uncle Danny appears in my vision. He is bending over, yelling something. I can't make out what he is saying, the noise of the tractors blends with another roar in my head, so I look past him and watch as the raindrops materialize in my vision and fall on my face. I feel each one as it lands. They feel so very warm. I close my eyes.

October 1969, Somewhere Outside Seattle

I had fallen into a rhythm with my steps, one, two, three, breathe in. One, two, three, breathe out. I kept my eyes focused on my steps, walking on the pavement when I could, stepping off onto the soft muddy shoulder as traffic passed. I was aware that in my olive drab army fatigue jacket that was soaked completely through, I only present a dark silhouette to oncoming traffic, which causes me to tense every time I hear the approach of a vehicle behind me. Traffic has thinned somewhat, and the rain has calmed but is still steady. A stiff breeze has come up, which causes me to squint when I elevate my vision.

Dimly through the rain, I get a glimpse of a dimly lit underpass ahead, close enough to see, but still in the distance. Along with my slogging march, I had passed two small trashy strip malls, some of their shops with boarded up, broken windows, all of them dark and silent. There had been an Esso gas station across the highway too that hadn't looked open for business.

The bridge's underpass promised to be the first shelter from the rain I had seen since leaving the airport and being left behind. Picking up my pace, I fast-walk the distance, but as I approach, I see someone standing alone under the bridge. I slow down unsure of whether to approach, cautious in my newly acquired fugitive status. There are bright lights underneath the overpass, and there is a wide paved sidewalk from one end to the other, with the road on the left and the cement pylons that support the bridge on the right. In the middle of nowhere seeing someone standing under the bridge, alone on a night like this made no sense to me. I chide myself for being a chicken-shit and begin walking at my regular pace again.

As I draw closer, the pastel blur caused by the rain in my eyes clears, and the situation under the bridge comes into better focus. The figure under the bridge is wearing a long trench coat, pacing. The figure arrives at the far end of the sidewalk, turns and retraces to the other edge of the dry border, a distance of about one hundred feet. Below the trench coat, a pair of high heeled pumps clack on the pavement. It is a woman, and unless I cross to the other side of the four-lane, I will have to walk past her. I drop my pace so that I don't arrive unexpectedly out of the rain until after she has reached the other end of the dry space and has turned toward me. I didn't see any reason to frighten her by appearing suddenly with her back turned. As it was, I was fairly certain just walking in out of the rain on this lonely stretch of road would be enough to give her pause.

She doesn't seem to be in any hurry as her pace is slow, leisurely. Once she turns and begins the return trip, I quicken my step and come under the shelter of the overpass. The relief is incredible. As soon as the rain is not pelting me, the air temperature feels ten degrees warmer. I cannot help myself; I stop and shake my head, my arms and stamp the mud off of my shoes.

Where I am standing, a puddle immediately forms, and there is enough water falling that it begins to run toward the edge of the curb and spill into the gutter. Perhaps predictably, I start to shiver. Whether it is from the cold, the wet, the fatigue, or just the situation I cannot stop, and it slowly spreads from my torso outward until my shoulders are quaking. The shaking is bad enough that I am having trouble maintaining my balance, and I stumble over to the four-foot-tall concrete base that supports the pylons of the overpass and lean against it as my thighs quake. With stunning clarity, I realize that I am royally screwed. I don't think I can go any further tonight, and I don't know where that would be anyway. I have been walking a long time, and it is too far to go back. I don't know what is ahead of me or how far.

In my compromised situation, I momentarily forgot about the woman in the trench coat. When I look up, she is standing in front of me. Still keeping her distance, she has her heels perched on the curb while I lean against the cement abutment five or six feet away. She stands, hands in pockets her head tilted slightly to the left as if trying to comprehend what just appeared. She does not appear frightened in the least, just curious.

"Balls! What beach did you just wash up on?"

I untie my hood and pull it back, wiping the hair out of my eyes and sweep my hands along the sides of my head, wiping the excess water back and down my neck. I blink away as much as I can out of my eyes, and my trembling slowly comes under control. Looking up I see that she is still standing there.

She's wearing the trench coat and black high heels. Her halo of curled hair appears to be suffering a little from the humidity, and she is heavily made up. I can't imagine what she's doing waiting here under a bridge in bumfuck Washington. She's not young as I am, but she is not old either—she is someplace in between. She's tall in her heels and the trench coat pulled up around her neck makes her seem taller.

"Your car break down or something?"

"Something."

"You live around here?"

"No"

"Well, you're not much for conversation I'll say that for you."

"I came from the airport. I walked."

"Holy shit! In this rain? The airport's about three miles from here. No wonder you're soaked. Why didn't you take a cab or somethin'?"

The traffic had continued to speed by in both directions, but the volume had tapered off significantly. Each car brought with it a mist of backwash rain that followed it into the underpass and the wet tires had soaked the pavement in damp streaks that petered out halfway to the other side. A car approaches on our side of the road slows as it neared the underpass. She immediately turns toward it and bends down to see the driver. I assume that her ride had finally arrived to pick her up. As the car passes the passenger side window rolled down, and the car does a slow roll by, the driver taking in both of us, and then speeds up and disappears back into the rain.

"Well, FUCK YOU TOO!" She yells as she gave the retreating car the finger with the hand that wasn't holding her purse.

"Shit." She reaches into her purse and pulls out a pack of cigarettes, shakes one out, then produces a lighter and lights up.

"Shit, shit and double shit. Crappy night all the way around. Fucking rain!" She turns back to me, and with the cigarette poised in the corner of her mouth she squints through the smoke and blows out a cloud of smoke.

"Lemme guess. No money?"

"Not enough. Could you spare a cigarette? Mine are soaked."

"They're menthol?"

"Okay with me, if you can spare it."

"It's been one shitty thing after another tonight, one cigarette isn't going to make or break the trend."

I push myself away from the retaining wall as my boots squish water. As I start toward her to get the offered cigarette she holds up her hand for me to stop.

"Close enough sonny. Just reach for it."

I take the cigarette, and my wet fingers immediately soak the butt end. Reaching into my pocket, I pull my trusty Zippo out and fire up.

"Thank you," regarding the cigarette in my fingers, feeling the tickle of the menthol in the back of my throat, "this is the first nice thing that's happened to me today."

"Long day?"

"You can't imagine."

I smoke in silence, and she went back to doing laps under the bridge. My options are usually limited and when in doubt, I try to push on. In silence, I finish the cigarette and flick it out into the street. I don't want to go back out into the rain again, but I'm uncomfortable settling down under the bridge with another person watching me. Walking to the far end of the dry sidewalk I feel defeated. As I stand dejectedly staring into the unknown beyond with my hands in my coat pockets, her voice came from behind me.

"Town's not too far now, but it's still a pretty long walk."

I turn around. She's finished her last lap and now stands in the puddle that I had dripped onto the sidewalk. She shakes out another cigarette and says, "Might as well have one for the road."

I was torn between the need to move on to I didn't know where, but the chance to delay the inevitable was too much to resist. I opted for easy. I walked back to her, and this time she let me approach and take the cigarette. She flicked her lighter and lit mine first and then her own. Walking over to the cement abutment she leans back and crosses her arms, holding the cigarette poised near her mouth in her left hand.

"It's a shitty night. I had a date, but like every other man, he got what he wanted and dumped me here. Looks like I'm just as screwed as you are, so I'm not going anywhere for a while. And you might say I'm a professional listener."

Close up, I could see that she was sort of good looking. Some lines branched out away from her eyes and around the corners of her mouth. Her hair was red but seemed to be flat with no highlights. I had seen enough dye jobs to recognize one when I saw it. Her trench coat was stylish but not new, and she had an aura of perfume that was strong enough to ward off the scent of tobacco smoke. She might have been in her late twenties or closer to forty for all I knew. All I could be sure of was some of those years were hard ones.

"What do you say? How about a little entertainment? I could use a good story and like I said," she smiles, with a glance at the oncoming traffic, "I'm not going anywhere just yet."

There was so much to tell and yet nothing to say. Suddenly, I really wanted to unload some of the baggage and let it all go, but it didn't feel like the right place. I hoisted myself up and stared down between my knees at the water that was starting to drip from my shoes a little more slowly. Involuntary shivers still flashed through my body, and my fingers and toes were too cold.

"There's no place to start and too much to tell."

"Oh jeez, give me a break. You're one of those."

"One of what?"

"One of those guys that want you to believe that they are dark and deep. The kind of guy that tries to impress the girls with your deep and troubled past, because you know that girls always go for the bad boys."

She said all of this while waving her hand that held the cigarette, her voice dripping with sarcasm.

"Well they don't go for me. Especially not for that."

"You queer or something?"

That question caught me off guard, and I snapped my head up and looked at her. She looked back with an open expression. There wasn't any sneer or smirk, so it was apparently an honest question but to emphasize it she shrugged.

"I doubt it."

With a deep sigh, I turned and looked to my right out into the storm, and whatever was beyond it.

"Let's just say I'm fucked if I go that way, and I'm more fucked if I go back that way." I pointed to my left.

"You in trouble with the cops?"

"Not yet. But it's just a matter of time."

"If you don't mind my saying so, you don't really look like the hardened criminal type, so how bad could it be?" A pause, and a deep long puff on her cigarette. "But I've been fooled before, and those guys were better looking."

"Thanks, if that's a compliment."

"Naw, just an observation. I bet when you get dried out and cleaned up a little you look a lot better."

She stood there and reached into her purse taking out her pack of cigarettes. Shaking two out, she put both in her mouth and lights them. Passing one to me, she again assumes her pose against the wall. With the cigarette in her left hand, she pauses with it near her mouth and again squints through the smoke,

"Well?"

I suddenly wanted as much sympathy as I could get. I was tired of feeling sorry for myself and wanted someone else to do it for me. In a rush, the events of the last week poured out. In a hurry to tell my story, I left large somewhat more incriminating pieces out, but I felt better just by getting it off my chest. As I finished, I could feel an awkward silence just beyond my tale of woe.

To avoid it, I slid down off the wall and looking toward the rain and town, I said, "Again, thanks. Thanks for the smoke. If I sit here any longer, I might be here in the morning, so I guess I'll be going."

With a sigh and a deep shrug of my wet shoulders, I added "Take it easy and thanks again."

I walked to where the dry pavement ended and stopped. Shoving my hands down into my pockets, I tried marshaling my resolve to step out into the cold and wet. I realized that I should have asked for directions, but now I feel that our relationship has been severed. I didn't want to turn around and go back. Yet the same time, I did. From behind me, a piercing whistle sounded and one of the cars coming from the other direction across the road slowed. As I turned to look, it did a wide U-turn and pulled up next to the woman. It was a good old Yellow Cab with its roof light on, probably headed back to the airport.

The woman stepped down off of the curb and opened the rear door and put one foot in the cab. Raising herself up above the open door she called,

"If you're coming you better move it and get in."

Margaret's Library

With minimal hesitation, I turned and sloshed my way back to the cab. By the time I got there, she was comfortably seated in the back seat behind the driver and making room for me. I was too wet to try and shake off any of the excess water and in too big of a hurry to bother. I climbed in and splashed down into the seat. The driver didn't even look at me in the rear-view mirror but immediately motored away from the curb and out from under the overpass into the rain. I hadn't heard any exchange between them, so I assumed that she had already given him a destination.

The inside of the cab smelled like every taxicab, all the odors that make them so unique; cigarette smoke, body odor, grime, and vomit. It was also incredibly hot. My clammy clothing was cold and wet, but the heat hit me in the face, and within what must have been a half mile, the water running out of my hairline into my eyes became mixed with sweat, and I began to perspire profusely.

I didn't pay any attention to the route we took until the cab came off of the main road. Making several turns, the driver eventually twisted down a street that glowed slightly from dull yellow street lights and beer signs in the tavern windows that stood shoulder to shoulder for the entire block. The cab pulled to a stop halfway down the block, and the woman pushed some money over the front seat to the driver and got out on the street side of the cab. With her hand, she shooed me out of the other side, and I clumsily climbed back out into the rain and stepped up onto the curb where she followed me.

"My name is Margaret, just Margaret. I must be nuts so before I change my mind, come with me."

She produced a set of keys from her pocket and approached a door that stood between two of the taverns. It took two keys to open the door; one for a deadbolt lock above and one for the keyhole in the knob. The door, swollen from the humidity, resisted opening at first and she had to throw her hip into the door with authority, and it burst open with a squeal. It swung open to reveal a steep staircase leading to the second floor, where a bare light bulb served to illuminate the long narrow ascending space. Without waiting to see if I was following, she hiked up the stairs and used still another key to open the door at the top. Like a lost dog, I followed her up the stairs and into the small entryway inside.

"Drop your coat there on the linoleum. Your shoes too."

I struggled out of the clinging, soaking wet coat and squatted down to untie my boots. After complying, I stepped through the alcove into the next room. With a snap, a lamp came on, and I was immediately taken aback by the sight.

A small living room with a high-backed overstuffed sofa against the far wall and a coffee table in front of it take up almost half of the space. A couple of high-backed wooden chairs and a patterned area rug cover the linoleum floor. A couple of doorways open toward the back of the building on my right and I can hear, and feel, the thump of the jukebox from the bar below. Two windows open out in the front and onto the street below.

The rest of the room is given over to shelves. There are even shelves above the two interior doors. All of the shelves are filled with books; hardcover and paperback books of every size. There are books on the coffee table, two lying face down and open. The lamplight is soft, and the room is warm and cozy. I haven't said anything since getting in the cab, but this is really amazing,

"Wow! It's like a library."

She smiled softly. "I work nights mostly; I don't own a T.V., so I have a lot of time on my hands. Never underestimate the power of a smart woman, I always say. Besides, you can never have too many books. In my line of work, I don't only need to be a good listener, but I have to be able to hold up my end of a conversation as well.

"Look you seem to be a pretty nice kid, a little misguided maybe; naïve for sure, but a nice kid. I must have a little nun in me, so you can stay here tonight and get your shit together. Through there is the bathroom. There's a tub but no shower; towels are in the closet next to the door. Take your wet duds and hang them outside the back doorway on the porch. It has a roof so it's out of the rain and they can't get any wetter anyway. Out there they can drip all they want. Once you're warmed up, there's a couple of robes on the back of the door. Put one of them on, and we'll run your stuff down to the Suds and Duds in the morning. You can rack on the sofa tonight, and I'll try not to wake you when I come in."

"You're going back out?"

"Honey, the night is still young. Who knows? Maybe I'll find my Prince Charming waiting around the corner for me," she said with a smile. "I'll be back after the bars close; after a night like tonight somebody's going to buy this girl a drink."

She hadn't taken her coat off but had kicked her shoes off the minute she stepped into the living room. Sitting on one of the wooden chairs, she worked them back on, stood and without a backward glance went out the door. I followed the sound of her heels on the wooden stairs as they descended to the front door, followed by the screech of the hinges and then the bolts being locked behind her.

June 21, 1970,
NSA Station Hospital, Da Nang

There are no drawn curtains in the ward. Sitting up in the hospital bed, I scan the bay around me. Opposite me, there are windows at head height that run the length of the room and open from the bottom out. All of them are open, but there is little air moving in the room. The wall behind me is similar, and the sound of the downpour outside is close, roaring on the roof and splashing outside of the windows. Hospital beds line both sides of the room. Each one holds a resident in various stages of undress; a few in hospital gowns, most in their skivvies. From my vantage point, I see some wear casts or bandages on various parts of their bodies. A few are lying down with their arms, hands or legs suspended from the ceiling. Some of them are reading; others writing letters and some of them just stare at the ceiling in studied subdued silence. Most of them are wearing bandages on their hands, legs, feet or heads. A few other fellows are sitting or lying on other beds around the room. Conversation is minimal. For the most part, I am alone with my dark thoughts. When there is talk, it is quiet and subdued as they trade books or show each other the pictures in their wallets. Above everything else, it is hot and sticky.

Looking down at myself, I examine the gauze bandage winding its way from my hands up almost to my shoulders. Raising my right arm, I peer closely at the wrap. A yellow stain had begun to seep through the gauze in various places, the result of the goop that they liberally spread over the burns on the backs of my hands and arms before they swaddled them in bandages. I am bare to the waist with a few sizeable square gauze pads taped in random locations. Some of these also sport yellow tint. One farther down on my left side declares its individuality by showing a dark reddish-brown stain. My right leg also has a large dressing, and this one too seeps the reddish-brown stain.

Through the double doors on my left, a female nurse dressed in fatigues backs through the doorway, pulling a wheelchair. Once clear of the door, she spins the chair around and drives it down the aisle. As she passes, she freely distributes sunny smiles and greetings to the men. The men, for their part, return the greeting each showing appreciation and respect, all of them glad to see her. She signals that the chair is for me when she stops alongside my bed. With some bustle and cheer, she assists me into the chair, ignoring my protest and request to walk by myself, with a smile.

"If I didn't do this, I wouldn't have anything else to do."

As she is wheeling me out of the ward, all of the men offer good wishes and support in spite of the fact that, before today, I've never met one of them.

After a brief ride to the end of the building and through some more double doors, I arrive in a room that smells like alcohol, soap and despair. The doctor, holding his hands at shoulder height with his surgical gloves on and his surgical mask hanging loosely around his neck, steps up to my wheelchair and checks my dog-tags. After reviewing the bags attached to my I.V., he walks around to look at my hand. The gauze, unlike the wrap that extends from my wrist to above my elbow, is brown with dried blood, and the bandage has become stiff. He carefully lifts it up high enough to look at the underside of the dressing and then sets it back down. Making eye contact he begins, "Good morning!" glancing at the name on a clipboard on a small stainless-steel table next to him, "Private First-Class Casey. This hand of yours is going to need some special attention. With the resources we have here, I'm not going to try and do anything with it today. I'm not a hand specialist, and I really can't tell if there has been any damage to the tendons or muscles with only an X-ray to go by. There is too much bruising on your knuckles and swelling. Also, you have a fracture to your index and fuck-you fingers." He added with a smile. "I would probably want to wait until that settles down a little anyway. Most likely, you are going to need a specialist for it. So you are going to need to go to Seoul or maybe even back to Madigan to have that looked at, and there's a chance that you may lose a finger.

"Which one? Cuz if it's the little one there's no loss there doc. It doesn't work anyway."

I can see you've had trauma to the hand and fingers before, what happened there?"

"It was a farming accident. They had to reattach the little finger and the tip of my first finger. For some reason, that little one never worked after that. I can move it sideways, but can't make a fist, so it gets in the way more than it helps out."

"I see. Well today, we are going to clean up your leg and see what we find. The X-ray shows no damage to the bone or kneecap, but there are a couple of good-sized fragments of metal that are in fairly deep. We will try and get those out for you. If we don't, they can cause you some trouble if they get infected. I see you've also got some pretty good scars going around your knee too. One of those is where we're going to have to go in." He looked at the leg with a wry smile, "Another farming accident?"

"I tried to nail a barn door to my leg. Almost did it too." "I'm noticing a theme here," he joked, "How are you feeling right now?"

"I feel great! Whatever the nurse gave me a little while ago is terrific stuff; anytime she wants to do that again would be okay with me."

"Well, that's a little something to get you to relax. I'm going to numb up your leg so that I can dig around in there, I don't want you moving around while I do it, so once we start, I want you to just sit back, cool out, and above all, lie still. Okie-dokie?" Before we start is there anything you need?"

"Smoke?"

Waving his hand around the room, "Not in here."

"How about some chow?"

"Not for a while. We can't have you vomiting while we work. We'll try and get you something a little later once we're done."

"Roger on that."

He secured his surgical mask in place and signaled with his hand to the nurse who also stepped up to the bed, her mask and surgical gloves also in place. She held out a towel with a hypodermic needle on it. He picked it up, held it up to his face with the needle pointed at the ceiling snapped it with his finger a couple of times and jabbed it into my leg. Although I was watching, I was surprised by how much it hurt.

"Jesus!"

"Yes, well this is the numbing medicine. It takes a while to work, so sorry about the stick."

"Thanks for the warning."

"We'll give this a few minutes. Try and relax some, if you can." With a pause in which his eyebrows furrowed, he added, "I heard about your buddies, I'm truly sorry. Your pal Dugan is over in the other ward you know. He's been pretty clear we need to take good care of you. You two pretty tight?"

"We are now."

After a few minutes, he poked around in a few places asking me if I could feel it which I couldn't, and then gesturing to the nurse, began working on my leg. The nurse draped the wound with a big square towel with a hole in the middle. Reaching into the hole, she spread the wound by placing her hands on either side of it. The doctor put some kind of stainless steel pliers with a bent nose into the opening and turning a thumb screw spread the hole even wider. Dropping the tool onto the table next to him, he dove in; brandishing what looked like a different pair of needle-nosed pliers. In a matter of seconds, he retracted the pliers and with a sucking, tearing sound, pulled out a jagged irregularly shaped chunk more than three-quarters of an inch in size and bright red. Holding it up for a better look, he remarked, "Wow! This is a rock fragment! On the X-ray I just assumed that it was metallic. Well, how about that?" He dropped it into a metal pan on the table where it made a distinct metallic clank. "Hmm, well one down and one to go."

I was suddenly very dizzy, and the room was sweltering.

Looking up at me through his eyebrows he said, "How you doing? You okay? You need a bedpan or anything?"

My vision narrowed into a tunnel as the outer edges darkened, "Fine doc, just gonna close my eyes for a minute. The rooms spinning a little."

October 1963, Darlington, Wisconsin, Emergency Room

Sitting in a straight-backed chair, I'm still confused. I can feel the seat of the chair under me and the back of the chair against my shoulder blades, but I am far from comfortable. Comprehension seems to elude me, and once more I move my eyes from left to right and back again. I can't seem to move my head because there is some kind of brace or collar that won't allow any rotation of my neck. Looking up and to the left, I see there is a contraption hanging from a trapeze with three or four ropes attached. They are connected to cloth sling, and my left arm rests on it. What appears to be what remains of my left hand lies palm up on a little, stainless-steel table. *What is this place?*

My arm hurts as bad as I can remember anything ever hurting. My face hurts, my head aches and something inside of me hurts too, but I can't seem to locate just where the pain is coming from. Suddenly I am sick, I try to lean forward so that I can vomit but the collar holds me firmly in place. As I begin to heave, a stainless-steel pan appears over my right shoulder, held by a hand connected to someone behind me. It is held under my chin. Rather than violently puke, my guts simply discard the contents of my stomach without much of a struggle. Even so, whatever it is that hurts inside me stabs me with excruciating pain, and I gasp for air for a few seconds while the violent spasm ebbs.

It is too much to take in, and the room spins and tilts. I close my eyes to stop the spinning. Immediately a hand grips my shoulder—hard.

"No son!" This voice I know, Uncle Danny. "Emmett, you have to stay awake. You must stay awake, stay awake with us now Emmett."

Then another voice, also familiar but less so. "That's right Emmett. I know you hurt, but we have some work to do, and I need you to stay with me while I do it."

This last statement is spoken kindly, and I open my eyes, in front of me is the portly frame of Dr. Mitchell. He and I know each other. On a few occasions, Dr. Mitchell has stitched and plastered me in a number of places. He had pulled nails out of me, casted me, and once even reattached my ear when I managed to separate it from the rest of my head. He stands in front of me in his usual attire, unbuttoned white rumpled lab coat, pinstriped white shirt with a loud, wide tie. The tie is tucked between two buttons of his shirt where his friendly belly gaps the buttons. I had never seen him in the clinic or on the street when he did not have a rubber cigar holder clenched between his teeth. On the street, it also had a cigar in it; in the clinic it was only the holder he clenched and chewed constantly. The holder never came out even when he was giving instructions to his patients. As a result, one side of his face was in a permanent squint from the effort of biting down on the foul pacifier.

"Your arm is broken in a couple of places Emmett, and I'm pretty sure that you've got another fracture in your face too. More seriously you have a concussion, and it is really quite important that you stay awake for us for a little while." He paused and pulled up a little round stool, which he sat down on, bringing him eye to eye with me. "I'm going to explain something to you. I know that you are hurting badly, but I cannot give you anything for it right now because of my concerns for your head. As soon as we can, we are going to take you in an ambulance to Madison, up to St. Mary's Hospital where they can set your arm and see to your face and head. Right now, we have you stable, and we need to keep you under careful observation so we know that you can make the trip. In the meantime, though, I am afraid we are going to need to do a little work here, and I'm going to need you to help me."

I couldn't nod my head, and for some reason, it didn't occur to me to say anything.

"When we took off your glove, two of your fingers were almost torn off. I cannot be sure of what other damage there is in your hand, but the other two fingers are broken as well. I am afraid if we wait too long we will lose them unless I do my best to reattach them now or at least restore the blood flow to them. Even so, I can't assure you of the outcome. One of the doctors who can see to your head and face is on his way from Madison and should be here in about an hour. During that time we are going to have a little sit-down, and I am going to try and sew your fingers back together. Do you understand?"

This time I croaked, "Yes."

"You know, I'm getting pretty tired of patching you up all the time Emmett." He said this with a smile he somehow wrapped around the rubber cigar tip. "That must have been a mighty wallop you took to the head. Does it hurt much?"

"I've had worse." My attempt to return the humor fell a little short.

"That would be saying something. I highly doubt it though."

"Check with my Da."

With a look of shock on his face, he looked up over my right shoulder what he sees there must have been confirmed, because he turned back to me, "Well, um, well, hmm I see. Well, just the same it's a doozy so stay with me."

On some level, it occurs to me that the someone standing behind me must be a family member because with another look over my shoulder he nods. There is some shuffling of feet, and a door opens and closes. I sense that whoever it was has left the room. The nurse bustles by. Pulling another stainless-steel cart up next to the one with my hand on it, she lays a rolled towel on it that she unrolls revealing an array of shining instruments. Tearing open a paper package of gauze, she covers it with brown Betadine and even though I don't seem to be able to breathe through my nose, I can taste the smell of the disinfectant immediately.

Doc Mitchell rolls up closer to me. For the first time, I see that he is wearing gloves. He takes the gauze from the nurse saying, "I think I'll do this one myself if you don't mind?"

She looks quickly at him and then glances at me and nods.

Holding the gauze in his fingers, he meticulously swabs my hand while at the same time moving with gentle care. I can't help it; I flinch. He looks up at the nurse, and she gently braces my wrist on the edge of the table. The pain that shoots up my arm almost makes my eyes explode.

"Sorry." the compassion is evident in her voice.

"We have to hold you still Emmett. It is important that you don't move and above all, we must keep you awake. Bear with it now; this is going to take a while."

For a long time, I sat and watched as he chewed his cigar holder and meticulously reattached tendons and stitched his way through my hand while the nurse held down my arm with one hand and wiped the perspiration from his brow, and mine, with the other.

December 1958, Kimball Square Neighborhood, Chicago, Illinois

On Monday, December 1, 1958, disaster struck. A fire broke out at Our Lady of Angels Catholic School in Chicago. The fire began shortly before classes were to be dismissed for the day and originated in the basement of the school near the foot of a stairway. The elementary school had an enrollment of almost 1,600 students. It was the heyday of parochial institutions after World War II. In the resulting panic, ninety-two children and three nuns lost their lives when smoke, heat, fire and toxic gasses cut off their escape through corridors and stairways. Even more were injured when they jumped from second-floor windows, which, because the building had a raised basement, were nearly as high as a third floor would be on level ground. The ancient school building with its years of varnish and wooden construction refused to be extinguished. Everyone watched their televisions in horror as it burned throughout the night.

Needless to say, the disaster was the lead headline story all over the world, and even Pope John XXIII sent his condolences, from the Vatican in Rome. The severity of the fire shocked the nation and surprised educational administrators of both public and private schools. The disaster led to significant improvements in standards for school design and fire safety codes, though too late for those tiny angels. The Caseys attended Our Lady of Grace across the city from Our Lady of Angels, but the similarity in their names fostered concern from our extended families. That evening and far into the night, the telephone in our little entryway rang as relatives and friends checked in to make sure we were alright.

The school was destroyed entirely, leaving the Archdiocese of Chicago with an educational dilemma. The remaining children still needed to be educated, and public schooling was out of the question. In addition, the archdiocese had already collected the tuition. The solution arrived at was to transport the remaining survivors to the many and various other Catholic schools within the Archdiocese. Although logistically difficult, it was arranged that the students would spend one day of each school day at another school, so that the burden would be shared equally by all Catholics. As a result, classes for the students at my school were dismissed every Wednesday for the entire day so it could accommodate the influx of displaced kids. This gave us a day off in the middle of the week, every week, for the rest of the school year. Every kid but me, that is, and as an unfortunate consequence, Kate.

I no longer remember whether I was behind in my studies, or whether they just kept me out of spite, but the nuns determined that I would also attend school on those Wednesdays. Sister Mary Loyola, my second-grade teacher, in particular, made a strong case for my attendance in the, by then, weekly Sunday morning conferences with my father, all the time never taking her eyes off of me. My father, well aware of my wandering attention span and penchant for nosing out trouble, determined that if I was to go, I would need to be chaperoned. Kate drew the short straw.

Those walks to and from Our Lady were both emotionally damaging and physically uncomfortable. Kate denied her day of freedom, never missed an opportunity to slap, pinch, poke, or kick me in the shins. Always blessed with the ability to save, she always had her own money and made it a point to stop at the bakery or ice cream shop to purchase herself something delicious, which she ate with the added enjoyment of doing it in front of me.

Our seats in the second-grade classroom were segregated in the back. So, we did not disturb the visiting children. Even that far away, it seemed Sister Mary Loyola's eye never strayed far from me. When she wasn't reading the book she invariably brought with her, Kate alternated her time between glaring at me and whispering threats which she intended to carry out as soon as we were out on the street. Threats she usually carried out.

To this day, I feel that apologies were inadequate for this cruelty I visited upon her. I also realized penance after confessional was wholly insufficient to save me from the hellfire that awaited me on the other side.

Why, I wondered, if God was all-knowing could he allow this to happen to me?

October 1961,
New Home in the Suburbs

Over the past few years, my time had been divided between the farm in Wisconsin and home in Illinois. I attended school for most of the year in Illinois and spent major holidays with my family. Vacations and the balance of the rest of the year I spent in Wisconsin. My father had wisely discerned that spare time and neighborhoods of Chicago were not a good mix for me. But after my harvesting accident, I moved back in with my parents full time. Back in school, the novelty of my sling, bandages and scars quickly wore off. I soon fell back into my old ways of garnering negative attention. In no time at all, I found myself back where I belonged, my desk placed out in the hallway of the classroom, sequestered from the rest of the students. My life returned to status quo.

In the fall of 1961, my parents had had enough of the city, and made the decision to relocate to the western suburbs of Chicago. After an extensive and seemingly endless search in which we were told to remain in the car, they purchased a brick, Cape Cod style house at the end of a seal-coated street, north of the railroad tracks in the village of Villa Park. The luck of the Irish, which was never far behind, followed them as much a part of them as an arm or a leg. Almost immediately after signing the mortgage papers, Da lost his job—a layoff of some sort. At the same time, his hated 1957 Pontiac Chieftain blew its clutch and was towed away to repair shop. The required down payment for the house and the loss of employment rendered Da unable to afford the hundreds of dollars needed to have the car repaired and would have been a total disaster if the shop owner had not taken pity on our situation.

The shop owner, a well-established former Chicagoan himself, understood the fix we were in and offered the use of a loaner car that he maintained at the shop for various purposes. My father was slow to trust him because, after all, he was a Dago, but eventually he had no choice. In fact, it was barely a car at all, a gigantic well-used 1948 Buick Roadmaster, with a monstrous chrome front grill that stuck out farther than my cousin's front teeth and appeared better suited as a battering ram then a luxury car of the day.

The reality of a mortgage burden, the prodigious cost of raising a large family that now numbered eight, the loss of Da's income and the blown clutch proved too much for my mother, and once more she needed to *go away* for a time. With the help of the Buick, the move was accomplished almost solely by my father with the little help that Kate, Andy and I could offer. The little ones were farmed out to friends and family to tend to while our transition was completed. Grandpa Quinn came down from Madison to watch us remaining kids, while Da was out looking for work. While there, Grandpa sanded all of the wooden floors in the house and then varnished them, revamped the furnace ductwork and installed all new cold air returns.

While they finished the floor and did some painting, we children busied ourselves arranging the furniture and playing in the new backyard. It was almost as if we had never seen grass before. It was not the farm, but it certainly wasn't the city. The far western villages were transitioning into a suburban identity. Agriculture had previously been its mainstay, but the land had become too valuable to waste on growing corn and beans. So, farming moved farther west as the Village readied itself for the influx of baby boomers from the city. The people and the subsequent building boom that would precede them had not yet begun. As a result, the western suburbs still had large tracts of undeveloped former farm fields that had quickly returned to their grassy, prairie roots. Situated on the northern edge of the town, our yard abutted a vast, open prairie that stretched for a few miles behind us and in both directions, to the west, north, and east. Free to explore something besides back alleys and crowded neighborhood streets, we launched ourselves into the undertaking with considerable enthusiasm.

The enormous task of moving out of our apartment required a Herculean effort of my father. He carried each piece of our furniture down the winding four flights of stairs at the back of our brownstone walk-up apartment and loaded it into a rented trailer, which in turn was hitched to the monstrous loaner Buick. He might have tried to tie other household possessions on the roof, but he would never consider damaging anything that he had borrowed, so he would not risk scratching the paint.

"Always return what you borrow in better shape than it was when you got it." That was his motto and one he absolutely lived by. Although I could probably count on two hands the number of things I had ever seen him borrow.

Once the trailer and back seat of the car were packed full, he drove the forty-odd miles to the new house and unloaded, wrestling each piece into the house and to their respective rooms. He repeated the process over and over during the evenings and nights after he returned from his job search. His days spent looking for work and nights spent moving the household soon took its toll, and dark shadows appeared under his eyes and his temper shortened even further.

The only thing he could not move by himself was Kate's piano. The big upright piano had been a major departure for my parents. For them, it was an expense that bordered upon a luxury and unusual when they struggled with so many other things. It was for Kate though, and because of that, it made all the effort necessary. My parents made monthly payments for several years so that Kate could take lessons from Mr. Kapinos, across the hallway. Even though Joe Kapinos was a Pollack, he fought in the war, so Da was okay with him, for the most part. In fact, almost our entire apartment building was made up of war veterans. Mr. Kapinos had fought in Poland, Mrs. Bronder's husband had been killed in Europe, and Mrs. Berg—who was a Jew and lived below us with her husband—had actually escaped from a concentration camp. Although she didn't speak very fluent English, she would proudly show us the dents in her legs from where she had been shot.

For the piano, Da hired professional movers to do the one thing that had defeated him. Because knowing him as I did, I am sure that he tried to do it himself first. In awe, I watched as three men hoisted the incredible weight of the monstrous piano onto the back of a fourth man and strapped a belt around it and the man's chest. Gripping the belt with both hands and with the other three men guiding the piano this man almost casually stepped down onto the circular wooden stairs that wound their way down to the ground with a landing on each of the lower floors. The man walked the four flights stopping only when he reached the safety and stability of the concrete at the bottom. If I had not seen it with my own eyes, I would never have believed it. I immediately had a new hero.

Suburban life was far different than city life but proved easy to assimilate. School had never been a challenge academically for any of us, especially Kate. But the requirements of school society still had to be met, and in that regard, the suburbs were no different than the city. Hierarchies had to be established and reinforced, and it took a few fist fights on and off school property to determine proper placement in the pecking order. Once these necessities were performed, then and only then could friendships and alliances be formed. Fighting was something that my brother and I had developed as a skillset inside and outside of the family. Both of us had more than enough competence to handle suburban kids who were expecting different results.

In a fist fight, it is important to never get into any fight that you know you can't win, so we had also learned diplomacy. Once in a fight, it is important to fight to win, which means make the first move, fight with a ferocity, and walk away when it was over. Once we had made our point, we were left alone, and for the most part, we Caseys liked it that way. We knew how to make friends, and we knew how to be friendly, but we didn't need either because after all; we were our father's sons.

With the move to the suburbs came a vast area to explore, with open spaces of prairie just at the edge of town, countless businesses, storage yards and buildings in town all with easy access to their roofs. And of course, all with lax security that we were happy to exploit. There was freedom even for Kate, and she would often accompany us on these reconnaissance forays, blowing us away with her intrepid nature, lack of fear and curiosity-fueled cleverness. A true beauty at almost fifteen, she seemed open to virtually any adventure and brought a devious and sometimes dangerous imagination with her. It was with some surprise that after all these years I discovered that she was immensely likable. It was also no wonder that the bicycle traffic in front of our house picked up with curious and hopeful boys.

October 1969,
Margaret

I sat in the bathtub until the water had cooled and was no longer comfortable, and I had stopped shivering. On the back of the bathroom door were two robes, both terry cloth, but one was decidedly larger than the other. An exceptionally soft towel taken from the closet gave me a quick dry. I put on the larger of the two robes; surprisingly it was actually too big for me. Exiting the bathroom, I suddenly realized how utterly exhausted I was and slumped down on the sofa, in the comfort of finally being warm and dry, my eyes began to close. With a start, I remembered my wet clothes, and after wringing them out over the tub again, I went through the kitchen and out the back door. Outside the door, a wooden porch about eight feet wide spanning the width of the building was set with a small wooden table that needed another coat of paint and two lawn chairs. Above the porch, the roof extended out beyond the building, covering it and back stairway completely. The roof extension was supported by four-by-four posts at about eight- foot intervals. The one window that faced the back of the building from over the kitchen sink sported a small planter, with a riot of philodendrons growing out and down and up the outside wall. The rain, still pouring down, created a deafening roar under the roof. To the left of the door, a long wooden plank had been fastened to the bricks. Several threaded hooks had been screwed into it. I hung each piece of clothing on a separate hook, turned and faced the darkness and wished for a cigarette and a reason for my latest predicament. With a sigh, I realized that the reason for my latest predicament was because I was a Casey, and a sinful one at that.

I slept the dreamless sleep of mental, physical and emotional over-load but awoke still on Central Standard Time. In spite of the rest I had gotten, my brain was slow and plodding, and the inside of my mouth felt like it was coated with cotton gauze. The bedroom door, which had been open the night before, was closed. I had a dim memory of her sil-houette backlit by the bulb at the top of the stairs when she had come home. While she slept on, I busied myself by looking at the hundreds of books that lined every wall of the living area. There were probably a thousand there were so many. The titles and authors spanned every-thing from fiction to two different versions of the Koran, the Bhagavad Gita, and an ornate King James Bible. Lao Tzu's, "The Art of War" lay open on the small table in front of the sofa along with Ray Bradbury's "I Sing the Body Electric." Since I didn't expect to be staying long, I didn't want to open a book and start on it. Instead, I rummaged in the kitchen and found a mostly full pack of cigarettes, which I carried outside to the back porch. I contemplated the back alley in daylight and chain smoked.

Margaret slept until after eleven by the clock in the kitchen. From out on the porch, I heard the bedroom door open and her bare-footed heel strikes as she hurried to the bathroom and shut the door. Moments later the toilet flushed, and the bathtub taps were cranked open. In a few minutes she started to sing, not loud and not harshly; in a melodious contented voice, her voice suiting the tunes she selected. She sang very well, and her bath lasted just long enough to go through a respectable Broadway Review. I was sorry when it was over. I found myself dreading a face-to-face meeting with her, ashamed of taking advantage of her hospitality, and even more ashamed of needing it.

Soon she was rattling around in the kitchen, filling the kettle, and set it on the two-burner stove, all the while humming one of her tunes. Eventually, I felt her standing at the screen door behind me; perhaps sizing me up, perhaps contemplating an appointment with a psychiatrist. When the kettle began to whistle, I felt her move away from the door, and she again bustled in the kitchen, rattling cups out of the cupboard before banging their doors shut. In a few minutes, she backed out the screen door with two steaming cups in her hands and a pack of cigarettes held in her teeth. She was clad in the other terry cloth robe from the bathroom door that reached about mid-calf. She smelled great, like fresh air. She clunked the two cups onto the table and dropped down into the remaining lawn chair. Modestly arranged her robe over her knees, she shook out a smoke and looked at me expectantly. It took me more than a moment to realize that she expected me to light it.

"Hope you like cream and sugar because that's what you got."

"This doesn't smell like tea, is it coffee?"

"It's better than coffee, it's Sanka. It's made out of coffee, but it is freeze dried." She huffed back into the chair and took a long hit off her cigarette. Squinting, she let the smoke leak out between her teeth and added, "And it doesn't cost as much as coffee."

"Thanks. I really appreciate you helping me out, I'm not sure I know how to thank you properly. I don't think words would do it justice."

After a long pause in which she smoked and regarded the alley behind the building, she spoke up.

"You're right, words probably wouldn't do it justice, I probably saved your ass, but that's what people do. Words hardly ever do a situation justice." She took another long pull on her cigarette and French inhaled the smoke up through her nostrils. Blowing the smoke out through her nose once she had gotten as much out of it as she could, she added. "People use words to show how smart they are or to convince you that their way of thinking is better than your own way. When something is important people should use as few words as is necessary and then they should shut up."

I got the hint and directed my gaze out into the alleyway.

I decided that the reason I didn't like the Sanka was that I had been expecting it to taste like coffee. It certainly didn't taste like any coffee I was familiar with, but once I came to that realization, it wasn't terrible. It was the first thing I'd put in my mouth in quite a while, so I threw it back and set the cup back on the table. Her cigarettes were awful, and besides having a thin flavor they were also the menthol, which made my throat tighten up when I tried to inhale a healthy amount. So I lit another one.

"I don't suppose you've got enough on you to spring for breakfast? Doesn't matter anyway though, no place around here to get it. Most everything along here don't open until bar time this afternoon. I'm gonna get dressed, so you rustle us up something out of the fridge. The eggs are pretty fresh and salami. Might be some cheese, and for sure there's orange juice."

She shoved herself up out of the chair, snatched the empty cups up off the table and whirled into the apartment. Over her shoulder as the screen door slammed she said, "No smoking inside."

She arrived at the breakfast table in a long-sleeved red and black flannel shirt and a pair of loose-fitting blue jeans. I served her breakfast of a pretty good salami and cheese frittata with some cilantro and garlic. She ate with relish and complimented me after she finished. She dropped the dishes in the sink and reached underneath for a large plastic garbage bag, which she tossed at me.

"Put your wet stuff in here. I guess that you wouldn't want to traipse all the way down to the laundry dressed only in my old bathrobe so while I'm gone, you clean up around here. When I get back, we'll see about getting you on your way. Last night you said California, but I don't think you realize how far away California can be." She paused and looked out across the backyard before adding, "It's a long way and not just in miles."

July 1963,
A Perfect Day for a City Boy

It is going to be a hot one. The morning dew on my bare feet is cold, but the air is already heavy and hot with humidity. While I milk the three cows that are my responsibility, the sweat is already running in my eyes, and the cows' tails are busy slapping me in the face due to the morning swarm of flies fresh from the manure pile outside the barn. By nine o'clock, the air will be wavering in the sunlight, and the heat will be on us in earnest.

"Larry has hay down today. You and your cousin Tom are going to go over and help bale after breakfast." My Uncle Danny's voice came from between two cows across the aisle.

Larry lives on the other side of town about seven or eight miles up, toward the settlement of Calamine. He's my cousin too, but older and married. He rents a big spread on the Pecatonica River and milks close to sixty cows a day. There is always more work at Larry's than one man can handle.

"Once Tom gets here you boys walk out to the highway. You can get a ride into town and then out to Larry's."

"I don't like those boys hitchhiking." Aunt Martha's raised voice came from the other side of the barn where she was feeding calves in the far corner.

"Well, that's how they're gonna get there. I can't let them take the truck. I got things to do, and I need to run to the mill in Argyle to

176

get feed ground this morning. That's the wrong direction. Let 'em use somebody else's gas. 'Sides, Emmett's twelve and Tom's eleven, they can't drive through town, 'thout somebody noticin'."

"Calamine's pretty far, and not just in miles Danny."

October/November 1969, Goodbye Seattle

Standing in the Seattle Greyhound station, my freshly clean clothes still smell like soap, my hair is still damp. Margaret had insisted I take another bath and shave with her disposable razor. "You don't know when you'll get the next one." Little pieces of toilet paper still clung to the various cuts on my jaw and neck. I look over the surprisingly busy waiting area. The floor is filthy from endless, wet, foot traffic and the room itself smells of stale cigarette smoke, dirt, diesel fumes and unwashed bodies, all competing for space in my nostrils. Fastened together, rows of formerly white plastic bucket chairs, now yellowed, grey and cracked are arranged back to back, filling the open area in the center. To my right is the ticket window, manned by a bored and detached agent, working with a cigarette clutched in the corner of his mouth, a half inch of ash hanging off of the end of it. To my left, an arrangement of vending machines ready to dispense any and all manner of junk food and drink. Most of the slots that are visible in the display window are already empty. The soda machines appear to be mostly empty as well. Interspersed along the outside of the seating area, small televisions are mounted on adjoining plastic chairs with small coin slots underneath to power up the set. In all respects, a typical Greyhound bus station.

Outside the double glass doors ahead of me, I see and smell the squad of buses parked diagonally with their destinations displayed on the marquee above their windshields; Portland, Coeur d'Alene, Vancouver, Eugene and a few more. Their headlights are bright in the darkness of a late fall evening. As evening had fallen, the rain had begun again, and the pavement around the buses is shiny with the wetness where the huge tires had tracked it into the garage. The wiper blades of the buses swipe lazily back and forth even though they are under the shelter of the metal bus barn roof.

I have my ticket in hand; she bought it for me, Margaret holding her cigarette in the corner of her mouth while she counted out the fare at the ticket window. Now she stands next to me, her right arm cradling her left elbow, her left hand holding her cigarette inches from her mouth, staring at nothing. I have no baggage, only a wool Army blanket that she rummaged out of her closet. She rolled it tight and tied the ends with a length of rope that was long enough to sling over my shoulder and carry across my back. The ticket says Portland; my bus is the second one from the left.

In the end, I had stayed with her for three days. Once my laundry was washed and dried, she took me grocery shopping, and I took over the kitchen to make first lunch and then dinner. She told me it was Sunday and she didn't work on Sundays or Mondays because business was slow and she usually went to church on Sunday mornings. Instead, we sat on the couch and talked about politics, the Vietnam War, hippies, and weather. She was smart and well-informed, and her opinions were thoughtful and objective. We never ventured into my situation or her occupation, although both hung in the room like cigarette smoke. Sunday night, I moved into the bedroom with her. Monday and Tuesday passed the same way, neither of us left the apartment unless it was out on the back porch in our respective bathrobes, to smoke cigarettes and drink Sanka. Now it was Wednesday, and the inevitable but dreaded conclusion of my stay had arrived.

We have no more conversation left to lighten the moment. Finally, she dropped her smoke on the floor and ground it under the heel of her sneakers, took a deep breath and sighed from deep inside of her. Turning to me, she stepped in front of me, cutting off my vision from anything else and made eye contact, her eyebrows pulled down and serious. I am stricken by how beautiful she really is. Reaching up she plucked a small bloody piece of toilet paper from my jaw, the result of using a not-too- sharp disposable razor and began. "Ok kid. Emmett, you're a pretty good kid, you're smart, and so far, you're lucky. But you're still a kid, so I'm going to give you a little advice. I think I've earned that right." She stopped to take a breath and fidgeting, she rummaged in her purse again and pulled out yet another cigarette. Lighting it, she again stared off at nothing and took a deep drag, while she tapped her foot impatiently. "So here it goes, listen up. I don't know where you're going or where you're gonna end up, and I can't tell you if you're making a huge mistake or a brilliant decision, but as long as you've made up your mind, for now, don't stop until you see it through. If you make up your mind to go somewhere or do something, then do it. Don't stop, don't hesitate. Trust your instincts, and if you fail at something, god forbid. Move on—quickly."

Then she turned away and directed her gaze out the double doors to the buses standing at the ready and started again. "There was another kid like you, a long time ago now. With big dreams and grand plans but when things got tough, she stopped. She took the easy way. She let the situation tell her what to do, the window closed, and those big dreams melted away, (sniff). Along with her self-respect. The next thing she knew she had one foot nailed to the floor."

She stopped and took a drag off her cigarette and once again stared off at nothing.

"The decisions she didn't make, became life choices." Another drag, another pause, and without the eye contact. "Her dreams faded when the going got tough, and then they died. She chose the easy way. She could have taken a chance, but she was afraid, she lacked self-worth, and as a result, her prophecy was fulfilled. Every day of her life was pretty much the same as the day before. Her sense of worth and self-esteem became shameful and bitter. I want you to keep your hopes up and your eyes open and don't be so trusting. Not everyone will be as nice to you as I am."

She looked away at her mostly unsmoked cigarette for a second and, with a sigh, dropped it and ground it out slowly. Then, she straightened her shoulders, suddenly realizing that she had slumped down, took a deep breath and I saw her mentally shake the memories away. Briskly she added.

"Now give Margaret a hug and tell her thank you and—even if you don't mean it—tell her that you love her and will never forget her."

I wrapped my arms around her and told her—and I meant it. I breathed in her smell of cigarette smoke and perfume. She put her face against my neck and laid her head on my shoulder. I felt her tremble under my hands. After a long moment, she released me and pushed me away, her eyes misty. She sniffled and took a tissue out of her purse, and without another word, she turned and walked away wiping at her eyes as she went.

November, 1969
Lost in Oregon,

Portland, Oregon, had proved difficult to navigate on foot. The streets were confusing and busy. It took almost the entire day to make it to the outskirts of town one short ride after another. Most of the traffic appeared to be local and what few rides I was able to catch only took me several blocks each. The streets did not seem to offer a clear way directly out of town, requiring me to resort to walking most of the day. Throughout that day, the weather alternated between a light rain or a cold, wet wind that I guessed must be coming from the ocean. Finally, reaching the interstate ramp at the southern edge of the city, was picked up by a long-haul trucker who said he was having trouble staying awake and could use some conversation. He was going to Grant's Pass and was almost home. He talked nonstop the entire ride, and I was saved from the need to hold up my end of the conversation or offer any background information.

Once at Grant's Pass, he deposited me at the bottom of the off-ramp where it joined with Highway 199. By that time night had fallen and I was spent. I was unwilling to accept another ride at this late hour without a clear idea of where I was, or where I wanted to go.

I climbed over the concrete pylon of bridge pillars and hiked up the embankment to where the underside of the bridge met with the street above. At the juncture of the steel support spans and the top of the embankment, there was a six-to-eight-foot space between the long I-beams that run the length of the bridge. The steel spans are three or four feet high and are set on a foundation of finished concrete.

The space between the I-beams and above the concrete foundation creates a small cubicle that is above the ground and out of any wind or weather. Up in this place, the bright lighting under the bridge was muted, but the noise and vibration of the traffic bumping up onto the deck above me were more imposing. I hoped as the hour got later, the interstate traffic above me would lessen enough to allow me to rest. I was thankful that I was going to stay dry, for now. Hoisting myself up into the space, I unrolled my blanket bedroll and wrapped it around my shoulders and settled in for the night. This was not the first time I had spent the night in a place like this, and every time I did it I hoped it would be the last. You don't sleep well in a place like that but by dozing in and out of sleep, the long nighttime hours passed more quickly.

As the light outside began to grow, I gave up trying to sleep. Hopping down off of the cement, I shook out my blanket and rolled it back up, securing it with my rope. Almost simultaneously with my arriving at street level, another hitchhiker climbed out of a car at the intersection. I could hear him thanking the driver for the ride as he reached into the back seat for a guitar that he then slung onto his back. He spied me and crossed the street said his howdies and bummed a cigarette. His dark brown hair was down onto his shoulders, and all he carried was a guitar strapped to his back. He said he was heading west to Crescent City and was looking forward to the bitchin' scenery on the road there. Without a map, I was at a loss as to where I was, let alone where I wanted to go, so as we both made our way to the nearby intersection. He was sure we would have a ride in no time and graciously admitted that since I was technically there first, then I should get the first ride that was offered.

He was right about getting a ride in short order because only the second or third car stopped and offered to take us both. A young guy, about our age, in a beat up 1960 four-door Chevy Biscayne that at one time was supposed to be white and was coincidentally going to Crescent City where he had been promised a job picked us up with a smile and a wave. While I rode in front, Willis (I found out his name when he introduced himself to the driver) sat in the back and strummed his guitar, occasionally pointing out the spectacular views as the scenery passed by.

Our driver was a rail-thin young fellow, about my age with a hawk nose and pink cheeks, from a recent shave, was wearing a light blue Firestone Tire work shirt that said Robbie over the left front pocket. His wet hair was pulled back into a ponytail that hung down between his shoulders and the hands that clutched the steering wheel displayed knuckles and fingernails that were dark from regular contact with grime. On the floor hump between the driver and passenger area was a huge bag of trail mix that he said he didn't really like, and on the bench seat between us a gallon jug of herbal tea.

"My girlfriend makes this shit for me. I keep telling her I don't like peanuts, but she keeps making it anyway." Between puffs on the cigarette hanging out of the corner of his mouth, he added, "Guess she likes me." He smiled.

I was practically starving and thirsty too and I gratefully and unashamedly stuffed myself on the trail mix and tea. I had never heard of either one of these things before and found surprisingly, that whatever trail mix was, it was pretty good. Both were satisfying and delicious and tasted a little like they belonged in a dessert category. I made a mental note that if I could ever afford it, I would acquire more of both.

The Wedding Party

Once in Crescent City, the three of us parted ways. Robbie was kind enough to detour himself and take me to the south end of town to where Highway 199 ended at Highway 101. With a smile and a wave, he yelled, "Keep on truckin' man," made a U-turn and headed back into the city. Late morning traffic heading south was light, and I waited impatiently for someone to take pity on me, trying different poses with my thumb and practicing different looks of sincerity and trustworthiness, hoping that my dedication to the craft would net me a ride. Neither my looks of sincerity nor my energetic thumb posture proved effective and after what seemed long enough; I started walking down the road in a southerly direction deciding that any progress was better no progress at all. I paused only when an oncoming car approached so that I could turn and execute my latest thumb-out pose.

Soon I just gave myself over to walking. I didn't think about my situation. I didn't think about my past or my future. I merely allowed my feet to create a rhythm that was taken up by my breathing and thought about nothing at all. The scenery was incredible, and I kept my head on a swivel, moving from one view to another, taking pictures with my eyes. One of the advantages of walking is when you see something of interest; you have plenty of time to look at it as you pass by.

While passing a roadside sign that told me that it was seventy-some miles to Eureka, California, an old delivery step van slowed behind me and then came to a stop in the traffic lane. The truck was ancient and had been painted over white with what must have been a paint roller. Still visible under the paint was a Sunbeam Bread logo, and several flowers and peace signs had been added by hand. The door of the van was open, and a kid with wild hair, a tie-dyed shirt and a pair of bell-bottom pants that sported a band of embroidered cloth around the cuffs addressed me from the driver's seat.

"Hey man, you need a ride someplace?"

"Sure do, where you headed?"

"Man, like we're goin' to a wedding man."

"That's cool, where at?"

"Oh man, it's like at this waterfall, you know, so cool man." He said, gesturing wildly with his hands.

"Okay. Where's the waterfall?"

"Oh? Oh yeah man I get it, like see it's outside of Eureka, down the road a ways," he pointed ahead through the windshield. "You dig a ride man?"

"You bet."

"Climb on in! Join the party, man."

I climbed the step into the van. There was no passenger seat, so I turned to look into the semidarkness in the back of the truck. As my eyes began to adjust to the difference in the light, the driver ground the transmission back into gear, let the clutch out and started slowly up and headed south. The inside of the truck was bare metal walls, and there was only the light that came in through the doorway and the two small windows, one in each door, in the back. The floor was covered by mattresses that were arranged in such a way as to completely carpet the space. Arranged haphazardly on these were five other inhabitants all roughly my age, two guys and three girls relaxing and smiling in my direction. They were all dressed in varying shades of the same outfits as the driver. Over the road noise and the sound of the truck engine one of them hollered.

"Hey far out man c'mon in sit down and hang out. The rides are pretty rough so you'll fall if you don't sit man. I'm Keith and he's Raimy, this here is Orange Sunshine, then Rose Petal, and that one's

Judith. The dude driving is Brian."

One of the women vacated a spot near the doorway and crawled on hands and knees, over to the speaker curling up under his arm, still dreamily smiling at me. I sat down on the mattress and leaned my back up against the vibrating side of the truck. Looking around, I took in the group one by one as they took almost no notice of me and again resumed whatever activity they had been engaged in before I joined them. The one name Judith sat cross-legged and stared out the windshield with no expression on her face, and her eyes didn't seem to ever blink. Even in the half-light, I could see that her pupils were huge. Keith added, "Judith's trippin' man, she's someplace far away. Got some righteous blotter acid, man."

The boy named Raimy was also cross-legged and rolling joints out of a grocery store-sized bag of weed, and when introduced only looked up and smiled before returning to his task. Orange Sunshine ran her hand up under Keith's shirt and cast a sly smile at me over her shoulder. Rose Petal was lying on her back regarding the truck roof and seemed lost in reflection.

"So, who's getting married?" I yelled.

"Oh man, Brian, man," waving toward the driver, "and Rose Petal, it's gonna be boss man, a total groove. It's gonna be at this waterfall place, like in the forest, dig it man, a real forest, and we're all gonna swim and hang, it's going to be a happening. You know man?"

"Sounds pretty cool, when's it gonna happen?"

"Whenever we get there, you know man, can't have a wedding without the bride and groom you know," he said winking at me. "There'll be people from everywhere, man, we're going to party har-dy. We're campin', you know, and we're getting back to the land, man. They can't start without us you know man? Hey man, why don't you come with, you doing anything? You could come and hang out, you know?"

"I'm not doing anything at all, but I gotta keep truckin'. I need to get some grits and some sleep." Lapsing into what could pass as the appropriate vernacular.

"Oh man, there's gonna be plenty of chow, we even got some here you can help yourself to. If you're tired man, I can help you with that, I got uppers and I got some mescaline too. You need to get up a little or a lot?"

"No thanks man, uppers make me paranoid, but I'd take some food if you can spare it.'

"No worries man, help yourself whenever."

Mid-November 1969, The Waterfall

The old bread truck rocked and swayed down the road demonstrating almost no life in the springs or suspension.

In spite of the general condition of the passenger-cargo our driver, Brian, seemed pretty together and he applied himself diligently to navigation and even passed on the several joints he was offered pausing only occasionally to swig out of the bottle of Boone's Farm apple wine that leaned up against the bottom of his seat.

It turned out to be a very long drive and was made even longer by the crowded compartment, their general lack of deodorant and the truck's lack of shock absorbers. My nervous system struggled to cope with the various stimuli, the lack of sleep and a healthy dose of very good weed. I gave up trying to catch glimpses of the scenery through the windshield or out the side door and leaned back in the corner, behind the driver's seat and fell into a vibration filled dreamless sleep.

The squeal of the tortured brakes woke me with a start as the truck slowed and took a sharp left. It jounced off the road the suspension system rattling ominously and onto a small lane that went straight back into a pine forest. Everyone in the truck, myself included, pressed forward peering out of the windshield as the truck chugged along. After about a quarter mile the lane opened into a wide parking area in the middle of a forest. There were several vehicles already parked haphazardly around the parking lot, most of them covered with peace signs and flowers—some were newer, most were older.

Shutting off the truck, the silence of the forest was almost a palpable presence. I was overcome by the quiet of the woods and the amazing shades of green and amber, so different from the road noise of only moments ago. The parking area was covered with long pine needles, and I was almost apologetic for any noise we created in the cathedral-like atmosphere of the parking area. For a while, the only sound we made was the ticking of the engine and exhaust of the old truck as it tried to cool down.

The quiet did not last long, however. Within minutes a large group of enthusiastic and jubilant people came pouring out of a small path in the far corner of the parking area and descended upon us. They had waited for our arrival more or less patiently, and their laughter and joy were utterly unconditional. I was embraced just as enthusiastically as the bride-to-be. Within minutes, the stores that were loaded in the bread truck were carried out by the group and they all, myself included, marched off into the woods on a wide, well-trodden path in a parade of color and laughter. Two of the people took charge of Judith, holding her hands and guiding her as she walked between them her head on a swivel looking at everything intensely, but what she was seeing was anyone's guess.

As they walked, they sang, surprisingly in harmony, and I would be lying if I didn't find the mood infectious. After a bit of a walk, we exited the woods at the edge of a large, rushing waterway. The water roared past us from right to left, making a tremendous noise. It was too large to call a creek, but it was too small to call a river. The water was deep and clear as it roared over and between rocks the size of a Volkswagen. It was difficult to judge its depth as it raced through the dells created by high water-worn stones that stood fifteen to twenty feet high on either side. The noise was loud and exciting, and we seemed to be a million miles from anywhere. There was a mist drifting down through the open space created by the waterway, and its cool dampness made the contrasting greens of the trees and ferns seem even more intimate. Although the sky was bright, any sun or clouds were obscured by drifting mists above us. Turning to the right, we moved upstream walking along the edge of the cataract on our left. The roaring of the water increased as we walked, and soon we rounded a stand of smooth boulders and arrived at the waterfall.

I had seen pictures of waterfalls before, but never actually seen one. None of the images in magazines or *National Geographic* could compare to the scope and beauty of the real thing, especially this one. Far above us, the water leaped far out from the sheer cliff face, crashing down and over the rocks and boulders below. As it struck obstacles, the water splashed into cascades, separating, flowing around them rejoining itself spreading out over the cliff face and forming multiple rivulets that in turn raced down the various grooves that had been carved into the cliff face over millennia. It cascaded and funneled its way down for at least fifty or sixty feet before rejoining for the last ten or twelve feet. That was a free-fall into a large pool at the base of the cliff. Over endless time, the water had carved the space into an expansive grotto with rock walls surrounding the edges of the pool, sandy with the debris of countless years of water pounding on stone. A constant mist boiled up out of the pool and into the still air, rising into a low hanging cloud that slowly drifted away, chasing the water downstream in slow motion. The water and mist disappeared around the turn in the river and against a backdrop of the deep greens of the dense stands of pine forest it vanished from view. The pool was a huge bowl of water that filled the entire space save the narrow edges of sand and was contained by the cliff face and the upright stones that stood shoulder to shoulder on the other three sides. The water was in constant motion as the ripples created by the waterfall pushed it on its way out of the narrow outlet at the foot of the grotto.

Those carrying supplies from the truck disappeared down a path that continued into the woods only to return minutes later having stowed their bundles. The rest of us took these moments to experience the peace and tranquility that the setting called for. Once everyone had reassembled at the water's edge, a small circle formed around the troth-plighted couple surrounding them in a tight arc of protection. With a nod from Brian our driver and murmurs of encouragement, he and Rose, (I just couldn't make myself think or say Rose Petal), stripped out of their clothes. Two of the girls approached the now naked couple and placed woven crowns of fern and leaves on their heads and then backed away. The two lovers took each other's hands and stepped into the water walking out to where they could no longer stand and had to swim. Dog-paddling side by side they swam directly under the falls making no attempt to avoid the splashing water and disappeared behind it. No one made a move to leave but instead waited almost breathless with anticipation. Long minutes passed with no sign of the couple. I did not have any idea what to expect, so my heightened excitement and curiosity was no less than anyone else's. The keen energy of the moment made time pass slowly and quickly at the same time, so it was difficult to tell just how long the couple remained out of sight. Then, once again, they emerged directly through the falls dog-paddling side by side, stopping only momentarily to push the water out of their eyes and their hair back from their faces. As soon as they reached a spot that they could stand, they held hands and raised them above their heads. Everyone cheered including me although I didn't understand. There was no denying that the moment was electric, so I joined in with enthusiasm. Later that night as we sat around the campfire, Raimy explained that Brian and Rose Petal made secret vows behind the waterfall and sealed them by making love. In their eyes and everyone present, they were now married.

The celebration after the "wedding" was truly a *Happening* and lasted three whole days. Small and large tents and canopies were set up in a clearing a short way up the path from the falls. In spite of the cool temperatures, people swam in the icy cold water of the pool beneath the cascading water of the falls, campfires burned nonstop to hang out around when the night became cold; there was plenty of weed, food, easy laughter, and free love. All of the above given freely and with no apparent concern for specific partners, and all with no strings attached. We were occasionally visited by Park Rangers in their Smoky-the-Bear hats, but it appeared they were more interested in the spectacle than whether our camping permits were in order. They stood at the end of the clearing with their arms folded across their chests and watched us like they had front row seats at the circus freak show.

I would be lying if I said that I joined in with enthusiasm completely. I was a little too Catholic for that. The joy and enfoldment that they all expressed to each other and to me made me uncomfortable. Having never experienced anything like this level of freely given affection and acceptance, my skepticism was on full alert. When the girls shed their granny dresses and tie-dyed shirts, I tried not to stare but did anyway, and my Catholic guilt rose in my throat, almost choking me. The kids all seemed without inhibitions toward touching, laughing, or modesty. I had a lifetime of reinforced taboo issues with all of those qualities so although I truly enjoyed my time with them; I enjoyed it from the fringe. Still, on the second day, I tried my best and actually swam in the pool with some of them albeit wearing my underpants and waiting until darkness had fallen. For their part, they all seemed to understand my reticence and made sure to allow me my space.

On the first night, everyone gathered around a large campfire. The frenetic pace of celebrating exhausted everyone's physical energy and most leaned against one another staring into the flames, content and comfortable with each other. A few had guitars that they strummed languid tunes on that apparently had no words to accompany them. There were enough people so that when the inner circle filled, another started outside of the first and when that one was filled a third was begun. I comforted myself in the belief that I was the original member of the third circle. I was close enough to be a part of the group but far enough away to avoid intimacy on most levels. Then, Lucille sat down next to me.

November 1969, Lucille

Lucille was a beautiful dark-eyed and a dark-skinned girl with obvious Hispanic or Mediterranean ethnicity. Her long, black hair appeared glossy in the firelight and was full and straight widening out as it got longer, falling onto her shoulders and down her back. She had caught my eye several times during the day as she had frolicked and danced with the others. A few times she caught me looking and smiled coyly back at me. Instead of the standard mode of dress for the event, she was dressed in stylish tight hip-hugger jeans and a flowered shirt that buttoned up the front but did nothing to hide her obvious charms. She exuded youthful innocence that was incredibly alluring, and I couldn't help but feel smitten with her from afar. Of everyone at the gathering, I found her the most interesting and attractive. So when she plunked down next to me that evening, my heart rate increased immediately. We did not speak. Instead, she sat close to me and leaned her head on my shoulder as we watched, hypnotized by the firelight.

For the next three days, we stayed together, holding hands and walking the amazing fern-lined trails through the forest that surrounded us. We would stop frequently, and kiss and she would hug me close and sigh, sounding like her heart was full. Her kissing was tentative and sweet never wandering into ardor. It was clear that her need for closeness and affection outweighed her desire for physical release. I was happy to oblige her, although, in the back of my mind, I held out hope for the carnal portion of her as well. Something about her innocence and naiveté told me not to pursue it. I was content with her company

194

and allowed myself to enjoy her happiness and her total attention. At night, we slept together fully clothed lying on my army blanket with her sleeping bag over us. We both felt the difference between being among the group and the separation that prevented us from being a part of it. She listened with total rapt attention as I talked. She was beautiful, smart and curious; in short; she was perfect.

When the fourth morning arrived, people began to pack up and stow their gear. In twos and threes, they shouldered their packs and with hugs and waves disappeared back to their homes in whereverland. Lucille too announced with tear-filled eyes that she had to leave as well. I had learned that she lived with her parents in Los Gatos and that it was a long way away to the south. I was somehow not surprised when she told me that she had to be back at school the next day. Her friend, whose name I couldn't remember if I had been told it at all, had gotten with one of the local guys and decided to stay on for a season and would not be riding home with her. Looking into her sad face, I suddenly realized how youth is not always measured in years. With the party breaking up and each departure, my immediate future was once again in jeopardy. I had enjoyed her company and didn't want it to end. Since I didn't know what or where Los Gatos was I asked if I might accompany her. She immediately threw her arms around me, and her smile sealed the deal.

In the parking area, she unlocked the trunk of a late model two-door Oldsmobile coupe, and I tossed my rolled blanket in with her backpack and sleeping bag. The car was a nice one spotless on the inside and out, with electric windows and the smell of clean vinyl and a pine air freshener.

"No smoking *anything* in the car." She said, with emphasis on the anything.

She asked me if I would mind driving to which I readily agreed. I have always had trouble trusting other people when they drive, spending most of my times with my foot pressed hard against an imaginary brake pedal or my hands placed firmly on the dashboard. Once on our way, while I drove she pointed out interesting landmarks and vistas, occasionally even telling me to pull over so that we could enjoy a particular view without the burden of simultaneously watching the road. Leaving the forest, we soon turned east away from the coast and began following the twisting canyon of the Eel River switching back and forth and crossing it many times. What she called foothills, my naïve Midwestern upbringing perceived as mountains and once again I was in awe of the beauty around me.

In less than an hour, Lucille directed me off what she called the 101 onto a smaller secondary road with the dubious name of Avenue of the Giants. If I had been blown away by the expansive vistas of the California countryside, it was nothing compared to what was contained on this side trip as we entered the magnificent Humboldt Redwoods, State Park. After repeatedly pulling over to the side of the road so that I could look at this tree or that one, she finally laughed. She said, "just you wait," and suggested that we would see plenty of trees and in a short while we would be able to get out of the car and walk among the giants themselves.

On a few cherished occasions, my father had taken us deep into the vast forests of northern Wisconsin, where we would trek cross-country through the vast trackless wilderness still contained there and known to very few. He was always completely aware of where we were and without the aid of a compass could invariably emerge out of a thick stand of the underbrush, within sight of where we had left our car, parked in one of the unmapped fire prevention lanes that pierced deep into the forests. He would do this after hours of seemingly aimless strolling. On those occasions, I was touched by the otherworldly substance and sentient awareness that I could perceive as I walked among the trees. That feeling paled in comparison to the emotions that were created by the stately presence of the magnificence that I discovered in the Humboldt. Once we parked in the lot provided, we embarked into a realm governed by spiritual substance. The gigantic, stately redwoods rose up endlessly, disappearing into the fog that lay over the top of the forest. As they rose to dizzying heights, they seemed to not lose any of their broad girth, no matter how far up I gazed. It was easy to imagine them reaching for the stars. Without the least bit of exaggeration, I could feel the age and wisdom of this forest, and immediately a resonance vibrated a deeper chord within me. I could feel the awareness of it. For the first time in my life, I recognized the life around me. Nature as it were, did not exist for my enjoyment but did so for itself alone. It lived as a singular unit, intermingling individual lives with all of the other component lives creating a vast interdependency of community. It was my first brush with the spiritual experience that was available for those that could see the life around them.

For a long time after we resumed our drive to the south, neither of us spoke, lost in thought and reflection. Sitting hip to hip on the bench seat, she would reach for my hand and clutch it in both of hers, not talking, but with long sighs while she took in the postcard scenery. From early morning until late afternoon, the drive consumed the entire day. Full dark had arrived by the time we had negotiated our way through the freeway jungle of the San Francisco urban area. The only other detour we had taken was to route ourselves so that I could cross the Golden Gate Bridge. The bridge was a magnificent testament to man's ability to create structure without life. Shrouded in fog, it was spectacular from an engineering point of view, but nothing could compare to the stately majesty we had left behind in the forest.

After the city, we soon began climbing the hills near Los Gatos in the dark. In the final hour of the drive, Lucille had become increasingly quiet and fidgety. Troubled by her sudden shift in mood, I broke with one of my unwritten rules and asked her what the problem was. At first, she laughed and changed the subject but finally, she turned in her seat to face me leaning back against the passenger door. With a deep breath and a sigh, and then another breath she began.

"I guess I have a problem." Another sigh. "You've never asked me about me, that's kinda another reason why I liked you. You know? You just took me the way I am." Another sigh, and now a tear.

"Well." Deep breath, "well." then another deep breath and finally in a rush, "The reason I still live with my parents is that I'm still in high school. I'm eighteen but my birthday was just this month, so I'm a grown up. My parents let me go to the wedding this weekend as a kind of, you know, as a birthday present sorta'."

I knew where this was going now.

"George and Phyllis," *her parents apparently*, "let me go with Ally because they thought we would keep each other safe, and not be stupid. We both know, or knew, Rose Petal from school last year, and she wanted us to be there. Ally is Ally, and she goes off on her own all the time. So my folks were a little worried about her, to begin with. Even though they won't have any way of finding out that Ally didn't come home with me, there is no way that they are going to let me come home with you, they'll freak. I'm scared." Sniff. "I don't know what to do. I love you Emmett, and I want us to be together, but I can't think of a way to make it happen. I want to go with you, but I'm afraid."

With this, finally off her chest she crossed her arms and dropped her chin down on her chest and quietly sobbed and sniffled while I, once again, immediately felt like shit. In the back of my mind, I had been wondering how it was going to go down at the end of this ride. My own fear of the unknown didn't help the situation. It would have been enough that I was getting farther and farther away from resolving my own life issues in any kind of satisfactory way. Now I had walked all over another person's life.

"Don't worry Lucy baby, it'll work out the way it's supposed to. Whatever it needs to be, it will be. I don't want you to cry. Neither of us has had enough sleep, and I know I'm tired and dirty. Maybe once we get some rest, tomorrow will show us a way."

"Tomorrow will be worse. I have to go to school tomorrow. My parents have to go to work; I'm so scared; my chest hurts."

After a long pause, while I chastised myself for the turd that I was, I finally started again.

"Okay, let's figure this out. When we get home, where do you park the car?"

"Mom and Dad's cars are in the carport, so I park on the street in front of the house. Why?"

"When we get there, you grab your stuff and go on in the house. I'll just sleep in the car, okay. Then in the morning when you go to school, we won't need to bump into your folks, and I can maybe drop you at school. How does that sound?"

"You're going to sleep in the car? How?"

"I've slept in my car all the time. I'll just get in the back seat. Even if they look at the car, they won't see me, and I can lock the car from the inside. I've got a blanket in case it gets cold, I'll be okay, I promise."

After a few sniffles she wiped her eyes on her sleeve and sitting up she took a deep breath. Looking out the windshield she said, "Okay if you're sure we can try that. Our street's pretty safe. You should be okay."

Once in Los Gatos, she gave me a quick tour. The bank where her father worked, the real estate office where her mother worked and the high school where she was an honor-roll senior.

After that, we went the few blocks where she pointed out her house from a block away; a neat little ranch house on a street where all the other houses were neat, little ranch houses as well, looked cozy, the front lawn and shrubbery well-tended. The picture of a happy household on a pleasant street where everyone mowed their grass on Saturday and grilled on Sunday. I pulled up to the curb and killed the engine and lights. She sat in the seat, tears again running down her cheeks staring out the side window at the front of the house.

"It's not going to get any easier the longer you wait, Luce." "I know, it's just, just. You know, if I go in there—it's like

I'm like different somehow. They know me so well. They'll see the difference I bet, and if they ask me what it is that's different, I'll have to lie. I don't want to lie; I don't even think I can. I want to just go away with you. Maybe I could call them from somewhere, far away, but that would be so mean. They're really good people, I couldn't do that to them." Finally, and uncharacteristically, "SHIT!"

In a rush, Lucy threw herself across the bench seat and wrapped her arms around me. Her recent tears were wet on my cheek, her arms held me affectionately, not with desperation. I kissed her forehead, and she raised her lips to mine, and for the first time she kissed me with real physical passion; her breathing quavering and coming faster. I could feel her heart beating under her shirt, and I felt myself respond in kind. As gently as I could, I pulled her away from me, afraid of starting something we couldn't or shouldn't finish. Her wide-eyed look of bewilderment searched my face for an explanation and then when it dawned on her, she dropped her eyes and nodded. She took a deep breath and slid across to the door and opened it. Reaching back over she pulled the keys out of the ignition and stepped out of the car. Going around to the back she popped the trunk lid and rummaged around. She returned to the car door and dropped my blanket roll onto the passenger side of the seat, then closed the door. She bent over and looked at me through the window for a long moment, then turned and slowly walked up the walk to the front door. Once under the porch light she gave a last look blew me a kiss and went inside. The outside porch light went out, and an inside light blinked on behind the door.

In case there might be a curious local police patrol in the neighborhood, I locked the doors and tucked the blanket behind my head on the armrest of the door behind me. Slumping down behind the steering wheel, I stretched my legs out onto the floorboard of the passenger seat, out of sight but able to watch the house—waiting. One by one, the lights went out.

The last lighted window was in the corner of the house, and I saw as the curtain was pulled aside, and a face appeared briefly, then the curtain dropped back in place, and shortly the light went out. I ticked off another thirty minutes in my head and then sat up, opened the door, and stepped out onto the street. Up and down the road, the neighborhood was already asleep. Stepping up onto the sidewalk, I slung my blanket roll across my back and looked left back toward the town and then turned right.

August 1969
And So, It Goes

And just like that Mrs. Riverton is nowhere to be found. I sneak back to the high school and look for her car. I have tried to call her but she does not answer, she does not respond. I have passed by her house, slowly. I have cruised the neighborhoods, grocery store, and shopping mall parking lots hoping to see her car. It is not there. In the crowded atrium of the mall, I imagine I see her briefly in every similar haircut or authoritative stride. I've walked the halls at the high school, while the summer school classes drone on in the stifling heat, but she is not there, her office is dark. She has moved on, I am old news. Another life lesson permanently etched by misery.

Adios Los Gatos

Walking the sleeping streets of Los Gatos, I attempted to adopt a gait that would appear casual. The last thing I wanted was to create suspicion in the mind of any rolling police patrol. All of the streets were well-maintained, the sidewalks were clear, the yards almost Spartan. I was aware of how a dark figure, walking at this time of night, might appear. After a few blocks, it seemed that each street curved slightly only to peter out as it intersected a slightly larger one. When the curve in the street was to the right I would turn left when I reached the next intersection. There was a sense that the streets slowly funneled toward a more central point. Eventually, I approached an intersection with a California Highway 17 sign and an arrow extending in both directions. To the right was the way back into town, to the left; darkness. The irony was not lost on me, and I smiled ruefully to myself. I turned left.

Every night since leaving Portland the low-lying fog was ever-present, but the hard rain of Washington and Oregon had abated. There had been mild showers most days, so everything had always been damp and fresh smelling, and my clothes never seemed to dry completely. When we had climbed up into the hills of Los Gatos the skies had cleared, and the stars were visible and bright as the lights of the town behind me faded. No moon was visible to give me an indication of direction. Uncle Danny's voice sounded in my head, "The bottom of any phase of the moon will always point south." I didn't have a direction in mind or a destination, but I felt movement of any kind was probably better than stasis. In the back of my mind, I could visualize a broken-hearted Lucy driving the streets of Los Gatos searching for me the next morning instead of going to school. It would be best if I got out of town altogether.

As soon as I was clear of the outlying buildings and small shops, the darkness was complete, and the sidewalks ended at the edge of town. The road almost immediately made a sharp turn to the left. I could feel more than see that it sloped steeply away. My internal clock told me that it must be close to midnight or at least getting close, and there did not seem to be any traffic coming or going. I debated whether to stand and wait for a ride or walk back to one of the little strip mall shops and try to sleep in a doorway. Both ideas sounded equally disagreeable. Walking down the hill into the deeper darkness with no sense of where it went didn't seem any better. Reaching into one end of my bedroll, I pulled out a dry pack of cigarettes that Lucy had bought for me and lit one. With no other available activity to distract me, I squatted down on the shoulder of the road to ponder my predicament.

Halfway through my cigarette, a pair of headlights appeared to my left, accelerating as it started to separate from the town. When it got within a couple of blocks, the headlights flipped up onto bright, blinding me. It was the first vehicle to pass me on the way out of town, so I rose from my crouch to tried and give it my best shot. I turned toward it full on and tried and look friendly, lost but safe. Even before I raise my thumb, the sound of the engine slowed, and the vehicle pulled up alongside me; an old Ford F-100 pickup, the rust in the fender wells evident even in the darkness. The driver struggled across the seat and hand cranked the passenger window down. As soon as the window was down all the way, the ugliest dog I may have ever seen shouldered its way past the outstretched arm of the driver and growled out of the window, a complete complement of vicious teeth visible.

"Where you headed?" The driver said.

"Down this way, a ways."

"I'm headed back to UCSC; been visiting my girlfriend, you know, I gotta be back to school in the morning. You're welcome to ride, but I can't let you in here," he added, "Cyndi—well she doesn't like strangers."

That was perfectly obvious; she was not only ugly, but she was also big too. She appeared to be some kind of shepherd- Sasquatch mix-breed.

"You're welcome to ride in the back if you want. This road runs down to Santa Cruz, and it's pretty quiet, especially at this time of night. I might be your last chance for a while."

"Sounds okay."

I threw my bedroll over the side and climbed the tire into the bed of the pickup. There was a flat spare lying on its side behind the cab and the usual trash that collects in the back of an open truck. It was getting pretty chilly, so I pushed the tire aside and hunkered down behind the cab holding the rolled blanket up against my chest. Cyndi immediately threw herself against the sliding rear window of the cab, just in case I wasn't already afraid of her. The driver smacked her on top of the head and yelled through the small opening.

"Road winds plenty so don't stand up or anything. Otherwise you'll get thrown out. I ain't gonna stop until I get to Santa Cruz so if you need something pound of the roof of the cab. Might snow a little before we get all the way down there; has before so, sorry about that."

Then he snapped the window shut and hit the volume on the radio. In seconds the sounds of the Rolling Stones, "Let It Bleed" vibrated through the night. Grinding the old Ford into gear, we chugged around the curve and into the darkness.

How he knew it might snow I had no idea, I didn't even know that it snowed in California, but as the truck veered through one turn after another, the flurries rushed up and over the headlights. My view out of the windshield was somewhat obscured by the massive head of Cyndi, but while braced into the front passenger corner of the truck bed I caught glimpses of the big flakes of snow as they were devoured by the bright headlights that illuminated the diamond-shaped highway signs with squiggly lines on them. Each sign advertising the next series of curves accelerated my heart rate and created a 4G centrifugal force against the solid truck bed rails. My damp clothes did nothing to ward off the chill; and with the snow falling, it seemed colder to me than it probably already was. Shortly I began to shiver, and my arms trembled in their grip on the sides of the truck. The ride went on for seemingly ever but in reality, was relatively short.

I had lost count of the number of back and forth curves however soon the road straightened out, and we emerged out of the hills into a broader valley. I could see the sides of it as we had moved in under the cloud cover again and the stars had disappeared, and the snow had stopped. Shortly we began to pass more houses and roadside enterprises and then stopped at an intersection. The rear window of the truck slid open again, and the driver twisted in his seat to speak through it.

"Hey man, do you know where you want to go?"

"No, not really. It's pretty late huh?"

"Yeah, it's pushing one o'clock. So, here's the deal man. This here is Highway 1, if you take that it goes along the coast. Left is south, right is north. Up ahead that's Santa Cruz, pretty cool place, you been there?"

"No man, I just got in from Oregon a couple days ago." "Oh, shit man, in the summertime Santa Cruz is where you wanna be. Babes man, babes everywhere, sand beach, boardwalk beautiful nights man. Not as much fun this time of year though, the water's too cold. Hey, do you have a place for the night?"

"Not really, I thought I sack out someplace quiet."

"Look, man, I live just off the campus, you know, my landlady lets me have Cyndi, so it's cool, but like I said, man, Cyndi doesn't like other people."

"Yeah, I get that."

"Look, the campus has all kinds of places to sack out. The dorms are pretty sparse, but you know people are starting to finish up for Thanksgiving in a week or two, so it's pretty loose. There's like this dining facility, and they never bother to check your meal card, so I eat there all the time. You can just walk in, you know. If you're cool about it."

"That'll work for me man, hey I appreciate the ride. I don't know how long I'd have been standing there." On the ride to Santa Cruz, we had not passed a single car.

"That's okay man, glad to do it. Listen I'll cruise up onto campus, and I'll let you off by the food building, sound excellent?"

I was wholly familiar with how to function on a college campus and stay under the radar, this sounded good to me.

"Fan-fuckin-tastic."

"Good as done."

Leaving the rear window open he drove on toward the lights of town. We were still short of the brighter lights of Santa Cruz but certainly within the city limits as I watched out through the windshield when we passed a fairly large sign indicating the University of California Santa Cruz was the next right turn. Taking the turn, we passed several buildings on the right-hand side that appeared to be mostly maintenance and facility support structures, and then approached a set of buildings that seemed to be bright white in the walkway and street lights sitting in a quadrangle.

The driver stopped and once again spoke through the rear window.

"This is Cowell College, there's the dorms over there, and the chow hall is straight ahead. Like I said, it's pretty loose so you should be cool man."

"Hey thanks, man, I really appreciate it. I'll give it a try."

I hopped over the side of the truck and reached back for my blanket. Once again Cyndi attempted to augment her diet with my face, snarling and growling at the window. Stepping back from the truck, I waved at him through the glass, and he gave me a 'thumbs-up' and headed up the street. I listened to the loud exhaust of the old muffler as the truck made its way around what was apparently an extensive circular route and soon it passed behind me before accelerating out onto the main road turning toward the remaining way into Santa Cruz.

I slung my bedroll and purposefully headed up the sidewalk in the direction of the dormitories. The food court would not be open before morning, so there was time to take care of other more important priorities. Approaching the first of the buildings I saw that they were arranged in a semicircle with a grassy area in the center. The whole campus seemed to be perched on the side of a fairly steep hill, and the dormitories had been constructed to match the grade of the ground around it.

There were no lights on in what I took to be the student's rooms; only the lights over the various exits of the buildings and the hallway lights beyond them shone brightly. It was utterly silent, giving an odd feeling of emptiness to the scene. The sound of my boots on the pavement was the only noise in the enclosed space between the buildings. Approaching the first doorway facing the direction I came from— south—I tried the doorknob and was greatly relieved when it turned. Pulling it open, I stepped inside and was surprised that it was much warmer than the outside air. Until that point, I had not realized that it was cold outside, and I was chilled. And hungry.

September 1969,
Barnard Residence Hall,
University of Wisconsin, Madison

I pushed my tray along the food line, loading it up with as much hot food and bacon as the service ladies would allow.

Grabbing a couple of waxy cartons of milk, I arrived at the cashier's register.

"Meal Ticket." The bored food service worker who really needed to discover the wonders of Clearasil demanded. He looked like a student working his tuition off. I handed him the wrinkled blue ticket.

"You only got one punch left on this ticket you know."

"Yeah, I'll have to stop at Student Services and get another one before lunch."

"Funny, you don't look like a Taylor York."

"Family name."

"Probably just a coincidence, but there's another Taylor York goes to school here too. What are the chances?"

"That would be a coincidence. I'd like to meet him."

"Well, the other one has tits."

He gave me a meaningful look, then just shrugged and punched the card.

Mid-November 1969, Cowell College, UCSC, Santa Cruz, California

$\mathcal{O}$nce inside the dormitory, I caught the door before it could slam closed and eased it shut. The building was absolutely quiet, which it probably should have been, but it made the need for stealth all the more obvious. Standing still in the doorway, I listened for any new sounds and to get a feel for the layout of the building. Caution is always better than surprises, and the quiet of the sleeping dormitory would allow me plenty of time to explore options and take advantage of opportunities as long as I was careful.

No matter what bricks and mortar you use on the outside of the building or how trendy you design its façade, the inside of a college dormitory is dictated by function and function dictates that they all follow the same general layout. The lowest floor usually contains a laundry room, utility room, a couple of gender-specific restrooms. The largest area is given over to a game room/television viewing area. On my right, the hallway showed a concrete block wall, painted in a glossy off-white color that reflected the light of the red glowing EXIT sign over the fire door at the far end. Halfway down the hallway, a large double door opening spilled soft light into the hallway, from the room inside. The hallway to the left went off at ninety degrees from the main hall and passed two doorways and then made a sharp right turn, out of sight.

The first doorway opened into the laundry facility. Three washing machines stood back to back with three more in the center of the room flanked by tables for folding laundry at each end. I had never known college students that folded their laundry, but the tables were there nonetheless. Four large dryers lined the outside wall of the building along with windows on both sides. The dryers were stacked two upon the other two, also flanked by two folding tables under the windows. Both sets of appliances featured the usual coin slide mechanism necessary to energize the machine. I desperately needed to do some laundry, but it would have to wait.

The room next to the laundry hummed like a utility room and was double locked. Proceeding around the corner, I found myself in a long game room. A television sat on a shelf on the wall I had just come past, with an array of couches and chairs haphazardly arranged more or less facing it. There was a ping-pong table along the wall on my right, and the entire left wall featured windows that looked out to what I imagined was the west. At the end of the room two restrooms—men's and women's—flanked a drinking fountain.

Taking the stairs to the second floor, I saw the hallways were the same, but residence rooms lined the outside sides of the corridor ahead of me and around to my left. Making a left then to the right, I found exactly what I had expected. The shower room. The room featured two shower stalls in an alcove with a mirror and two more stalls. None of the shower stalls had a privacy curtain. A floor drain in the center of the room and three toilet stalls on the right and three sinks on the left completed the hardware in the room. A large purple towel was hanging on a towel hook next to one of the showers.

Crossing to the towel, I felt it. Dry. Smelled it; not musty. With a sigh, I squatted down and unlaced my boots. I stripped down piling my clothes in one of the sinks and stepped into the shower as soon as it ran hot. An abandoned bottle of Prell Shampoo sat on the floor with just enough left in the bottle that, when mixed with a little water, lathered well enough to give my hair a thorough washing. A small sliver of unknown but flowery bar soap provided enough suds to wash my way down the rest of my body. The water was hot, and there was plenty of it, so I stood still for quite a while.

Finally, I shut the faucets off and stripped the water out of my hair. As I was blinking the last of the shower out of my eyes, the door burst open and a girl in panties and a T-shirt shuffled in, zombie-like. One hand scratching a wild mop of blonde hair while her head bobbed about, as if balanced precariously on her neck, her eyes still closed. She didn't look around; just moved into the first stall, not bothering to shut the door behind her. Her feet reversed themselves, and then a voluminous splash was followed by the incredibly noisy flush. She emerged from the stall, pulling her panties up over her butt, still with her eyes barely open. She grabbed the door handle and shuffled back out of the room.

Uh-oh, wrong dorm.

I had realized any quick movement, like grabbing for the towel, would have gotten her attention, so I remained absolutely still. Once she was gone, I quickly dried and contemplated my next move. Should I change dorms, or keep on going? I didn't want to put the damp, dirty clothes back on yet, and I didn't want to walk to the next dorm. I simply picked up my things and tucking them under my arm, stuck my head out into the darkened hallway. With the coast clear and the towel wrapped around my waist, I retraced my steps to the laundry room.

There were a few mostly used up boxes of laundry detergent, and one almost full bottle of something called fabric softener that smelled pretty good but for sure wasn't soap. Dropping my laundry onto the farthest folding table, I got down on my hands and knees and with my head as low as I could get it, moved along the further line of washers. Almost immediately, I was rewarded. Retrieving one of my boots I returned to the first machine and lifted the front side of it high enough to kick the toe of my boot underneath it, I repeated the process with the other boot. Then once again dropping onto all fours I was able to use a discarded wire coat hanger to slide out five quarters that had been dropped between the machines and forgotten. I now had enough to do my laundry and legally raid the vending machines in the television room.

Once the washer was chugging along through its wash cycle, I took two of the remaining quarters and turned to check out the vending machines. I stopped dead in my tracks and was pretty sure that my heart did too. A girl was leaning against the door jamb idly swinging a bottle of Coke by one finger that was stuck down into the bottle in one hand and scratching her stomach with the other. She did not appear frightened, just curious.

"You lost or just a pervert?"

"Are those the only choices?"

"It's three o'clock in the morning. You're in the girl's dorm, in a towel. who does that? Perverts! You look like trouble to me, so I think I better drop a dime on you."

"I'm not trouble, I just need to get my clothes washed and then get out of here. 'Sides, I thought I was in the men's dorm."

"So? Are you lost or are you some kind of pervert?"

"I guess I would have to put myself somewhere in the middle of the two."

"I didn't realize that you were in the shower room until I was almost back in bed, then I couldn't figure out if I was just dreaming it or not, so I went back in there. It was still all steamed up, and your big wet footprints led me right down here. Please tell me that you're not a serial rapist or something."

"I'm not a serial rapist! I'm not even sure what that is."

"I'd explain it to you, but then you'd probably think it sounded like a good idea, pervert."

"Not really a pervert either."

"You watched me pee."

"I didn't watch, but it was impressive nonetheless."

"Pervert."

"Look, I'm tired; I'm hungry. I just need to have something clean to put on and then I promise, I'm outta here."

"Where'd you come from?"

"Fifteen minutes ago, you were dead asleep, now you want to play twenty questions." I paused, then sighed, "I came from Los Gatos."

"Nope, you didn't"

"Why not?"

"Los Gatos is about forty-five minutes away, no way a fortyfive-minute trip would make you all tired and hungry."

"Okay Sherlock Holmes, I came from Eureka by way of Los Gatos."

She brightened, "You got a car?"

"Nope hitchhiked."

"Too bad. Wow, that is a long day."

She took a drink of her Coke and looked at the other door jamb for a few moments. Then brightened again and said,

"I'll be right back."

And with that, she was gone. She returned in only about a minute and a half struggling with a large cardboard box and dropped it onto the nearest folding table.

"Lost and found box. There should be something in there that you can put on instead of Angie's good bath towel."

"Who's Angie?"

"The girl who owns the towel you're wiping your dick all over."

A little shocked, "My dick, as you call it, is perfectly clean."

"Well, you can bet I'm not going to check."

She tossed things at me as she started to dig through all of the discarded clothing in the box throwing the various possibilities onto the nearest washing machine. I circled the washers and looked through the pile, selecting a sweatshirt with the sleeves removed and Grateful Dead on the front of it, surprisingly there was also a pair of cut off jean shorts in almost my waist size.

"Who loses a pair of shorts?" I wondered out loud.

"More importantly, who loses a Grateful Dead sweatshirt? People just don't have any respect." She countered.

214

I gathered them up and headed for the nearest restroom.

The sweatshirt was really loose, but the shorts were a perfect fit, showing off my lily-white legs. Returning from the restroom, I found her with her head in my washing machine.

"What're you doing!?"

"This is fabric softener, you put a capful in with the rinse cycle. Makes your clothes come out not so stiff. Don't they have fabric softener in Eureka?"

"Uh. I actually don't know. Are you always this rude?"

"You need to lighten up, buddy. Okay, I'll admit you look better dressed than you did with that towel—maybe not a rapist after all but still a pervert. And yes, I'm always this rude."

"Ok, I'm not a rapist. I do act like a guy most of the time so most of you girls would call that a pervert, I guess. Look, I'm really too tired to be really conversational, and I really appreciate your help and all, but once I get my stuff out of the dryer, I'm gonna head over to the boys' dorm to try and find an empty bed someplace."

"Don't bother. The boy's dorms are full, more men than women on this campus and there were a lot of freshmen this year so no dice there. Upstairs on the second floor, there is a room that's empty that we use for smoking reefer in. It's got a bunk with a couple mattresses that you can roll out and get some sleep if you want. If I put a scarf on the doorknob, nobody will bother you."

"How does that work?"

"The scarf means that somebody's in there fucking."

"Oh. Okay, that sounds pretty good. Thanks for being so cool."

"Hey man, we bonded right, I even let you watch me pee."

"I didn't watch you pee."

"Whatever pervert, I gotta study, that's why I'm up so early. Gotta cram for an exam this morning. If you're gonna go on up to the room, turn left at the top of the stairs it's the second door. If there's a scarf, you'll have to come back here. I'm gonna study in the Rec Room so when these are done I'll put them in the dryer. When they're dry, I'll bring them up. Got any quarters?"

"Wait, how do I know you'll do that?"

"Shit, how do you know I won't call the campus cops is the question that you should be asking. Go to bed."

I kept one quarter for a Snickers Bar and gave her the rest.

Chrissy

dreamt that someone was hammering, maybe nailing up siding, or nailing down shingles. For some reason, the insistent pounding made the dream uncomfortable and disquieted. I began to get annoyed but couldn't seem to find my voice to yell, to tell them to stop. In fact, in my dream, I suddenly became aware that I couldn't breathe either, and I bolted upright in bed panting and disoriented. I was in a tiny room, in the lower of two bunk beds, the air hot and airless and the sun streaming through the window bright and intruding. Before I could figure out where I was, what day it was, or what time it was the insistent knocking on the door began again. Swinging my legs over the side of the bed, I dropped to the floor and peeked under the door. There was a pair of feet on the other side of the door in a pair of girl-sized sandals. I staggered back to my feet, unlocked and opened the door a crack.

As soon as the door moved, she shoved it in and whooshed into the room, tossing the wad of clothes onto the desk chair in the room. She fixed me with a look, and said

"What? You thought I was gonna fold 'em? You wish. Dude, you must sleep like the dead. I've been pounding on the fuckin' door for five minutes."

Same girl, same mouth. Feeling half catatonic, I sat down on the side of the bed and couldn't think of a single thing to say.

"Whew, that test was a breeze. I was freaking out man, then Prof blows my mind with a complete skate."

I rolled that statement around in my head for a few moments

and no matter which way I rotated it, I couldn't make head or tails of it.

"What? I didn't understand a word you just said."

"Geez pervert, I said I studied, and the teacher gave us an easy A test. Pissed me off."

"Why didn't you just say that?"

"Why don't you just learn to talk? Or don't they teach that at pervert school?"

I ran my fingers through my hair, this chick was too much work for my head. Sighing I decided that I should at least give it a try. I was just too tired to fight it anymore.

"Look, uh, Blondie…"

"Names Christine. Call me Chrissy." She flipped her hair off her shoulders. "Or not."

"Okay, my name's Emmett, but everybody calls me Hole. Anyway, it's like this…"

"Wait! What the fuck kind of name is Hole?"

"Family name, long story, okay? Listen up for a minute, geez. Anyway, I'm not from Eureka or California, or Oregon or Washington although I came that way to get here. I'm from Chicago by way of Wisconsin. Used to go to U.W. until my shit hit the fan."

"U.W.! Seriously? Dude, the TV's full of the serious shit going down at U.W. They show the anti-war demonstrations from Madison and Berkeley all the time on T.V. If I was Tricky Dicky I'd be freakin' out."

"Yeah? I've got my own shit to worry about, I'm not too sympathetic about what Dickwad Nixon is shoveling. You probably got to see me on TV then, you just didn't know it."

"Whoa, you were one the demonstrators?"

"Well, I don't much look like a pig, do I?"

"Did you get arrested? That's so cool."

"It's not so cool if you're the one getting arrested. Anyway, that's why I'm here."

My stomach gave a very audible grumble, which got the attention of both of us.

"Hey," she said, "Let's boogie over to the chow hall and get some grub. Those boots ain't gonna go too well with those cut- offs so grab your jeans. I gotta hear the rest of this. The food's okay and you can eat all you want."

While I stuffed my face with everything I could reach, she sat across from me with one foot up on the chair and her knee even with her chin sipping another bottle of Coke and ate her way through an orange. Through it all she watched me pack the food away with wide eyes, but didn't say anything, content to wait until I was done. After I set down my third empty carton of milk and had a good belch, her patience ran out.

"Okay pervert, I bought you lunch, now let's have it." She even readjusted her chair so that she was facing me full on, elbows on the table chin in her hands.

Without dragging out too far, I gave her the basics of the last two weeks. At least the high spots. She was dumbstruck by the whole saga. For my part, I was amazed at how much had happened in those few days too.

"Wow, you're a fugitive from justice! That is way cool, beyond far out man; that is heavy. Good thing I didn't finger you to the Five-Oh last night, huh?"

"I'm not sure campus pigs and regular pigs are the same things, but yeah, I'm pretty sure that wouldn't have ended very well."

She shoved her chair back and jumped to her feet, "Let's go! It's time you got some California into your system."

She had me wait in the quad while she made a quick dash into the dorm and returned in less than five minutes with my brand new/old cutoffs and jingling a set of keys.

"Since you borrowed her towel last night, I figured I'd borrow Angie's car today. Don't worry she won't miss it, she's a real airhead. I borrow it all the time and 'sides it's too far to walk down to the Boardwalk."

Angie's car was an older Datsun, the red paint job faded to into lackluster magenta and sporadic ulcers of rust, bubbling up through the hood, roof and trunk. The lock on the driver's door had been shot, and the empty keyhole showed rust too— evidence that the lock had been absent for some time.

"Angie kept locking her keys in the car, so her boyfriend just popped the lock. Nobody'd steal a piece of shit like this anyway. C'mon get in. Just throw the shit on the seat in the back."

There wasn't much space in the back for any more shit, but I cleared the empty food containers, soda cups and bottles off the seat and enough room on the floor for my feet. Chrissy fired up the beast, and in a cloud of dark oily smoke we backed out and headed off campus. When we got to the road I had come in on the night before, she turned right in the other direction from where I'd arrived. Crossing a wide but very shallow river, we entered Santa Cruz city proper and drove straight through. The sun beating down lit the buildings so brightly that the shadows between them were eerily black. The elevated light and color contrast making everything I looked at seem like an endless series of Kodachrome photographs. Above the rooftops ahead of us, a Ferris wheel and rollercoaster track appeared as we drove, apparently west. Within a block of them, she pulled over to the curb and shut down the poor thing, and I had the mental image of it standing by the curb panting to catch its breath.

"We'll walk up from here, but first we got to get you some sand skis."

"Sand skis?"

"Sandals! Geez, you gotta get with the program dude."

Jaywalking across the busy street, we entered a small inconspicuous head shop, and I was immediately immersed in a totally different, more Californian culture. Back in Madison, Wisconsin, we had shops where you could get bongs, and pipes, maybe buy some incense or a black-light poster, but they usually masqueraded as a record album store—a completely legitimate business. This shop was wholly devoted to just counterculture, and I was lost in sensory overload.

Patchouli was the dominant aroma that emanated from various joss sticks burning in intricately carved incense burners randomly placed around the shop. Every square inch of the walls was covered with Jimi Hendrix, Jim Morrison, and Janis Joplin posters, T-shirts with marijuana leaves screen printed on them. There was every kind of black light, lava lamp, and reefer paraphernalia. When I stopped to examine an ornate hookah that stood near the front window, the dude wearing a dashiki and working behind the counter spoke up.

"You wanna' try it out and see how it works man?" He tilted his head toward the beaded curtain leading to the back of the store.

I was saved from the dilemma of deciding when Chrissy barged into the conversation.

"Here put these on and pay the man." Hanging from her fingers were two flat pieces of leather with a loop sticking out of one side near the wider end.

"Put what on, these aren't sandals. How much do these cost?"

"Just shove your big toe into the loop and voila-sandals! They're three bucks. Pay the man. C'mon we're burning daylight dude."

I still had the twenty Da had given me in Chicago, and now it became seventeen dollars. The proprietor refused to charge sales tax because he was, "stickin' it to the man," and I didn't have the heart to explain the revenue sales tax system to him, so I put the seventeen dollars—all one-dollar bills—back into my wallet. He pointed to the back room full of boxes with a toilet stool in the corner behind a shower curtain and smelling delightfully like urine and weed, where I shed the jeans and pulled up the cutoffs. Sticking my toes into the sandals produced the uncomfortable feeling that they would fall off at any time and Chrissy and I flapped back to the rusted-out Datsun on the street. The hygiene situation in the back seat looked a little too iffy to throw my jeans into, so I rolled them tightly and wrapped a loose bootlace around them and threw the boots over my shoulder.

Sunshine and Wine

Two empty bottles of Annie Green Springs apple wine sat between us in the sand as we watched the sun begin to set into the gray ocean. We had walked the boardwalk, through all the stores hawking their tourist kitsch and Rat Fink airbrushed T-shirts. We had walked the long pier with starfish that clung to the pylons just below the surface of the water, and I had reveled in its fishy ocean smells. I had seen squid and octopus and all manner of disgustingly fascinating creatures. My head on a constant swivel; everything I had seen was alien to me, new, interesting, and exciting. I wanted to spend hours looking at each new thing. Chrissy feigned disgust, though with a half-smile of satisfaction, had continually dragged me away from one spectacle after another.

I had waded in the frigid water. I had jumped into the waves attempting to body surf. I had felt the wet sand as the riptide pulled it out from under my toes. I had tasted the salty brine with complete fascination. I stood on the very edge of the world that I knew. Now sitting on the sand, my shorts wet and clingy, I reached for my sleeveless sweatshirt chilled in the fading light.

We shared a small bowl of weed and already buzzed from the wine, my turmoil and anxiety seemed far behind me.

"So really, I guess I can't keep calling you pervert. No way I'm calling you Hole unless it means something different than what I think it means. You said your name's Emmett; do you want me to call you Emmett?"

"My real name's Robert, my school teachers called me Robert, nobody else has ever called me Robert, or Bob, or Bobby unless they never wanted me to trust them again. When my mother calls me she just rattles off the name of every one of my siblings before she gets to Emmett, my father calls me Hey you, if he calls me at all. I've been called Hole for a long time. Whatever it used to mean, it's comfortable to me. Whatever you like, I'll still answer to it. Pervert's as good as anything else."

"I guess Hole isn't that different from pervert."

"Yeah, like synonyms."

I looked across at her and took in the view. Her long, tousled blonde hair hung loosely, below her shoulders and she continually pushed it back off her face. Her face was heart-shaped with a perky, slightly upturned nose and big, long-lashed blue eyes. When she laughed it was hearty and honest and when she smiled her evenly spaced white teeth only accented her sparkling eyes. Her skin had a healthy golden tan and was well-toned. She wore dark blue bikini bottoms under her shorts and sweatshirt, with no apparent self-consciousness. I had never experienced a combination of beauty and outspoken confidence; I was quite taken with her. I thought she had real substance. I suspected her rough vocabulary was primarily used to shock people and not part of who she really was. She seemed much too smart for that.

"Like the view, pervert?"

"Honestly? Yes."

"That's what they all say."

"Who's all?"

"Just every boy I have ever known since I was like ten. Listen, dude, don't think I don't know I'm pretty; believe me. I know I hit the gene pool jackpot, nobody is more surprised when they look in the mirror than me."

"You make it sound like you have it rough."

She pulled her knees up and put her arms around them, resting her chin on them and gazed out at the fading sunset.

"Yep, when you look like this lots of doors get held open for you that's for sure. Being pretty, life's good right, but everybody wants a piece of pretty Chrissy. Everybody wants to get their picture taken next to pretty Chrissy, be with pretty Chrissy, be seen with pretty Chrissy, or fuck pretty Chrissy."

I didn't say anything. I waited for the rest.

"In California, if you're blonde and pretty, brains are a liability, you dig? Listen to any Beach Boys song. Blonde hair, blue eyed, chicks in California are supposed to be fashion accessories, not have opinions. As soon as I open my mouth, people turn off. They get that look, like I'm some kind of being from outer space."

I watched the perpetual waves roll in and out and said nothing.

"Oh sure, some of them are willing to be *just friends* but they still want a piece of pretty Chrissy's ass, they're just willing to wait for it. Some chicks too, you'd be surprised.

I can't seem to make myself play the mindless dumb blond like Goldie Hawn on *Laugh-In*. I've tried you know? Back in school, to try and fit in, you become one of the many, no opinions, no personality; another vanilla person in a world where people are comfortable with sameness."

I decided that I liked this person, and not in a way I usually liked most girls.

"I know exactly what you mean Chrissy. I've spent my whole life living outside of the lines. I've always wanted to make the box bigger; you know, push the limits just to see what there is on the other side. And you know what I learned?"

"What's that?" She asked the question like she was afraid of the answer.

"That it's harder to be lonely in a group of people than it is to be lonely when you're by yourself. Being alone and being lonely are two different things, I know, but it's easier to handle when you are alone because then it's a choice, instead of expecting some random group of friends to fill a hole that's inside of you. I'm a big fan of easier."

I watched her out of the corner of my eye and saw her slowly nod.

The sun finished extinguishing itself into the ocean in a stunning display as the last rays painted the undersides of clouds in fiery oranges and soft pink on a bright pastel blue sky. The waves continued to roll in, and our shadows began to appear stretching out in front of us as the dancing neon lights of the boardwalk behind us took over. The silence between us lengthened as the daylight faded.

"Shit! C'mon, I'm hungry, got the munchies. Unless you've got more scratch than I think you do, we need to get back to campus before they stop serving dinner."

The exam that Chrissy had taken was the last one for the school's term, so she was on a break between quarters. The campus became semi-deserted as students fled for a last fling of warmish weather before the rains of late fall set in. Her roommate had gone home for the entire week. Chrissy said she never went home on these breaks; she much preferred the solitude. I suspected there was more to it but figured that if and when she wanted to share, she would.

Returning from the beach and after dinner, in the dining facility, I needed to shower off the salt water and sand. Chrissy stationed herself at the door and said she would guard the door of the shower room in case someone tried to walk in on me. I lathered up and washed my hair, but as I rinsed the shampoo out of my hair and eyes, I felt her join me in the shower stall. Looking down into her eyes she smiled back. Her fabulous wet skin was slippery and smooth as she pressed up against me. Reaching down she got a good handful of me and shook it in a simulated handshake. In her best east Texas accent she smiled and said;

"Howdy partner!"

When she grabbed me, I jumped but not too far, and she again looked up, smiling shyly,

"What are you looking at, pervert?"

"Everything." It's hard to argue with perfection. "Turn around, I'll wash your back."

I moved my things into her room.

Friday Morning, Cowell-Stevenson Dining Hall

The morning sun streamed in through the crack in the drapes, lighting the dust motes as they drifted aimlessly dancing through the pall of my cigarette smoke in a constant lazy motion. As she lay with her head on my chest, I could feel her heart rate slow and her breathing return to normal. "Jesus! Where'd you learn to do that?"

"Hmmm?"

"You know, ... that."

"I read a lot of books."

"I gotta get me one of those books. Holy hell."

She idly twirled the hairs on my chest and sighed. Neither of us was in any hurry to move as we shared a cigarette and watched the dance of the dust motes and smoke, content with our own thoughts comfortable in the afterglow of the moment. The calm of the moment though was in direct conflict with roiling confusion in my head.

It was two weeks since I had walked away from the airport in Seattle. Two weeks that I had been missing and, most likely, two weeks that people were looking for me. It seemed that no amount of emotional or physical distraction could pull me away from the concern and the inevitable conclusion. As a professional procrastinator, I was willing to give it my best shot at distraction; however, in truth, I had no idea how to solve the dilemma. I had no idea how to go about going back and facing the music, and I had no idea where this was going. I did on some level know how it was going to end though.

We spent almost a week together. Chrissy wanted me to see

California the way she saw it, not just from the perspective of a tourist. In addition to walking the boardwalk and lazing on the sand of the beach in the cool late autumn sunlight, we had driven up to Napa and Sonoma in the sorely taxed Datsun. We saw the vast vineyards, where row upon row of pristine vines marched up and down the hillsides, and people and equipment were in the constant motion of commercial viticulture. That is what the tourists saw, but Chrissy was not content to have me see only that. She seemed to know someone just about anywhere, and she knew someone in Napa as well who worked in the vineyards. With his influence and direction, we worked an entire day, stacking wooden crates of grapes onto wagons, and then unloading them back in the sheds where they were to be processed. It was hard, hot work and by the end of the day, the dormitory shower was a welcome refuge.

On another day we drove to Castroville, The Artichoke Capital of the World and watched as the hundreds of migrant workers picked artichokes. I learned that picking them and knowing when to pick them is an acquired skill and difficult. I learned it the hard way. I once again worked in the sheds where forklifts zoomed in and out with pallets of harvested vegetables. I helped load them onto conveyors where other workers sorted them and boxed them, and I watched as they were whisked off into still other storage sheds to wait for the trucks that would take them back to Wisconsin and Illinois.

We had walked the streets of Carmel and watched the upscale tourists as they aimlessly strolled the streets, diligently searching for overpriced mementos. She showed me the beginning of the road into Big Sur; the rugged coast road that wound through the coastal wilds one hundred and fifty miles to San Luis Obispo. We had looked down from the hills at the vistas of the San Joaquin Valley, everything bright in the sunshine with the smell of the ocean in the air. All of it foreign to my eyes, and nothing that tugged at me enough to make me want to live there.

"You're thinking about it, aren't you?"

"Wouldn't you?"

"I wouldn't have walked away in the first place. If I had, I'd have walked the other direction, north. You could have walked across the border and been safe in Canada, no probs man."

"Well, we both know that you're smarter than me. Besides if I had, then I wouldn't have met you."

"Well, it isn't like we've got a future. Unless you want to go down to Castroville and pick artichokes for the rest of your life."

"I'm not sure my poor hands could take it." I joked

She was right. There was no place for me to hunker down or start a life. I couldn't get a job or a driver's license because I would have to supply my Social Security number. We were both sure that my number had been flagged and would lead the authorities directly to me. My money had run out; I was not just a fugitive, now I was becoming a desperate fugitive.

"If I keep moving I don't know where I'll go. If I go back or turn myself in I don't know what they'll do to me. I'm too pretty to go to Leavenworth, you know."

"You're pretty all right… pretty stupid. What messes, geez, is this one-time deal or were you always this stupid?"

"Pretty much always."

"Well, we don't have to decide this morning. If you don't know where you're going, pretty much any road will take you there."

"Wow, that's pretty heavy. You think of that all by yourself?"

"Yep, just now, don't make fun of me, pervert. Not unless you want me to yank your crank off? Hmmm?"

"Not just now, please. I've got plans for it in the immediate future."

"Mmmm, me too."

We couldn't stay in the dorm room forever, and eventually, hunger forced us out of the room and into the dining hall.

"Today is Friday, there's this place we like to go up in San Jose on Friday nights. It's a big empty warehouse-like place down by the wharves and the old shipyard. On Friday night, they get a couple of outstanding bands, and they crank it up to about two-hundred decibels. Everybody goes; you can hang out and dance. Gets pretty wild."

"I don't dance."

"Huge surprise. You're so uptight, I'm surprised you can squeeze shit out of that puckered asshole of yours."

"What a sweet talker you are."

"Anyway, it gets better see? My old man, he lives up in Fremont. He's always is saying that he wants to spend time with his little Chrissy, except he really doesn't. He just says that, so I won't tell mom to jack up his alimony again."

She paused for a second and let me chew on that statement while she looked someplace else. *Which is worse*, I wondered, *emotional distance like the Caseys practiced or faked emotional enfoldment.* I decided that the Casey way was more honest but just as unfulfilling. Then she continued with a show of enthusiasm and energy.

"So, I can give him a call see, and he'll come down here and pick us up, and you know, like, take us out for dinner and lay some bread on me, and then we can go to San Jose and make the scene at the warehouse. He may even let us use his car. What'dya think?"

"What is daddy gonna have to say about me?"

"Are you kidding? Most of the time he's happy if the guy I'm with can speak in complete sentences."

I didn't think this sounded like a ringing endorsement; she was trying awfully hard to infect me with her enthusiasm.

"Okay, look, my dad really likes to own things. He especially likes to own things that cost a lot of money. I'm not sure what he does to make it, but he makes a lot of money. He thinks I am one of the things that he likes to own." She picked up the orange peel she'd left on the food tray and started tearing it into little pieces, intensifying the aroma around us and collecting her thoughts. "He thought he owned my mother, and believe me, she did cost a lot of money. But she was like trying to catch liquid mercury. As long as I stay in touch with Daddy, he likes to wash and wax me and keep me on display. Makes him feel like he's somebody."

"Where's your mom in all of this?"

"You mean, Pretty Penny? Well, Pretty Penny likes things too, different things. Different men mostly, and she likes money—a lot. She just doesn't like to have to make it herself. So Pretty Penny lives in Carmel in one person's house, or another's depending on who is offering the most and the best of things."

"Sounds kinda shallow."

"Vapid would be a better word. She was completely clueless about why I would ever want to go to college. That's why I ended up at UCSC instead of Stanford or UCLA where I wanted to go. She wouldn't cover any of my expenses, and Sheldon wants me to be close by, so he can showcase me when he wants to."

"Sheldon?"

"Yeah, Sheldon." She made a whatever face. "So what d'ya say we give old Shelly a call and we party tonight?"

"If you think it will be okay with your dad, sure let's give it a whirl."

Meeting the Parents

Apparently, Sheldon had flexible work hours because in a couple of hours, he pulled up in front of the dorms where we were sitting in the grass under the trees and honked. He was driving one of the most beautiful cars I had ever seen, probably one of the most boss cars ever to roll off of an assembly line. It was an atomic red Oldsmobile Cutlass 442 convertible, hubcap spinners, with white vinyl seats and trim to match the white top. The engine rumbled just enough to give me a jolt of testosterone in my crotch.

"Hey, Sheldon! How's it hangin'? This is Bobby." She smirked and I knew she'd been waiting to do that to me. "Can we put the top down daddy? It's too nice a day not to have the top down. Please?" And then she added, "Happy Thanksgiving, daddy."

She popped open the passenger door and leaned in and made a kiss noise near his face, then pulled the button on the seat and pulled it forward and vaulted into the back seat. I reached in and offered my hand to Sheldon, but he looked at it like he didn't know what to do with it, so I stuck it back in my pocket.

"Sure Princess, no probs."

He reached up and flipped the roof locks above the visors and hit the motor switch to lower the roof. Chrissy busied herself with the roof cover snaps in back, and in no time, we were on our way. While he drove, he made meaningless small talk about people and places I knew nothing about and could tell from her responses Chrissy didn't give a shit about. He threw in a smattering of hip terms like far out and cool man in a way that didn't fit with his establishment haircut and button-down oxford shirt. He wasn't trying to impress her, so I assumed the feigned with it vocabulary was aimed at me. I, in turn, smiled and feigned interest when he aimed a comment toward me, but mostly I enjoyed the bitchin' ride.

It was mid-afternoon, and the high-end restaurant that he chose was nearly empty. It was too late for a lunch crowd and too early for evening diners. The maître d' seemed to recognize Sheldon or at least his mode of dress and guided us to a choice table in the back at the windows facing out onto an ocean vista. A bow-tied waitress, in a spotless shirt set water glasses on the table before we were even seated. The menu didn't have prices on it, and I was afraid to order anything for fear of offending Sheldon. Chrissy spared me the embarrassment and ordered for me, making eye contact to assure me that I would like her selections. While we waited for our food, the small talk continued centering around Pretty Penny; who she was with, what she was having done to herself most recently, and how soon her attorneys would hit Sheldon with the next alimony hike. I had never considered sea bass as an entrée, but I had also never tasted anything like it. It was fabulous.

After dinner, Sheldon convinced us that we needed to run up to Fremont to see what he had done with the cabana and patio deck around the pool. On the way up to Fremont, I was amazed as we passed row upon row of parked and mothballed battleships in the shipyards. Massive grey steel boats beginning to show their rust, retired veterans forgotten and without purpose.

At his home in Fremont—which was constructed of as much glass as it possibly could be without collapsing on itself—we both ooh'd and ahh'd about the expansive cabana, which was appropriate because it was pretty amazing. The postage stamp of a yard was completely paved with expensive brickwork with the kidney-shaped pool as the centerpiece, and the cabana with its striped awning and lounge seating were nothing short of opulent.

Reaching into his pocket, Sheldon pulled out a wad of bills fixed with a gold money clip and peeled off about a dozen twenty's and handed them to Chrissy.

"Since you and Bobby want to go down to San Jose tonight this should be enough for a couple burgers and a few sodas. I'll use the Benz if I need to go out tonight so why don't you take the Cutlass?"

Chrissy didn't even pretend to act like that was too magnanimous a gesture. She grinned and jumped up from the lounge chair and this time gave Sheldon a real kiss on the cheek. She hooked the keys out of his outstretched hand and pocketed the bills,

"Thanks Sheldon, see you in the morning! C'mon Bobby, let's hit it!"

On the way to the driveway she flipped the keys to me, "Think fast, pervert!"

"Hey! I can't drive this thing! What if I wreck it?"

Chrissy climbed over the passenger door and plopped down in the seat. Reaching into the glove box, she pulled out a pink visor and pulling her hair into a ponytail, pulled down the visor and said, "C'mon let's go! I got something I want to show you, and you'll need to be driving."

 The Warehouse, San Jose

wo hours later, we pulled into the parking area of a massive
warehouse on a street lined with several other abandoned warehouses. The expansive lot directly across the street from the buildings
had been paved but time and neglect had taken its toll, and it now
sported potholes and crops of vegetation of varying height along with
more than a hundred cars. The dust kicked up by the arriving vehicles
hung in the cool evening air, illuminated by the headlights as more cars
continued to arrive. The lot was alive with people, walking through
the headlights as they roamed from car to car, smoking, talking and
laughing. There was a general flow toward the entryway, but no one
seemed to be in a hurry. I pulled the keys from the ignition and dropping my hands into my lap, I sagged back against the seatback. "Jesus!"

"You're not the only one with skills.... Bobby."

She primped in the visor mirror pulling her ponytail out and
touching the corners of her mouth with new lipstick.

"Nice to know I still got it." She smirked with a self-satisfying smile.

"Believe me, you've definitely still got it."

"Okay then, let's get loaded and have us some fun." Then she added, feigning concern, "That is if you think your legs will still work."

She did a quick swivel with her gaze and then leaned across and
hit the horn, one short and one long. Moments later a short, skinny,
Hispanic dude in a leather jacket that was at least two sizes too large
for him, swung into the headlights and up to the car. Sweeping his
long black slicked-up hair back, he dropped his elbows down on the
window sill on Chrissy's side of the car, "Hey Chicka, where ju been

lately?" Stepping back, he took in the car, sweeping his eyes from front to rear and back again. "Madre! What a bitchin' ride! Where'd ju come by this? This is serious iron, man!"

"Hey Luis, I go to school you know, I don't get to stand on street corners makin friends like other people."

Little Luis puffed up like a proud rooster, "Hey, Ju gonna hurt my feelings, Luis don't stand on no street corners. Maybe you wan' me to move on, eh? Ju better watch your mouth Miss Prissy-Chrissy. Maybe, Luis, he goes somewhere else to do business, huh Chicka?" Then as if he hadn't noticed me before, "Who's the vato?"

"Be cool Luis, I didn't mean anything, just jivin' with you man. This is Hole. I wouldn't fuck with him if I were you." Then she went back to business. "We're lookin' to get down man, you know, down."

"Dude!?! Ju're name is Hole? For real man? How ju get a name like that?"

I looked across at him and narrowed my eyes. "It's short for Asshole."

"Never mind man don't tell me, just bein' curious, ju know." He backed away from the car waving his hands in front of him. "I don't know nobody else name of Hole that's all, never heard of it before." Then to Chrissy, "I got what ju need Chicka, ju want up," he pulled the left side of his coat open, "I got ups. Ju want down," he pulled open the right side of the oversized coat, "I got jour downs. Just how down ju wanna go."

"Down enough, so I don't have to spend all my bread on the over-priced brews inside."

"I got reds man, those work great for that, especially if you throw a couple brews down on top of 'em.

"Tell you what Luis, I'll take six, and I'll throw in another twenty if you'll keep an eye on the Cutlass while we're inside. Deal? Six."

"Six!?! Shit girl, nobody needs to get that far down, ju serious?"

"I'm havin' trouble sleeping. Mind your own business, beaner."

"Okay, no sweat. Geez, you are one touchy bitch."

The exchange took place while I feigned indifference and continued to watch the roiling crowd through the windshield. Smoking pot was a relative novelty to me as I was only recently initiated into its social application. At first, when I was offered a passing joint I had politely deferred, satisfied with alcohol-related buzzes. Eventually, my abstention became a cause for suspicion, and subsequent paranoia among the people I was socializing with, so I had buckled and joined in. I immediately appreciated the difference between the high that marijuana provided, which was very different than the loss of inhibitions experienced with alcohol. This was especially true when the two were mixed together.

During my high school career, I had always had a healthy respect for my personal limitations when it had come to drinking. My almost magnetic attraction for trouble caused me to be paranoid enough to appreciate the possible consequences of capture while intoxicated. Knowing your alcoholic limit is not a talent that you are born with, no matter what your ethnic heritage. I had become an expert at knowing where the line that I should not or could not cross was without jeopardizing myself. It is a developed skill based on many trials and more than a few incredibly wretched errors. Those who do not—or more important, will not—establish those skills, soon fall prey to social predators of one type or another. My past history and choking Catholic guilt had honed my survival skills to a very fine point. I rarely let my guard down for fear that someone would try to take advantage of me. So drinking with temperance became a necessary skill. By the time my senior year had rolled around I had become expert at holding my liquor and in controlling my alcohol consumption. Subsequently, I also made it my creed never to take advantage of anyone else in similar circumstances for which I had earned the respect of those who knew me.

I did not know anything about drugs. I had no idea what the six, little, round red pills were that Chrissy showed me in the palm of her hand. I broke another of my cardinal rules, and rather than wait to find out, I revealed my ignorance and asked.

"What do you do with those?"

"These are reds man. You know, downers. Seconals. My mom eats these things like candy. They help you sleep, but you gotta be careful with them, they'll kick your ass."

"No thanks then."

"C'mon Emmett, drinks inside are gonna be expensive, and I only got the one I.D. so you can't even buy any. If we're gonna get a buzz on, you're gonna need a little help. You know, like the Beatles say, 'I get by with a little help from my friend.'"

"Alright, but just one."

"You're a pretty big guy, you better take two."

⸺⸺◉⸺⸺

The next hours evolved into a whirling blur of colors, bright lights, and laughing faces. The vast interior space was too large to ever be crowded, but even so, there were presses of people everywhere. Mirror balls suspended on long cables from high above in the girder ceiling caught the strobes from the stage and flashed in my eyes no matter where I turned. Chrissy alternated between gyrating with unexpected energy in the area reserved for dancing and slurping beer while yelling at me at the top of her lungs, while drunkenly waving her arms for emphasis. For my part, I slowly became a part of it all. The lights, the hard metal music, the mass of humanity all absorbed me. It was not possible to rationally appreciate the music; it did not enter through my head. Instead, it penetrated me on a primal level. I found myself as a single cell in an amorphous organism that pulsed in time to the background of sound

The need to remain on the outside looking in no longer necessary.

There was just too much going on to feel any separation from it all. I took my turn on the dance floor.

Eventually, the bands burned themselves out in a spasm of flashing lights and feedback, and the silence that replaced them rang like a bell. The exhausted revelers slowly shuffled out into the night and onto the rest of their weekend. Chrissy—almost incoherent—hung on my shoulder and struggled to keep both of her feet going in the same direction at once. Upon arriving at the 442, I found Luis asleep in the front seat. When I pulled open the passenger door and poured Chrissy into the front seat, he practically vaulted out of the car with bulging eyes.

"Hey man, she tol' me to keep an eye on the car, ju know man? Nobody touched it, ju know? Luis was on the job."

"Hey, no sweat Luis, thanks for your help."

Looking down at Chrissy slumped against the car door Luis crossed his arms, "That girl sure likes to get fucked up. How many of them reds did she eat?"

"Don't know. Probably all of 'em."

"Chicks with that kind of problem, I dunno, man, look at her, she's got the world by the ass, ju know?"

"She's compensating for a bad childhood."

"Jeah? Shit, who isn't?"

"I wonder if I'm supposed to take her home, or back to school."

"Whichever is closer man, you look pretty fucked up too, ju don't want no 5-Oh stopping ju."

"School then I guess; Fremont's farther than Santa Cruz, right?"

"Jeah. But not by much. Hey man, jou be careful with her, okay, don't be no pendejo with her, she's good people, jou know?"

"Hey dude, watch it. I ain't that kinda guy."

"Jus' sayin' Hole, no offense man, we're cool, right?"

"We're cool, dude." I fired up the duel exhaust of the 442.

Then remembering my manners.

"Adios amigo."

Time to Move On

I woke up when the Cutlass vaulted the curb, just in time to see the first Keep Right road sign disappear under the hood. The car had careened up over the curbed median and now was barreling down the middle of the divided highway at an exceptionally high rate of speed with one wheel on each curbed side. By the time the second white rectangular sign arrived at the bumper, I had become conscious enough to release the gas pedal, and we were going noticeably slower. This time the road sign broke off above the hood and shot over the windshield and hit the trunk lid before exiting the vehicle. Finding the brake pedal, I bought the car to a stop in the middle of the highway still straddling the curbed median. I was sobering up in a hurry. The racket of the road signposts being mowed down by the car had roused Chrissy as well. Together, we stumbled out of the car and staggered around to the front of the vehicle, where we stared stupidly at the ruined perfection of the 442.

"Hijo de la chingada! Whoa! Man, that is not cool!" Chrissy apparently had a gift for understatement.

"Indeed." I couldn't think of anything more profound than what she had just said.

Two vertical creases at least four or five inches deep and just as wide were etched into the previously pristine bumper, the inside headlight on the driver's side dual headlights was broken, and the driver's side of the grill was gone, most likely lying on the pavement somewhere behind the car. The hood had two ax wounds; the first above the injured headlight and the second was directly in line with the driver's seat. I realized it was probably a good thing that the second sign had gone over the car instead of through the windshield, at least for me.

In our favor, there was no steam escaping from the radiator, and as far as I could tell in the dark, no other fluids leaking onto the ground underneath the engine. There was an unmistakable fast tick coming from under the hood which could only mean that the fan blade was making contact with something in there, but the engine was idling smoothly, and all of the tires appeared to be intact.

"Sheldon is gonna have kittens."

——————◦((◦))◦——————

Several minutes of pounding on Angie's door back at the dormitory finally yielded results when the boyfriend answered the door dressed in nothing but a sleepy scowl. "What!?!"

"Hey, Roger. We need a little assist with a prob, man." Chrissy was now almost entirely awake but still slurring her words and in full planning mode.

Roger proved to be a godsend. Once he was fully awake, he proved to be a competent thinker and planner, which made one of us. With him following behind in the broken-down Datsun I piloted the Cutlass back to Fremont. Shutting the engine off out on the street, he and I pushed the poor injured beast up the curved drive to Sheldon's house and into its parking space next to the blue Mercedes Benz 280SL convertible under the open carport and dropped the keys onto the front seat. The foothills to the east were brightening as the rising morning sun backlit them with a bright glow. By the time we returned to the UCSC campus, it was full daylight. Roger didn't even say goodbye, as he turned and stumbled back to Angie and bed.

Letting myself into Chrissy's room, I gathered my meager possessions. The Grateful Dead sweatshirt I pulled on over my shirt. With my new cut-off shorts and sandals in addition to my old army field jacket the bedroll had expanded in girth making the rope that I used to tie it shorter so that now it would only fit under my arm like a fat purse. Dropping the finished product onto the desk chair, I turned to look at Chrissy. She was lying on her stomach, her open-mouthed face turned toward me fully clothed with her feet hanging over the side of the bed. Her hair was a rat's nest of disarray, and her snore was reminiscent of a diesel truck. Pretty Chrissy had left the building. I decided, what the hell and gave her shoulder a shake.

"Hmmpf. What?"

"I gotta go, Chrissy." Her eyes popped open, and she pushed herself up and swung her legs over the side of the bed and stared stupidly at the space between her feet her disheveled hair hiding most of her features. "What?"

"Look, Sheldon's going to be justifiably pissed off about the car. You'll be okay because he'll cut you slack. After all, he needs to use you as a weapon against your mom, so even if he's pissed off, he still needs you. But if Sheldon thinks I was driving, then he'll have someone to take it out on. I don't know what he'll do, but I promise you it won't be good for me." I let out a long sigh. "So, I gotta get bookin'."

Still, with the same expression, she reached up and scratched at her scalp. "Hmmm...what?"

I said nothing. Then she used the other hand to pull her hair back on both sides and tuck it behind her ears. She fixed her eyes on my face, and I waited as rational consciousness appeared in her eyes. She slowly nodded, swiveled her eyes around the room and fixed them on the dresser near the foot of the bed.

"Right. Bummer. Yeah, I guess you're right, but that kinda sucks. You sure?"

I said nothing, recognizing that it more than kinda sucked. I knew she was trying, but she couldn't seem to muster any expression in her voice.

"Up there on the dresser is Shelly's bread. Take it." I started to protest, but she shook her head. "He's got good insurance. Probably the best that money can buy. He'll be pissed for about twenty-four hours. Then he'll start to miss me, so he'll buy me something expensive. I can always get more money. Take it, you're probably gonna need it more than me. You know which way you're goin' yet?"

"South, I guess." I went to the dresser and picked up the wad of crumpled bills, counting them as I separated and straightened them out, one hundred thirty-six dollars. Lying next to the wad were three little red pills. I swept them off the dresser and into my pocket, not because I wanted them but to keep Chrissy from taking any more of them.

Taking a deep breath, she pushed her hair back out of her face, and when she looked at me, she was once again, Chrissy, smart and rational.

"Okay but remember what I told you, don't take the coast road until you get past Fort Ord, you might get nabbed goin' by. Go through Castroville and Salinas. Don't talk to anybody in Salinas, that's an Army town. I hear it can be pretty rough. Lots of prostitutes and MPs."

"Hey! Everybody's a prostitute in one way or another; don't be bad mouthing them, they're probably the most honest people around."

"Hey okay, geez, kinda' touchy aren't ya?"

"I haven't slept all night" I almost added not like someone else, but common sense told me that was not a good direction to take. "Not touchy, tired." I was remembering Margaret, feeling guilty about Lucille, and already missing Chrissy. Most of all, I was feeling sorry for myself. Shit, I needed some sleep. I shouldered the bedroll and looked at her one more time. Once again, she was staring at the far wall slumped into an exhausted slouch. "See ya babe."

She turned and gave me a long look, then in a very quiet voice, "Yeah. See ya pervert."

I closed the door behind me as quietly as I could.

The Pink Dolphin, Santa Cruz

I spent most of that Saturday sleeping on the beach, below the boardwalk in Santa Cruz. The beach had never been crowded, but there were more people on Saturday than there had been on the weekdays. Many of the newcomers were obviously soldiers up from Fort Ord. They were easy to spot because of the white wall haircuts, and they traveled in packs of four or five. Between naps, I watched them as they tried one ploy after another with the local female beach population. For their part, it was obvious that the girls were far too smart to be pulled in and the result was that as the sun began to set the boys were still packed up, but their spirits were decidedly lower. Although they had passed near me most of the day, none of them had paid me any mind, and I had been happy to keep it that way.

The retail establishments on the boardwalk all sported window placards that stated No Public Restroom. Chrissy was not about to use some outside Port-a-Potty so naturally, she had a well-established alternative in place. Directly across the street from the roller coaster on the boardwalk there was reasonably-sized saloon with the dubious title of The Pink Dolphin. During the time that I had spent on the beach and boardwalk with Chrissy, we had frequently used the restroom facilities there. The patrons and the management had seemed accepting of whatever intrusion we created as we breezed in relieved ourselves and breezed back out into the sunshine.

I had at first been confused by the signage used for the restroom designations. Although there were two separate bathrooms, both doors featured the same symbol. A circle with an arrow pointing up and to the right at a 45-degree angle with a cross at the bottom, where the six is on a clock face, the universal symbols for male and female but both on the same door. Both bathrooms featured the same fixtures, a couple of urinals on one wall a couple of sink stands and a couple of stools enclosed by closable stalls. I figured it was just one more quirky California affectation, and used whichever one that Chrissy didn't.

The Pink Dolphin establishment was bright and friendly. Windows facing west supplied bright, indirect light and the wood-paneled walls reflected and softened it into a warm, mellow glow. The entire wall behind the bar was mirrored, amplifying the lighting and open airiness of the immense room.

Enough tables to be adequate for a large crowd were well spaced to allow plenty of traffic between them. A large square of parquet flooring opposite the bar provided a good-sized dance floor, for those in the mood to shake a leg if that was your thing.

Above all else, the Pink Dolphin had nonstop music. Behind the bar on a shelf, a large reel-to-reel tape player turned constantly, and the music had encouraged me to linger and listen. Whenever I had gone through to use the bathroom, the music was always blasting out of strategically placed speakers in every corner and behind the long bright bar that covered the entire back wall. The music genre was new to me; both loud and rhythmic, a far cry from the bubblegum pop and commercially lucrative crap that steadily poured from AM/FM radios that I was used to.

On my own again and needing to relieve myself, I decided to go back across the street. I had money in my pocket for a change, so although I didn't have enough to rent a bed for the night, it was enough for a beer and sandwich. It would be nice to sit somewhere besides the hot sand, and I was looking forward to the music. The bartender had also never asked me for an I.D.

Once I had a cold beer in front of me, the accommodating bartender told me that unfortunately, they didn't serve food, but that I could step around the corner and grab a burrito and bring it back and eat it at the bar.

It was my first ever burrito—it smelled wonderful unwrapped on the bar in front of me. I relaxed and sipped the ice-cold beer and experienced the wonder of heavy metal rock and roll. It was not afternoon anymore, but it was a long way from the probable crush of the evening and night revelers. The bar patrons, although not sparse, were spread out so that each was able to enjoy its leisure without intrusion. The reel-to-reel tape player had entire albums recorded and played through one after another. By the time I was into my third beer, I had listened through Uriah Heep, Atomic Rooster, and was thumping my way through Black Sabbath and thoroughly grooving. And then everything turned to shit.

Three young men raucously entered the bar, laughing and generally enjoying themselves, making a point of being noticed. Everything about them said, Army—from their white T-shirts and unlaced boots all the way up to their regulation haircuts. The center guy was big—not much taller than I was, but a good fifty pounds heavier and with very little extra weight around his middle. The other two were typical sycophants, tagging along behind at a respectful distance and letting the big guy make all the decisions and most of the noise. And his opening statement spoke volumes.

"Jesus, will you look at all of the queers in here! Somebody should call the cops and have 'em clean this place out."

One or two of the people in the bar shifted uneasily, and a few got up from their stools and made ready to leave, one or two slipped quietly out the door behind the three. I took a deep breath and sighed. All my life I had known this guy in one form or another;

bullies who were big enough and loud enough that they rarely had to demonstrate any physical skills. They were always accompanied by some sort of entourage—hangers-on that drew their strength from the proximity of his. The arrival of this trio signaled the end of my musical education and the time for my departure. I still had half of a beer and a ten-dollar bill on the bar, so I took a swallow and reached for the ten.

"How's about it faggot, you gonna buy your new friends a beer?" He boomed as his hand came down to my outstretched hand.

I pulled my hand out from underneath his along with the ten. "Sounds reasonable."

"See that? Fuckin' queers don't want trouble. They're smarter than they look. Right guys?" The two boat anchors both smiled and agreed in mumbled words. "C'mon bartender, three beers and three shots. It's on this faggot here."

The bartender hustled pouring the beers and the three shot glasses full to the rim, his hand shaking noticeably. He gave me a sympathetic glance left the ten where it lay, and quickly moved to the other end of the bar, where he busied himself washing glasses that were already clean and trying to avoid any further eye contact. After distributing the shots, the three fellows saluted each other and threw them back and immediately erupted in a coughing spasm and a frantic reach for the three beer mugs.

With his eyes still watering the big fellow regarded me in the mirrored wall behind the bar, "Something funny, ass fucker?"

I returned the look without expression and instead of a response, took a sip of my own beer. One of the other boys spoke up then.

"This guy thinks he's big stuff, Spaulding. Look, he's some kind of hippie faggot; geez he could sure use a haircut, you know? And a shave too. He's kinda pretty with that long hair don't ya' think?"

That drew a laugh from all three, and Spaulding walked around behind me in mock examination of my now shoulder-length hair.

I watched him in the mirror, and he smiled and nodded his agreement to his two buddies.

"Yep, it would be a public service. Cleaning up a filthy hippie and teaching him a little respect, all at once."

Shit, I thought, *why is it always me?* It was clear that the situation was not going to resolve itself, and it was starting to escalate. Too much testosterone and sun, augmented with a dose of whiskey bravery is a bad mixture when you blend in ignorance and stupidity. Especially when there is more than one of them. It is never a good idea to let an antagonist get behind you, and even though I could see him in the mirror well enough, I didn't trust him to not sucker punch me. I noted that he held his beer mug in his right hand as he stood behind me with his arms crossed, that would be his dominant hand, so it would be the one he would want to use. The beer mug was a formidable weapon if he chose to use it as one, so I was going to need to keep an eye on it.

I took a breath and sighed the storm was about to break, but it was not going to strike where he was expecting it to. I was not afraid of him or his friends but I was angry, angry at my situation and all of the circumstances that brought me into these dead-ends. I felt it start under my sternum. I felt my heart rate increase. I felt it climb up the arteries in my neck, a pink mist that flooded into my brain. I felt my mind awaken to the flood of endorphin, my vision narrowed, and my focus became total. I had known this kind of rage all my life. I feared it myself, so I sighed and swiveled up off of the bar stool and turned to face him all in one motion, not fast, smoothly and deliberate.

He was taller than me by a few inches, and the muscles in his upper arms told me he was no stranger to the gym and a severe bodybuilding habit. Big muscles do not translate into fast reflexes. He would be slow, but he was confident that he didn't need speed. He was used to overpowering his victims not out-quicking them. It would be a huge mistake to get inside of his reach where he could get his arms around me, and his arms were much longer than mine. When I stood up, he immediately switched the beer mug to his left hand to free up his dominant right one and he squinted at me as a big smile opened the bottom half of his face to reveal exceptionally bad teeth. The Army was going to have its work cut out for them with this orthodontic disaster.

"Look boys, the faggot's got a little rooster in him." Turning his attention to the bartender at the end of the bar he added, "You keep out of this you hear? Or you're next. Stelter, you keep an eye on him. If he reaches for that phone talk him out of it."

The one who must have been Stelter had been switching his weight from one foot to the other, and his face said he was nervous about the whole situation. He was too dedicated to Spaulding to try and stop him, but he was not a willing participant. Spaulding had just handed him a way to be in on the fun and still save face without getting his hands dirty, and he nodded and grinned at me and then drifted off in the direction of the bartender.

Winning in a fight has a few essential rules. If you expect to win a bar fight, never wait for the fight to come to you. Don't wait for the attack, always throw the first punch. Attack completely, with your whole being, mind, and body. Attack without mercy and attack until the fight is over. Finally, always fight with the expectation that you will win. It had been a very long time since I had had the shit kicked out of me in the passageway near Our Lady of Grace and my skills had experienced several upgrades during that time. I did not like to fight. In truth, it somewhat sickened me, and I would have much rather reasoned my way out of a confrontation of any kind. This was not going to be a situation that reason was going to work in and just because I did not like to fight didn't mean that I didn't know how.

With the beer mug in his left hand, he was prepared to block any roundhouse or uppercut punch that I might throw with my right hand. His right hand was already clenched and preparing for the knock-out.

Once he had me down, I was confident that the other two would wade in as well. Still smirking at what he assumed was misplaced bravado he took a swig of his beer as he watched me over the top of the mug.

The shortest distance to anything is a straight line, and a wide swing with my hand would have taken much too long. Instead, I just dropped my stance and threw my open hand straight forward from my shoulder with as much force and speed that I could muster. Striking the bottom of the mug, I drove it up and it into his face. There was the satisfying sound of bone and teeth crunching and blood spouted out of his mouth and nose, his eyes went blank and rolled up somewhere behind his eyebrows. He did not crumble into a heap; instead, it took a moment for the message that he was no longer awake to pass from his consciousness all the way down to his feet. He fell backward slowly at first like a tree falling picking up speed as he went. He hit the floor with another crack to the back of his skull and still holding the beer mug.

My pulse was racing, and my ears were singing with all the negative energy of it. It had been awhile since I had engaged any kind of personal fighting. It was something that I always feared and hated, no matter how necessary or unavoidable it may have seemed at the time. It frightened me that my muscle memory embraced the violence. It terrified me that somewhere inside of me existed a force of violence that slept with one eye always open. That rejoiced in the explosion of energy and dripping with the joy of release. In a way, it was like someone who never wanted to keep a gun in the house, not because of the danger it presented but because of the fear that they would always want to use it.

My feet were still spread, and my weight balanced on the balls of my feet with my hands held wide and in front of me. I rotated my gaze from one to the other of the two remaining G.I.s making sure to catch their eyes. The fight was over. Without their leader, the other two spread out and put their hands up shaking their heads.

"Hey man that's not cool," said the one on the right. "Yeah, we're gonna call the cops." Said Tweedledum.

"Probably a good idea, it looks like he might need some medical attention."

The one on the right turned and headed to the payphone near the front door while digging into his pocket for loose change. The other dropped to his knees next to his buddy, and so did I.

"We better roll him up onto his side, so he doesn't choke on that blood," I said.

He looked at me like I was some alien life form but then nodded. Squatting next to him we heaved the inert supine fellow up onto his side. I turned his face further toward the floor and listened to assure that he was breathing without restriction.

"Don't want him to suck any of that into his lungs. He'll come around in a minute or two so just let him lie there for now."

Rising up I turned to the bar only to make eye contact directly across the counter space with the once friendly bartender. He didn't look friendly anymore, he looked terrified.

"Dude! Dude, you gotta get outta here! Right now!

"I was pretty much planning on it. Can I just catch my breath?"

"No dude! Those cops get here, and they find you still here they'll bust your head wide open man. They come in here all the time and clear the place out. They're trying to get our license pulled because of the, you know, kind of people that hang out here. If they find you here that will give them the excuse to shut us down for days man. It's the weekend man, we're supposed to be busy. Dude. You gotta go."

"Great. Only I don't know where that's gonna be. Not sure where I'm heading."

"Anyplace but here man. Look he's on the phone right now. Either he's calling his friends to come in here and finish kicking your ass and break the place up, or worse he's really calling the cops, and they'll come in here kick your ass and shut us down."

I looked around the place for the first time in a little while, and it was utterly empty. The patrons had melted into the bright sunshine outside the front door.

"Look, dude, you were right and all. This big fucker here, well he had it coming, but that isn't going to matter in about five minutes. C'mon man, come this way." Going to the end of the bar he waved his arm in a come-on gesture. I left the ten-dollar bill on the bar and crossed to the table near the wall where I had parked my bedroll and shouldered it. I took one more look at the two boys still standing and the other one who by this time was sitting up and looking around like he couldn't figure out where he was. Then I turned and went through the swinging doors at the end of the bar.

Following the bartender, I walked through a maze of beer kegs and shelves lined with boxes of beer mugs, and glasses, and to the metal security door at the back of the bar that someone had written on in felt tip marker, "Fuck you, Stanley." Pushing open the door, he stepped out holding it for me. The back door opened onto the service alley behind the motel around the corner. "Take a right and head south down beyond where the public beach ends. Then you can turn back into town if you want but man, for now, stay off the city streets. You dig?"

"I dig. And thanks." Whenever in doubt, turn right.

"Just get outta here man. Go!"

Back on the Boardwalk

efore I got to the end of the alley, the red mist of anger had ebbed out of my brain, and I was rapidly becoming rational. I listened for the distant sound of a police siren approaching but heard nothing yet. When I reached the street corner, I eased up to the edge of the building and took a quick peek around the corner. To the left, the street carried into the town proper and meant going backward. To the right, the boardwalk and the beach sounds reached me from half a block away. Straight ahead across the street and continuing down the alley was south. I reasoned as I began to exit town the buildings and busyness of the town would start to peter out. An individual on foot would become more conspicuous and much easier to apprehend.

When in doubt, I turned right and eased myself down the side of the Pink Dolphin. At the corner, I again peeked around the building and watched a police officer climb out of his parked cruiser, square up his utility belt and walk around the front of the car and into the Dolphin. As soon as he entered the building and before any other cops arrived, I crossed the street and climbed up onto the boardwalk. Digging into my pocket, I made my way to the roller coaster kiosk and bought a ticket. I rode the roller coaster three times in a row and the Ferris wheel twice. The top of both carnival rides offered a perfect bird's eye view of the Dolphin directly across the street in a brief photograph that sequenced as progressive events took place. The roller coaster was a good one that rattled around its course and had plenty of twists, and stomach-churning turns and at one point actually dropping straight in a below ground tunnel that was as black as night, so the time spent scouting wasn't a total loss.

The first snapshot view at the top of the roller coaster showed the squad car still idling at the curb. It was the same on the second ride. The Ferris wheel offered a series of stops as each seat, in turn, was emptied and subsequently filled with fresh riders, leaving me free at the top to watch with interest. In short order, I watched as the policeman exited the bar ahead of the three boys. The big one was still a little unsteady on his feet, and one of the others had him by the elbow to keep him stable. They turned to their left and made their way down the sidewalk and around the same corner that I had just vacated, making their way back in the direction of the alley and out of my sight. The policeman stood in the street in front of the squad while he wrote in his notebook and watched the boys make their way around the corner. He then climbed back into the car and began using his microphone. The next ride on a rollercoaster, the cruiser was gone.

I rode the rollercoaster one more time because it was higher than the Ferris wheel, and I could see farther into town, and the Ferris wheel one more time because it offered an extended look during the pauses at the top. I saw no flashing lights and heard no sirens, so I retrieved my bedroll and bought another one of the burritos at the stand next to the T-shirt shop. I walked to where the boardwalk ended and out onto the sand heading south. I ate the burrito and tried to stroll as casually as possible.

As I was just finishing my dinner a voice shouted from behind me, "Hey you, hold it a minute."

Swallowing my mouthful and my suddenly pounding heart at the same time I turned slowly around. A lifeguard had followed me down to the end of the beach and stood pointing at the trashcan next to him.

"This is the last trashcan going that way buddy, don't take that wrapper down there, I don't want to see it blowing down the beach."

"Yeah? Okay, I'm done with this anyway." I threw the wrapper into the can and gave him a nod turned and headed south trying to look purposeful in case he was watching me.

The reason that it was the last trashcan on the beach became clear shortly. In less than a quarter mile I came upon the estuary of the San Lorenzo River. The river flow was steady if not brisk, and although it did not appear particularly deep, it was broad enough to present an effective roadblock. In the growing darkness, it was clear that the tide was drawing away from the shore and the river chased it into the sea meandering out over the sand. Across the river from where I stood, the beach trickled away to a rocky shore, and homes pushed their way out vying with each other to be closest to the sea. This was not the place to cross. With the prospect of a walk of any length ahead of me this night, I didn't want to spend it with wet boots and jeans, and I didn't trust the river bottom to not have enough discarded trash to risk wading it in my bare feet. Looking upriver I could barely make out where the river curved back to the north and into Santa Cruz in the gathering gloom. I feared that walking any distance along the river's edge out in the open might invite attention from the authorities on the alert for other vagrants or me.

Near where the curve turned out of sight a bridge spanned the river running north to south. Under normal circumstances, I might have considered sheltering underneath it and spending the night there, but now with my senses on alert, I assumed that those were places where people would be expected to hide out so I could not chance it. The bridge did offer a way to cross the river with dry clothes, so I turned that direction. Keeping away from the river's edge and hugging the sand drop off at the edge of the town approaching the bridge, it became clear that it was a railroad bridge, the tracks heading south out of the city. If I waited another fifteen minutes, I reasoned it would be dark enough so that I should be able to cross without being seen. I hunkered down in the scrubby rocks halfway up the embankment and waited.

The light lingered for a long while, and with each minute my anxiety increased. I spent the time rearranging my pack and smoking a couple of cigarettes and slowly counting to one thousand. Once it was dark enough, I climbed the rest of the way up the embankment and up onto the rail line. The lights from the boardwalk and the city itself seemed overly bright after sitting in the dark. I was feeling conspicuous standing alone on the edge of the railway trestle, so I didn't hesitate but hurried out between the rails and began my crossing. Railroad trestles are all the same. The railroad ties are a standard distance apart, and there is no stone roadbed under them, rather the space between them is open to whatever is below. The space between the ties is either too close together or too far apart to accommodate an average stride. The individual is obliged to either shorten their steps into a hurried tiptoe or lengthen them into an exaggerated stride. Both are difficult when you are in a hurry and even harder to do in the dark. Catching your boot between the ties would result in a face-first fall onto them or worse the steel rail and quite possibly hobble you with a sprained ankle. I opted for a hurried tiptoe.

Nearing the far end of the crossing, the front of my thighs were starting to ache with the effort of keeping up on my toes and the exertion of trying to hurry without hurrying too fast when I heard the familiar two longs, a short, and another long blast of a railroad locomotive signaling its approach to a bridge or trestle crossing. The sound was behind me and uncomfortably close—and loud. I wasted no time looking over my shoulder. I knew the train was going to get here in short order, and I couldn't hurry any faster than I already was. I concentrated on finishing the crossing then turn to look back. When I did the incredibly bright headlight of the lead locomotive was lighting the last buildings at the edge of town before reaching the river bridge, it was still around the curve to the left, but it would only be a moment.

The locomotive was laboring along relatively slowly, perhaps fettered by a speed limit imposed when passing through a town or city and much slower than the open country speed I was used to. As it appeared past the last buildings, I closed one eye to prevent the head-light from completely destroying all of my night vision and stepped down off of the right-of-way and squatted into the scrub that lined it. With an incredible racket, the engine roared out over the water followed by three more. The bridge added to the noise by groaning and creaking with all of the sound echoing back up off of the river. Blinded by the headlight, I could not estimate the length of the train, but it was moving at speed—about as fast as I could run. With a rush of wind and sound, the engine and its companions roared past me and around a bend to the right, pulling the rattling cars behind it.

If you want to get on a moving train, the first thing you need to do is forget everything you thought you knew about getting on a moving train. It is not like they do it in the movies, there are no open boxcars moving along at a speed slower than a walk. There are actually almost no open box cars—ever. If you want to wait for one the chances are you are going to wait for more than one train. Even if you spy an open boxcar, the doorway is a long way up off the ground, and the railroad bed slopes steeply away from the rails making it even farther above your feet. If the train is moving at any speed whatsoever it is more likely that you will end up under the train instead of on it.

Secondly, a moving freight train is an enormous amount of mass moving with enough inertia to run completely through a charter bus without losing any speed at all. Your body mass has as much effect upon the movement of the train as a gnat hitting the windshield of your car moving at seventy miles per hour. Everything the train is built out of is unforgivingly solid. Therefore, it is essential that you match your speed to the train as closely as possible. If you do not, the force exerted when you grab hold of it will pull your shoulder right out of the socket and you will end up under the train instead of on it.

Last and most important; if you decide to hop a freight train, you have to totally commit to it. If your attempt is half-hearted or if you are at all hesitant, you will end up under the train instead of on it. Even so, committed or not it is good to have a healthy amount of fear and respect for the attempt. I had hopped freight trains before and knew what to look for, but I had never done it in the dark. Rising up out off of the sandy scrub, I stepped up next to the moving train. I looked back down the track to where the cars rounded the slight bend emerging from town. There was enough light from the town itself to make out each individual car as it rounded the corner. I reasoned that once the last car made the river crossing the train would begin to pick up speed and I would have to abandon the attempt.

By my count, thirty or more cars had rounded the corner when the first of the hopper cars appeared followed by three more. A hopper car is used to transport large loads of anything that can be moved in bulk, such as coal, grain, ore or even the broken rock used as ballast to build the roadbeds for the railroad track itself. The car is loaded from the top. The loose product is poured or dumped into it top of it either by massive conveyors designed to handle large quantities of loose products or massive end loaders. A large conveyor loading coal can fill one of these monstrous freight cars in under five minutes. When the car gets to its destination the underside of the car is then opened, and the contents rush out into pits that are dug under the track bed. In essence, the car unloads itself. To facilitate this, the ends of the car are sloped at approximately a forty-five- degree angle so that whatever is in the car is funneled into the openings under the car. The end of each car is supported by large angle iron braces which hold up the upper part of the 'bucket' and are welded to the bed of the undercarriage. That would be my target.

The sloped end of the car, supported by the angle iron braces formed a good-sized space big enough to move around in, and also provide shelter from weather and the wind that the train itself produced. The cars traveling in tandem had ladders for the workers to climb from the ground up to the top of the car. These ladders when the cars were coupled in tandem were close together within ten to fifteen feet of each other which would allow me to possibly miss the first one but be in a position to catch the next one without breaking my stride or my arm. Making sure that my blanket roll was securely slung onto my back I set my feet and got ready to sprint.

I let the first car clear the trestle, and as soon as the second neared the end, I started my jog. Picking up speed, I was at a dead run when the first car began to pass me by. Running as fast as I could made the passing car appear to be going relatively slowly. As the end of the first car came into my peripheral vision, I swerved closer to the train and got ready to commit. As soon as the first ladder came into view, I stopped pumping my arms and raised them up to shoulder height, calculating the height of the third ladder rung, and when the second of the two ladders was almost upon me, I jumped for it. As soon as my hands came in contact with the warm steel, I left my feet and allowed the impetus of the train to swing my legs up and away from the ground neatly landing on the bottom rung of the ladder. I was on.

Riding the Rails

Quickly climbing the bottom two steps, I stepped into the alcove created by the sloping side of the end of the railroad car, and before I lost my nerve stepped across the coupling and into the alcove of the lead car. The shelter was better in the lee of this car and after leaning out and checking to see if the train was indeed going to pick up speed and not slow to a stop, I dropped my blanket roll into the corner and sat down on it to catch my breath. The night was warm, and I was dry.

Within minutes, the freight train began to pick up speed, and in a very short time, we were flying past the remaining buildings and road crossings, hurtling south. Just because it was out of any weather and protected from the wind did not make my little alcove comfortable. Freight cars are not cushioned to absorb the incredible vibration of the speeding mass of iron and steel like passenger train cars are. The vibration and tremendous clickety-clack noise and constant sway back and forth on the rails take some getting used to. Pulling my bedroll out from under my butt, I quickly retrieved my field jacket and put it on before once again sitting on the now tighter blanket roll and settled in for what I hoped was a good long ride.

It was not to be, less than an hour into my trip the train began to lose speed. The horn again sounded two longs, a short, and then another long. Grabbing onto the cold angle iron brace of the hopper car I leaned out far enough to look forward. Coming up out of the night a hazy glow lit the sky to the east and far ahead of the train. Ahead, the rumble and racket of the track changed its sound and the clickety-clack crescendo as the train progressed ever more slowly. A switchyard was approaching, identified by the overhead semi fours with light banks of red, yellow and green. Several lines broke off to the left from the main line, and that was the reason for the racket increase as the train rumbled over the switches that could guide traffic onto the redirected lines. As we approached the first of these lines, I followed the siding lines as they veered off and then disappeared under massive cyclone fenced gates, a high cyclone fence that vanished into the distance to the left and right, the expanse of fencing topped by stretched concertina razor that coiled its way along the entire length. The entire area was lit by tall steel light poles spaced throughout the area featuring a bank of four bright yellow spotlights that after the previous darkness of the train ride made it appear almost daylight bright. The air above the lights was thick with fog that hung down into the upper reaches of the light giving the impression of a closed space. A small white sign was centered on the fencing midway between each fence post was much too small to read at this speed and distance. I didn't need to read them anyway. Inside of the paired gates that hung on a massive roller assembly stood a well-lit shack with two army jeeps carefully parked next to it, their rear spare tires and squared off boxy frames just visible beyond the shack—Fort Ord.

The train's speed had slowed significantly but was still moving at a pretty good clip and did not appear to be going to slow any further. The area both in front of me and behind was desolate with rail sidings paralleling the main line and scrubby weeds springing up in the spaces between them struggling for survival through the rocky railroad ballast that covered most of the ground. The speed of the train and the absence of any kind of open place to land a jump from it without breaking a leg or my skull made egress out of the question. The well-lit area and the presence of the guard shack along with my complete ignorance of the surrounding area made the decision to stay on the train for me.

As the train continued through the switchyard, it began to pass flat cars with military vehicles loaded on them, dozens of deuce-and-a-half trucks, jeeps, and three-quarter ton pick-ups all with their white stars painted on the doors lined the cars from end to end. As I watched the cars pass by I was suddenly stricken by the revelation that I was indeed a fugitive. Surrendering myself had not really been a serious consideration. Instead, I had immediately switched to survival mode, determined to avoid or elude capture. The nauseating thought suddenly created a sense of separation as real as the cyclone fence I was looking at. I was on one side of the fence, and the world and society were on the other. At that moment's revelation, I recognized, maybe for the first time in weeks, that this time; I had gone too far and that maybe I was not going to be able to come back. Instead of being liberating, the realization of it made me feel sickened with fear and dread—and shame. The game board suddenly tilted away from me as rationality rushed in. Instead of maneuvering within the structure of society unconsciously being steered by circumstance, I had in my unthinking way allowed myself to be pushed beyond the familiar boundaries that I usually used for my own entertainment. I was on the outside looking in, and the game had suddenly become real.

The train continued at the same steady pace that it had achieved approaching the switchyard, passing a couple more gates with the lighted guard houses. At one of them, I glimpsed two soldiers standing on the other side of the gate, idly watching the passing train while they enjoyed a smoke. They appeared comfortable, casual and secure in the knowledge that they had a job and a place to sleep tonight or tomorrow morning, unaware of my passing. I watched them until the train passed back into the darkness and the fog blurred my view.

Very shortly after, we left the cyclone fences and glow of the streetlights of Fort Ord. The train radically reduced its rate of speed, slowly breaking down the massive impetus of the iron and steel and was soon moving at less than a walk and readying to stop. The train stopped completely for whatever reason, so I tossed my bedroll off on the western side and then lowered myself to the bottom step of the ladder and jumped down. If the train came to a full stop and then left again, I could still hop back up into one of the following hoppers if I chose to. In the meantime, I stretched and looked around. On the opposite side of the train from me, the sky glowed brightly—a town, with its night lights illuminating the foggy night sky. To my left, the string of cars that had followed me this far stretched into the darkness and disappeared. To the right, the great headlight of the train lit the fog ahead in an unearthly bright light, but the engine itself was not visible. Behind me, the blackness of the night hinted at how far it was to anything tangible.

The distance of the engine, fully thirty cars away, muted the rumble of the engines, and the fog made space seemed confined. If it hadn't been for the softening of the sounds out in the foggy night, I might have missed the crunch of boots on the rocky ballast coming closer at a fast walk. I turned my head from side to side trying to pinpoint the direction that the owner of the boots would appear from, the sounds reflecting off of the hollow rail cars next to me. As I tried to listen, I slowly crouched down to hear better. I realized that the person would pass me on the opposite side of the train, moving quickly from the front of the train and toward the rear. I eased myself up against the closest wheel of the car I had just jumped from and put my back up against it. The boots quickly came closer, their owner idly whistling and bobbing the beam of a flashlight along in front of him and crunched their way past my position, walking on the rocky portion of the roadbed. As the sound began to dim they stopped. Within seconds the sharp metallic clang and squeak of the couplings being released signaled the imminent separation of two sections of the train. The sound was quickly followed up by a piercing whistle and the waving of the flashlight beam toward the front of the train. The train was preparing to switch out, and in a few moments, I would be standing directly across the open space and looking directly at the lone switchman. I turned my back on the train and walked as quickly, and quietly as possible, into the fog.

Beyond Carmel-By-The-Sea

It took almost no time at all for me to see that Monterey and Carmel held nothing of interest for me. There were certainly plenty of things to see. The towns were meticulously sculpted to appear on the expensive side of quaint. The people strolling the streets were stylishly hip, preferring to carry their dogs rather than walk them on a leash. Restaurants were classy and expensive. The beach was rocky, very public, and well-patrolled. I had spent two sleepless and very frigid nights, wedged into cramped places away from watchful eyes. Walking the streets, I was ever aware of local Serve and Protect cars that slowed their already leisurely cruising speed as they crawled past me, window down, mirrored sunglasses fixed on my progress along the sidewalk. My long hair, beard, blanket roll and army jacket jarringly out of place in this upscale slice of Americana.

It was time to move south again. It took me the better part of the morning to traverse Monterrey and Carmel, as the towns fell away, the transition into sparsely populated California was surprisingly quick. By mid-afternoon, I reached Highway 1 again, and once I was assured that the city limits were behind me, I began hoisting my thumb at each passing vehicle. Out of habit, when traffic becomes sparse, I turned and walked substituting idle waiting with physical activity, turning only when the sound of an oncoming car or truck approached.

As I marched along, to my Midwestern eye, every direction I look is a picture postcard. The highway itself a thin two-lane surface with narrow sandy shoulders that at first ran in a straight line but quickly transitioned to curves that meandered in and out of the sight of the ocean to my right. Some trees lined both sides of the road, but not enough to block the view of the endless sea to my right, the rugged brown mountains to my left. Mountains, or at least very high hills that I have never seen before, marched off to the south—steep, treeless, brown and seemingly uninhabited. In my Midwestern ignorance, I scanned the sea constantly, hoping that I might glimpse a whale spout yet knowing that the distance was vast beyond my comprehension. I consciously took pictures with my mind of the scenery, hoping to commit as much as I could to memory.

A dark, dusty sedan eased to a stop beside me, almost expectantly, and the driver leaned across and rolled down the window. Leaning down to peer in I was surprised by the driver, his shirt collar conspicuous with its reversed appearance, the dreaded Roman Collar—a priest.

"I'm not going far, but I can give you a ride for a little way if you like?"

Putting distance between myself and Carmel-By-The-Sea was a priority, and without any hesitation, I tossed my shoulder bag over the passenger seat and climbed into the much less dusty inside. The priest, his left hand on the steering wheel offered his right one.

"I'm Father Lamb, but if you're uncomfortable with that most people call me Father Tom, or if that's uncomfortable, just call me Tom."

A lifetime of Catholic guilt, past and present, rushed up into my throat like a bad case of acid reflux as I took the offered hand, and replied, "Casey; Robert Emmett Casey, I'm Catholic Father, er, Father Tom."

"Well now, good to know, not necessary, but good to know. That's a lot of names, do you go by anything shorter?"

"Yes sir, Emmett."

"Please, no sir, either Father Tom or just Tom, okay Emmett?

"Alright."

"So where are you heading?" He asked pointing through the windshield.

"I'm hitchhiking down to Big Sur. I kind of want to see it. I'm from the Midwest, and I've heard the name before, so I wanted to see it first-hand."

My mouth was just puking information; I almost couldn't wait to answer another question.

He put the car back in gear, and with a careful look in the rear-view mirror started back down the road and accelerated south. Once we were back up to speed, he put an easy hand on the top of the wheel and took a long look at me then went back to the road and the scenery.

"Pretty country. I never get tired of looking at it. I'm from back east, New Jersey, so I've seen the ocean, but this one is decidedly different. And mountains, you never get tired of those," he added with a wave of his hand. "I'm just down from Castroville, a little ways back that way," waving toward the back of the car, "My middle of the week is a little slower than my weekends, so I thought I'd drive down and see the Carmelite Mission. I understand it's pretty special."

"A mission? Like a Spanish one? Where's that? The mission I mean."

"Oh, it's a couple of miles back that way, but I just can't get enough of this view, and I also wanted to see what the big deal was about Big Sur, so I was kind of detouring. So, for a little bit, you and I are partners in discovery, what do you say?"

"Sounds good. I don't really know what it is, Big Sur, I mean."

"It means, Big South, in Spanish. Originally, according to the Castroville Public Library, it was originally called El Sur Grande. They called it that because the coastline is too rough to provide any harbor, so it was wild and unexplored until really only the past few decades. It was a mystery, and from Carmel and Monterey all the way to the cities and towns in southern California it's a long ways, so it was the Big South, Big Sur."

"Well, you do learn something new every day. So, there's really nothing out there?"

"Bears, cougars, snakes probably, mountains, but no, there's really nothing down there."

"That should be interesting."

"Not frightening? Just interesting."

"Sorry father, behind me is frightening, in front of me is just something new."

I got another long look while he casually steered around the curves with one hand.

The constant vista out of both sides of the car and the gently winding road occupied both of our attention for a few minutes. The three-dimensional scope of the mountains on the left gave a deep impression of vast distance and the ocean that disappeared to the distant horizon both combined to minimize both my problems and my sense of personal self.

"You know, it's gonna be evening soon, and I'm a little hungry, and you look a lot hungry, how about I buy you lunch or dinner?"

"You said there's nothing down here."

"I'm sure there's something, besides," he said patting the dashboard, "that's why we have a car."

Another few curves, some more monotonously spectacular views later we came upon a large wooden sign outside of a large wooden post and beamed building, trumpeting our arrival at The Gateway to Big Sur. The parking lot was empty enough to give the impression that the establishment was closed, but a small sign on the front door said, OPEN. Without hesitation, Father Tom wheeled into the lot and parked right outside the door. We climbed the tie-cut steps and clomped across the wooden porch. Tom opened the door, which tinkled a small bell as it widened, and held it open for me to precede him into the entry, carefully closing the door behind him. It seemed unearthly quiet in the building, and shutting the door too quickly seemed like it would have been an assault on the solitude.

It was neither cool nor hot inside. The air had that quality that you didn't need to get used to, leaving your senses to take in everything around you instead. All of the woodwork was darkly stained and fragrant with the smell of varnish, the ceiling was latticed with massive beams that were fastened at the ends to posts which matched them in girth. The work was of the old- fashioned mortise and tenon construction that I had seen for years in the barns back in Wisconsin. The matte floors were tiled with caramel colored ceramic, and the seams were grouted to match the hue of the woodwork.

A well-appointed middle-aged man glided into the entryway, with an air of calm and not a hint of haste.

"Afternoon gentlemen, would you prefer the dining room or perhaps the lounge?"

"The dining room please." Replied Father Tom, equally cool.

"The dining room it is. Would you like an early dinner menu or a late lunch?"

"What would you recommend?"

"The avocados are particularly excellent, and the sea bass is on both menus today sir. I recommend it highly."

"Sounds great! We'll have that, and a couple of tall, very cold beers, please. How's that sound, Emmett?"

I felt entirely out of place in my jeans and dirty sweatshirt not to mention in a restaurant that I probably couldn't afford to even work at.

"Sounds great!"

The dining room was completely deserted, the tables were arranged well apart from each other to provide plenty of travel space between. There were no booths. To my right, double glass doors opened into the lounge. Beyond that, mammoth glass windows opened out to reveal the constant motion of the ocean as it ran to the horizon. We were seated in the back left corner in exceptionally comfortable chairs, and the windows on our side of the room were darkened by verdant forest growth that grew right up to the glass.

I am not an adventurous eater, tending to stay in the burger and fries food group. The beer that arrived was not a familiar brand but was ice cold and very good. While we waited for the food to arrive, we sipped the beer and engaged in small talk about California weather, or the lack of it, and the difference in agricultural approaches out here as opposed to back East. Then the food arrived, and I watched Tom carefully and aped his movements so that I did not appear awkward or out of place. The avocado salad was foreign in every respect. The avocado, being green and slimy and surprisingly tasteless, was served on a bed of a type of lettuce that was definitely unfamiliar to me. Romaine and Spinach was Tom's response to my quizzical look and when you ate it with the avocado was terrific. When sea bass arrived, it was another story entirely. The first bite exploded in my mouth with such an overabundance of flavor that I am sure I made a noise because Father Tom burst into peals of laughter, stopping only when he had to take out his handkerchief and wipe the tears out of his eyes.

"Tastes pretty amazing, right?"

"I can't even think of a word for how good this tastes. I've had sea bass only once before, and it was good, but nothing like this."

"Well enjoy, we'll talk afterward."

I started a little, so he added with a broad smile spreading his hands wide, "You didn't think an amazing meal like this wouldn't come without a price did you, Mr. Casey?"

The food was much too delicious to eat it fast, even so, it was gone much too soon, and the wait staff quickly whisked the dishes away, providing small mints on an individual plate, and disappeared. Father Tom excused himself to make a phone call. When he returned he placed two packs of cigarettes on the table one in front of me, and one he opened himself after regaining his seat. After signaling for two more beers, he shook out a cigarette and produced a very fine gold lighter and took a deeply satisfied drag. He held up the cigarette in front of himself and looked at the burning end.

"A minor indulgence. I keep quitting and then when I have one I'm never quite sure why I quit in the first place."

Taking another satisfied puff, he crossed his arms and look at me through the exhaled smoke.

"Now, it's time for you to sing for your supper, Emmett. I don't mean that in a bad way though. You seem like a pretty smart, well-educated kid from the Midwest, and you're a long way from home. So, I like to hear stories, the more of them I hear, the better a priest I think I become. So if you please, I'd like to hear some of what brought you here."

"I don't want you to hear my confession, Father."

"Goodness, is there something in how you got here that is deserving of confession? Oh! This really is interesting." He smiled a Cheshire grin and added, "No, no, no, I'm just curious. There seems to be more to you than just an aimless hitchhiker, more than meets the eye as they say. No, I'm just nosy."

I took a good drink from the newly arrived beer and then I started to talk. I talked about draft cards and whores. I spoke about hippies and college students, I talked about rednecks and retribution, and the more I spoke the more I couldn't stop. I filled in the blank spaces that had been hanging loosely in my mind. I gave background. I voyaged into the past. I talked about pain and beatings and loneliness. I talked until I didn't have anything left to say. Through it all, Father Tom sat and smoked, sometimes gazing up at the beamed ceiling, sometimes out the windows at the now darkened trees, sometimes with kind eyes aimed directly into my own. The evening dinner crowd arrived and was seated, far enough away from us as to be unobtrusive. They dined quietly and departed. The beer gave way to coffee, and the coffee gave way to pie and coffee. When I had finally run out of topics and was done, I looked across at him not knowing what I wanted him to say.

He unfolded his arms and lifted the coffee carafe pouring another cup for himself and took a drink before carefully placing it back in the saucer.

"Well, I guess I have a question."

I just raised my eyebrows but remained silent.

"How far is far enough, when you are running from yourself?"

Carmelite Mission

That night was spent at the Mission. The phone call Father Tom had made was to let them know that there would be two guests instead of one. The showers were hot, and the soap was rough. The sheets on the beds were clean, crisp and smelled of the outside air. I slept like the dead. The next morning, I went to mass with Father Tom before daylight and then had a most splendid breakfast with the nuns, already dressed in their signature habits. They each engaged me in candid and lively conversation, something I had never experienced with a nun; they were nonjudgmental, curious, and funny. Returning to the tiny cell-like bedroom, one of the nuns with a soft smile and softer voice accompanied me, but before we got there, she redirected me to a small room near the front door. Inside was a treasure trove of discarded, lost-and-found items.

"Tourists come and tour the Mission often. It's surprising how many things they leave behind. For a while we keep them here in case they return for them; then we take them into town to donate for the homeless." She paused and moved a few items around, then produced a like-new army surplus canteen, and from another pile an excellent canvas carryall with a shoulder strap. "This had some food in it when we found it, we had to discard the food, but it might be easier to carry your things in this, than with that rope tied around a bundle."

Father Tom drove me south, down past the restaurant from the night before, and well on my way to Big Sur. At a pullout overlooking the sea, he pulled in and offered his hand.

"We come to a parting of the ways, Mr. Robert Emmett Casey. God moves in a mysterious way. If you keep your eyes open, you'll see it happen." Then he added. "Think about what I asked you last night."

I climbed out of the car and shouldered my pack, all of it freshly laundered. It was now bigger and heavier than it had been. Along with the canteen, a sack of sandwiches, dried raisins with nuts and seeds, dried apricots, and some oranges had been added. I bent over and looked at him through the window from across the car, he smiled and so did I. Without another word, he looked over his shoulder and backed out onto the highway, steering the car north. I watched the car until it rounded the first curve and waited to watch it reappear before disappearing around the next. I looked at the ocean, and I looked up at the mountains, and then I started walking south.

With my stomach full and the sun on my shoulders, I walked lost in thought. Traffic was almost nonexistent; cars that did pass did so slowly. Their out-of-state plates spoke of how they happened to be on this stretch of road, and their long looks over the dashboard at me suggested that I was yet another spectacle that California provided. At no point did the thought of picking me up seem to occur to them. I contented myself with just walking, in no hurry for a change. The scenery kept its promise. The sea always on my right and the impressive hills on my left I took as many pictures with my eyes as I could. By the time the sun touched the ocean I had probably covered twenty miles or more of steady thinking and had begun to think about a place to spend the darkened hours.

Shortly before dusk, the unmistakable sound of running water signaled another of the many rocky springs that bubbled out of the hillside sometimes, on one side of the road or the other. Crossing the road, I discovered a little spring pouring out of the rocky ground on the embankment only feet from the shoulder of the road. Without hesitation, I dropped to my knees and had a long drink of the icy spring water. Once I was quenched, I quickly rinsed my face and refilled the canteen. This would be a good place for the evening and night. Being aware that night creatures would also be coming to the spring I crossed back over the roadway and stepped over the guardrail. At first slipping on the slope, I dropped down well below the level of the highway to where the slope lessened and gave way to scrub brush and the weird succulent growth that seemed to serve as ground cover in California. I didn't bother with a fire but sat down and watched in awe as the sun extinguished in the sea. This view hands down beat sleeping under an overpass.

After dark, the breeze changed from the sea and came in with a chilling fog that crawled up out of the ocean. I slept in my clothes, all of them, with my blanket around my shoulders and in the morning the fog was thick and chilly. In the pockets of the field jacket, I had discovered two packs of cigarettes, a tin of waterproof matches with a small Saint Christopher medal inside, and a small, holy card with a note penciled on the back, "How far is far enough?" Finally, there was a twenty-dollar bill. I ate a sandwich with some of the trail mix from the bag of food that Father Tom had somehow procured from the Mission, grateful again and almost tempted to even offer a prayer of thanks—almost.

With the chilly air showing no sign of lessening as the light grew, I climbed back up to the roadway and after stiffly climbing the guardrail, started walking briskly to warm myself. Walking in the cool fog narrowed the world to a muffled forty or fifty yards in every direction and stole the scenery. There would be no traffic at this early hour; it would be a morning of walking and thinking. Eventually, the fog began to thin, giving occasional glimpses of the backlit mountains with the sun still behind them as the fog slid away into wisps in the hills and vanishing clouds.

When traveling cross-country, you have plenty of time to look at the scenery as everything approaches in slow motion. Obstacles in the distance offer ample time to consider alternative approaches. Unique things that appear ahead are given leisurely consideration for identification, and reflection. That was the case as I slowly rounded a bend in the road and in the distance of maybe half a mile saw the vague shadowy figures of two people sitting alongside the road. At first, they were just the silhouettes of two people, but as I closed the distance, I could see that they were a male and female. In the five minutes it took to draw still closer, I could see that they were also watching me as I drew nearer. A male was sitting on the guardrail; a female was sitting cross-legged with her back propped against a good-sized backpack, which was resting against one of the guardrail posts. Both were smoking, but their posture did not indicate they were smoking casually; they were tense, on their guard.

I didn't slow my approach, pretty sure that if I did that they would be even more suspicious. Instead, I strode right up to them and gave them a howdy. The girl wiped her eyes, sniffed and returned my greeting trying to smile. The boy, his eyebrows drawn down in a frown, also said hello, but reluctantly. Up close they were both very young, younger than me. I guessed his age to be sixteen or seventeen maybe eighteen—maybe. Californians didn't seem to physically age as fast as Midwestern kids, the girl was younger, maybe a lot younger than that. He wore what seemed to be standard issue dress for coastal males; worn jeans, sneakers that were sort of tied, a T-shirt with a colorful logo and a worn denim vest over it. His hair was longish, but not very, and he had a serious acne problem. She was dressed in high top, P.F. Flyers sneakers that looked almost new. A blue- flowered granny dress that even sitting on the ground like she was, covered her almost to her ankles. The sleeves were short, and she had a woolen Indian blanket wrapped around her shoulders like a shawl. She rubbed her hands up and down her bare arms to warm them against the chill damp air. Her hair was long and loose, down between her shoulder blades and even in the subdued light of the foggy morning glowed reddish gold. Her face and exposed arms and hands had more freckles than open areas of skin. Her eyes were bright, deep brown and puffy. She was pretty. The boy stood up and placed himself between myself and the young lady, and then surprisingly; wiped his hand on his pants leg and offered it as a greeting.

"I'm Tim, this is Angela, Angie. We're camping, and heading to L.A."

"Nice to meet you Tim; Angela/Angie—um Emmett. I'm heading south too, but not all the way to L.A. I don't think." Then remembering the note from Father Tom, "Guess I'll see though, I'm not going anyplace in particular."

I parked my ass on the guardrail and fished out a cigarette, after lighting it, I looked up and down the highway.

"I haven't seen a car so far this morning, looks like another day of walking. How'd you guys end up here so far?"

"We got a ride yesterday, but the man was kinda' creepy, and so Tim made him stop and let us out. We spent last night just over there." Angie's voice was young and shy. She indicated a place across the road and up the hill a little.

"He was creepy alright. He wanted Ang to sit between us in the front, and then he kept touchin' her leg, 'by accident'."

"Well, that's not cool man, probably good that you got out then."

"Got a smoke that you can spare?"

"Got some." I gave each of them one.

"We brought papers and tobacco in a bag, but they don't smoke the same. Thanks, man."

As we sat and smoked what little conversation there had been fizzled out completely and an uncomfortable silence started to stretch out. I was tired after a long cold night and have never been particularly talkative anyway. I didn't feel much like it now either.

For their part, I could tell they were uncomfortable. I stared up into where the rising hills disappeared into the fog, thankful for once that my back was to the chill breeze and steely-gray ocean. I'm not a big man, but I'm not small either, at five-feet-ten and pushing up near two-hundred pounds, I was two or three inches taller than Tim, and outweighed him by thirty pounds. I had more than a week's beard growth and couldn't recall when my last hair-cut had been. By comparison, these two were young, alone, afraid and in the middle of nowhere. I was probably pretty high on their list of things they didn't want to see, walk out of the fog.

I figured that my appearance and presence was daunting enough, but with their events of yesterday probably even more so. I didn't spend any time on whether they were too young to be out here alone, or if the story they told was true. It was their business, not mine. As the tension of the silence increased, I also recognized that the tension was not of my creation, but was here when I arrived. So when I finished my cigarette, I rose and shouldered my pack. The lack of conversation had stretched to the point of discomfort, and the cold and damp of the morning had extended the distance between us.

"Not gonna be too many rides today, I'd guess. Any movement is better than no movement, so I'll keep on truckin. Good luck. If I get some distance ahead of you, you'll be first to see anyone that might be pickin' anybody up." I started to walk away, then turned around and added, "If today is like all the others lately, the sun will burn off this fog by mid-morning, and it will probably warm up."

I turned and started walking, not in any hurry. A few years of hitchhiking had taught me that when there were no rides, sitting and fretting was just an invitation to more sitting and fretting. Walking, on the other hand, guaranteed that you were making progress, even if it was maddeningly slow. Walking also helped me to think. I could control my breathing, set my pace and space out. All manner of revelation had occurred to me while I walked, and the opportunity for inner-reflection was never time poorly spent. 'How far is far enough?' That thought alone was going to cover a few days walk.

I walked about to where I thought might be the edge of my visibility in the fog before I looked back to see the two kids one last time and turned around, maybe to wave, maybe to just see someone else. I was surprised by what I saw. They were not still sitting on the side of the road, they had picked up their things, and the two of them were walking in my direction, both with their heads down, Tim carrying the backpack, and Angie still wrapped in the blanket. I watched them long enough to see her, wipe her eyes one more time, and for Tim to look up and see that I was watching them. I turned and set my own pace and walked until the sun started to peek through and the last of the tatters of fog drifted down the hills and out into the ocean.

Once the fog was off and the sky was sunlit again, I walked until I found another spring and filled the canteen that I had gotten from the Mission. A small nearby rock slide that seemed to tumble out of the hills at random intervals provided a good-sized stone, so I sat in the sun that had finally risen above the mountain ridges to the east. I had some trail mix but needed to keep as much food as I could in reserve. I was not in dire need yet, and you could never tell what was around the next corner. Within ten minutes Tim and Angie trudged up and she immediately threw herself down on the ground. After I offered her a drink from the canteen, and Tim had one too, they proved to be much more talkative. At first, Tim wanted to know how I kept the water so cold, so I showed him the spring. He was flabbergasted that I thought the water could be safe coming out of the ground like that. Then he was fascinated. So, I showed him how to widen the opening in the ground a little and then wait for the water to clear out the sediment before catching it in his hand to drink. His face lit up with a bright smile that showed perfect teeth.

Finally warmed up enough to take off my coat, I tied it around my waist and made ready to be off again. The warm sun seemed to have made both of them much perkier, and when I shouldered my bag, they both got up and made ready to move again too. I didn't really mind, but I was a little surprised. When I started out, they fell into step behind me and matched my pace. Through much of the morning, they walked with me, Tim occasionally pointing out things that he knew about.

"We're in the Pfeiffer State Forest right now."

Or

"There's a little town up ahead, can't remember the name, but it's right after you leave the forest." He knew where he was.

These information bursts were preceded and followed by long periods of quiet, broken only by the sound of my boots on the sandy shoulder of the highway and my measured breathing. As long as I could hear them behind me, I didn't bother to turn around to check on them, and they never seemed to be very far back. For her part, Angie did not speak. In what must have been early afternoon, there was the distinct sound of Tim's backpack hitting the ground and a long sigh. Turning around, I wasn't surprised to see that they were both looking done in and had dropped along the roadway with the backpack. I decided it was as good a place as any to take a break and walked back to them. Somehow, we had become a group.

"That little town's gotta be kind of close now. We don't wanna go through there on foot."

"Seems to me that's the only way we're gonna get from one end to the other."

Traffic had continued to be sparse. After all, it wasn't exactly the tourist high season. By my guess, it must be getting pretty close to Christmas. I realized that I hadn't even thought to ask Father Tom what the date was. I hadn't noticed an Advent Wreath in the little chapel at the Mission.

"Do you know what date it is, or day?"

"Uh, yeah, umm, it's Wednesday. Maybe the 16th or 17th."

"Of December? Right?"

"Like wow man, are you for real? Yeah, December."

"Well, that helps to explain why the traffic is so light. What's the deal with the town?"

"Nothin', we just don't want to walk through a town like we're bums or something. People might think we're suspicious—or something."

"Would the something be a something I should be worried about?"

No answer.

"Well then, I guess I'll be seeing you. Depending on how much farther it is, I want to be well clear of it before it gets dark. Sun goes down around 4:30-5:00 this time of year. Gotta be after 1:00 by now. You two take it easy. Keep watching out for strangers that don't look cool."

I gave them the rest of my pack of cigarettes. I knew I didn't have to, but I was starting to feel bad about leaving them alone, again. I picked up my shoulder bag, turned and walked away. Tim had been right about the town. In another thirty or forty minutes I passed a sign on the road that told me I was entering Posts Unincorporated. There was also a sign advertising the Post Ranch Inn. I just kept walking and in short order went on to the town on my left, which proved to be hardly worthy of the sign. After that, the road began to curve back toward the sea and opened into a vast nothing of wilderness frontier. There was a whole lot of nothing as far as you could see. I walked until the sun again touched the ocean, and I came upon another small spring. Then I once again decided on the ocean side of the road to stop for the night. The road was close enough to the water to hear it breaking on the rocks below, and already the breeze was picking up from the ocean with a cool damp. Tonight, I was going to have a fire.

It took the rest of the daylight to scrounge deadfall wood.

Apparently, there are not many trees that enjoy the rocky bluffs along the ocean, mostly scrubby pines. The dead limbs below the upper greenery were tough to break, and there weren't many that had been dropped to the ground. There was a lot of scrub brush, tinder dry and woody, and pretty soon, I had enough to keep a little fire burning at least until sleep took me. I used one of the waxed papers that the nuns had wrapped a sandwich in to help light the fire. Once it was going, I leaned back against a rock and ate the sandwich.

Full dark had fallen when I heard voices above me. They were talking quietly, and they were still ways off, but they were definitely approaching on foot. I stood up, then decided that I shouldn't stand with the fire behind me and instead I hiked myself up the hill as quietly as possible and back out onto the highway. They were coming from my left, and I could barely make them out in the complete darkness. Crossing the road, I stepped down into the ditch graded into the steep hillside of the foothills making the road surface at about chest level and waited for them to arrive, or hopefully; pass by.

As they drew nearer the voices became clearer. One was angry, and one was afraid. Tim was upset, Angie was afraid. When they came even with the glow of the little fire, they stopped. The argument changed, "Don't stop Tim. We don't know who it is. Come on, I don't like this." Her whisper was low and harsh.

"It might be him. I don't want to keep walkin' in the dark Ang. I can keep you safe, baby."

"No...please. Let's go, or we can go back. C'mon Timmy."

I didn't know what else to do, so I spoke up from the ditch.

"It might be who Tim?"

Angie screamed, and even in the dark, I could see them both jump. They had been more or less facing away from me thinking that their trouble would probably come from the direction of the fire, and both whirled around.

"Hey! Mother-fucking shit! Is that you, Emmett? Jesus-fucking-Christ shit you scared the shit out of me—us."

"You guys looking for me?"

"No. Well yeah, kinda. We decided to walk through the town, and then we couldn't catch up to you."

Score one for bravery. Deduct one for lack of it.

"You're welcome to the fire if you like. It's better than not havin' one."

They didn't respond, didn't even wait for me to cross the road. They just climbed the guardrail and scrabbled down the rocky bank, toward the fire.

Burnt Tortillas in Big Sur

I followed and sat back down on my rock to watch. Tim dropped the pack and plopped in an open space amid the scrub brush, and Angie got busy. Opening the pack, she pulled out a small frying pan, bowl and a couple of plastic bags. She asked to borrow my canteen, and then from one of the bags, she filled the bowl about a quarter full of what looked like flour. She mixed it with some of the water. After examining its consistency, she poured it into the pan on the fire. Reaching back into the bag, she pulled out a small spatula and watched as first the pan got hot, and then the paste in the pan began to steam. It smelled exactly like hot flour. When she tried to flip it over, she discovered it had glued itself to the pan and it crumbled into small burnt up shards. She began to sniffle, and another tear rolled down her freckled cheek.

"What'cha cooking Angie?" I couldn't resist.

"Tortillas, but it's not working." Big sniffle.

"Is that corn flour or wheat flour?"

"It's white flour."

"I'm kinda new to California, but I'm pretty sure tortillas are made with corn flour. Corn flour is yellow, kinda."

"This is all we've got." Another sniffle, she wiped her eyes again. "I'm so hungry Tim, we're gonna starve out here. Oh my god, I hate this. We need to go back, Tim."

"We're not goin' back."

"Okay, just a sec." I reached into my bag, and without showing the rest of the contents, I pulled out one of the sandwiches. Opening it up,

I smiled when both of their eyes fixated immediately on the contents of the wrapper. But their eyes got even bigger when I pulled it apart and looked at the inside.

"Here, Angie take this piece of bread. It's got butter on one side, rub it on the back of the pan, all over it."

She looked at me like I was crazy.

"Go ahead, first scrub the soot off of the bottom on the sand. Don't worry the sand's clean enough. Once it's good and covered, hold it over the fire upside down."

Another you-must-be-crazy look. As the butter on the back of the skillet began to melt, I added.

"Now put a little more water in your flour and pour it onto the back of the pan." She poured it on the skillet, and it immediately began to set up.

"You see that Angie, you're making crepes, instead of tortillas. To do it right, we would need to have some eggs, but we'll see how this works out. Now we'll make a few of those, and then we'll take what used to be in this sandwich, and we'll wrap it up in your new crepe. A gourmet meal, out in the middle of nowhere."

She looked up at me through her hair, and for the first time, she gave me a huge smile. After a dinner of burnt flour and bologna crepes, she squatted down next to me and showed me how to roll a cigarette from loose fixings and cigarette papers. A skill I had never picked up, although I had watched it plenty of times. She was happy and warm and full. We smoked, and I told them about life in the Midwest, anti-war demonstrations, and draft boards. They listened like I had just told them that Martians were real.

Later that night I woke to their struggles. In the dying light of the fire embers, Tim labored and grunted over her as she lay inert beneath him. Her dress pulled up around her hip she lay spread eagle with her fist balled in her mouth, and her eyes pressed shut. Something alerted her to my intrusive stare, and she turned her head and opened her eyes. Her big, dark eyes glistened as she looked across at me. She took her hand away from her mouth and gave me a small, weak smile, then closed them and again bit down on her fist. I turned away and listened, as Tim finished and rolled away. Soon his breathing became regular, but her sobs continued. Eventually, I went back to sleep.

———— ⚫ ————

For a change, the morning fog had not settled down around us. Instead, it hung above our heads as the light grew. The air was almost dry. I shared the oranges and dried apricots, and then made ready to go. While they were packing up, there was a thump as something heavy fell out of the big backpack, and I heard Angie let out a gasp. Lying on the ground between them was a great big .38 Special Colt Trooper. I looked down at it even as Tim dove to scoop it up, which he fumbled and it dropped again. Finally snaring it, he looked up at me, and then down at the ground, and then finally in the protracted silence reached up and offered it over to me.

"I promised to keep her safe. I needed to be able to defend her."

I squatted down next to him and took the gun turning it over in my hand—loaded it was a handful. I grew up around guns, they didn't scare me. The grips and butt had seen plenty of use, but the weapon itself was well-oiled, clean and looked to be in good order. I flipped open the cylinder, all of the chambers were full. I plucked one of the shells out of the gun and palmed it into my jacket pocket, then closed the cylinder and rotated it so that the empty chamber would line up with the barrel in case he dropped it again. I handed it back to Tim.

"Always keep the empty chamber at the top, helps prevent accidents, especially if you keep shoving it in and out of that pack, or dropping it."

Then, I looked him in the eye.

“It’s just as likely that you can be shot with your own gun if you’re not careful. Find someplace to get rid of that thing and do it soon. Handguns are trouble waiting to happen. It’ll bring you nothing but trouble. If you need to keep someone safe, get a shotgun.”

“It’s my dad’s. I can’t get rid of it just like that.”

“You’re dad a cop?”

He was surprised, and it showed, then he looked away; out toward the ocean and nodded.

I shrugged, “It’s a cop gun. Try and find a way to give it back to him. My advice would be to do it in person. In the meantime, stop handing it to strangers.”

I turned and picked up my bag and headed up the hill. When they saw me ready to move out, they shoved their things into the backpack and followed. Once on the highway, I didn’t hesitate and turned south and began walking. They followed immediately, and we fell into the march formation of the day before. This time, it was different. Within the first few miles a car slowed down and then came to a stop next to them. With the briefest of conversations, the driver, a middle-aged man whose car sported Oregon plates, reached across and unlocked the doors, and with an excited wave to me to join them, Tim and Angie piled into the back. I looked through the windshield at them, at the man behind the wheel, at the smile on Tim’s face and the anxious look on Angie’s face and decided another day of walking would do me better. I waved them off and silently wished them well.

When the car pulled away, I turned and started walking after the car. Good luck Tim and Angie, but mostly good luck Angie. A cop gun. Well shit.

July 1966,
J. C. Penney

When I turned fifteen in July, the first thing I did was go to J.C. Penney and fill out a job application. It was opening a new warehouse outlet in my parent's neighbor-hood. On the form, I listed my age as sixteen, old enough to work without a permit. In the midst of a frenzied hiring spree to staff the endeavor, they hired me on the spot as a warehouse man and never asked me for any proof of age. The job of the warehouse men was to unload, by hand, the trucks and railcars that brought the surplus merchandise Penney's could not sell in its catalog stores and stage it so that the other workers could reprice the items and put it on the floor for sale at ridiculously low prices, allowing the chain to recoup any losses they might have due to overstock surplus.

The work took place in the evenings, after hours, and for me; after school. Unexplainably, I was the only teenager that they hired for the crew. The crew consisted of mostly young married family men moonlighting from their other occupations and trying to make ends meet. We arrived in the early evening already tired from the efforts of a full day and began a shift of heavy manual labor for minimum wage. For the other men it was criminally small money. For me it was a fortune.

The trailers were loaded to their ceilings, stuffed with a potpourri of anything that could be jammed into them. The heavy boxes were hand carried to the end of the container, then lifted onto hand trucks and dragged into the storeroom, hand stacked as high as possible. The operation was repeated over and over, in whatever weather there was. After a day in the sunlight, the temperature in the trailers was hot and stifling. At other times, the temperature was well below freezing. It was brutally hard work carried on at a frenzied pace. A race against the clock to finish each unit before the truck or engine arrived to pull it away and replace it with the next.

The men were all young, diligent and irreverent of authority. I had already spent most of my life working alongside young men and boys much older than myself. They were my kind of people, and because I worked diligently and was equally irreverent, they took me in as one of their own. In the heat of the summers, there was always a cold case of beer stashed in one of the cars or trucks. In the cold of winter there were always a few pints of whiskey handy, all shared equally. I quickly learned how to marry the disciplines of hard work and alcohol consumption and remain functional. They liked me for my quick wit and shook their heads at my lack of respect for authority. We quickly worked out a side business agreement involving brokering sales to underage drinkers, which provided me a guarantee of invitations to the popular parties and them with a source of vicarious entertainment when I regaled them with the hyperbolic tales of teenage parties and mating rituals.

To maintain security, JC Penney also took on a few local policemen who were interested in moonlighting. It was easy work for them. They were encouraged to wear their uniforms to work, and as long as they remained visible, there were no real security issues. Their primary job was to just be visible. They strolled back and forth along the registers and leaned up against the service desk, occasionally accompanying one of the full cash drawers to the back office. There was no real excitement, and they soon became sufficiently bored. When that happened, it was a short walk to the loading docks to check out the security in back. Back at the dock, they drank coffee, kibitzed with the men and/or made my life a living hell. These cops all knew me for one reason or another, but mostly for the one reason. To the men, it was funny and broke the monotony for both the cop and the dock workers.

One, in particular, enjoyed it more than the others. Where the others just thought it was fun to give me shit in front of the men on the dock, Larry Johnsen took it to a whole other level. Larry was a big man on his way to getting bigger. His uniform was stretched at every seam with newly laid down layers of fat, and his gun belt continually dragged his pants down. Larry had a mean streak about a mile wide, and I was a welcome break from the boredom of hitting on the cash register girls up in front. Larry was the type of cop who was not a crooked cop yet, but he would get there eventually.

Larry had made it his business to learn everything he could about me. Over the years I had been picked up for any number of things. Everything from throwing snowballs at passing cars and out after curfew up to shoplifting, destruction of private property and defacing public property. In the latter incident, Larry had been the apprehending officer, to his utter joy, arriving just as I rolled and heaved a final huge snowball into place, to become the left testicle of the seven-foot fully erect male sex organ I had constructed around the base of the flagpole at the high school. As usual, there had been no arrest, after being duly handcuffed and transported to the station a phone, a call to Little Mick had sufficed. But Larry knew fertile ground when he saw it.

For Larry, entertainment to relieve boredom consisted of him catching me from behind when I was busy, bending my arm up behind me and forcing me over a pile of boxes. He would then pull his revolver and lay it along the side of my face, close enough that I could smell the oil of the gun. Once he had me in this position, he would deliver his latest monologue of how he would catch me one of these days. The monologue usually ended with some dire bodily injury that I would sustain, up to and including taking one right between the eyes or up the ass. It only really served to convince me that he was a coward, but I never forgot the smell or the look of the cop gun.

December 1969, Heading South Again

uesday turned out to be an excellent day for hitchhikers. Within an hour, I got a ride that took me as far as Moro Bay. Highway 1 turns away from the sea for a while there. Finally by early afternoon, I was at the junction of Highway 1 and the 101 freeway and a real bottleneck. Highway 1 and the freeway run together for a while in San Luis Obispo, both turning south together. A familiar green billboard-like sign with a white arrow indicated that Los Angeles was to the right. A small crowd was gathered at the near end of the ramp, and as I approached they appeared to be waiting for something. I walked up to the ramp and was greeted by a group of fellow hitchhikers all standing behind the guardrail, except for one. He stood on the roadside of the guardrail, holding up a small hand-lettered sign with a hoped-for destination displayed on it. The rest maintained their distance; some eagerly watching the numerous cars taking the ramp up to the freeway, others laying down resting their heads onto whatever qualified as backpacks, others still sitting in groups and talking. The size of the group was confusing to me as I reasoned that all of them could not be hitchhiking from this one point. It also boded poorly for me as the last arrival. There was no sign of Tim and Angie.

Crossing the guardrail, I joined the small crowd on the other side, dropped my pack and sat down on the edge of the loungers. I attempted to look casual and self-assured, so I placed myself where I could observe the travelers protocol, hoping to learn vicariously without having to appear to be a novice in this uncertain situation. All of them appeared to be about my age, but their appearance and mode of dress varied across a broad spectrum. There were cut off jean shorts, and long denim jeans with embroidered cuffs, T-shirts, flannel shirts, sweatshirts and no shirts, sandals, sneakers and high-top work boots. No one appeared in a hurry, yet all of them turned and craned their necks when a car stopped on the shoulder. The protocol seemed to be a casual first come, first served ride arrangement based on the honor system.

Among the group of people, the conversation was comfortable. There was a free exchange of information, as well as joints and cigarettes. They were well-seasoned travelers, and from the sounds of it, hitchhiking was their primary source of transportation. They talked about dead spots where a ride was almost nonexistent, good spots where a ride could be gotten within minutes at times. They shared their lore of best places to sleep if they got caught on the road after dark, and where to get free food if they got hungry. They were almost all pros. I fished out my almost empty pack of cigarettes, but my Zippo was out of fluid. Almost immediately someone offered me a light, and after I mumbled my thanks, I became part of the group. Everyone shared the origin of their trip, and without hesitation I offered mine. Most had traveled less than one hundred miles and the rest not much more. By my guess, I had traveled over a thousand, and everyone was duly impressed. I became somewhat of a celebrity.

One by one, when their turn came, they would gather their things and step across the guardrail—some traveling alone, many in pairs—would raise their signs or thumbs and soon be off. The early afternoon passed in a quiet, restful peace the sun was warm, and since I wasn't going anywhere, I dozed.

"Hey man, get up! It's your turn man."

I came up out of sleep with a start to a long-haired freak squatting down beside me.

"Already? Hey cool man, thanks."

I grabbed my bag and jacket and started looking around me. The crowd had dwindled. Where there had been ten, now there were only a few. The sun was well on its way toward the horizon, and the shadows were longer. The air had turned chilly. I clambered across the guardrail and prepared to stick up my thumb. As usual, I adopted my usual habit of beginning to walk up the ramp while I raised my thumb at the passing cars. Immediately, the long-haired freak ran up beside me but on his side of the guardrail.

"Hey man, like you can't go up the ramp man. It's against the law, no hitchin' on the freeway, they'll pick you up."

"What do ya' mean, there are a lot more cars up there."

In answer he pointed at a large rectangular sign, still another twenty yards up the ramp from where we stood, with a lot of printing on it, some of which said that bicycle riding, horseback riding and most particularly hitchhiking beyond this sign was prohibited.

"Well shit."

"Yeah man, and it's gettin' late. Traffic's gonna get less and less, gets really hard to get a ride after dark. So good luck man, I'm next, so hope you get one soon."

"Hey man, why don't you just come on with me? Might be just as easy for two as for one."

He didn't even think twice. He turned and ran back to his backpack, shouldered it and grabbed a small cardboard sign, turned and returned at a slogging run hindered by a huge backpack. After clumsily climbing into the roadway, he thanked me and flipped up his sign, which read...

Hollywood.

Christmas? 1969, Fresno, California

Three weeks later, I was standing on the on-ramp of the freeway again, just outside of Fresno. Since hitching a ride in San Luis Obispo, I had looked down in absolute wonderment at the seemingly endless urban sprawl of Los Angeles as I crested the hills surrounding the city and beheld the night-time lights of the City of Angels. I had learned to panhandle in bus stations and shared rides with many strangers. I had walked in fear down Hollywood Boulevard totally unprepared for this icon of Midwestern dreams to be actually a filthy, littered armpit of low-level social strata and despair. I had worked day labor, raking lawns and building backyard tool sheds in Long Beach. I slept on couches, floors and once even a storefront doorway. I ate Christmas dinner at a food kitchen in Inglewood.

One of the nights, I was startled awake by the tremor of an earthquake under my shoulder blades while I slept on someone's living room floor. I became aware just in time to roll away from the monstrous Harley Davidson motorcycle that was parked inside next to me as the house shook it off of its kickstand and it crashed on its side, onto the spot where I had been asleep only a moment before. I had seen the awesome aftermath of that tremor in the buckled pavement of the streets and overpasses.

It was an anonymous existence. There was no chance to create lasting relationships, each person I met, each place I found to sleep was doomed to last no more than a day or two. Every day was marked by hard physical labor and the constant anxiety of where the next meal would appear, or where the next place to spend the night hours would be. I could get by, but just and there was never a hope that anything better was forthcoming. Through it all there was the realization that I could not make a home there or anywhere else. I decided it was time to leave La La Land.

Most of all, I had walked. I had walked miles upon miles, through towns I didn't even know existed, Cerritos and Norwalk, Downey and Pomona all towns, all really just another name for Los Angeles. Each one with a different culture, and each one with specific rules for its own neighborhood. I made sure I didn't linger.

Now it was early evening, and I was tired. It had been a long day of walking to the freeway from Long Beach and Signal Hill and then half-listening to the many heinous sins of a trucker's wife. I had shared lunch in Bakersfield with the lonely over-the-road trucker who hadn't finished his monologue while we drove from the city. He bought lunch so he could finish explaining why his wife was a total bitch. Now two more rides later, the sun was edging down toward the horizon, and I was antsy to get beyond Fresno before full dark set in. The south end of a city is a hard place to try and hitchhike to the north. Most people are local, and the rest don't like to pick up strangers when darkness is about to fall. In my haste, I violated a cardinal rule; I started walking up the ramp.

Long before I approached the freeway proper, but probably far beyond the signpost prohibiting such behavior, I saw the flash of brake lights above me on the roadway. The brake lights were followed-up by the brighter back-up lights as the car shifted into reverse and began a high-speed maneuver down the ramp in my direction. I was optimistic for only seconds before the gumball lights on top of the vehicle switched on and the California Highway Patrol Car slid next to me and braked hard.

"Get in," He barked as his passenger window came down.

He was the perfect stereotype of a CHIPS officer. Khaki uniform, dark aviator glasses and a perfectly trimmed mustache over a tight-lipped scowl. It appeared that I was going to be the evening's entertainment. I reached for the front door to get in the vehicle.

"Get in the back."

Once in the car as I shut the door, he once again punched the accelerator and sped backward down the ramp until we passed the Pedestrians Prohibited sign where he once again braked.

"See that?"

"See what?"

He adjusted the rearview mirror a little so he could make eye contact.

"You some kind of smart ass?"

"No sir."

"Do you see that sign?"

"Yes, sir."

"Do you see what it says?"

"Yes, sir."

"So, you can read. Did you read it before you strolled on by it?"

"Yes, sir. I'm sure I did. I guess I was in a hurry. I haven't done much-hitchhiking sir, and I wanted to get home before it got dark. I really didn't mean to do anything wrong."

"How far is home then?"

"Not too far sir. I was down here looking for work. It's tough to get a job right now because nobody wants to hire me on account of my draft status is 1A. So, I gotta look harder. I'm really sorry sir. I promise I just made a mistake."

The police scanner under the dash was quiet except for the occasional static blast. He focused his gaze up the ramp toward the freeway for a long second and then sighed. Taking his foot off the brake, he eased down the ramp toward the intersection and threw the car into park. Exiting the car, he stepped out onto the pavement and opened the back door on his side of the car, and waved me out across the seat.

"Step back behind the car and put your hands on the trunk. Let's see your ID."

He did a thorough search of my pockets, sleeves and pants legs, and then turned his attention to my wallet, removing and laying out each item on the trunk lid next to my left hand.

"Driver's license, Illinois, Student ID, University of Wisconsin, hmm, pretty girl, this your girlfriend?"

"No sir, my sister."

"You said you were almost home. Illinois and Wisconsin aren't really very close. Where are you going in fact?"

"My girlfriend's, uh sir, there's no work back in the Midwest, so I came out here to look for something. She lives in Madeira," remembering the big green sign at the top of the ramp indicating mileage to the next proximate cities. "Her name's Lucy."

"Where's your draft card?"

It would probably not be a good idea to tell him that a full explanation of this absence was in some Army personnel file back in Chicago, but I hadn't prepared an explanation for its absence either. In fact, it hadn't occurred to me until just now that I might need to have an explanation for its absence at all.

"What? Is it not in there? I used it for I.D. this afternoon at the employment office, oh my God, I must not have put it back in my wallet. Let me check my pockets?"

Leaning back from the trunk of the car, I began patting my pockets and rummaging into the depths of them. My search was unsuccessful, however, since said draft card no longer existed on this plane of being.

"Oh shit, I'm going to have to go back."

"Employment office will be closed by the time you get back there. Look, I stopped you because you can't walk on the freeway. It's too dangerous, especially now that the light is fading. Hitch all you want, it's not illegal, but stay on the ramp."

"Yes sir, officer. Thanks, for understanding. I was just in a hurry, and I kinda forgot what I was doing exactly, you know, thinking and walking, they kinda go together. I'll stay down at the foot of the ramp. Thank you."

He wasn't impressed by my mollified expression as far as I could tell. He just stood there motionless, his gaze hidden behind his aviator glasses, a starched uniformed manikin. He knew I was completely full of shit but was probably trying to decide if I was worth the hassle of doing something about it. Then still, without saying a word, he gathered my personal debris off of the trunk lid and bunched it with my wallet, cigarettes and lighter, and handed them back to me.

"Stay off the ramp."

I carefully stowed my picture of Kate, my license and ID back into the wallet as he marched to the driver's side of the cruiser and without even looking back, opened the door and slid himself back into the driver's seat. The MARS lights on the roof flicked off, and the back-up tail lights came on. As I stepped aside onto the graveled shoulder of the ramp, the cruiser hit the gas and sped past me careening down the ramp in reverse only to come to a halt on the shoulder at the base of the ramp and went silent. I was now going to be a supervised hitch-hiker, which, I was sure, would help immensely with ride acquisition.

I had to assume that the cop was watching me, so I diligently reassembled my wallet and stood still waiting for cars. Amazingly, there was quite a bit of on-ramp traffic, and within ten minutes a beat-up Chevy Monte Carlo chugged to a stop in front of me on the shoulder. I sprinted up on the passenger side as the window came down and I was assaulted by the incredibly noxious fumes of body odor, garlic, and stale cigarettes. The driver smiled and waved me in as he shoveled debris off the passenger seat. It took me a few seconds to take him in. He was huge. Not big as in hunky or muscular; immense in girth and bulk. His seat was ratcheted back as far as he dared to allow his belly to clear the steering wheel. Where his shirt and his pants didn't meet a considerable landscape of hairy skin striated with stretch marks soaked up the light of the evening sunset. His hands appeared tiny because of the swollen fat on the backs and between his fingers. He held a half-smoked cigarette in his right hand and reached across his massive man breasts with his left to shake hands which forced me to lean further into the swamp gas that surrounded him.

"Name's Bob. Where you headed?"

Fully aware of the cop sitting back behind us, I said, "Madeira, at least."

"Sounds good. Why don't you toss your pack into the back?" I twisted and dropped the pack into the alley dumpster that was the back seat and Bob pulled out onto the ramp, and we were off. I was glad to put the cop behind me. In the weeks that I had been on the move, this was the first law-enforcement person who had shown an ounce of interest in me, and even though I thought it had gone well, it had unnerved me. I had too much history with cops who showed interest to trust to providence, so I gave a little nod to fate.

Moving at freeway speed did nothing to dispel the stench in the car. In fact, with the air pouring in from the dashboard vents, I expected to have no appetite for a few days. Once installed in the flow of traffic Bob attempted some small talk, asking about where I was from and headed. He nodded at my answers but didn't seem particularly interested in them either. After a couple of miles, he flicked his cigarette out the cracked driver's side window and shifted his immense bulk toward the center of the seat. With no preamble, he placed his right hand on the inside of my left thigh and gave it a squeeze. Taken by surprise, I looked at his face, and above his three chins, his mouth split into a wide grin that lacked most of his lower teeth.

"What in the fuck!"

"Come on dude, you ain't gonna get anywhere tonight. Might as well shack up somewhere you can get out of the weather and get a good meal. I can rock your world dude." He released his grip and moved his hand north, way up north.

"Bob! Stop the car! Stop the car now!"

"Come on man, how 'bout a quickie then. I know a place. come on. How ya' gonna know if you'll have a good time until you try it? You won't be sorry."

"Bob!" I pulled his fat baseball glove of a hand off of my crotch. "Stop the car, or I'm gonna knock the fuck out of the rest of your teeth!"

"I can't stop here, let me just pull off on the next ramp. Then we can talk."

I turned my back to the door and leaned forward grabbing several yards of his overstretched shirt, he flinched and yelped, "OUCH."

"Stop-this-fucking-piece of shit- car – NOW!"

That was enough for Bob, and he pulled onto the shoulder and stopped. With my right hand still on his chest, I leaned far enough forward to pull my pack off the backseat with my left. Maintaining eye contact, I let him go and opened the door. I stepped out onto the shoulder and grabbed a breath of fresh air. I slammed the door and yelled.

"Andela mother-fucker!"

Bob gave me a pleading look and looked like he was going to say something else, so I started around the front of the car. His eyes got even bigger than they already were, and he headed back out onto the freeway, the beat-up engine leaving a slick of oily, black air in its wake.

"FUCK!"

I was completely unnerved, my thighs trembled with the effect of adrenaline and something else. I had known people back in the neighborhood who were queer, both men and women. Hell, everyone in the neighborhood knew about them, and what team they played for. For the most part, they were friendly people, and for the most part, everyone left them alone, and as far as I knew they hunted in different neighborhoods. I liked sex personally, but had never really considered the possibility of a homosexual experience. If I ever had, this one episode permanently cured me of the urge. This had been a wholly repugnant encounter.

The half-light of the evening was leaning toward full dark. The headlights changed from twin pinpoints of light to glaring, too-bright beacons as they rushed toward me and blasted past in a whirlwind of dust and sound. I could imagine a driver seeing a dark figure along an empty stretch of highway, and feared that if they fixated on me, they could steer directly into me. So I reasoned I should try and get off of the road as soon as possible.

My breathing began to slow down, and the blood pounding in my ears ebbed away. It was best if I started walking to give my legs something to do besides quake. I shouldered my pack and turning right and staying well to the far edge of the shoulder, I set my pace and started. In a short distance, my brain began its argument. I should have said something else. I should have seen it coming. An endless loop of shoulda', coulda and woulda. An age-old argument that my undisciplined brain dallied in far too often. I walked faster.

The first quarter mile of a long walk is the hardest, you set your pace, and you push on. But it takes that long for your breathing to match your pace. After that, you settle in, and your steps and breaths match and become an unconscious movement. The rhythm of your heels matches the in and out of your lungs—step, step, step breathing in, step, step, step, breathing out. It becomes a dance, music that your lungs and heart resonate with. It frees your mind to take whatever direction it chooses.

I resolved my internal discussion about my foolishness and was just getting a good meditation going about destinations when the next set of headlights bracketed me as it slowed and veered off onto the shoulder behind me. I stepped farther off onto the meager verge of the shoulder and turned to squint into the beams as the car slowed and came to a stop. Any thoughts of a potential ride died in my breast as the MARS lights mounted on the roof flashed on and began pulsating.

Late February 1970, Fort Lewis, The Hammer Falls

The chair is uncomfortable not just because of the steel construction and the green leather vinyl seat, but because of where the chair is sitting. Across the desk from me is a military guy; an officer. His green fatigues are starched stiff and shiny, and an eagle is perched on each of the collar points of his shirt. The nameplate on the desk reads Colonel John Smolders. In my stressed-out state I assume that his name probably also describes his temper. Behind the Colonel is an array of framed black-and-white photos. From my vantage point, they all feature Colonel John Smolders in various poses with other soldier types; all of them armed with rifles and pistols, looking tough. Just like all of the pictures, the Colonel is not smiling this time either.

Since I was shown into his office, he has not made eye contact or even looked up. Instead, he has a brown folder open on his desk, and is reading it intently. With a wave of his left hand, he pointed me to this chair. The MP who accompanied me from the stockade made no sound. After removing my handcuffs, he is standing directly behind me as I sit in this uncomfortable chair in this uncomfortable place. To the left, there is a clock on the bookshelf under the window on a stand with crossed cannons that ticks the seconds off loudly. Five minutes pass.

The past five days have flicked by in a whirlwind of angst, regret and desperation. True to their word, I had been picked up by the California Highway Patrol for hitchhiking on the freeway. My feeble attempts to explain my presence on the highway anywhere near an on-ramp had been ignored, or worse, sneered at. I was taken into the headquarters office, fingerprinted and put in a holding room where at first, I'd hoped that I would be harassed and put back on the street. But as time passed, that option became increasingly unlikely. The longer I waited, the more my level of paranoia increased.

Inevitably, the subject of my draft card, or rather the lack of it, became a point of interest. In the almost three months that I had been on the road, the local draft board back at home had plenty of time for the paperwork of my induction and the story behind it to catch up with the bureaucracy of government paperwork. Although I was ignorant of the process that took place, once the link was made my travels were officially over. I was booked and held without preamble or benefit of an explanation. I had waited in silence, ignored for several hours, without the offer of food or a bathroom when finally, two military policemen, MPs, and a CHIPs officer, clipboard in hand, appeared at the door of the holding room. It was all too familiar to me. Cops with clipboards seemed to figure into a lot of my recent history.

Once handcuffed, I was escorted to a green panel van with U. S. Government plates and deposited in the back behind the screened grate that prevented me from attacking anyone in the front seats. The sun was lighting the horizon of the new day as we got underway. The two MP's talked and joked with each other and ignored my presence for the most part. The van stopped only for fuel, during which bathroom breaks, snacks and drinks were acquired. Then we were back on the road. Two fuel stops, two piss breaks, two bags of peanuts and a coke. I'm sure the two had probably switched off driving, but I wasn't really keeping track—or interested for that matter. It was evident that they had someplace to be and it was time-sensitive because there was no wasting time. It was almost midnight when we were waved through the gates of Fort Lewis outside of Tacoma, Washington, and my trip had come full circle.

The next three days were spent in what the army called a stockade, in other places it is called—jail. I spent the three days being sprayed with an ice-cold fire hose while I showered, scrubbing the floor of my cell with a toothbrush, and going outside in the rain in my underwear to exercise and other fun get-acquainted activities. My hair had been buzzed right down to the scalp, "*to prevent fleas*". The most amusing of these pastimes occurred during the night, so I was also running low on sleep. There was nothing I could do about it. As the jailers were fond of telling me, "*My ass was theirs now*". The treatment had the desired effect; I was scared shitless, tired and beaten.

Now in this uncomfortable chair and in this awkward place, the hammer was about to drop on me. I could feel it coming. It was going to fall on me from a very high place, and the two eagles on the collar lapels across the desk from me were going to make sure of that. I rubbed my palms on the knees of my filthy jeans to dry them and swallowed the lump in my dry throat. With a deep breath through his nostrils and a long sigh through his clenched teeth, the Colonel closed the file, and made eye contact—at last. His eyes were so dark I couldn't make out any pupils. At least he didn't appear to have a weapon anywhere handy.

"I've been reading your personnel file." He pushed it across the desk in my direction for emphasis. "It's not a long read." For not being a long read, it had certainly taken long enough.

I didn't have anything to say, so I said nothing. The silence stretched out in the room and the clock ticked on.

"I have never been presented with this particular problem before. I would have been happy to keep it that way."

I still didn't have anything to say, so I said nothing. The clock ticked, the MP shifted his weight behind me.

"The Uniform Code of Military Justice, which has jurisdiction in situations like this, gives the commanding officer guidelines for AWOL cases. But for the most part, it is up to the commanding officer to make a ruling. However, your particular case does not fall into the UCMJ guidelines completely. I would say it is unique, but I don't want you to take pride in the accomplishment, so I'll just say it is un-usual. You have been missing for eighty-one days, an accomplishment in itself. I could say that you have been absent without leave, but that is not technically true, as you never really arrived. Did you?"

He made eye contact with me, daring me to respond. I did not.

"There are many cases where the military code goes so far as to impose a death sentence on deserters, which technically you are."

Pause. Eye contact. The lump in my throat was now the size of a baseball, but I refused to swallow it in front of him.

"Unfortunately, there doesn't seem to be much chance of that hap-pening given the temperature of the political scene in this country that would be seen as too inflammatory. Not that you might not deserve it, but it would offend people's sensitivities. Everybody's a candy ass peacenik these days. Understand though, this is a serious situation. Whether we hang you or shoot you or whatever decision is reached, you have no one to blame for your fate but yourself. You have com-pletely stepped on your own dick, you got that?"

Eye contact again.

"Yes, sir."

He held my gaze for a long moment, and his eyebrows pulled down, and his face got even tougher. Here comes the hammer, I thought.

"According to the guidelines, if you have been AWOL for a short period of time, a few days or a week or two. You can be fined, or re-duced in rank. But you don't have any rank, do you?"

Eye contact.

"If your period of absence is over thirty days you are to be reduced to the lowest rank and given a less-than-honorable discharge and sent home. A dishonorable discharge will follow you for the rest of your life, you can count on it. Good luck finding a job. You can also be given time in the stockade, and forfeit your pay, but you've never gotten any of that either."

The phone on his desk jangled causing me to start. He reached for it, and said, "Yes? That is correct, please come right on through."

He hung up the phone and addressed the MP behind me, "That will be all, wait for Private Casey out in the clerk's office."

Boot heels clicked behind me, and the colonel saluted him over my shoulder. The door opened. One went out, and one came in—different boots. The other soldier entered and immediately came around to the Colonel's side of the desk. He had a clipboard.

"Stand up Private Casey. At attention."

I didn't know what to expect, but it was clear that it was about to happen right here right now. I stood up and did my best to stand up straight.

"Don't eyeball me, Private Casey."

I fixed my gaze on the middle black-and-white photo over the top of the Colonel's head. In it, Colonel Smolders is holding a rifle in one hand and brandishing a forty-five automatic in the other, in what looks like a jungle setting.

"Since it is up to my discretion and this particular dilemma requires a resolution that benefits the cause of the United States Army, I have the perfect solution. No, I am not going to send you home. You've already spent too much of Uncle's money getting you here. You were a draft resister back at home and you engaged in rioting and anti-war protests. I would imagine that pukes like nothing better than for us to throw you out of the Army and send you back home to a hero's welcome. So no, I will not grant you your wish and send you home. Corporal Simmons will witness these findings, and a record of this hearing will be placed in your already troubled personnel file."

Taking the clipboard from the Corporal, he read:

"You are to be transported to the first basic training rotation available. You will take basic training in that rotation and company. That company will be Company B, and you are to be placed in 1st Platoon. You will be under the training guidance of Staff Sergeant Drill Instructor, Foster and Company Commander Captain Alexander. You will pass every test, you will conquer every hurdle and you will learn what being a soldier is all about."

He handed the clipboard back to the corporal and continued looking directly at me with his lowered eyebrows and angry countenance.

"I will personally watch your progress, and I will be getting regular reports. If you set one toe out of line, if you give me one single solitary reason, I will throw you in the stockade until you get your head screwed on right. If that happens, we will start the process all over again. From the beginning, in a completely different rotation. If it takes you the entire duration of your enlistment, the next two years, to get through basic training, that will be just fine with me. Is that abundantly clear?"

"Yes, sir!" I couldn't believe it. They weren't going to shoot me, well maybe not today anyway.

"In my opinion, no duty will be too menial, no amount of discipline if necessary will be too extreme if we are to make a soldier out of you. I expect you to measure up, and I expect you to understand the error of your lazy ways. I expect you to be tested and I expect you to toe the line or learn to bend. If you break, so be it. Your ass is ours. You have done the crime, and now it is time for you to serve your penance."

Penance? An interesting choice of a word and one that I was wholly familiar with. Now I knew I was going to be okay. *Penance. Shit I know all about penance; bring it on the motherfucker.*

February 1959, Our Lady of Grace Rectory

"Bless me Father for I have sinned it has been one week since my last confession."

It is Friday afternoon, and I am a familiar position. For all good little Catholic boys and girls who attend Catholic school, Friday afternoon is part of a dreaded routine. On Fridays, classes are dismissed early. At the end of the Friday school day, the nuns march the students from the school across to the church, so we can all go to confession. It is a weekly ritual that gives us plenty of time to consider our sinful ways as we wait in single file for our time in the confessional. Each class from second grade through eighth contains somewhere in the neighborhood of fifty to sixty students, and each of those students must take confession every Friday. Friday afternoon confession can last as long as two hours as each one of the young sinners extols the transgressions of the past six days. On occasion when I have had a particularly productive week, which was frequent, I and a few others of similar ilk, are escorted to the rectory rather than the chapel. It is the rectory that we fear. In the rectory, Monsignor Lavin takes our confessions, and this is one of those weeks.

The rectory is the residence of the priests who work at our church. There are five priests in our parish, and they are ever present around the city block that comprises the campus of the church, convent and school. Monsignor Lavin is the pastor and spiritual leader of our church and school, having been elevated from Father Lavin shortly after our arrival in the neighborhood. Father Lavin wore the full black cassock of a priest, but with the elevation in rank the cassock was now trimmed in red and sported red buttons. The Monsignor was acutely aware of his rank and authority and took tending to his flock, especially its transgressors seriously.

The full front porch was roofed and sported several upholstered chairs and had large heavy double oak doors complete with two stained leaded glass inserts. Once inside the entrance of the rectory, a wide staircase with red brocaded carpet and darkly polished banisters rose to the second floor on the right-hand side. The corridor then continued into the back of the residence. Directly under the staircase, a small alcove had been furnished with a padded kneeler and prayer rail that faced an overstuffed wing chair. Monsignor Lavin sat in the chair and chain-smoked cigarettes while he heard our confessions.

Each of us waited our turn in the sitting room, which opened immediately to the left of the front door. There were usually four or five of us and very rarely was one of them a girl. The arrangement lacked the usual trappings of a true confessional. Where the confessional provided privacy and also featured a screened grill that the confessor pled his case though, this required a face-to-face confrontation with the scowling smoking face of the Monsignor. Those waiting for their turns in the sitting room also had the benefit of overhearing both the sin and the penance, which made the waiting time much too short. The reasons that we were in the rectory was already well-known to the Monsignor, having been fully briefed by a note from the various teachers, not all of which were nuns. Hedging our confession was not an option, and the procedure was more a formality than an actual confession. In the rectory, the penance was significantly different.

As I am currently a third grader, my turn in the queue comes early. I have been here before, and I know what to expect. I know the reasons for my presence are similar to those of the past. But as in the past, I have no idea how to stop breaking the rules. I seem to have trouble with turning my letters around. Js look just like Ls to me, and bs and ds look the same and so on. Sentences can be confusing for me so when I read, which I like to do, I have developed a way of looking at entire sentences and paragraphs rather than individual words. In this way, I get the context rather than the wording in the sentence. I can read a whole page that way in a matter of seconds. As a result, I have been apprehended again reading ahead of the class in the material. This is strictly forbidden. In addition, although I have attempted to explain the problem to the teacher, the diagnosis is inevitably that I am feigning stupidity to garner special attention. Also, strictly forbidden.

"These are my sins." I recite from my position on the kneeler. My eyes squinted to avoid the cigarette smoke, and my nose was assaulted by the overfull ashtray to my left.

"I disobeyed Sister Mary Allen two times.

I disobeyed my father twice

I disobeyed my aunt four times

I am sorry for these, and all my sins so help me God."

I couldn't be sure about the sins I was claiming about my father or aunt, but I threw them in, just in case.

"And how were you disobedient to Sister Mary Allen?"

"I read ahead of the class Monsignor."

"Yes, and you and I have talked about this before have we not?"

"Yes, Monsignor."

Once I detail to the best of my ability this disciplinary faux pas, Monsignor Lavin assigns the requisite penance. This almost invariably consists of five Our Fathers and five Hail Marys after making a good 'Act of Contrition'. These prayers are the most basic and rote pillars of the Catholic religion, and any kindergarten child knows them right from the start of their spiritual indoctrination.

The penance is to be performed while on the kneeler, and once the recitation begins, Monsignor Lavin vacates the chair and walks behind me. Each prayer is concluded with my solemn "Amen". As soon as I utter the Amen it is punctuated with an exclamation point by the whistle of the cane and the resounding snap of it against the backs of my legs. Although I knew it was coming, I have managed to hold back my tears until now. There will be nine more, ten in all, one for each amen, each carefully in a different place. If I lose my place in my prayers or have to start over, there will be one extra. Tonight, my Da will yell at me, again. My Mom will cry in the bathroom, again. In the morning my pajama pants will be stuck to the open cuts, and Kate will have to help me dress.

March 1970, Fort Lewis, Washington, North Fort

The Colonel had been as good as his word. Drill Sergeant Foster was a man in his element, the bastard's bastard, and he was diligent. Capable of artfully intermingling rigorous training with talented sadism he created a hellish basic training experience that even raised the eyebrows of the other drill sergeants in our company. In what meager defense I could offer, he was hard and mean on all of us but true to his assigned mission; Foster never passed an opportunity to single me out for ridicule or extra duty. I was on K.P. two times for every one time of any other recruit. If an area needed policing for cigarette butts, I was his man. If we were not marching, running or exercising the military low-crawl became my primary mode of transportation from point A to B. I pulled fire guard duty at least once a week even though he had sixty men to choose from. One time he caught me smoking behind the latrine while on a nonsmoking break, so I stood in front of the entire company and ate my pack of cigarettes, including the half-smoked one, for his enjoyment and my disgust.

To my surprise, and his frustration, with the exception of eating the cigarettes, I loved it. I loved it all. I reveled in all of it, the running and climbing, carrying the backpacks and equipment. It was an exhilarating test of my physical capacities, and I surprised myself as well. It challenged me, and my body answered the call. When the running became too much for others, I shouldered their packs. When others couldn't get over an obstacle, I gave them the needed boost. My body sang with the joy of physical release and the rhythm of my boots on the ground was the song of my soul. I found a physical aspect of release, that I had never known before. My body, already hardened by real work and a few months of foraging on the road, grew muscle and sinew and flexed itself in narcissistic splendor. Where the others lost weight and slimmed down, I packed on another ten pounds of muscle. Following his instructions to the letter Drill Sergeant Foster dogged me every step of the way. He tested me as hard as he could, but he could not break me.

I was issued my M16A1 rifle. It was rifle number 117. It fit my hands, and it suited me. On the range, number 117 was uncannily accurate. I had never held such a fine weapon. I was miles ahead of most of the other recruits since I already knew how to shoot. Number 117 and I became a deadly duo. The range fire required one hundred rounds fired downrange at various targets. After a couple weeks of practice, we were taken to the ranges for record fire. On two separate occasions, recruits took a foxhole position and were given pop-up targets at various distances. The man-sized and man-shaped silhouettes were spaced at fifty, one hundred, one hundred fifty, two hundred, two hundred fifty and three hundred yards. During your test, the targets would pop up at random intervals and in random order stand for a few seconds and then drop back down into the brush. The shooter had five seconds to see the target, aim and fire. Hits were recorded by a range spotter standing directly behind the shooter. On the first round of forty, I hit forty. I only got credit for thirty-nine however, because the bullet passed through the fifty-yard man silhouette so cleanly that he didn't fall down.

"No credit for that one Casey, he didn't die. Miss!" yelled the spotter.

On the second round of forty, I missed… none. The last record fire was forty rounds, fired at night, at a rigid silhouette, at one hundred yards, on full automatic. A full clip of ammunition and one in the chamber come out of an M16A1 at a rate of three rounds per second.

On the third record fire, the target had to be hit twenty times out of forty rounds to pass. On the third record fire I passed, and then some. The only shadow of a dark spot in my basic training rotation occurred at the grenade range, and because of it Foster and I came to a visceral understanding that carried me to the end of the rotation and ended my extra duty purgatory.

Weather in the winter at Fort Lewis was consistently miserable. Days without hard steady rain were rare. Often the reason it did not rain was that it was too cold. The combination of wet and cold often required, in addition to our green fatigues and winter outerwear, us to also be dressed in heavy gear—rain pants, parka, and rubber buckled boots worn over our combat boots. Once dressed, not sweating was no longer an option. It couldn't be helped. It was mandatory and immediate, and added extra weight to our field packs, gas masks and rifles.

Grenade training was one day and one day only. Recruits were bussed to the grenade range in thirty-foot truck trailers that we called cattle cars. Upon arrival, we sat in outdoor bleachers and received indoctrination about the wonders of grenades: there are colored smoke grenades for signaling; and white phosphorus grenades, nicknamed Willy Peter that will burn a hole right through you; and the most common grenade, the fragmentation grenade or frag. This grenade has a core of high-power explosive enclosed in a steel cage that comes apart in small sections so that when it explodes, these tiny fragments spray out in a 360-degree radius of razor-sharp death.

Once sufficiently impressed with the firepower of the little baseball shaped devils, we were taken into a cement bunker with a thick concrete roof overhead. Each individual recruit was then escorted around to the front of the bunker and was given a live grenade. He was then to execute a grenade thrown by the numbers. When my turn arrived, I was escorted by Foster out of the bunker and around in front of it to a small ten-foot long concrete trench. The trench was chest high facing out into a large blasted outfield and backed by the bunker where the others wait their turn. The Drill Sergeant then instructed me one more time;

"Take your glove off the idiot string and put it in your pocket, then grip the grenade in your throwing hand. One, grip the safety lever and then pull the pin. Two, cock your arm, Three, throw it as far as you can, Four, duck behind this wall. Clear?"

"Yes, Drill Sergeant."

That is where the trouble started. With a smirk and a shrug, the clerk who had issued my uniforms issued me a field jacket that fit me across my broad shoulders but with sleeves that might have been too long for a gorilla. Immediately upon being issued our field jackets, our Drill Sergeant ordered us to pull out the bottom string, which was used to tie the bottom of the jacket snug around one's hips. We then threaded the string through the sleeves of the coat and out each side where we attached our government-issued leather gloves with one hundred percent wool liner inserts. This was meant to ensure that we didn't lose our gloves, but what it also insured was our gloves, whenever we weren't wearing them, dangled at the end of our wrists like fish at the end of a line.

Step one and step two went according to plan. Step three; not so much. When I brought the now live grenade forward to throw, the too-long sleeve of the jacket flopped down over my hand, and the grenade, now missing the safety lever, got caught in it. Instead of throwing it as far as I could, the grenade dropped out of the sleeve and landed on the wall in front of us spinning like a top off of a string. There is a ten-second timer on the grenade. Suddenly ten seconds seemed like a very short time indeed. Instead of rolling down the slope of the cement bunker and out into the blasted area, it sat there spinning right in front of us like a Hanukkah dreidel.

The first thing Foster did was look at the grenade, then he looked at me, his wide-eyed expression matching mine I was sure, then back at the grenade. Two seconds gone. The next thing he did was hit the deck. Flat on his stomach in the bottom of the trench. Three seconds gone. In my shock and surprise, hitting the deck didn't occur to me, so I looked at the grenade again. The concrete bunker wall sloped smoothly away from me toward the range for about six feet; then apparently just dropped off toward the ground. How the grenade had not just rolled down the slope of the wall was a puzzler, and I thought about it for a tick. Four seconds. Then reflexively I swept the grenade off toward the range with the sleeve of my coat, almost afraid to touch it with my bare hand. Five seconds. I looked at Foster again, and then I fell right on top of him in the small space there wasn't room to lie side-by-side.

KABLAM!

The concussion of the grenade that couldn't have been ten feet away from us was impressive even with the impact shielded by the thick concrete. Still lying stunned in the trench, it was only a few moments and dirt, and fragments began to rain down on us from the blast being directed straight up into the air. In a few more moments Foster started to struggle up, and I slid off of him into a crouch. Hunkered down, he faced me in the cold, damp concrete ditch his eyes wild his face pale.

"Holy mother of God, I practically shit myself. Geezus!"

I was beyond speech.

He reached out and grabbed the front of my coat and pulled me up on my toes, off balance his face close enough to smell his aftershave.

"Casey, I swear to fuck, if anyone, and I do mean anyone, hears about this I will shove the entire U.S. Army right up your ass." He paused long enough to take another deep breath and shake his head. "Listen, it's bad for me that this happened, but it's worse for you. Especially with your record, all I have to do is say you tried to kill us both, and your ticket is punched, kapisch?"

Well, shit, my head wasn't working that fast, but I hadn't even considered that angle.

"I get it."

"You've busted your ass, I have to admit it. I was looking for a fuck-up when they showed me your file, but you've busted your ass. You've earned your stripe, and you're almost out of here so let's leave it here, deal?"

Up on my toes and leaning to close to him, my body was just starting to realize what I had just tried to do and began to quake. I didn't know what kind of deal he was talking about, but any alternative probably featured someone with a clipboard. I didn't know how to deal with this suddenly sane and reasonable version of Foster either.

"Deal."

Graduation day arrived, and Foster ceremoniously handed out private stripes at morning formation to a select few of us, I got my stripe on graduation day. The lousy little stripe meant a raise in pay, so I gladly accepted it. Many of the other graduates had friends and family that had traveled to the ceremony on what was the first sunny day I could remember; mine did not. We stood on the parade ground and heard profound wisdom from some high brass officer and then saluted the flag, anticlimactically.

As we milled about exchanging last words of friendship and expressions of relief the sea of new dress green uniforms parted, and Colonel John Smolder's dark face and aura strode through corridor repulsing graduates with negative energy. Resplendent in his dress officer uniform with enough medals on the left breast to sink a small boat he stopped directly in front of me and waited. I did not forget to salute.

"Congratulations Private Casey. It would appear that our little rehab program was a success. Honor graduate no less. I could have happily gone either way, but this way Uncle Sam wins too."

I had learned my lessons well enough to not say anything.

"As you already know, your ASFAB scores are impressive. IQ level

142 is uncommon and with a score like that you should be in the OCS program at least."

He paused for effect and then with a smile that only took in the left side of his mouth,

"You and I both know that you might be soldier material, but you are definitely not officer material, are you? Honor graduate or not, I still would not trust you. So, before you start thinking too much of yourself, remember. A screw-up will always find a way to be a screw-up, and you're a smart screw-up. Let's see how long it takes you."

I didn't know whether to respond to the positive or the negative to that statement, so I took a chance.

"Yes, sir."

"Obviously lots of MOS possibilities for that kind of score, but since we only have you for two years," and then with a little smile, "at least for now, I think you've proved sufficiently what you are best suited for. Congratulations, private. Now we'll find out what you're made of."

He saluted again, turned on his heel and with his little retinue of sycophants breaking trail retreated.

Later that morning, I received my orders for my AIT. 11B infantry, fourteen weeks of more of the same I had just finished. Well played mother-fucker, well played.

June 1970,
Sea-Tac Air Force Base,
Tacoma, Washington

I am ready; we are ready. My gear is packed it sits on the floor between my feet. My new jungle fatigues are stiff and smell new. I miss my good boots. The bird is sitting on the runway. We know it is waiting, we can smell the jet fuel. I made my last phone call last night, waiting in the rain for my turn at the phone booth. Ma cried into the phone, Da told me to watch my six o'clock. Kate came on just as the operator asked me to "deposit sixty cents for additional minutes." "Come home to me, Emmett."

I am going to war.

August 1970, Stateside—For Now

Back in the States again, Fort Lewis, Washington, another full circle and back to the beginning. The issues with my left hand proved to be largely unfounded, and in the end, the doctors opted to let it heal by itself. I had the stitches in my leg and hand taken out the same day. My broken fingers stayed sore longer than my hand did. The Army was not about to let me lie around and feel sorry for myself. After a short stay at Madigan General, I was sent back to the Intake Station at Fort Lewis and assigned night CQ duty. With my bandaged hand and other spots that were still not quite ready for action, it seemed that the only thing I was suited for was to run errands and perform other gofer duties.

The long nights were dull and boring. The only break in the monotony of sitting next to the phone came when a new influx of recruits arrived on buses from the airport in the middle of the night. They had to be escorted to the chow hall and what would be their temporary quarters before processing them in. Ironically, this was the exact process that I had missed out on several months back. In all ways, it was a typical Army job; dull and mindless.

On the plane back to the States I had had an awful nightmare. A blind, nameless terror that stayed with me even after my seatmate shook me awake. The manic racing of my heart made it almost impossible to remain seated and not jump up and pace the aisle of the aircraft. I stayed awake the rest of the flight afraid that the dream would return. But the dream returned, again and again. Sleep proved difficult with my fear of the dream, and I became afraid of my bunk. Instead, I took long rides on the buses that shuttled around the main and north fort and back and forth to Madigan General Hospital, dozing with my head against the window.

I just could not get enough sleep, and I asked the doctor for something to knock me out. He gave me a piercing look and questioned me about why I needed them. I knew why he was asking and recognized that the correct answers would land me an immediate psych appointment, so I told him I was having trouble with the time change. Once I had the prescription, I discovered almost immediately that one pill worked okay, but three absolutely did the job.

Since I did not know anyone and because I was only on a temporary assignment, no one tried to get to know me, which I liked just fine. I began to settle in and adjust to my routine. Each day after lunch, I took the bus from the intake station back to Madigan for therapy. An Army corpsman checked me each day and then sat me at a typewriter. For the next hour, I typed variations of A quick brown fox jumped over the azalea bush. I had taken an entire year of typing in high school because there were mostly girls in the class, and it was an easy A.

My fingers already had plenty of muscle memory to master the exercise, and once the soreness faded, my speed increased to the point where the corpsman and I drank coffee and shot the shit for an hour, and I didn't have to type anymore. I began to drift into a routine that would have been just fine with me for the duration of my enlistment. I had plenty of free time, plenty of chow, and there weren't any people fucking with me. The only fly in the ointment seemed to be not sleeping. Insidiously, however, the isolation of being alone among so many and insomnia allowed the darkness to creep into my daily thoughts.

After a month of my existence in limbo, I was woken from a narcotic-induced sleep by the company clerk one morning. His schedule and mine were opposite of each other, and I had only met him in passing, but when I did see him, he had seemed like a pretty stand up kind of guy. Once I recognized my slide into depression, I had considered asking him if there was anywhere I could score some weed. On this morning he was noticeably excited, and as soon as I sat up on the side of my bunk, he dropped down on the opposite bed and brandished a sheaf of papers at me.

"Dude, I've got your ticket out of here, and man, you are gonna like it."

"I got orders? I was hoping they forgot me."

"Naw, I think they may have forgotten about you. At least for now. That's never a good thing man, cuz once they do find you, you definitely ain't gonna like it."

"So? What is that?" Pointing at the papers, he was still shaking at me.

"This is really cool man, you'll dig it!"

"It's my discharge, right?! Tell me it's my out-a-here!"

"Bullshit on that motherfucker, me first."

"Ok, what is it?"

"Dig this man, the mother-fuckin-Army is abolishing the draft, you know, and so now we got the Volar Army. All volunteers, right? "

"Too late for me."

"No shit too late for you, but hold on a minute. The fuckers are trying to improve their image because of the war, dig? And so, they're getting rid of the draft, so they need to improve their recruiting."

"And that's good for me, how?"

"Get this man! The Army wants guys who will go back to their hometowns and work with the recruiting stations."

"Fuck that! You're shitting me, right?"

"No, it's real man. Maybe you could get into it, might keep you out of going back over there." He finished this with a sideways cock of his head in the general direction of Asia.

"What's the catch?"

"Well, I think you gotta try to recruit your old friends 'cuz that's the idea. Aaand, it's supposed to be only for guys who are just finishing AIT."

"First part's easy, I don't have any friends. As for the second part, why even talk to me about this then? I'm not just out of training, and I've got a fucked-up attitude on top of it."

"First off, they don't know that you don't have any friends fuckhead. Second they expect all of us to have a bad attitude. All we gotta do is change your MOS, and bing, bang, boom, you just finished training. What'dya think?"

"Sure, change my MOS, that sounds easy." *Sarcasm at its finest.*

"It actually is man. See, there's this 71U class that only lasts a couple of weeks. It's a pretty new MOS so not too many are in it yet. You apply for it, take the class and your MOS changes. Then the company clerk, that's me, puts you up for this hometown bullshit thing. You get three things for the price of one, you get outta' here, you get to go home, and you get a different job when it's over. I don't know, but maybe if it works out, you might even get to stay home and work out your time. Where were you from anyway?"

"Chicago, so I'm not too big on having to go to work there for the rest of my time. Just a different kind of jungle. What's 71U?"

"Keypunch operator. Uncle Sam's getting into computers. They need people to put the stuff into 'em. Computers read cards, not print. You can type right?"

"I took typing in high school. I was the only guy in the class, so that's why I took it. Took it twice actually."

"That's all you gotta do. The C.O. sends a request over to battalion, it gets approved, there's a typing test and if you pass, off you go."

"Easy peasy, right? How do I get the battalion to approve it much less the C.O., who I've been avoiding ever since I got here?

"First of all, I prepare the paperwork for everything that happens around here. The C.O. signs whatever I put in front of him. Second, the same thing happens pretty much over at battalion, except the clerk has to get the OK from the X.O."

"The XO? That ain't gonna happen, Jesus, fuck me, what'd you get me all excited for?"

"Well there's this thing, the battalion clerk and the First Sergeant got this thing. If the First Sergeant gives the okay, then the XO will rubber stamp it."

Shit, here it comes.

"What thing?"

"You gotta talk to First Sergeant. He's the man. If he says go, you go. If he says jump, you fuckin' jump."

"I gotta kill somebody?"

"No man, geez, no. But you gotta go see the First Sergeant. He called over this morning, and wants you in his office at 1400 hours, today."

"I don't get it."

"Well, you gotta go see him now, so suck it up buttercup."

# Battalion Headquarters, 1400 Hours, First Sergeants Office,

After I came back from Madigan, I detoured to battalion headquarters and presented myself at the orderly room. I was expecting the usual Army hurry up and wait, but I was admitted straight through. The room was the typical army office—light gray walls, dark gray steel desk, gray steel chairs and gray steel bookshelves. It was as neat as a pin. No memorabilia, no pictures, nothing fun. First Sergeant Frank sat behind his desk his hands relaxed on the desk in front of him, his eyes on me. The look was relaxed, no animosity or curiosity revealed. His eyes were lidded casually taking me in and aware of his power. He had me sized up three paces into the room. This man was a good judge of people and character and definitely not one to be fucked with.

First Sergeant Frank was a very big man and not just in size. When people referred to him they usually just called him The Man. He was tall, wide and tough. He owned the place and everything in it, and everyone knew it. His fatigues were starched within an inch of their lives and tailored to match his frame. His frame would have been impressive even on a younger man. In the Army, sergeants make the world go round. Officers have meetings and make decisions. Sergeants make or break those decisions. Sergeants know everything about everybody, and they know how to get things done. The longer they serve, the more comprehensive the network of sergeants they create. Thirty seconds inside the door, I already knew First Sergeant Frank held the strings on a lot of nets.

I stood at attention, and he let me stand there for another long five seconds.

"At ease Private, take a seat."

This guy knew how to handle people, but oddly I felt completely at ease in his presence.

"How's the hand?"

"Good, finished my P.T. last week."

"I know. I also noticed that you didn't bother to tell battalion that you were finished."

"Well First Sergeant, I've been pretty busy with CQ."

The small smile that formed on his face just made him look tougher.

"Gonna jump right into the bullshit, are we?" He picked up the black phone on his desk, and I heard the response both through the door behind me and the receiver that he didn't quite have up to his ear. "Please bring in some coffee." And to me, "Cream and sugar?"

I shook my head. "Just coffee."

The coffee arrived in steaming mugs emblazoned with 101st Airborne wings, and a carafe. The SP4 orderly set one cup in front of me while he sized me up out of the corner of his eye. Once he stepped back from the desk, he waited.

"That will be all Cutler, hold my calls and see that we are not disturbed for the next thirty minutes."

Once the door closed, Frank took a drink from his coffee and made a face. He leaned back in his chair and gave me a long considerate look, over the coffee mug. The more he relaxed and got comfortable the more tension in the room he produced. I didn't know what I was expecting, but the situation had subtlety shifted. The initiative was his, and he knew it, but this was going to be something different.

"It's a real shit storm over there."

If over there meant Vietnam, then that statement stood on its own.

"You walked in, and you walked out. There's something to be said about that."

I would gladly not have had experience under my belt, so my level of thankfulness was abbreviated.

"I spoke with an old friend of yours today, Colonel Smolders, he remembered you. Didn't send his regards though."

That got the reaction out of me he had hoped for. I was surprised. It seemed ages ago that he had sealed my fate and dismissed me like I was nothing.

"I've also had a good look at your personnel file. A good long look at it. It makes for some interesting reading really. You've had quite a colorful trip to get to the chair you're sitting in right now. In fact, I'd say, I've never quite seen anything like it, and that's saying something. Thanks to you and some of those events, I've made some changes to the way our reception protocol at the airport is being handled. So in a way even that part of your journey was a service."

He took a drink of coffee and made another face. "Stuff tastes like shit."

I tried it and had to agree. He still hadn't said anything that required a verbal response from me, so I nodded instead.

"It would be an understatement to say that you have had an interesting recent history. The Commander at the 503rd has, in addition to your CIB and Purple Heart, made a glowing recommendation for a Bronze Star. So apparently, even though according to Colonel Smolders you are a smart-assed little pissant, you have done some good things." Then he added, "and some not so good things.

Now it seems that we should invest more of Uncle Sam's money in giving you a new MOS and finding you a job that would be more to your liking apparently. Even though you've only got about eighteen months left to serve. So, it sounds like you'd like us to do you a favor?"

He had spoken with his eyes lidded while he gazed into his coffee mug. With the end of the statement, he raised his eyes and eyebrows at me, looking the question.

"No First Sergeant, I'm fine right where I am, but if the Army can use me some other way, then I'm okay with that too." He snorted through his nose, and then looked at me. He transferred the coffee mug to his left hand and pointed over my shoulder. "See that?"

I turned around, and there was nothing there except the door of his office.

"That door is closed. We can speak freely with that door closed. I'm not interested in hearing any bullshit, or any what you think I want to hear. I'm interested in what you think and feel because it matters as to how I make up my mind."

"Okay First Sergeant, then yes, I'd like to get out of here. This sitting on my hands and not doing anything is murder. But I also don't want to go somewhere or do something that might be worse."

"Amen to that, and there're plenty of those jobs available. But you're a pretty sharp fellow, aren't you? According to Smolders, a real smart fuck-up, so I'm to watch my step with you. But it would be a waste to not use that to our advantage, so I want to have this little conversation and let's see where it takes us. Okay?"

He leaned over to his right and opened one of the lower drawers on his desk. Reaching in, he lifted out a bottle, unscrewed the cap and poured a healthy amount into his coffee, replaced the cap and then returned the bottle. After that, he took a good pull on the coffee cup and sighed.

"Much better. Alright, first of all, I see you've been asking the docs over at Madigan for narcotics. Oh, don't make a fuss, I've been in this man's army for almost twice as long as you've been alive. I have very long arms, and I can reach just about anything I want to reach. Narcotics is a slippery slope Casey. Don't fall too much in love with them, if you're having trouble, let someone know. That shit is ruining a lot of good men.

"Second of all, like I said, I've been in the army for a very long time, and the military's been good to me. But it's only been as good as I made it be. The army is a lot like life in general, there is a lot out there if you want to take the trouble to take it. Most people just want to get through it. So they don't work for what they want, and they take what they get and complain about it instead. I take what I want, and because of that, the army's been a good place for me. I'm getting long in the tooth now, and my retirement is right around the corner. It's my retirement that I'm concerned with now, and that is what I'm currently pursuing.

You need a favor, lord knows you could also use a break. I am in the business of handing out favors, but only when it suits me." Pause, another long pull on the coffee mug. "Favors aren't gifts though, favors cost something. So naturally, I need something in return from you. I have a job that needs to be done. You are in the perfect position to do it, and if you do it, I can grease a lot of rails for you. If you don't want to do it, I will understand, but I will also be in a position to find you a job and a place that will absolutely guarantee that the next eighteen months will be the most miserable shit detail you can possibly imagine."

Well, this was shaping up to be a fun little talk. He was only moments away from handing me a great big slice of shit cake, or bending me over his desk and jamming the telephone up my ass. My choice.

"I don't suppose I get some time to think it over?"

"You suppose correctly. In my experience, when faced with two very tough choices the longer you consider it, the worse they sound. In addition, due to some unforeseen circumstances, time is an issue."

"So, I choose between the devil I know or the one I haven't met yet?"

"Good choice of words, but not quite. This is not a tough job and the reward for a job well done is a guarantee. I can change your MOS. I can find you a good duty station, and if I so choose, I can also make sure that you aren't fucked with anymore, by anyone. Remember, I have very long arms, and I've been around a very long time. I will still be in this man's army even after you aren't. Would you like to hear the details?"

"No, but yes I think." Something didn't smell right and just by being here Frank already had me firmly by the short hairs.

"First of all, remember I can make you sweat blood if I want to, so what I tell you now is between you and me. If you so much as talk in your sleep about this, you are still within my reach and vengeance will be mine. Clear?"

"Yes, First Sergeant." Fuck.

"As I said, I have given more than three decades of my life to Uncle Sam. Now as my retirement approaches, I am working on making that retirement as comfortable as possible. The Army has developed a significant problem and the Vietnam War and the high brass's inadequate preparation for the aftermath it has created has made it worse. There is no fix for the problem. And like most problems, if you can't fix it you find a way to embrace it. The problem is drugs. They are illegal, and they are everywhere. You boys coming home from over there are bringing both your habits, and the need for them with you, and it is contagious.

"The growing appetite for marijuana and other things is swelling out of control, and the search for those things is taking our men to places and to people that are dangerous and difficult. Too many of our boys that deserve better are struggling with this problem and some are being arrested and serving time. Too many are stepping through doorways that lead them into much more dangerous levels of addiction. Like narcotics," he added making eye contact pointedly at me. "I have created a solution that seems to be working while at the same time helping me with my own situation.

"The intake station is a vast installation, a labyrinth of barracks and warehouses, filled with supplies of every kind imaginable. I have merely arranged to provide one more kind of supply and help keep our men out of harm's way. It works, but I have a problem. Demand has exceeded current supply, and that is where Private First-Class Casey fits in."

Dread is a traitorous thing, it makes sweat bead on your forehead and spring out of your palms and armpits.

"The door behind you is closed for a reason. There will be no record of this meeting. If you agree to our arrangement, then all is well. If you have a moral dilemma and decide that you want to share our discussion, it would be the word of a documented narcotics user versus a decorated and respected career veteran. Therefore, I can trust you so I will continue.

"Purchase of supplies has been arranged. It is a large purchase, and it involves a considerable amount of planning, arrangements, and money. For reasons that should be obvious, I cannot play a role in the transaction. This is an army base, filled with enlisted men who have never been away from home before. Or if they are experienced are transitioning from one place to another. We need a go-between we can trust and who is under the radar of suspicion. We need someone who is not just smart, because smart people are not necessarily quick thinkers. We need someone who is also clever, in case clever is called for.

As I understand the narrative, you survived on your own for almost three months with only a couple of bucks in your pocket. That kind of clever is hard to teach. That sort of smart can get a person into trouble or out of it. You've proved your capability as a soldier, and you survived a situation that by all accounts you should not have. I think this is something you can do, and I think you are right for the job. In addition, you do not exist on anyone's books right now; in a limbo of unassigned duty and temporarily forgotten. If you get it done, you have my word. I'll not ask you for anything else, and I will be an ally that you'll be glad you have."

I tried to swallow the lump in my throat, but I didn't have any spit to lubricate it.

"When is this supposed to happen?"

"That's the spirit, tomorrow night. The log will show that you were on CQ all night. You will be picked up outside the gate at 2200 hours, and the driver will take you to the buy. He will also be armed and provide back up if it comes to that. He is not there to make friends, and he doesn't want to be yours. Clear?"

"Okay. Um. Anything else?"

"I expect you to be armed as well. What is your weapon of choice?"

"Won't they search me?"

"I would. I suspect if they don't find a weapon on you they'd be suspicious."

"So armed, but soon unarmed."

"Exactly, but keep an eye on where the gun goes. Just in case."

"No revolvers please. I like a semi-automatic, a .38, Walther or a Beretta?"

He cocked his eyebrow at me, a little surprised. "Done." He picked up the phone and was immediately answered.

"Get me Dunn on the phone. Show yourself out Casey. If all goes well you and I will not be speaking again."

July 1959,
Kimball Square Neighborhood,
Chicago, Illinois

As darkness fell the air cooled and the day's humidity settled into a grey fog that hovered above the streetlights softening the light and creating bright halos around each. Three steps into the alley the softened light disappears. In comparison, the alley is inky black and silent. It smells like garbage and dog shit, which has been cooking in the heat and humidity of the summer sun. I carefully walk hugging the row of garage doors that line both sides of the alley, their pale faded paint glowing in the dark. I am careful with my feet to avoid tripping on the cracked and heaved cement garage aprons. The paper bag in my hands rustles as I roll and unroll the top of it with nervous anxiety. During the day we played softball in the alley, but no one dares the darkness at night. The bag is heavy both with the weight of it and what it represents. I am almost more afraid of it than I am of the fearsome darkness of the alley. This is not my first job, but it is my first big one that I get to do by myself.

Little Bobby Fiore had given me the bag and my instructions, and I repeat them in my mind over and over hoping the mantra will calm me.

"Okay R.E., take this and give it to the guy waiting for you in the alley on Kimball Street. He's gonna have something to give you in return. Bring that back to me. If you think you are gonna to get pinched, lose the bag. You understand? Do not get caught with it. Lose it. The guy in the alley is expecting you, and only you. Make the exchange, then get out of the alley and come back on the street. Stay in the light. Don't stop to shoot the shit with anybody, understand? Come straight back. Capiche? We're trusting you to do this and if you do, we'll give you something else that we can trust you with. Understand? Say 'I understand.'"

Little Bobby is one of the big kids. He's in high school, and Bobby controls what the boys in my neighborhood get to do and not do. He also sees that things that need taking care of get taken care of. Everybody listens to Little Bobby. They look to Little Bobby, and things go right. Little Bobby's father is a big shot down at the Italian-American Club up on Fullerton. The Club is where all the dagos hang out. Big Bobby takes care of the big things in our neighborhood. Little Bobby handles the little things.

"Take it to the guy in the alley on Kimball. Take it to the guy in the alley on Kimball." The voice in my head matches the sound of my feet as I shuffle along hugging the garage doors.

I know what is in the bag, I looked. It's a gun. It has a cylinder that is full of bullets and a little short barrel. I've seen them before. It is an ankle gun; some of the men in the neighborhood carry them all the time. It is meant to be strapped to your ankle under your pants leg. Sometimes one of the big boys has one that he shows us. The bag is heavy, and the top is getting soft from my sweaty hands rolling and unrolling it as I walk carrying it in two hands.

I slow as I approach the end of the alley that opens onto Kimball. It is late enough so there is no cross traffic I can see or hear on the street beyond. I don't see anyone, maybe I'm early. The last building at the end of the alley is a brick brownstone apartment that faces the street at the end of the alley. My shoulder scrapes along the bricks as I try to get as much light as I can from the end of the street so I can make out anything. But there is no one there. Slowing down my already slow pace the thought of waiting in the dark alley for a stranger increases my fear and anxiety. I hate the alleys at night. Just as I decide to stop walking near the end of the alley, I kick something soft with my feet and look down. With my gaze fixed upward looking for a person, I had not thought to watch where I was going. Propped in the doorway of the furnace room of the apartment building is a man and he wheezes from the kick. I turn to run.

"That you R.E.?"

The voice is not familiar, but whoever it is he knows me. "Um yeah, who is it?"

"Hey man, it's me, Ronnie Mencorini, you know from Our Lady. Little Bobby said it would be you."

A relief, I do know this kid, he used to go to Our Lady of Grace. He graduated a couple of years ago.

"They shivved me, man. I'm stabbed," he took a long breath, "robbed me too. They were waiting for me, God, I'm in a bad way R.E., you gotta go get Big Bobby. You gotta go to the Club and get Big Bobby. Can you do that?"

I squatted down and dropped the bag. Maybe to assure myself he was real and not just another spectral terror that lived in the alley. I couldn't be of any help to him, but I reached out and put my hand on what I thought was his chest. My hand came back wet. That was enough. I was overcome with a wave of dizziness and spots danced in my eyes in spite of the darkness of the alley. I stood up and put my hand on the building bricks still warm from the heat of the day until the nausea passed.

"I'll get Big Bobby." I ran to the streetlights and turned left.

1970, Seattle, Washington, Mr. Dunn

The rains had returned to Washington, and they poured down relentlessly. It was cold with little wind. The rain fell like it was coming out of a bucket. The driver never introduced himself and did not have much to offer in the way of conversation. I assumed he was the Dunn that First Sergeant had called. I was almost afraid to take a good look at him, so I tried to get a picture with my peripheral vision. Square jaw, high cheekbones, and big hands but that was it. After he had picked me up outside Main Gate in a nondescript late model coupe we rode up the highway for a few miles and then pulled over into a wayside.

Reaching into the back seat, he retrieved a pretty little .38 caliber Walther PPK and handed it to me along with a full clip. Since I was already in over my head and way out of my league I had decided that the best thing to do was act as much as I could like I knew what I was doing. There wasn't any turning back, so being afraid would just keep me from thinking on my feet. I racked the slide and checked the chamber, and dry fired it a couple of times and then popped the clip into the gun. Racking the slide one more time I put one in the chamber then made sure the safety was on before leaning forward and shoving it down into the back of my pants.

Next out of the back seat was a typical Army AWOL bag, except this one was heavy. I unzipped it, and in the dim light of the dashboard I looked in at more money than I had probably seen over my entire life.

"Jesus!"

337

"Jesus has nothing to do with it. I hope you're up for this. Remember I got your six, but you're on point."

He reached one more time into the back and pulled an M16 out far enough for me to see it, then replaced it and removed a very nasty looking, sawed-off 12 gauge out and showed that to me too.

"Wanna trade for one of these?"

"Nope and nope."

Fort Lewis to Seattle is not a long drive, and once in the city, we negotiated the back streets wallowing our way through the standing water and peering through the fogged windshield to read the street signs. Once we located the correct street and block for the address, we circled the neighborhood. Then checked to see if there was an alley behind the building we were looking for, which of course there was. Dunn pulled up across the street from the address. We sat there for a full five minutes just looking at the door.

The building was a small townhouse, jammed between two others, which were identical in a block of identical ones. There were three apartments one on top of the other, and one that had a small outside stairwell descending to an underground level. Lights shone through the windows of the basement apartment. Finally, Dunn popped his door and announced,

"Showtime."

My stomach was churning, and my bowels suddenly felt loose. I opened the door and stepped out into the pouring rain and stood on the opposite side of the car and looked at the door. The Walther was digging into the small of my back, and I fought the urge to reopen the door and pitch it onto the seat. Walking around the car, I slid up next to Dunn who was leaning against the fender of the car with his arms crossed. He was a good four or five inches taller than me, and the sleeves of his raincoat were tight across his biceps.

"If I hear a gunshot, I'm coming in. If I don't, you're on your own."

What if they just knife me and drag me out the back door, I thought as I sloshed across the street wishing it was farther. It wasn't very hard to understand why Dunn wasn't tapped to do this part of the operation. He was across the street from me, and I was almost afraid to turn my back on him. On sight, I would have been concerned about being left alone in an empty room with him.

I paused one more time and looked back at Dunn. He gave me a thumbs up. I didn't feel like returning it. I opened the thankfully silent wrought iron gate half expecting it to squeak loudly enough to wake the neighborhood and descended the eight steps and faced the door. Taking a deep breath, I rapped the brief code on the door that I had been given. The lights in the window immediately went out. The only sound was the rain pouring down the stairs behind me. Suddenly in a rush, the door swung open, and a hand grabbed the front of my coat and yanked me inside. The door was quickly closed behind me.

"Do not speak. Stand very still with your hands in the air." The disembodied voice, calm and composed, an Asian accent.

An oil heater against one wall huffed and produced an awful smell and an eerie glow that danced across the floor in front of me. Other than that the room was black. Hands began to run down my sides, armpits, and across my chest, then around me down my back and immediately happened on the Walther, which was pulled out of my belt. I was slammed hard against the front door behind me.

There was an explosion of language that sounded Chinese to me.

"Of course, he is armed, and he probably expected us to find it. Please assure that he has only one weapon."

The search resumed this time much rougher, and much more probing. My Zippo lighter was fished out of my pocket and into the rough hand behind me.

"Hey, is this a business deal or a date?" I kept as much fear out of my voice as I could and was a little proud that I thought I pulled it off.

"No funny business. We decide if this is a business deal.

What do you have for us?"

"It's in a satchel in my left hand."

The bag left, and footsteps shuffled away. A light came on farther down the hall, a door closed, and the darkness returned.

"Please have a seat while we assure that you have complied with your end of the bargain."

"Shouldn't I see the product before you take your payment?"

"As you say."

A table lamp in the room clicked back on, and the room came into sharp focus. Two men stood at ninety degrees to me, one to the left and one to the right. The one on the left got my immediate attention because he was holding a huge handgun that was pointing at my guts. Both were Asian, by my guess Chinese—definitely not Vietnamese or Korean. Neither of them was anywhere near as young as me. Behind the second man stood an entire wall of marijuana in plastic-wrapped bales. In the corner next to the floor lamp was a stack of burlap wrapped bundles. The whole room smelled so much like grass that I was surprised I hadn't noticed it before.

"Whoa, that is a lot of shit! Is it any good?"

"The very best Michoacán brought in from western Mexico only yesterday. You must try some."

"No, I think I'm good."

"It is not a request, you must try some. If you did not, I would suspect you are not a very good businessman. I am a businessman, not a thug, I hope that you are one as well." Then he took a step closer and added, "You are quite young for this kind of thing, so I assume that you must return and vouch for my product to your superior."

He produced a switchblade from his pants pocket, and it flicked open. Turning he sliced open the nearest bale and pulled a small pinch from the bulk of the contents. Crossing to the opposite wall, he lifted a bong from the bookshelf and stuffed the weed into the bowl. Replacing the knife, he patted his pockets, apparently looking for a match.

"I had a lighter in my pants pocket if you will let me have it back?"

"Certainly."

The Zippo appeared in the hand of the gunman on the left, and he handed it to him. He turned it in his hand.

"I have always admired the Zippo, it is said that it will light even in the wind."

He squatted down in front of me snapped it to life and turning it on its side set it on the weed and took a long hit off of the bong. Once it was going well, he handed it to me, while he held his breath. I took a tentative hit, and the result was incredibly instantaneous. I was high before my lungs were completely filled. This was some excellent shit. I was immediately racked by spasmodic coughing as I tried to hold the smoke in my lungs, and I could feel my eyes turning red. Chinaman smiled at me as he exhaled. He took another hit and finished the little bowl of serious weed. He squatted there in front of me rocking back and forth on his heels allowing me time for my brain to reset.

"It is good, this I know. Now you will try the hashish."

"Yes, it is good. Hash, you say?"

Turning he lifted one of the burlap bundles from the corner and unwrapped it. It was sticky and had a beckoning resin fragrance that smelled heavenly. Inside was a block of the pressed resin, vaguely resembling a football that had been deflated and pressed flat. Taking my lighter once again, he flared it and held it to the corner of the block for a few seconds. Closing the lighter, he squeezed off a thimble-sized chunk of the hash and pushed it into the already hot bong. Once again, he lit it and took the first hit, drawing in the lungful and closing his eyes for a moment. Then he handed it to me.

The hash was a completely different experience, the high more intense. I could feel my mind both slowing down and speeding up all at the same time. Involuntarily I closed my eyes and sighed, for the first time in almost a year my body relaxed. The current geography of my situation aside, I experienced momentary bliss.

"You are a professional? Few can handle this one; you are a dealer yourself, perhaps?"

"No sir, I am not."

In actuality my brain was having trouble remembering my name.

"But I can surely appreciate a good product when I experience it." I could have added that I'm an Irish Catholic, although he probably would not make the connection behind my ethnic proclivity for substance abuse.

"This is quite excellent."

If you didn't have anything to do for the next three to five days.

"Please do not think me impolite now, but I must not have any more, or I will not have my wits about me." I do know how to be polite when the time comes for it.

"If the counting proceeds as it should you have nothing to fear from us, Private First-Class Casey."

Even in my euphoric state, an alarm went off. I started.

"It is alright, I insisted that your handler inform me as to whom I would be entertaining this evening. For my own protection, you understand."

The counting apparently went according to plan, twenty minutes and one more toke of hashish later I shook hands with the *Chinaman*, in exchange for the satchel. Everything on the wall now belonged to me. It would fill the trunk and crowd the shotgun in the backseat of the car with little room to spare. I went outside to tell Dunn to pull around to the alley and found him standing in the rain right where I had seen him last, arms still folded, no expression on his face, with a single addition. A sedan was now parked directly behind the car that Dunn was leaning against, and napping in the front passenger seat sat a man taking his ease and definitely not taking any notice of his surroundings.

"Nosy neighbor?"

"Nosy cop."

On the way to the alley, Dunn made a short detour. I helped carry our sleeping companion to an apartment foyer three blocks away, where he could finish his nap out of the cold and damp of the Seattle winter. Dunn dropped his keys into the storm drain.

Once Dunn, always with his hands-free, had supervised the loading of the car but before I crammed myself back in, I asked Dunn to wait for a minute. He gave me a look, he didn't look put out or angry, I assumed he might not be capable of showing emotion, so he just gave me a look and then nodded. I went back to the back door and knocked. One of the stooges answered, angry as always. I asked to speak to the Chinaman one more time. When he came to the door with a quizzical look on his face, I handed him my Zippo. He was surprised as he turned it over in his hand, and then he smiled.

"May I have my gun back sir?"

⸺⸺)(()(⸺⸺

Two nights later I was once again pulling CQ duty. The night had been quiet. No calls, no intake from the airport or bus terminal. The on-duty Spec4 had taken off to sleep down at the barracks. Bored and alone I tilted my chair back and put my feet in the bottom drawer of the Orderly Room desk. With nothing but the sound of the rain outside the open window, I dozed. Something woke me with a start, opening my eyes to my first really good look at the guy whose name might be Dunn standing opposite me across the desk, his raincoat dripping, seemingly taller and wider from my seated vantage point. His face and crewcut hair wet from the rain outside. He might have just arrived, or he might have been standing there ten minutes, no expression on his face—waiting. He reached into the inside pocket of his dripping raincoat and produced a thick manila envelope, which he first pointed the end at me and then dropped on the desk. No greeting, no Howdy, just point and drop. Apparently an emotional avalanche coming from him. With that done, he turned and went back out into the rain.

I turned the envelope over, but it was blank on both sides. It was sealed, taped closed and thick. Tearing open the top of the envelope, I dumped a fat bundle onto the desktop. A bundle of money over an inch thick was secured by a rubber band, all mixed bills of different denominations, which I counted; twice; five hundred dollars. There was something else in the envelope, and I shook it out too, and it rattled onto the desktop, my Zippo lighter lay there the side with my date of birth engraved on its face up shining in the light of the desk lamp and a small piece of paper with a handwritten note.

"A favor for a favor."

November 1970, Merrill Barracks, Nuremberg, West Germany

Another quiet office behind another Orderly Room, another First Sergeant, another clipboard. First Sergeant Sinclair lounged across the big wide desk rocked back in his desk chair flipping through the papers on his clipboard. My personnel file lay open on the otherwise empty desk in front of him. NCOs reach high rank because they are tough and savvy, but the Lord doesn't build them all the same. Sinclair was short. He was sitting, but I could tell that his feet didn't reach the floor when he rocked back. He was also thick—not fat, just thick. With his high and tight military haircut he looked like an artillery shell, thick and solid rising to a point up at the business end.

He had not spoken in five minutes. I had learned to wait; fate has its own timetable. Finally, with a sigh, Sinclair flipped the clipboard onto the desk with a clatter while he rocked back into an upright position. With his arms spread and his elbows bracketing my file he bent his head and scanned the top page, silent still. Finally, without changing his position, he raised his gaze and looked across the desk at me through his shaggy eyebrows. I found myself wondering why they didn't trim his eyebrows when they shaved the rest of his head.

"Well Private, this is a puzzle." He just left that statement hanging in the room for a long pause. This was our first meeting, and I knew enough to just wait.

I had arrived in Germany three days ago. True to his word, First Sergeant Frank had followed through, and my orders for keypunch school had come through in a week. The class was given at Fort Ord in California, and I had been flown there in no time at all like a migratory bird following the same southern path I had walked the previous year. Only this time when I arrived, I was on the inside of the security fence. The class was scheduled to take two weeks and consisted of mainly learning about the keypunch machine and how it worked, and then learning how to type/punch the cards into an orderly deck that could be fed into a computer. I had finished the class in four days. Most of the other students had been mostly clue-less and poor typists. I made them all nervous sitting on my hands in the classroom and started pulling CQ for a couple of nights. I had become an expert on CQ by this time. Then miraculously the Army, or the long arm of First Sergeant Frank, showed its infinite benevolence. I was awarded honor graduate status and offered an opportunity to become a Home Town Recruiter.

With those orders in hand, I had caught the red-eye flight out of San Francisco after paying a taxi driver fifty bucks to drive me all the way from the Ord. My Da met me at the airport. He was dressed for work and smelled of his Old Spice aftershave. At the arrival gate, he had gotten out of the car and walked around to the curb where he had taken my duffle bag from me and then squared his shoulders and looked me up and down. He shook my hand holding it for a long moment, turned and walked back to the car.

Once home, he had insisted on lifting my duffle bag and car-rying it into the still sleeping house. Once he had carefully placed it on the floor at the base of the staircase, I followed him to the kitchen. The coffee pot was still warm from him having made it earlier, before leaving for the airport. Instead of coffee, he reached up into the cupboard and brought out his bottle of Early Times and two shot glasses. Wordlessly, he poured two shots filled to the brim and then spilling only a little, handed one to me. He raised his own while looking me in the eye. I did the same and we both threw them back. Turning, he rinsed his glass in the sink and set it on a prefolded towel next to the sink, gave me a nod and left for work. Standing in the living room window, watching as he receded down the driveway, I couldn't recall whether he had spoken a single word during the entire encounter.

On the following Monday, I took the train to Elmhurst and presented myself to Staff Sergeant Reed at the local Army Recruiting Office. It was evident that Reed was not pleased with the situation, and I could tell that he had an instant dislike for me, personally. The feeling had been mutual, so we had a nonverbal understanding immediately. After a short orientation, Reed drove the two of us into the AFEES station on Van Buren in Chicago, where long ago I had stared at the front door before leaving my father standing on the sidewalk and walked away from my youthful ways.

The recruiting gig was scheduled to last one month. There was no mention of an extension if things went well, and the entire operation had seemed unorganized and futile. Reed had not liked me, and he had liked the situation even less. He went out for a walk every afternoon leaving me to man the phones. He also did not appreciate my methods or level of enthusiasm for the task at hand. Especially, once he heard me openly tell two young men that the Army was no place for an intelligent human being. Apparently telling a potential recruit to "Run, run now, run fast and run far," is not technically the language choices he would have preferred or used himself. I must have been the honor graduate of recruiting because I got orders for

Germany in two weeks instead of the month I had been scheduled for.

After reporting to Fort Dix, outside of Trenton, New Jersey, I was flown to Frankfurt, Germany, and an extended bus ride later, I was parked in the grey steel chair with the slippery vinyl seat gazing at the shiny top of First Sergeant Sinclair's bald head.

"I did not submit any requests for a keypunch operator. I have a perfectly fine one already, and I only need one."

He straightened up in his chair, leaning forward just enough for his feet to make contact with the floor. He gave me a long look up and then down, sighed and closed the file. Sliding the file into the upper corner of his desk and squaring it precisely to the corner, he meticulously placed the clipboard on top of it and sighed once more.

"I don't suppose you know anything about ordnance. Or for that matter what we do here."

I tried to look intelligent, which meant not opening my mouth.

"This is the 182 LEM Company." he spun his index finger around in the air above his head like a guy who is ordering a round of drinks for the house, "We're part of the 303rd Maintenance Battalion. Here we fix the things the Army breaks, and they break a lot of shit."

I tried not to look at the fly that was crawling up the wall behind him, and appear fully engaged. So far, the fly was more interesting.

"I don't need or want soldiers in my company. The 182nd's mission is to fix technical components, radios, radar, generators. Expensive shit. The technicians that work here are just that."

He paused, reaching into his top desk drawer he pulled out a pack of Lucky Strikes, shook one out and then rocked back in his chair again so he could fish a Zippo out of his pants pocket. After he lit the cigarette, he took a good hit off of it and blew it toward the ceiling, seemingly unconcerned that he had not offered to let me have one. Rocking forward to get his boots back on the floor he continued.

"They've traded three or four years to Uncle Sam for a guarantee that they'll comfortably retire twenty or thirty years from now. They're smart and skilled, but they are worker bees. The last thing I need is soldiers; guys like you, fully equipped with give-a-shit attitudes and nothing-to-lose opinions."

The fly made a couple of loops and then accelerated out the open window. There was nothing to do now but listen.

"The jobs these men do are routine. What they do every day is what their lives will become in the real world, eight-hour days of nothing special. I throw a guy like you into the pool with them, and all of a sudden, things get interesting. Guys like you, with your wild tales and your go-fuck-yourself attitudes are like a virus. Attitudes become contagious, because it is different from what they see every day, and as a result, more interesting. I am not interested in having to become a hard ass to everyone just because some dipshit troop wants to liven things up a bit."

He paused to slightly realign the files in the corner of his desk.

"Not only that but according to your own track record, you are the worst possible case for what I just said, a pariah. You have managed in a very short while to become singularly everything I don't want in this company." He made solid eye contact. "So, I have no use for you Private Casey."

Well, this was going to be fun.

"But—and that is a big but—it seems that you also have made a friend or two along the way." Putting a thick finger on the top of the clipboard, he added. "This is a 'Confidential' telex that I received yesterday. I don't get many of those, and I most certainly don't get many of those regarding incoming replacements."

He rocked back in his chair again and looked down his chin and broad chest at me, his arms on the armrests of the chair.

"What qualifies a PFC, with less than a year in service, who has already been in three different duty stations to be the subject of a classified' message I would wonder? But then I could also wonder why the message would come directly from the Commander of the U. S. Army Intake Station at Fort Lewis who needless to say, I have never heard of before, or could give two shits if I ever do."

He raised his eyebrows at me and paused long enough to let that sink in and to see if I was going to illuminate him on the subject. He had my attention.

"Now that is strange in and of itself, but then I get another telex this morning, this time, from someone I know very well and also strangely and coincidentally from Fort Lewis, Washington. I get one, maybe two, confidential telex's a year if that. In the space of a day and a half, I've gotten two." He stubbed out his cigarette in what must have been an ashtray also in his top desk drawer slammed it shut and dropped both elbows onto the desktop. "So, what I've got is a keypunch operator that is not a keypunch operator, a soldier who may be an excellent one and maybe the worst one, a one-eyed Jack. I'm thinking I need a guy like you like I need three assholes and then, I'm thinking maybe three assholes isn't so bad."

He took another long look at the stack of paperwork on the corner of his desk, coughed and cleared his throat.

"The company supply clerk downstairs will issue you your footlocker and room assignment. For now, you are assigned to the tech supply platoon under Lieutenant Kyle. The Platoon Sergeant, Staff Sergeant Viero, will meet with you sometime today, so once you're in your billet stay there. Can you drive a truck?"

"I can drive anything with wheels and an engine First Sergeant."
Probably true, but not technically true.

"Report to the orderly room tomorrow at 0800. If you are going to grace us with your presence, then it's gonna be my job to keep you out of everyone's way until we see which side of the fence you wind up on. If you don't give me any trouble, we're gonna get on swimmingly. If you do give me trouble—Well, I have a particular skillset as well, and you won't like it. Clear?"

"Yes, First Sergeant."

"Private Casey? What is the regulation position for displaying your rank on the collar of your fatigues?"

"I, ah, about an inch from the corner of the collar."

"Not about an inch, exactly one inch. No more, no less. Would you say that your PFC bars are one inch from the corner of your shirt collar?"

"I don't know, First Sergeant, I didn't measure it."

"I could measure it, right here, right now, but for the sake of argument, they are not one inch, no more, no less. They're not even the same from one side to the other. You have arrived in my orderly room, technically out of uniform, on your first day under my command. I won't have that, as a disciplinary precaution for you Private Casey, and just so you know I mean business, every time, all of the time; this time it just cost you fifty dollars. You may be dismissed, report to the orderly room in the morning, and this time with your lapels measured. Clear?"

Fifty bucks? Just to show me that he could fuck with me anytime he wanted. The gauntlet was down. I could leave it there, or I could pick it up. If I picked it up, there would be no half-way. I smiled at the little bald Napoleon,

"Absolutely First Sergeant."

At least I wouldn't be bored.

Two-Days Later, Merrill Barracks, First Sergeant's Office

A little over forty-eight hours later I was sitting in the same chair in First Sergeant Sinclair's office off of the orderly room. Those forty-eight hours had been eventful and trying. Since pulling away from the motor pool the morning after my entry interview, I had not slept, showered or had a satisfactory shit. Stale sandwiches and water had been it as far as breakfast lunch and dinner. The Sandman had dutifully packed my eyes full of sand, and the grit and fatigue scraped my eyeballs every time I blinked. Even I could tell that I was seriously overdue for a shower.

In contrast, Sinclair was fresh as a daisy. That is if the daisy was shaped like a spaghetti squash. He was again tilted back in his chair, slowly swinging his short legs back and forth, rocking the chair. He held his cigarette in the corner of his mouth and squinted his eyes as he read. His ever-present clipboard was braced on his lap, and he studied it silently, flipping back and forth between pages.

"I think we could say that that was an unmitigated disaster."

An understatement to be sure.

"Two five-ton semi tractors, dead lined, and one thirty-foot S & P trailer totally destroyed. Yet you somehow managed to save the cargo?"

The thanks were one hundred percent due to the response time of the German Fire Department, but then why not lighten the mood.

"Yes, First Sergeant, the six M60 tank engines were off- loaded and delivered to the 42nd HEM this morning; all consigned to 2nd Armored Cav."

"And this is somehow thanks to you, but no thanks to you."

"Yes, First Sergeant. The semis were not up to the trip I guess. The brakes on the trailer overheated in the mountains and caught fire, once the tires caught fire the trailer was a goner." At this point, I was pretty sure that the semis were probably not damaged, and likely would be found to be out of fuel. It wasn't until they had brought me the last one that they explained how to switch the fuel tanks from one side to the other. The trailer might have caught fire because the air hoses were hooked up backward, which kept the brakes set instead of released. Another gap in my preliminary trucking education and a detail during this particular interview was better left out of the explanation.

"Tell it to your grandchildren Casey. Shit, this is a cluster-fuck of supreme proportion. We are in the middle of Reforger II. This country is crawling with all these fucking weekend warriors who are over here to play war games with the Germans. They're busting up shit faster than we can tow it away, and now I have to explain why we don't have any more tactical vehicles to haul their sorry-ass busted-up shit out of their way."

The gravity of the last two days were not lost on me. I had been there for every miserable inch of it. However, I could see that he might be in a mood, so I let it go. When in doubt, say nothing. His next question caught me by surprise.

"How many coupons did you burn?"

"Coupons?"

"Gas stamps. Didn't Sergeant Samuel down in the motor pool issue you a book of stamps, so that you could get fuel?"

"Oh those, yeah, he gave me a whole book of them, but I didn't know how to use them since I don't speak German, and I couldn't read any of the signs. I just fueled up at the Air Force Base outside of Frankfurt, and then again at K'town. Nobody asked me for stamps."

"Well, what do ya' know, a silver lining. Did you turn them in yet?"

"No First Sergeant. Sparks told me that I had to see you ASAP, so I came here right from the 42nd. Samuel, Sergeant Samuel told me to guard them with my life, so I got 'em right here in my backpack."

"Let's have 'em"

I picked up my pack that had been resting between my knees. The insides smelled of warm apple core and cheese, which is what was left in there along with a large and thick book of the gas coupons. The book was about the size of a McNally Road Atlas, each page was divided into individual coupons three to a page, which was perforated so that they could be individually torn out and used to buy civilian gasoline. The book was primarily money that could only be used for fuel; thousands of gallons of fuel. I dropped the book halfway across his desk, and he rocked back onto his feet and flipped open the outside cover to see if any had been removed. Satisfied, he rocked back in the chair and lit another cigarette. This time he shook out another one and offered it to me. Unprepared for this gesture I wasn't too exhausted to have alarm bells ring in my head, but I took the cigarette anyway. I had run out of my own brand sometime yesterday.

"Don't drop ashes on my floor, use your hat."

He rocked back again and swiveled his chair to look out the window, his left hand resting on the book of stamps, his right one slowly absently stroking the shiny top of his head for a long minute. The window was open, and the bright sunshine and warm fall air wafted in, bringing the street noises from beyond the compound fence with it. Halfway through my cigarette, I was already hoping for another. Even in my sleep-deprived state, I knew that whether I got another one depended on how satisfying Sinclair's head rub turned out.

With a sigh, he swiveled back to center and eyeballed me again. Reaching down he pulled open his top drawer and pulled out his pack of Lucky Strikes and flipped them across the desk until they slid to a stop in front of me.

"Go get a shower and get yourself presentable. You've already missed formation, so you're late for work. Don't ever show up in my orderly room without a shave again Mr. Casey. Sadly that will cost you another fifty bucks. Report for duty at tech supply ASAP."

Well shit, another exciting and productive interview.

I got to my feet and grabbed up my pack, zipped it and came to attention. I saluted him, which he returned without a hint of nonchalance. He looked down at the pack of cigarettes and then pointedly back up, meeting my eye. I looked down at the cigarettes and then turned and left the room, leaving them on the desk.

Lieutenant Kyle/Tech Supply

First Lieutenant Jimmy Kyle was tall, wide and handsome.

As the Tech Supply Officer, his desk sat at a head of a long wide bay that stretched from one end of the building to the other. Along either side of this space, countless racks of component parts were arrayed each aisle between them opening out into the main corridor. The far end of the building was given over to the tech shop where their machinists, welders and mechanics could fabricate pieces necessary to finalize repairs that were otherwise unavailable. The shelving was divided into small cubbyholes. Each cubbyhole was given over to a particular repair that technicians in other locations were working on. As repair parts were finished or as replacement components arrived, they were collected in the cubbyhole until all of the necessary elements were collected, then delivered to the appropriate technician for installation. From his vantage point, Kyle watched with evident pride as his men went about the complicated logistics of assembling the orders. It was routine work, mind-bendingly mundane and unnecessarily complicated by military paperwork and sameness.

When I arrived at the platoon, the work was proceeding in a subdued and shuffling fashion. Kyle stood in front of his desk, hands on his hips, surveying his realm. He returned my salute with vigor and with a last look of pride and a deep sigh of contentment he took his seat and genuinely welcomed me into his fold. It took me thirty seconds to size him up. He lacked any animosity or guile. He was friendly and proud of his job, his country, and his men. He probably loved his mother and apple pie too. In short, he was just a nice guy, unlike First Sergeant

Sinclair. I realized I would probably feel bad about disappointing him, which was inevitable.

My new job, I learned, was to take the parts that came in every day from the various supply sources and match their invoice number to the work order number in a cubbyhole somewhere in the vast shelving system. As each part was placed in its cubbyhole, I was to mark it off of the manifest. If it was the last part of the manifest, I was to take the completed order and place it on the will-call counter for pick-up.

It was a typical military job, dumbed down enough to bring tears to anyone with an IQ above seventy, and made inefficient enough to fill the available time space of an eight-hour day. I had not slept for more than forty-eight hours, but it took me less than ten minutes to learn and master the extent of what was supposed to be my job for the next eighteen months. Except that it wasn't.

In the Army, individual soldiers are just a component of a larger organism. As an individual soldier, you soon learn that you are government property and that any individuality that you may hold onto in your imagination is not the way you are viewed or managed by the powers that be. Sometimes those individual components become injured and cannot function adequately enough to perform their required duty. When this happens, they are sent to the dispensary for repair. If the repair is not complicated, they are patched up or medicated to the point where they can be reinserted into the machine. If the repair is more complex, they are exchanged for a new component and returned to a larger more competent facility for further repair or simply scrapped. In the case of an individual soldier that might mean discharge or possibly a stateside hospital.

The Army has lots of components, not all of which walk on two legs. At the 182nd LEM Company, many of the more complex and by extension; expensive, pieces of equipment are sent for repair. Radio equipment, radar, generators as large as 45KW, everything electrical was its bread and butter. Some things could be repaired, and some things could not be. Many of these essential-to-the-mission pieces of equipment required extremely complex components themselves that were too complex for repair at my new installation. When that happened, they had to be exchanged for new. Most of these components were not just essential to the mission, they were also considered too valuable to fall into the wrong hands. This was accomplished only if you surrendered the now dysfunctional component directly. This process was known as direct exchange or DX.

The 182nd was a part of the 303rd Maintenance Battalion, other companies in the battalion fixed other things. Things that fit on a workbench went to us, but some things had to be towed into a garage or hauled in on a truck bed, those went to the 42nd or 66th HEM, heavy equipment maintenance. Things like armored personnel carriers and tanks fell into this category, and two-legged military components were just as adept at damaging these as they were radios and generators. The 303rd fixed it all, and by extension exchanged it all if they couldn't fix it.

The company, and for that matter the battalion had technicians, machinists, mechanics and logistics galore. What it did not have were drivers. The exchange points for all things technical were located at massive supply depots. During World War II, these supply depots were moved forward behind the advancing military, close enough to be accessible but far enough in the rear so that they could not be taken in the event of a counter-attack. When the war ended, and now in position, they became permanent installations for the new mission, the Cold War, the purpose of VII Army in Europe in this new era of strategic warfare was too display military readiness along the eastern border of West Germany and Czechoslovakia. The military front was stationary as they watched their counterparts on the other side of the barbed wire. As a result, the depots remained far to the rear.

Posturing is for diplomats and generals, not every day soldiers. With no real activity other than standing in formations and starting and stopping their assigned machines of war, motivation for the soldiers stagnated and boredom ensued. Unless you were a technician learning an occupational skill, there was no real thing to do. There was nothing to do after work, and nothing to do during work. For soldiers of moderate intellect, the frustration and boredom demanded diversion and not surprisingly Army life offered a remedy. Old school soldiers learned how to become alcoholics and younger more efficient ones got stoned, many did both. All day, every day. Not surprisingly equipment began to break down. It broke down mostly because it gave the soldiers, something to do and it broke down because most of them did not give one single shit about it.

Pirmasens, Kaiserslautern or K'town, and Germersheim were the major hubs for repair parts and heavy supplies but were hundreds of miles to the west from Nuremberg complicating the DX process. Drivers had to be able to leave at a moment's notice, depending on the 'criticality' of the part, drive to these remote locations, and then maintain their wits and competence to accomplish the complicated paperwork process of acquiring the new parts and then boomerang back often in time for the next workday. It was simply not possible to make it to all three of the depots in one day, often not even in two. As the need for parts and experience increased so did the need for a different kind of specialist.

What was needed was a small group of men that were independent thinkers, resourceful and capable of operating outside of the parameters of company life. It also required a fleet of vehicles that could be adaptable to short hops and long hauls, transport delicate instruments and five-thousand-pound tank engines. Although I truly think First Sergeant Sinclair would much rather of had three assholes, what he needed was more people like me, and it tightened his already too tight butthole just thinking about it.

Nonetheless; First Sergeant Sinclair had been in this man's Army for a long time and a sergeant in the Army for any length of time has a very long reach. There is ample opportunity for a man to improve his lot if he has a mind to. All he need do is see a situation for how he may benefit and then employ what means he has available to take advantage of it. Sinclair was a man of means and had the mindset to use it. In the end, an elegant solution to his dilemma was right there, and he didn't hesitate, he extended his reach.

March 1, 1971, Southern Bavaria

Three months later I was parked in a 'Rastplatz' on the E50 Autobahn somewhere west of Ludwigshafen. The deuce and a half signal van ticked loudly as its massive engine cooled in the evening air. Rather than the standard flatbed with its canvas tarp stretched over it this truck was equipped with a full signal shack, with sliding windows on either side and a lockable rear door to provide access to the interior. It was heavy as only military equipment can be, and inefficient as all military equipment used for peacetime is designed to be but excellent for the purpose that I employed it for.

The back of the truck with its enclosed cabin was loaded with electronic 'DX' equipment, all carefully arranged to prevent damage, spread out across the floor on packing blankets. The truck provided cover for the equipment should the weather turn sour and also make-shift sleeping quarters for the over-the- road drivers when the need presented. For me, the need presented itself often. Thanks to the casually sadistic efforts of First Sergeant Sinclair I had not been paid more than a fraction of my military pay since I had arrived in Germany. I had been dunned for uniform dress violations, not shaving properly, not having a military enough haircut and not showing up for formations. Spare cash for food or showers was a luxury that I could not afford, and I was beginning to see the sense in Sinclair's approach to life in the military.

The 'Rastplatz' was familiar to me. In less than an hour, I can be at the Kaiserslautern depot if I keep going west, a little more than an hour to the east lays Frankfurt where the military presence is too dense to perform the operation I am here to do. I stop here often as I go and come on my route. Located at a high elevation in the surrounding steep hills the daytime view is nothing short of spectacular to the east as the entire Rhine Valley lays out in front of you with its sloped mountainous hills covered with vineyards and cropland. It is an excellent place to eat my lunch and smoke some dope.

Tonight, I could not drive further even if I wanted to. Tonight, as the truck ground its way up the steep grade into the hills, we had climbed up into the clouds, and now the dense fog was too thick to clearly see much farther than the long hood of the vehicle. I have an appointment in Kaiserslautern in the morning, but tonight I will sleep in the shack. Another time I would have been content. Instead, I am tense, I am waiting for someone. Sitting on the back of the truck in the open door of the signal shack, I dangle my feet in the heavy damp of the fog, and let my hand stray down to the .45 resting on the step beside me assured by its presence.

In the truck, there are dozens of pieces of expensive 'DX'. Most are bound for K'town, and a few for the next depot in Germersheim. A few have arrived at their destination now, along with three books of fuel coupons, one for each company in the battalion, the 42nd, the 66th, and the 182nd. Thousands upon thousands of gallons of fuel. I have no idea whether the electronics or the fuel is worth more, and I am pretty sure I do not care. I do not like this part of the job.

Occasionally, the glow of headlights flash past on the roadway to my right beyond the trees that screen the Autobahn from the Rastplatz, rarely one will pull into the parking area only long enough for its inhabitants to relieve themselves of any bladder or bowel urgencies and then move on. Finally, a car with a full array of massive headlights and fog lamps pulls in and drives directly up to the back of my truck, blinding me within the glare of the sun bright lenses.

Keeping the lights directly in my eyes, I hear more than see as first one door, and then the other open and close, followed by the sound of heels on cement as the two inhabitants approach on opposite sides of the car. I have no chance to palm the gun. Then the lights are turned off leaving several bright blind spots in my night vision. A flashlight blinks on from the person on the right.

"Jump down from the truck please."

Jumping down I realized that my legs had fallen asleep, and I was a little unsteady, but I kept my arms held up where they could be seen as empty.

"Are you alone?"

"Yes, are you here to see the opera?"

"No, I only like ballet. Please move your pistol farther away from your hands and assure yourself that the safety is on. You are as safe as your mother's house."

Knowing my mother's house, the way I did that was not particularly assuring. The other person had remained beside the passenger door of the car, not speaking, but his posture spoke volumes.

"You have something for me I believe?"

"Yes, in the truck here. The things are marked with a blue ' on their parts tag, and these." I carefully reached around the corner inside the door and produced the three large books of fuel coupons.

"And I have something for you." He stepped forward and handed me a stiff vinyl AWOL bag that was quite heavy. "Here is a flashlight if you don't have one of your own. The Deutschmarks and Swiss francs are bundled separately, the American dollars are bundled by denomination. You, of course, will count it while we relieve you of your inventory."

"I think I will count it first. Would you mind holding the flashlight?"

"Not at all, but let's get into the car just in case someone should arrive."

"No thanks, I'll take care of it right here."

"You are cautious?"

"I'm careful and cautious."

The money counted, the products exchanged, the late model Audi backed away from the truck and then flipped on its impressive headlight panel and powered out and around the deuce-and-a-half and with throaty acceleration disappeared into the fog and out onto the Autobahn. I reclaimed my seat on the high tailgate of the truck and listened to the singing of the blood in my ears. Reaching into the truck, I retrieved the .45 and dropped the magazine out into my hand. I placed it in my shirt pocket and produced my already prepped hash pipe and lit it with my Zippo. After two hits, my heart began to calm and the fear that had been clutching at my groin faded. I gazed out into the impenetrable fog and thought about life as thunder began to roll across the hills. As the dope did its job, I settled into a some-what peaceful state.

Suddenly my hair began to rise on my head, and arms and a feeling of uncomfortable pressure came over me. Without warning, there was a sizzle and a bolt of lightning seemingly three feet wide flashed from right to left through my vision followed by the concussive blast of thunder so close that there was no pause. The shock wave of the concussion hit me full in the chest and scared me shitless. The impending storm had arrived and almost immediately another scene appeared in my mind's eye, impenetrable fog, searing flashes of light, noise and violence, terror and hopelessness. Death coming at speed.

I scrambled back into the truck as more flashes, and more thunder crashed around the truck. Slamming and bolting the door I could not stop the tears that streamed down my face.

Thoughtlessly I pulled the magazine from my pocket and shoved it into the pistol. Racking the slide, I thumbed off the safety as I backed into the far corner of the little shack. The storm raged all around me, and I panted with the fear it brought. I pulled my sleeping bag open and covered my head; trembling uncontrollably, racked with sobs, I sank into the corner and curled into a ball. The nightmares of my sleep had come alive as the storm outside matched the one in me.

Saturday, March 18, 1971, 0630 Hrs, 182nd EM Company Orderly Room

My vision is still slightly doubled as I regard Lieutenant Kyle across the First Sergeant's desk. He is not happy, and he is out of his element. His nice-guy persona doesn't easily assume the role of disciplinarian. It's also early Saturday morning, and he's been called back to post to deal with this crisis by Battalion. This is the part about being a commanding officer that he likes least. It is not a comfortable role for him. I'm just happy that it's the weekend and the First Sergeant isn't in that chair instead. I'm not sure that he would try to be understanding of the situation. Kyle ran his hand over his already rumpled hair. I had never seen him when he needed a shave.

"So," he began with a sigh, "Anderson and Boyden got into a fist fight in the barracks?"

"Yes sir, they did."

"I thought they were friends?"

"Yes sir."

"Why would they get into a fistfight, then?"

"Well sir, they had been drinking."

"So then Younger tried to break up the fight?"

"Yes sir."

"And now Younger is in the hospital."

"Yes sir."

"So how did Duncan end up in the hospital too?"

"Well sir, he had been drinking too."

"Emmett, that is hardly an excuse. I have been known to have a few beers once in a while, and I don't recall ever getting into a fistfight with any of my friends."

Lieutenant Kyle had called me by my given name ever since I had joined the Company. He had even had me to his home for dinner with him and his wife. Somehow, he was under the impression that I was worth his time. I, on the other hand, still called him sir.

"Well sir, it was St. Patrick's Day yesterday, and it's pretty rare when the whole squad is on post at the same time, you know. Usually, some of us are on the road, even on the week-ends, so we all went downtown and had a little St. Pat's party."

Kyle had inherited the squad of drivers as part of Tech Supply. The drivers were all the soldiers who didn't fit in where they were supposed to. Troublemakers and misfits like me, in a company that had no real job for them. To the man, they were trust-worthy, smart, exuberant and permanently doomed to never rise in rank.

"So, you went to a Gasthaus for some drinks and then came back to the barracks according to the CQ log at," he looked down and consulted the log, "0240?"

"That sounds about right sir."

"Then according to the log, a fight broke out between Anderson and Boyden, which Younger then attempted to intercede in, whereupon Younger was injured enough to go to the hospital. And Younger is also a friend?"

"That's correct sir, but there were a few other injuries that required hospital attention."

I was fairly proud of myself for being able to hold up my end of the conversation so far. My vision wasn't coming around very quickly, but I didn't think I was slurring my words too badly.

"Where was the CQ during all of this?"

"He was standing right next to me sir. It was a heck of a fight."

"Right, so the CQ woke the driver to transport the injured parties, and another fight broke out? This time Ryan and Duncan sustained injuries."

"That's correct sir. Anderson wouldn't ride in the same vehicle as Boyden. Tempers were getting a little short all around."

"Why not? I mean, why wouldn't they ride together? They do it every other day."

"Well sir, they had just gotten through beating each other up." I added, "and they had been drinking."

"That level of drinking—I can't understand it. So, then the Battalion CQ driver was detailed to take half of you, and the rest went in the company Suburban correct?"

"Yes sir. I went with the Battalion driver. I needed a couple of stitches too."

"You were injured?"

"Yes sir, those are my squad. I'm responsible for them, so I sort of had an opinion about the proceedings myself."

"Alright," he held up his hands for me to stop, "tell me what happened at the hospital because I don't think I can be getting the story straight from the orderlies I spoke with."

"Well sir, when we all got there it was pretty empty. It was after all pretty late, anyway Anderson needed stitches in his head. Boyden had cut his hand pretty badly on a wall locker door, so they put them on gurneys but right next to each other, you know, with one of those curtains that hangs down between 'em." Younger needed X-rays, so they took him away in a wheelchair.

So, Ryan, Duncan and I waited our turn, just talking to the guys on the gurneys. Well, I don't remember who said what, but an argument started through the curtain between Anderson and Boyden, and the next thing you know they were up and fighting again. Well sir, I'd had about enough, and Ryan was pretty mad by that time, too, so we both waded in again. I'm afraid there was quite a bit of, um, damage—sir."

"I've already gathered that from the discussion I've had with the hospital. The captain I spoke with was extremely upset." He rubbed his forehead. "How are you going to be able to work together this week? I mean seriously, you guys fighting like that. How do I put you all back on the road together? Not to mention, I have one man in the hospital with broken ribs and another man with a broken bone in his face. First Sergeant is going to have a cow when he gets here on Monday."

"No, we're good sir. Anderson and Boyden are both tucked in, down the hall, sleeping it off. They both shook hands and had a joke on the way back from the hospital. I'm pretty sure they got it out of their systems. We'll be good to go, sir."

"When I got you promoted to E-5, I thought you'd be able to handle the responsibility, Emmett. These boys are a rough bunch, but you're smarter than that. I don't want to hear about this happening again. I hope that's clear. I'm very disappointed."

I knew the day I had met him that this day was coming.

"How many stitches did you get?"

I don't know, twelve or thirteen. Woulda' been maybe five or six but I think I got hit with a bedpan or something. I'll probably feel that tomorrow."

The room was quiet for a full minute while Kyle looked out the window, and then down at the log book, then up at the ceiling. Finally, with a sigh,

"Okay, now off the record..." he leaned forward and put his elbows on the desk, "what's it like? What's a free-for-all fist fight really like?"

"Well sir, like I said, we had been drinking...."

January 1973,
15th MP Brigade, 42nd MP Group,
Heidelberg, Germany

I slowly rub my hand back and forth across my sore head. There is only stubble where there used to be hair. Some of the deeper cuts still feel wet and open. With my tongue, I work the loose tooth on the upper left side of my jaw, the inside of my cheek exquisitely tender. From the side of the cot, I levered myself up onto my bare feet and take inventory of sore places but lose count in my confusion and give up as too depressing. Instead, I limp to the door of the little cell and look out through the bars, something has awoken me. There are no windows I can see, and the lighting never changes but there is a feeling of activity beyond the locked doorway, maybe it is morning.

Pressing my face to the cool metal I hope it is, the nights have produced another kind of terror.

At night the guards take me for a shower; and another beating. The first shower had also featured a haircut, of sorts. They are democratic in their approach, each one allowing the others a turn. They express their anger with vigor. At first, I gave as good as I got but in reality, I knew I probably deserved it. Eventually, I concentrated on showing as little impact as I could from their treatment. I counted the days by the number of interviews.

Ten days, ten interviews with different JAG lawyers or Military Police. And just to mix it up a little, eight showers so far. I was probably glad that I was not allowed a mirror.

It had been a deal that had gone wrong, in fact it had gone FUBAR and taken a sharp left. It had been set up in a small Gasthaus in Furth. The hour was late, and the tavern was empty of other patrons. Seated at the table in the far corner we had greeted the three men when they arrived. A lot of product and a lot of money was to change hands, and I was working with a new partner, their count came up short. An argument had begun and quickly combusted, both sides on edge in such a public place. One of the three strangers emphasized his dissatisfaction by standing and pulling his sidearm. I had no way of knowing that he was undercover CID, but he had shown his hand too soon. My new partner jumped to his feet in angry surprise and had taken two .45 slugs to the chest at close range, dead before his body slammed into the wall behind him.

In the ensuing confusion and melee, the beast had awoken. The CID dick died later of head injuries at a local hospital and two others were incapacitated and apprehended at the scene, one of whom was apparently critical. The German Polizei had been only too happy to turn me over to the American MPs when they signed for me. The MPs, for their part, were delighted to make my acquaintance and continued to express it in numerous ways.

I watched the progression of the rank of the individual JAG and Military Police as they took turns each day interviewing me. The first was a delightful female Lieutenant, flushed with the new responsibility of a big case, genuinely interested in my interests and therefore completely unacceptable to the Army. She had expressed deep concern for my appearance but was assured that they were injuries that I had suffered during the altercation in the Gasthaus. The second day, two captains had taken her place. Then I had gotten different captains for a couple of days, and now I had progressed to a series of gold leaves and full birds. Their concern was limited to a few snide comments and a deeper concern for my slow-healing abilities. Each day, each interview a replay of my statements as they picked each sentence apart and meticulously attempted to catch me with any inconsistency.

I had begun the series of interviews with banalities and professions of self-defense. Now miserable and exhausted I had eventually given up the pretense. My shit was weak, and I knew it. They were not as interested in me as in my story but would be all too willing to lay it all at my feet if I did not cooperate. There was no getting around the fact that two Americans had died, one of them a police officer. In addition, two known criminals were in custody and presumed to be doing business with none other than me. There was not going to be a good cop/bad cop scenario. They were all going to be bad cops because they didn't have to be anything else.

A doctor had checked me in the hospital and determined bruised ribs, loose tooth, fractured nose, probable concussion and once again a broken finger. He sighed and gave me some aspirin and released me to the arresting officers. The guards at the stockade had promptly confiscated my aspirin and Zippo and very shortly afterward my confidence and self-esteem. My head hurt, and my jaw throbbed. I thought about sleep constantly and feared what each night would bring.

With the morning, the guards would change. The night shift, which I feared the most would be relieved, and the day shift would ignore me unless I was to be interviewed yet again. There were few other prisoners in my block that I could see, and I doubted I would have talked to them anyway. The only break in the monotony of limping from the bars to the wall and back was the arrival of the metal tray with food that I could not chew.

The now familiar rattle and clunk of the key turning in the block door signaled activity, and I quickly made my way back to the bunk and sat down. More than one set of footsteps began the trip from the doorway, and clearly, there was no place for them to be going than to me, so I took a few breaths and prepared for the worst. One set of boots, breakfast; two sets; shower time; more than two, unknown fate. I looked down at my feet as the boots arrived outside my cell. Unknown was almost never good these days.

"Prisoner stand up and go to the back wall, place your hands on the wall and spread your legs."

I complied with the instructions, gasping slightly as I leaned my weight on my swollen hand and finger.

"Open the cell please."

"Sir?"

"Open the cell, Corporal."

"Sir, we have to handcuff the prisoner."

"Corporal, open the cell and stand down. I don't think we will have a problem with Specialist Casey today."

"Sir, yes sir."

Again, the keys rattled, and the sound of the cell door swinging open was unmistakable. Shoes not boots entered the cell and stopped.

"You may stand at ease soldier. About face."

The unknown is almost never good. I pushed off the wall and turned. The first thing I saw was two pairs of very shiny low quarter shoes, then two pairs of impeccably pressed dress green pants, one with stripes down the outside. These were followed by two dress uniform jackets, both with enough tossed salad ribbons and citations to sink a small boat, and finally to two very tough looking faces. One of which, I recognized immediately although the full bird on the shoulder epaulet had been replaced by a silver star.

"Corporal, round us up some chairs and bring coffee. The sergeant here will assure my safety I am sure."

The Sergeant was a Command Sergeant Major with enough service bars down his sleeve to indicate that he had been in the Army since the Korean War at the very least. He, in turn, nodded to the Corporal who was at first shocked and then moved with speed back down the hallway. Even in my confusion, I snapped to attention and saluted them both.

Returning the salute, the General began.

"At ease Specialist, take a seat on the cot before you tip over."

"Sir?"

"Sit down Casey."

"Yes sir." Only too happy to oblige I eased down on the cot, but I couldn't get them in my vision without looking up at them, which hurt my neck and made my headache worse.

"You look about as rough as the first time we met Casey."

I couldn't add to that, there was no mirror in the cell after all. On the other hand, General John Smolders looked like he had just stepped out of the showroom. Two chairs clattered down the hall carried one in each hand by the Corporal hurrying back. Once he set them down in the cell and the two new arrivals had taken seats it was too crowded for him, and he was obliged to stand in the open cell door, not sure of his role and obviously ill at ease.

"I accepted a post at XII Corps six months ago, and was posted here, in Stuttgart. Like many of us, we have been riveted to the extent that this tale of corruption has uncovered. Since you are in the middle of this fiasco, I am not concerned about telling any tales out of school here. Not only is this a scandal of the highest proportion, but it involves layers upon layers of corruption and collusion that only the military can propagate. Because of the hyperbole that surrounds something of this nature your own personal story although central to the investigation has garnered little interest with one exception. That exception it turns out owed you a favor, and that favor has been called in."

I was listening, but what he had said made absolutely no sense to me. It just seemed like words with no connection to my situation. Like a politician warming up an audience.

"In other circumstances, or perhaps in another time, you would have been an admirable addition to this man's Army Casey. I said as much to you two years ago, but you have a cloud that keeps pace with your every move. For my own entertainment, and for Command Sergeant Major Tuttle's information allow me to recap what I mean.

AWOL before you were in the Army more than half a day—not just for a few days, or weeks, but for three months. Arrested for vagrancy and served time in the stockade. An honor graduate of basic training, promoted to PFC upon AIT graduation, battle-tested with a Bronze Star, Purple Heart, and Unit Citation. An honor graduate of yet another AIT, home town recruiter, and then a string of Article 15s that could take up an entire personnel file all by themselves, and finally look who we find at the very bottom of one of the largest Black-Market scams to rock the U.S. Army, since Berlin. None other than you, my friend.

"It is with a somewhat perverted sense of pleasure that I am both pleased and pissed off to be sitting here across from you. As far as I was concerned when I last saw you that was the end of you. I never gave it or you another thought. But you have kept popping up on my radar. And as I said, a favor has been called in, and now we will see what is to become of you."

Coffee arrived and a cup, a real coffee cup, not the tin cups I had been drinking out of, was handed to me. It smelled like the shit coffee in the army is supposed to smell like, but it was hot, and it tasted fantastic. I relished the sting of it on the cuts inside of my cheek and bad tooth.

"This, as I said, is Command Sergeant-Major Tuttle. CSM Tuttle is heading up the investigation with the Judge Advocate's Office and is the final word on what is going to happen to you. I have no dog in this fight, but I have asked CSM Tuttle to look into you personally, as a favor. What you have to say to him, and what you say in this room today is going to make or break you. I would not try and bullshit him, and I strongly advise you to be truthful to a fault."

With that, he turned to the CSM who cleared his throat and began.

"Specialist Casey, we have your sworn statements as an official record in this investigation. It is saying something that you can and did recall even the license plate numbers on many of the vehicles you came in contact with. Over the course of roughly the last two weeks you have been questioned by the some of our best, and with almost no variation your testimony has been consistent. In the short amount of time that has been available, we have been able to corroborate many of your statements.

Today multiple task forces are deploying—both military and civilian. And by the end of the day, we expect dozens of arrests and property seizures to take place. Without the window that you have provided, it would not have been possible, especially given one of our own agents lost his life and is unable to offer further evidence. Your testimony at trial will be necessary, and as a result, I imagine your life will be in danger.

"On a personal note, I could not care less what anvil falls on you, as you seem to have the makings of a lifetime criminal, but there are some who have made a case for your immunity in exchange for some of the names that you have up to this time withheld. Immunity, however, is not a get-out-of-jail free card. There is still the matter of a manslaughter charge at the very least, and as the ranking NCO, you also bear responsibility for the death of Private First-Class Biddle. You currently have at least ten outstanding charges of felony theft, smuggling, damage to government property, good grief the list goes on and on. Even if you slide on half of them, there are enough others to lock you away for most of your life."

"Excuse me, sir. Don't the other charges carry something like a life sentence?"

"Wouldn't that be nice? They could, but it would be unlikely."

"Then I think I may have told you as much as I am able."

"Excuse me," the General who had been leaning back in his seat with his arms crossed across his impressively ribboned chest broke his silence, "I have something here which may or may not be helpful. I had been asked to deliver it to Specialist Casey only if he was reluctant to fully cooperate. Would you indulge me?"

"What the hell, I can't wait to see this." CSM Tuttle didn't seem overly patient this morning.

Reaching into his breast pocket Smolders produced a business-sized envelope which he looked at briefly and then passed to the CSM who was closer to me. After a brief look Tuttle handed it to me. The envelope was blank there was no logo in the corner or name on it anywhere. It was sealed, and the seal had then been taped. I looked at it, curiously afraid of what it contained.

The CSM leaned back in his chair and fished into his pocket. His hand came out with a small pocket knife that he opened and handed to me. The Corporal almost came out of his shoes.

"Sir?"

"AT EASE Corporal, stand down!" the General boomed.

I slit the envelope open and pulled out a single sheet of paper. In spite of themselves, both men leaned forward in their chairs. Letter stock, good paper, written in a slanted hand that would do any Catholic schoolboy proud. Two simple sentences, over a neatly penned signature.

"Casey, tell them what you know. A favor for a favor."

The signature at the bottom?

Dunn

Well, shit...

I turned the paper over to make sure there was nothing on the back, then looked at the signature one more time. I took a deep breath and fixed my gaze on the corner where the ceiling met the two walls of the cell.

"I will tell you what I know."

The Nightmare

The guards no longer bothered with me; they ignored me. After a while, they even stopped locking my cell door. I roamed the hallway at night; I did push-ups until my arms shook, ran in place and did sit-ups until my belly muscles hurt.

Eventually, though I would have to lie down on my cot, and try to sleep. But sleep did not come.

Sleep never comes. Instead, the nightmare. Always the same, wrapped in a ruthless dread. I can see nothing, the light is dim and grey, impenetrable fog; but 'It' is there. With absolute assurance the 'It' is there, just beyond the threshold of perception, breathing, pressing in, coming. 'It' is huge, an immense shapeless mass, unstoppable, relentless. Paralyzing dread flows from it, and it is near, always coming ever nearer, coming for me. It is malevolent, its progress inexorable, the slow, unrelenting speed of fate itself.

In the dream, the air surrounding me is hot and moist, suffocating. My arms and legs are trapped, paralyzed, wrapped tightly in a blanket of flannel air that I cannot breathe, claustrophobic and defenseless. It is coming, always coming. Coming for me. It will engulf me in misery, suffocate me, and drown me with fear and grief. There is no escape; there is no defense. I feel it approaching a crossing point in the time-line of my life, a crossroads, somewhere in the near distance where we must inevitably meet, approaching with the speed of the hour hand of a clock.

The endless terror of its approach mobilizes every fiber of my be-ing to struggle awake but when I do the terror of the dream awakens with me. My entire body is bathed in sweat and I burst from the bed, trying to pull air into my lungs. In my frenzy, I pace the small cell, attempting to walk off the panic, my heart racing, my ears singing with the energy of my fear. I squat into the farthest corner of the room facing the cell door. I balance on my toes, ready. I pant rapid breaths waiting for the something that will, that must, burst through the doorway. I must fight, but I cannot win. Even with my eyes wide open the nightmare never ends.

Court Martial

In the end, it all came out. It might have anyway, but my testimony filled a lot of holes and showed them where to look. It was revealed that the CID agent—whose name was ironically, Smart—had been anything but smart. He had been playing both sides of the fence. He had made enemies. It was Smart's weapon that had killed PFC Biddle. There was a gray area regarding the exact nature or origin of Smart's fatal injuries since there were no witnesses who were to be trusted. Only the beast that slept with one eye open clearly remembered, and he was better left alone. A vast network of sergeants from the depots and various ordnance companies that spread out across Germany and all the way back to the states was uncovered. A mammoth degree of commerce had been conducted through the black market. The loss to the government was staggering, both in materials, dollars and technology. The extent of the corruption was vast. It was a big reveal, and it did not make the evening news.

The tribunal ruled Smart to be the crook he undoubtedly was and hung the murder of Biddle on him posthumously. His death was regrettably ruled as self-defense as far as the panel could determine. It was regrettable because of the loss of the person, but more importantly, because they truly wanted to hang me for it. They conceded that I had acted under duress while obeying what were undoubtedly illegal orders from a superior. As the case dragged on it became clear that although they tried diligently, they were going to have trouble pinning anything more on me. There was little doubt that I was culpable on several levels but behind it all there was the undercurrent of a hand pushing them away from me. In the end, they threw in the towel. I was to be given a general discharge with four years of conditional probation. I would be in the service two years, three months and thirteen days.

Two military police officers escorted me from Stuttgart all the way through my processing out at Fort Dix. At Fort Dix, thanks to my lengthy stay under arrest I passed my exit drug test. The two walked me right up to the boarding gate at the Philadelphia airport. I didn't know if they suspected that I might have one more shoe to drop, or if they just wanted to be assured that I was gone for good. Together we ran the gauntlet through the airport. The invective thrown at us as we walked the concourse was augmented by thrown cups of soft drinks, and people who refused to step out of our way. Some actually spit at us. In our dress Class A uniforms, the history of service to their country was written in the combat ribbons and citations on each of our chests if they had chosen to read them. Instead, we presented targets for everything wrong with America, and they were diligent in exercising their First Amendment rights. It was scant comfort to know that the two would have to return by the same route we had just suffered through together.

March 1973,
My Father's House

I am still on European time, so I awaken before three a.m. Central Standard Time. As quietly as possible I dress and make my way from my bedroom and down the stairs to the kitchen. The steps and floorboards all still squeak in the same places that they always have. I am careful to avoid them sometimes lowering myself two steps at a time on the stairway to not rouse the household. As I pass my mother's bedroom, I silently pull the door shut and cautiously continue my way through the house. My father sleeps in a separate bedroom, the smallest one in the house, tucked under the gables in the upstairs of the house. I can't say when they stopped sleeping together, but it's not a new development.

The old percolator coffee pot still sits on the back of the stove and after a major search to determine the latest hiding place for the ground coffee, I find it in the freezer and measure the necessary amount into the sieve and fill the pot with water. The process of brewing coffee in a percolator coffee pot is not quiet because once the water begins to boil the inside spout spits and gurgles the water into the waiting grounds. The noise alone is bad enough, but you cannot conceal the permeating smell of freshly brewing coffee. I comfort myself knowing that it is barely three o'clock in the morning and my parents should be difficult to arouse. I stand patiently while the old percolator grunts and coughs its way through the brewing process. Opening a cabinet I take a cup from the prodigious collection that memorializes every vacation and filling station that my folks have ever visited. I fill it and with it in my left hand, I snag my duffle bag from where I dropped it in the entryway upon my arrival yesterday afternoon and make my way to the basement staircase.

Once in the basement, I dump the few remaining personal items that I have brought with me from my duffle bag. The first thing I select from the pile is my two pairs of OD boots. They are easily the best pair of shoes I have ever owned, and the leather is soft and supple from constant loving care. I remove the low quarter dress uniform shoes and take a seat on the third step from the bottom of the basement stairs. Reaching into my front pocket, I fish out my small pocket knife. I glance quickly over my shoulder up the stairs to ensure that I am indeed alone. My Da also knows where all of the squeaks and groans are in this house. Carefully I pry off the heels of both shoes. Wedged tightly in each hollowed-out heel carefully wrapped in plastic rests a package containing fifteen grams of pure, blonde hashish. I put one package into one of the army boots and push it as far into the toe as possible. The other goes in my pocket. I align the nails in the heel with the holes in the bottom of the sole of the shoes and press them back into place rapping them on the stair next to me to firmly seat them back in place.

I remove the brass insignias and ribbons from my dress greens and toss them in the trash container next to the dryer in the laundry area. Gathering the fatigues, dress greens, and other remnants—reminders of the last two years, three months and thirteen days—I exit the basement through the door that leads to the backyard. Daylight is still a long time off, but the proximity of Chicago produces enough light pollution, so it is never totally dark. The air is cold and damp as only Midwestern winter air can be. On the way across the patio, I hook the bottle of lighter fluid that sits on the ledge near the charcoal grill and walk to the back of the yard where a rusty fifty-five-gallon oil drum stands at the limits of my father's property. The paint long since burned off from countless trash fires, the drum has begun to rust through at the base and it tilts against the steel cyclone fence that surrounds the garden. The drum is decorated with numerous holes, all put there by my father's 38 revolver at close range to provide adequate ventilation for the trash fires.

I unload the pile of clothing into the can and liberally douse them with most of the contents of the lighter fluid. Standing back, I look out over the expanse of open ground beyond the fence, pausing for a moment to offer a benediction to what is behind me but will always be in me. Having been relieved of my precious Zippo lighter, I pull a book of matches out of my shirt pocket along with my pack of Lucky Strikes. Mostly for my own amusement, I open the matches with one hand, bend one match down to the striker on its front and with my thumb snap the match into fire. I shake a cigarette up out of the pack and taking it in my lips I light it with the match. After a deep and reflective puff, I watch the match burn down while holding the cigarette in the corner of my mouth skillfully so as not to dislodge the tobacco onto my lips from the nonfiltered cigarette. Once, now so long ago, I had stood and watched something else burn down in my hand, time measured by experiences. It was such a small action then as it is now, but the small acts seem to account for the most significant consequences. When the match ignites the entire matchbook in a smoky flare of fire, I flip it into the barrel.

Sadly, the clothing does not explode in a soul-satisfying huff of flame. Instead, the lighter fluid slowly ignites and quickly crawls across the creases and folds. It gives off a noxious black smoke that is somehow fitting, and without another thought, I turn and follow my own tracks in the snow that covers the yard. As I approach the house, I naturally look up and there on the back step sits Little Mick barely visible in the dark. As I get closer, I see he is in his pajamas and bathrobe, his bare feet encased in his old moccasins. His pipe is tight in his teeth but unlit. His eyes meet mine then moving his head a little he looks over my shoulder and regards the smoke and fire pouring out of the top of the barrel. He looks back at me, looks me up and down, and with no other expression his lips tighten into a thin line, and he slowly nods his head up and down a few times. Wordlessly he stands up, glances one more time at the fire, then at me again. I think he may speak because I feel that we are sharing a moment. But, he lets out a sigh and turning he climbs the six steps to the back door and lets himself into the house. In a moment the light over the kitchen sink goes out. I sit down on the step he recently vacated and finish my cigarette. The fire inside of me has burnt out, so I watch my past burn instead.

Civilian Life and a Cup of Coffee

It is a Monday morning, my brain and body still on Western European time. After a shower in the bathroom under the eaves of the silent and too empty house, more out of habit than self-respect I shave too. Once dressed, I let myself out the back door as quietly as I can. My sister Kate's durable 1962 Rambler American sedan sits abandoned in the driveway. She left it behind when she departed for married life, and her escape. With the keys liberated from the hook in the front closet, I start the car and let it idle for a few moments to allow the oil pump to work lubrication back up to the top of the engine. I have no way of knowing how long it has been since it was last driven, so I check the tires to make sure they at least don't appear low and light a cigarette. Shifting into reverse I back out of the driveway before turning on the headlights. However, even with this precaution I glimpse the spare figure and face that regard me from the upstairs bedroom window.

As soon as I turn left out of the driveway, I drive the three short blocks to the train station. The parking lot is largely empty at this early hour. However, I pull to the back of the lot and back into an empty stall the chain link boundary fence behind me and the majority of the lot and station in front of me. Reaching into my pocket, I pull out the plastic wrapped packet, my small pipe and a book of matches. Quickly unwrapping the package, the aroma of the hashish caresses my sinuses, and immediately my head and senses begin to awaken. Striking a match, I hold the hash in my left hand and gently heat the sticky nugget until it blackens slightly on edge. The heat is necessary to make the sticky dope dry enough to crumble a small amount into my pipe, and I break off a small crumb the size of a pencil eraser and drop it into the pipe.

After carefully rewrapping it, I reach behind the pull-out ashtray on the dashboard and yank it free. Behind the vacated space of the ashtray I push the small package of dope up behind the wiring for the heater and radio. Making sure it is secure, I replace the ashtray and pick up the pipe. After a brief reconnaissance of the area, I light another match while missing my precious lighter with the tortoise-shell embossing. I place the small hash pipe between my teeth, set the match over the dope and draw the hot, pungent smoke as deeply into my lungs as I can. The result is almost instantaneous, the rush of the drug absorbing into my body starts in my mouth and throat before my lungs can process it into my bloodstream. With an involuntary sigh, I breathe out and drop back in the car seat, closing my eyes and feel-ing my body and mind sync up to the normal they have been missing. The tiny amount of hash is smoked in four or five deep draws, but it is enough to restore my equilibrium and calm my stress. Finally, I feel in touch with reality, and I reflect on how different my reality is, from everyone else's.

That necessity accomplished I shift into drive and pull out of the lot onto the streets of my abbreviated adolescence. Driving through the streets of town has a surreal quality. Although everything around me is familiar and seems unchanged, everything inside of me has. I pass by many places of memory as I aimlessly tour about taking ran-dom turns, smoking cigarettes one after another, unconsciously look-ing an anchor that can ground me back into this new, yet old reality. Everything is the same as it was when I left here on a foggy November morning. Nothing has seemed to change, and driving the car seems such a regular activity, yet I do not feel normal. I doubt that I will ever understand what normal is again.

I pass, one by one, the homes of the few friends I used to have.

After that, I tour the houses of all the girls I wish I had known better. I assume that they no longer live in these quiet suburban houses on these quiet, comfortable, tree-lined suburban streets. They have all moved on I am sure. They have gone to college, or steady jobs, they have married, they have had children. They have achieved that elusive experience they call normal. They have not experienced the intense fragility of life or the horror that can spirit it away in the blink of an eye. They work, they vote, they go to PTA meetings, they make their way through this life in the ignorant bliss of mortality, and they eat their dinners in front of the television each night.

I soon exhaust all the touring possibilities and feeling wired on too many cigarettes and coffee, I look for a parking place outside of the familiar diner, which has been downtown since before my parents moved to the suburbs. The windows bright against the darkness of the winter morning are steamed over, so everything inside has a blurred pastel appearance of a French impressionist painting. Pushing in through the door, a small bell hanging over the doorway tinkles my arrival. All conversation pauses, as the regulars glance up through the haze of cigarette smoke but seeing no one to greet who they know they resume their routines. Feeling uncomfortable and conspicuous, I walk past the occupied stools the length of the counter keeping as much distance from them as I hug the booths on my left and sit on the farthest stool.

A matronly woman, with a bad dye job and a pink waitress uniform, which bulges against the buttons across the chest and over the strings of her apron, bustles down the counter toward me. A white plastic name tag with Addy, punched into a blue labeling tape rests precariously over her left bosom. Clutching the ubiquitous coffee urn, she clanks a coffee cup in front of me and with the skill of a sharpshooter dumps coffee into it stopping only as the coffee reaches the brim and without spilling a drop on the cracked but spotless counter.

Without preamble, "Menu?"

"No, thanks. Just a couple of eggs over easy, bacon, toast, and a side of pancakes."

"Hungry?"

"Bored."

"You a G.I.?"

I look up at her with a question. "No, just got out."

"The haircut kinda gives it away. Coffee's on the house. When'd ju get out?"

"Yesterday, and thanks."

She ambles off with the coffee urn in hand and begins refilling cups as she moves down the counter, making small talk and smiling at rude jokes, never spilling a drop. Then she glances at me and speaks under her breath to a few of the men at the far end of the counter. They lean back far enough to see behind the other men leaning over their breakfast plates. They do not acknowledge with eye contact, and they resume their friendly banter with Addy. *Good to know.*

Within minutes the food arrives; nothing special, but plenty of it, along with a bowl brimming with little plastic tubs of make-believe butter and a silver decanter of syrup, which is probably make-believe too. I reach across to the napkin stand and grab the ketchup bottle and after dousing the eggs, I dig in. As soon as I get a good mouthful going, one of the men, the largest one, spins out of his stool and starts down the counter in my direction.

As soon as he moved I was aware of him, loose and comfortable as he hitches up his Levis onto his belly. He takes his time, a big man, almost as wide as he is tall, but not tall. His neck is almost as wide as his head, and his big arms make the sleeves of his long sleeve shirt look too tight. When he is within six feet, I'm off my stool backing to the booth behind my stool fork clutched in one hand, my knees bent and ready. I cannot allow him to walk behind me. I am thinking about which eye my fork is going into.

"Holy shit! Hey, take it easy, dude!" His hands up and facing out in surrender he backs up a step or two.

"Jesus Christ! Fuck! I'm just trying to get to the john, man."

I knew the restroom was behind me, without lowering my gaze I straighten up a little and shuffle a little on my feet, embarrassed.

"Sorry dude." I toss the fork onto the counter where it clatters off and lands on the floor on the other side, the noise too loud in the suddenly quiet restaurant. I shake my head and relax my shoulders. Unnecessarily I say again. "Sorry."

"Shit! I almost don't need to go anymore."

Looking past him, I see Addy frozen with the half-empty coffee urn in one hand. All activity in the room has stopped completely and there is dead silence, every eye on me. After shifting on his feet for another second, he slides past me on the side of the empty booths and bangs into the bathroom. Almost immediately he starts pissing loudly into the water in the toilet bowl. I can feel my face is hot and probably bright red. Avoiding the staring eyes that I know to be still there I stare down at my shoes waiting for him to finish. After a noisy flush and obviously without washing his hands, he pulls open the door and hesitates as he sees I'm still standing, waiting for him to pass again while I face him. Instead, he stops in front of me again.

"Just out huh?"

"Yesterday."

"Kind of a bitch isn't it?

I have nothing to say to that.

Now that he is not surprised, he is back to his confident, self- assured personage. There probably isn't very much he is ever afraid of.

"Not the most popular thing these days, being military. Not like it was."

He looks down the counter at the other men who are starting to go back to their coffee.

"Listen you've got nothing to worry about from these guys or me. Most of these guys are way too lazy, or too old, but they think what you've done is a good thing. Hell, if they were younger they would have gone to 'Nam with the rest of you boys."

I shrug and look at my food. "There was nothing good about it."

"Okay then, I don't want to hear any war stories, but if you're looking for work, I maybe can steer you in a good direction. If you're interested?" Then with a little smile, he adds, "But you are going to need to learn to relax."

For the first time since I was afraid I might need to stab him, but still not trusting him, I look him in the eye.

"What kind of job?

"The place I work, it's good work, a machine shop. The boss makes a point of hiring vets, honest son, it's a good place. Pay's okay."

"I don't know machining."

"No sweat, they train people who want to work. You can do a lot worse. 'Sides there's a lot of you guys coming out right now. The jobs are hard to find."

I look at my food. I look at the shelves behind the counter lined with boxes of crappy coffee, and paper products, not altogether ready for conversation.

"Okay, maybe. Where's this shop at?" I tried to make my voice sarcastic, but I was honestly interested, so it came out somewhere in between.

"Bensenville, up on York Road and Thorndale. Flick's, worth a try?"

"Maybe. Not sure if I'm staying around here. I haven't made up my mind."

"No skin off my nose, but if you are thinking about sticking a fork in everybody you meet, one place is as good as the next I'd guess."

"Yeah, sure. Hey, I'm sorry dude, guess I'm a little jumpy. I'll try and check it out."

In spite of whatever danger he had sensed, he puts his hand on my shoulder and says,

"Tell them Andy Panko sent you, it might help a little. Good luck."

And then he grips my shoulder tighter and drops his knees a little, I am a little surprised to realize that I am taller than he is and looks up into my face and his face tightens and he says,

"Death from above?

I am sure he feels me start, and I know my eyes widen in surprise. How does he know?

"Shoulder patch." He points to the tricolored patch with a sword pointing up in the middle on the right shoulder of my army field jacket. Hooking his other thumb at his own chest, he says, "Chu Lai, '67."

With that he walks back to his stool, slapping a few of the men on the back as he passes. He picks up his check and goes to the register. Paying his bill, he shrugs into his coat and with a look at me gives me a thumbs up and goes out into the cold, the tinkle of the doorbell signaling his departure. I'm still standing where he walked away from me.

First Paycheck in Two Years

The interview at Flick proved to be a formality. I was hired on the spot and started the next day. After three days of training, the employer was assured enough that I could spell, and do simple math. He put me on the shop floor where I began my experience as a machinist. The shop itself was vast, fully an acre under one roof, with row upon row upon row of brightly lit engine lathes, turret lathes, drill presses, band saws and warehoused steel. The bright lights illuminated the drifting smoke of hot cutting oil and hotter metal, and the sound of the industry was loud and comforting; the smell of hot steel, familiar. It was too noisy for anything less than shouted conversation.

The larger the machine, the more interesting the part was that the machines produced. I was started on one of the smallest, making some of the simplest pieces. Hundreds of them in one day, thousands in one week. It proved to be easy repetitive work, with no real sense of satisfaction in accomplishment, one piece in, one piece out over and over and over, ten hours a day, six days a week. Business, at least for Flick's, was excellent.

In short order, my production numbers outstripped my fellow machinists of small parts, and I moved up to a bigger lathe, and then a bigger lathe. The bigger the piece, the fewer there were, but the process was still the same. Always the same. There was a rhythmic satisfaction in the constant motion, which required a minimum of interaction with other people, and captured my conscious attention and focus. It became a competition with myself on each piece. Each piece a race against the production rate, each piece identical to the last, matching my hands to the rhythm of my heart and lungs, a dance that freed my thoughts to walk the roads of my mind. But most of all; it filled my day with structure and activity.

Each day was the same as the last. Each day, I packed my lunch, put my boots on and arrived before daylight. Each day I raced myself relentlessly, manic to produce a little more, to finish a process a little closer to maximum tolerance. Each day I ate my lunch standing at my machine. Each day I punched out and went home to my bed and my chair in the early darkness of the early spring nights. Each day, taking comfort, that tomorrow would be the same as the last. Each day, dreading the next.

How Far Is Far Enough?

shed my jeans and oily shirt on the small linoleum square inside the door and step back out into the hallway long enough to shake out all of the metal chips and grindings that have found their way into my pockets and waistbands. Once satisfied, I carry them into the bathroom to hang on the hooks on the back of the door, ready for another tomorrow. Turning, I spend a solid five minutes with dish detergent and a nail brush on my hands until only the cracks and fissures, and nail beds alone are highlighted by the black machine oil that they now bathe in daily. I don't bother to put anything else on, the curtains provide complete privacy. No one will be visiting. The phone will not ring.

It is much too early for dinner. the sun will not set for another hour or so, but I survey the refrigerator out of habit. I guess it is heated hot dogs or cold bologna tonight. It will depend on how stoned I am by then. From the butter compartment, I pull out a baggy of pre-rolled joints and light one up with my new fancy butane lighter with fake tortoise-shell finish. I lean against the stove, taking a much-needed hit. My brain sighs in relief.

I select a couple of joss sticks from the utility drawer. *Balsam and cedar tonight*, I think. Lighting one, I place it in the carved dragon incense holder on the counter. In the living room, I pull the chain on the red glass lamp that hangs from the ceiling next to the recliner and place the other joss stick in the ashtray on the single end table. A used sofa makes up the rest of the room's furnishings except for the massive component stereo system—my pride and joy.

The system is the only thing I brought home from overseas that I view with pride. It sits on two 2' X 6' planks supported by liberated bricks along the wall under the window. Two massive Bose 501 speakers sit on the floor at each end, their deafening output capable of vibrating the paint off of the ceiling in the third-floor apartments far upstairs. But sadly leashed in this environment, they are hardly ever allowed to show off their skills. Firing up the receiver, I turn on the reel to reel, put on my headphones, and sit down in the recliner. The cold pleather is stiff and hard against my bare back and legs. In the headphones, Deep Purple launches into the long, frenetic guitar solo of "Highway Star." I close my eyes while I finish smoking the dope. The roughly two hours of music on the tape will take me past sunset and into the night.

Later, I eat the last three hot dogs cold while standing at the open refrigerator door. I might need the last of the milk in the morning, so I drink water straight from the tap—all of the glasses are dirty. In the bedroom, I open the drawer of the dresser designated for socks and lift out the .38 Ruger long barrel revolver and make my way back to the recliner, which is still warm against my bare skin. In the red darkness of the lamp, I release the cylinder and drop it into my hand. Dumping the bullets into my open palm, I select one, replace it back into the chamber and line the other five up in formation on the table beside me. I reassemble the gun almost unconsciously, the movements automatic.

Settling back into the chair I lean it all the way back. With the headphones back in place, I listen as Pink Floyd begins the iconic "One of These Days"—a fitting song to match my mood. I rotate the cylinder by rolling it down my bare leg, each chamber distinctly clicking into position in line with the barrel and firing pin. I light another joint and fill my lungs, holding it tight in my chest. Closing my eyes, my demons are immediately present in the dimly lit room— night time companions of terror and remorse. Lifting up the almost

two-pound handgun, I place it under my chin, the end of the barrel
cold against my skin. I exhale the smoke and close my eyes. The
headphones mask the sound of the clicks as I thumb back the double-
action hammer.

"If bad luck knows who you are
Become someone else."
--Jandy Nelson

For I Have Sinned

———⬤———

A preview of the next book, *'For I have Sinned'*, coming soon!

Prologue

My name is Emmett Michael Casey. Depending upon the station of the family member I'm with, I'm Michael, or Mick. People who work with me call me Mick or Casey. I stand five-feet-seven-inches tall and weigh on both sides of one- hundred-thirty pounds, depending upon the time of day. My friends and close relatives call me Little Mick. I don't mind. People that don't know me very well think I'm an asshole. I don't give a shit what people think anymore, I mind my own business.

Diary of Mick Casey, Army Air Corps Tail-Gunner, The Flying Ass

JANUARY 15, 1945, TRENTO, ITALY

We hung for dear life while the Captain throttled up the four big engines. We were seriously overloaded with fuel, with ammunition, with eight tons of one-hundred-pound bombs, and us. We would need every inch of the runway we could get. The old girl shook like she was going to explode. I could feel myself leaning against my harness, just like we all were, just like she was, pushing hard against the brakes. She wants to go. Just when I thought it wouldn't take anymore, the brakes released and we were off, hanging on tight, deaf from the roar of the four engines going full tilt into hell, down the metal track that is the runway; thirty seconds behind the last bomber and thirty seconds ahead of the next one.

We're belted to the bulkhead, in our crash positions; three on one side, three on the other side, facing each other across the bomb bay, the racks of hundred pounders within an arm's reach as we were thrown into our harnesses with the force of the release and the rumble of the runway. We felt every bump and rough spot as we pounded along, too fast to abort, daredevils to the end. I didn't think she could lift her ass. I was praying, thinking come on baby, get up, get up, come on baby. I couldn't hold on any tighter. I didn't think we could possibly have enough runway and still we kept pounding along. Then we

400

were up, and then we bounced back down and raced on. Then we're up again. This time the landing gear ground its way up into the belly, and the engine noise changed pitch. The Captain pulled it into a hard bank, and we began the long spiral up to the other planes. We're off, all of us, brothers - not knowing what is ahead—all of us ready, all of us sudden converts to Jesus, if we weren't already.

I had left my parachute behind me in the bomb bay and crawled down the tight passageway into the turret at the back of the plane. Once I got my flight suit plugged in and my oxygen hooked up, I started to warm up a little. An hour out we got the OK from the Captain, and I cleared my two fifty-caliber Brownings, firing a long burst from each one, and settled down to watch my piece of the sky. This was our second mission and I prayed to God that it would be like the first one. I'm not a kid anymore, I'm nineteen, and I want to live long enough to see twenty. The first mission was a piece of cake the Captain had said. We dropped down, unloaded and got out of there. The flak was light and all the birds flew home. Today we're heading into Austria, the city of Vienna. At the briefing at three a.m. they said we'd see stronger defenses and concentrated flak. It was a beautiful sunny day, and I watched the Alps as we crossed them and out of Italy. Looking down I thought about how my brother-in-law Charlie is down there somewhere. He's walking behind Patten, I'm flying. Which is worse I wondered?

As soon as the mountains get a little behind us, the intercom blasts in my ears. Janssen yells, "Bogies, eleven o'clock high, they're comin' around!"

Janssen mans the upper turret so I can't see the eleven. In the tail-gun turret, I ride backward facing where we just came from. I pull my helmet back off of my eyebrows a little and get a good dose of sun in my eyes. I didn't see the bogies. They're using the sun as cover to get behind us. Then I did; three little dots right dead in our six o'clock and getting bigger real fast.

Then Janssen yelled, "Three at six o'clock, three more coming in on the starboard, four o'clock low! MEs, (Messerschmidt 109s).

The dots get bigger, we were in the starboard group today flying tight getting close to our I.P. (initial point). At the I.P., the formation will turn to the target, drop altitude, arm the bombs in the bay, and line up for our run. The group is vulnerable at both ends of the run. The tighter the group, the more firepower we can bring. During the run, we string out. They don't call these babies Flying Fortresses for nothing though. The wings and tails of the oncoming fighters define themselves in my vision. They aren't just dots anymore, they are trouble and they are bringing it with them. I swung the guns up. Six-hundred yards is the effective range for the Browning .50 caliber and they will be there soon. I know what six-hundred yards looks like and I wasn't going to wait until they got there. I was ready, I pull the triggers and the twins roar to life, a spray of tracer rounds racing off toward them, five-hundred rounds a minute.

The trio behind don't reach the gun range barrier. Instead they peeled off away, two to my right and one to my left. I couldn't swing my turret toward the other three MEs, I only have ninety degrees of rotation in the turret. I have to watch as they make their run. I could see the muzzle flashes of their guns as they swung into attack mode, concentrating on the waist and tail of the right-most B-17, Moaning Lisa. They attacked from a lower angle to avoid as many of our gun positions as they could and almost immediately fragments of the her started to peel off the fuselage along with sparkling Plexiglass from the gun mounts. They're tearing her apart. The first fighter split away, up to where I could lay strafing fire out for him to fly into, and I opened up on him. Then the second ME made its run, targeting the same position. This time her number four engine belched black oily smoke and the right wing dropped. The bomber heeled over to her right and away from the squadron. Moaning Lisa turned nose down and spun down into the cloud cover, out of my sight. They had cut one of us out of the herd.

"Stay tight, close up the formation, steady ahead. Any parachutes on that bird?"

"Negative." Shouted Taylor from the Sperry-Ball turret. "No chutes. Three o'clock, three o'clock level, he's gonna take us end to end."

I couldn't watch for chutes, I picked up the ME as he passed. "Two more, ten o'clock high, one at six o'clock level, you pick him up Casey?"

"Yep, I see 'em."

Then, just like that they're gone. None of them in the sky. Captain Brinker came over the intercom, "Damage check?" He's a lot older than the rest of us, he's almost twenty-five but he's still a pretty neat guy. I couldn't run any damage check because I'm on my knees strapped into the turret and the plane is behind me. But there doesn't seem to be any when the rest of the crew checks in. He told us we were approaching our I.P., which meant I had to get out of the turret and crawl back into the bomb bay.

Once in the bay, the Sperry-Ball (belly turret) gunner, Taylor, and I pull all the pins on the bombs so that they are armed and will explode on contact. We have to put on our chutes and hook up portable oxygen tanks first. We hurry our way through the process. You don't want to be in the bomb bay when the doors open, and our oxygen bottles don't have very much air in them anyway. Although we've practiced it a hundred times, it's hard to do in our parachute gear and oxygen tank. The catwalk between the bombs is narrow, ten inches wide, and the footing is icy this high up in the air.

Once I get back in the tail-gun turret, we turn hard to port and start our bomb run in earnest. The fighters will wait until we come back out on the other side. Now it will be anti-aircraft defenses, and flak—it started immediately, and it started heavy. The poor ship rocked up and down, back and forth. There is no defense, we're big dark silhouettes in the sky just asking for them shoot us in the ass. We have to take the pounding. Even with my harness cinched tight my head was snapping around on my neck like a punch-drunk prize-fighter. Behind us, I watch as the sky turns black with the smoke of the explosions and the flash of the flame when they detonate. We are in the lead group, and I can't imagine what the last group through was going to get as the blackness got thicker and thicker. I imagine this must be what hell looks and feels like. There are no atheists during the bomb run.

Suddenly a piece of my turret shatters and hits me on the side of my head, knocking me silly for a minute. I am ok, but my head hurts a lot. There is so much noise in the plane I could barely hear "Bombs away" coming through the headset. But the light on the floor between my feet flashed so that I would know, just in case.

We were ready for the MEs as soon as we cleared the flak. But there aren't any. They had vanished. We make it home safe, and at the debriefing we are told we lost three planes. They lost five. Just for laughs the chief from the grounds crew told us we won the award for most holes punched in the fuselage today. He asked if we wanted to know how many. We all told him, NO. We were in the air seven hours and fifty-five minutes. It felt like a lot longer than that. It took twelve stitches to close the gash in my head. That night I crawled into the tent and got in my sleeping bag. It gets cold in January in Italy. I couldn't sleep, I looked up at the canvas and thought we go again—tomorrow.

About the Author

Michael Deeze is a natural-born storyteller—in life and in print. A child of the sixties, he draws extensively from his own diverse life experiences and subsequent education to introduce the hapless Emmet Casey. A Viet Nam vet and Doctor of Chiropractic, Deeze weaves the history of an ill-fated child's transition from a lonely, inner-city rebel, decorated war veteran and into a man who looks all too familiar to him, a man like his father—all earned the hard way. After spending decades living near the forests of rural Wisconsin, Deeze now lives and maintains a small, private practice in Illinois. He's a devoted father to his three children, a magical daughter, two grown sons and his dog.

About the Cover

The incredible art of this book spins its own tale. Woven as a mural of runes, the tale entwines the branches and roots of Mighty Yggdrasil. Each rune carries meaning in one of the oldest of written languages. Like Yggdrasil, each represents a key aspect, or character point, within this book, offering a clue to a deeper, hidden meaning—and perhaps, a hint to the character's fate.

CPSIA information can be obtained
at www.ICGtesting.com
Printed in the USA
BVHW031432120419
545355BV00001B/23/P

9 781977 208576